CORPORATE SHADOWFILES

A SHADOWRUN SOURCEBOOK

Berry 93

FASA CORPORATION

MW00446464

TABLE OF CONTENTS

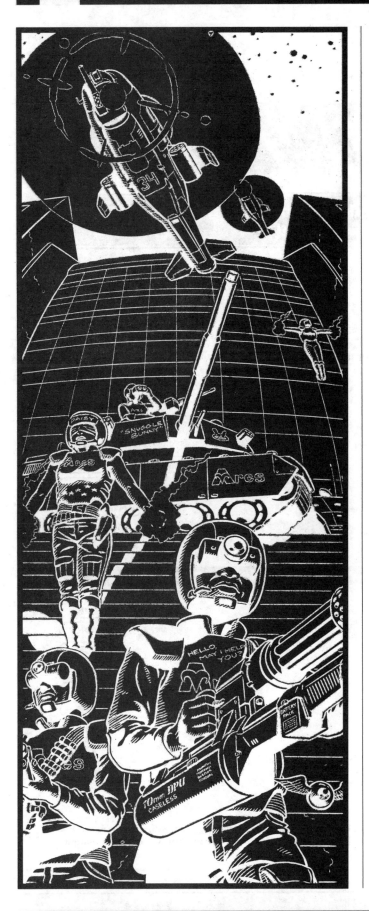

CORPORATE SHADOWFILES

Design and Writing
Nigel D. Findley

Development
Tom Dowd

Editorial Staff
Senior Editor
Donna Ippolito
Associate Editor
Sharon Turner Mulvihill
Editorial Assistants
Diane Piron
Rob Cruz

Production Staff
Art Director
Jeff Laubenstein
Project Manager
Jim Nelson
Cover Art
Rick Berry
Cover Design
Jim Nelson
Illustration
Janet Aulisio
Tom Baxa
Joel Biske
Mike Jackson
Tont Sczczudlo
Karl Waller
Color Section:
Design
Jim Nelson
"Shiawase" Photo
Jill Lucas
Layout
Mark Ernst
Keyline and Pasteup
Ernesto Hernandez

SHADOWRUN, and Corporate Shadowfiles are trademarks
of FASA Corporation.
Copyright © 1993 FASA Corporation. All Rights Reserved.
Printed in the United States of America.

Published by FASA Corporation
P.O. Box 6930 Chicago, IL 60680

WELCOME TO...
SHADOWLAND

> "I have taken all knowledge to be my province."
> — Francis Bacon, 1592

CATEGORY

	GO TO:
Message Base/Mail System	OK
Special Categories/ Topics (SIGS)	OK
Library Archive	OK
Information Base — SPECIAL FEATURES! (Limited Duration Posting)	
ARES Winter Catalog 2052-53 (Annotated)	OK
Paranormal Animals of Europe (Don't say we didnt warn ya . . .)	OK
Corporate Shadowfiles (Corp dirt ! Dig In!)	**OK**
Shadowtech Compilation (Weird Science 101)	OK
Tir na nÓg (En Route!)	NOT AVAILABLE
Real Life Compilation (Real Cool!)	OK
Germany (En Route!)	NOT AVAILABLE
Tir Tairngire (Those Wacky Elves . . .)	OK

CORPORATE SHADOWFILES

Introduction	OK
Big Brother Is Here	OK
Megacorporate Primer	OK
Doing Business	OK
Competition	OK
Economy	OK
Zurich-Orbital Habitat	OK
Rating the Corps	OK
Corporate Profiles (Color courtesy of Black Isis!!!)	OK

DOWNLOAD ALL?   OK   NOTE FROM CONTROL—Anyone with any knowledge regarding sabotage to this system should contact me ASAP. Censorship will not be tolerated!

INTRODUCTION

orporate Shadowfiles is a supplement to the **Shadowrun** game system. This sourcebook gives gamemasters and players a working knowledge of how megacorporations function in the **Shadowrun** world. **Corporate Shadowfiles** includes detailed information about the workings of megacorps, extensive profiles of major corporations, and game mechanics for determining how individual shadowruns affect individual corporations.

The first half of **Corporate Shadowfiles** explains how the megacorps of 2054 make money, interact, compete, and influence events in the world of **Shadowrun**. Gamemasters can use this information to design interconnected series of adventures or complete campaigns based on intercorporate maneuvering and competition. Rather than running individual adventures in isolation, the information in this book will help gamemasters to create shadowruns as part of a network of causes and effects. These interconnections add a new level of depth and complexity to the **Shadowrun** game. Throughout the book, various shadowrunners have annotated the files with opinions, anecdotes, and additional information they consider of interest to the reader. The gamemaster must decide whether to treat these opinions and evaluations, inserted by individuals who may hold a biased view, as valid. These opinions and anecdotes also suggest starting points for several complex and sinister adventures.

The second part of this book provides comprehensive profiles of some of the Sixth World's major corporations. As with most **Shadowrun** source material, the information given may represent nothing more than rumor or semi-educated guesswork by those who compiled the data.

Finally, the book includes a short rules section that quantifies a corporation's assets and activities in game terms. These rules give the gamemaster a tool for ranking the corporations, charting their overall successes and failures, and tracking the effect of any given shadowrun on its megacorporate target.

Much of the material in this book provides bits and pieces of intriguing information on which to base individual adventures or an ongoing campaign. How complex such adventures become, and how much trouble unseen corporate enemies may make for unsuspecting players, is up to the gamemaster.

This book is compatible with both the original **Shadowrun** rule book and **Shadowrun, Second Edition (SRII)**. Page references for both versions are given when applicable.

BIG BROTHER IS HERE

>>>>>**[Just when you thought it was safe to go back to Shadowland...**

A little friendly warning from your kindly SysOp: the Neo-Anarchists are back. Those of you familiar with the Neo-A party line should find the content, tone, and lack of internal consistency in the following diatribe all too familiar. Personally, I've identified at least three and perhaps four distinct points of view and writing styles in the files that follow. Anarchic or not, Neo-As don't seem to have anything against working together when it suits them.

As much as most Neo-As tick me off on a personal level, I have to admit that they've got a good (if slightly twisted) take on what's going on in the shadows and out of them. If you don't mind putting up with their pseudo-anarchic babble and gleeful hatred of all authority, you can learn plenty from what they put out.

Take this blather, for example (which some nameless Neo-As uploaded through a back door that scared the living drek out of some of Shadowland's tame deckers). Everyone in Seattle, and everywhere else, knows the megacorporations exist. They buy from them or sell to them, work for or against them . . . and, in the case of shadowrunners and SINless folk, frequently run from them.

But not many people know how the corps work. Corporate structure, how corps make their money, how they interact . . . maybe the CEO and a few other big shots know. But Joe Shadowrunner? Nah, he doesn't know. Most of the time, he doesn't care; but he should. He should care, because only by knowing how the corps operate can anybody understand what they're *really* doing to life in these United Canadian and American States. And everywhere else, for that matter. So read on, and maybe you'll learn something.]<<<<<
—SYSephan OPus (17:00:53/3-4-54)

>>>>>[Frag you and the hog you rode in on. Thank you.]<<<<<
—The Neon Antichrist (21:43:51/3-6-54)

>>>>>[Oh, yes, another thing. I don't know who among the local Neo-As actually uploaded this screed, but I would fragging well *like* to. . .as would the security boys who protect Shadowland from corporate intrusion. I think there's a job offer in the works.]<<<<<
—SYSephan OPus (23:21:31/3-6-54)

>>>>>[Offer gleefully accepted.]<<<<<
—The Neon Antichrist (00:00:32/3-7-54)

The megacorporations are a fact of life. They are as inescapable as gravity, as pervasive as air, and as necessary as both of those things for the continuation of life as we know it.

Not a politically correct viewpoint these days, but correct nonetheless. Most people prefer to view the megacorps as a facade or veneer over what they prefer to call "real" life. They think the corps don't affect the way things *really* work. This comforting fallacy represents a dangerous refusal to face an unpleasant truth. In significant ways, the megacorps *are* reality. The corps drive the world economy, from macroeconomic trends that change the face of the globe to seemingly minor occurrences that alter the price of your favorite stuffer. The corps pay the tab for all significant research and development programs; their money produces all the technological advances that the public takes for granted.

>>>>>[Hold on just a tick here. What about independent, private research labs?]<<<<<
    —Nat (12:22:47/3-9-54)

>>>>>[Point one out to me and we'll discuss it.]<<<<<
    —Archangel (15:04:16/3-9-54)

>>>>>[What about university research labs?]<<<<<
    —Nat (16:24:59/3-9-54)

>>>>>[No way you can call them independent, Nattie ol' chummer. Research labs answer to the university president and the board, who answer to the corporation that owns the university.]<<<<<
    —Ribald (16:42:19/3-9-54)

>>>>>[Corps don't own universities.]<<<<<
    —Nat (17:44:12/3-9-54)

>>>>>[Not outright, no. But they donate huge sums of money to keep the universities going. They lend equipment, they second personnel to the university staff, they provide other services when and wherever necessary. In return, the university jumps when the corps croak frog. That's reality.]<<<<<
    —Archangel (20:32:23/3-9-54)

>>>>>[Okay, what about that independent think tank in Kent—PensoDyne or whatever it's called? They do pure research.]<<<<<
    —Nat (23:46:30/3-9-54)

>>>>>[PensoDyne isn't independent. Yamatetsu Seattle owns it, through three shell companies. Nat, as far as I'm concerned there are *no* independent research establishments. *None.*]<<<<<
    —Archangel (02:12:33/3-10-54)

The corps dictate social trends, and to a great degree control the way many people view the world. To a certain extent, things happen in a certain way because the corporations have *willed* them to happen that way. Wars, civil unrest, insurrection, and other calamities all occur at the behest of the megacorps. Even shadowrunners, the one segment of society that considers itself beyond corporate control, exist only through the forbearance of the megacorps. If the corps should ever decide that the shadow community has become more of a hindrance than a help to their operations, they can send any number of corporate hit squads to exterminate shadowrunners without a second thought. Even more easily, the corps can eliminate the shadow community simply by ignoring it. Without corps to hire them for shadowruns, street ops face a brutally simple choice: find other employment or starve. The shadow world as we know it exists by corporate whim, and corporate whim can just as easily make it disappear.

>>>>>[I don't think I like this guy's arguments.]<<<<<
    —Blake (16:08:32/4-1-54)

>>>>>[I think the truth hurts, Blakey. Interesting how our nemeses, patrons, and reasons for existing are all the same, hm?]<<<<<
    —CySky (23:47:14/4-3-54)

CORPS AS NATIONS

For those of you who plaintively ask about national governments, I respectfully suggest you face facts. In today's megacorporate world, national governments are anachronisms. The Shiawase Decision of 2001, granting extraterritoriality to corporations, simply made official a condition that had existed *de facto* since the end of the last century. For the past fifty-odd years, the megacorps have played the most influential roles on the global stage. Though national governments and most of their citizens prefer to believe that the world runs by the rule of civil and criminal law and by international policy, in fact these forces pale in significance when compared to the rule of *corporate* law and *intercorporate* policy. In the 21st century, the old distinctions between social groups have started breaking down and reforming along new lines. Where a person might once have defined himself based on his geographical location, these days he might belong to a so-called "electronic tribe" or other previously unheard-of group. In this modern world, the megacorporations have taken on the same significance that belonged to emerging nation-states in the 19th and 20th centuries.

>>>>>[Does that mean the Corporate Court is the first true world government? Gotta give that one some thought . . .]<<<<<
    —Hart (22:13:45/3-24-54)

>>>>>[If national governments are so fragging irrelevant, why do the oh-so-mighty corps deign to let them exist?]<<<<<
    —Marjorie Morningstar (05:23:15/3-26-54)

>>>>>[Stripping away the sarcasm, you raise a good question, Marj. Try this for an answer.

The corps leave national governments in place because they perform a useful function. National governments handle a lot of functions that the corps don't want to bother with. Governments provide a social safety net (effective or otherwise), keeping people more or less happy who might otherwise vent their frustration against corporate assets. Governments maintain roads and data highways the corps use to carry out their business. And govern-

ments do all the scut jobs the corps don't want to touch, like making sure the garbage gets picked up. If the corps ever decided to get rid of the governments, they'd have to do all this work themselves, which would distract them from the profitable business of gouging the consumer.]<<<<<
—Bowers (13:53:27/3-27-54)

>>>>>[A colleague of mine told me once that when the world went to drek after the VITAS pandemic of 2010–11, the megacorps had the chance to become the world's official governments. They decided against it solely for the reasons Bowers described.]<<<<<
—Dirk (01:30:01/3-29-54)

Few people accept this reality, of course, for several reasons. First of all, it frightens them. More than half a century into the new millennium, most people view the world in 20th-century terms. They see themselves as citizens of a nation-state, and the nation at least partly defines them. When asked who they are, they say, "I'm an American," or "I'm from Pueblo." Most people find it disturbing that nationality no longer means much.

The ugly reality of the corporate world view also offends people. Megacorporations see individuals as assets, liabilities, or potential purchasers. Corps classify people into large groups, the better to accurately analyze and predict consumer behavior. The fact that individuals no longer matter *as* individuals disturbs many on a profound level.

Finally, the effort of understanding this frightening and ugly reality intimidates people. The prime movers of the world are not the politicians, those reassuringly well-known actors on the world stage. The geopolitical maneuvering that still fills most news media is akin to the ripples caused by something large moving below the surface of a still lake. Penetrating this surface to find out what's actually causing those ripples takes considerable effort. In order to understand the truth, people must make the effort to educate themselves. They must learn how corporations actually work, and what so-called "natural laws" they operate under. Intimidated by their own ignorance, most people cannot conceive of the effort it takes to understand how the world actually functions. Coupled with the fear that knowing the truth might make things worse, remaining ignorant becomes the only way most people can cope. Like the ostrich, the average joe prefers to stick his head in some nice, warm, comfy sand.

That judgment applies to most people. However, one of the tenets of Neo-Anarchism states that some people always stand out from the herd of humanity. These people want to understand, and are willing to act on what they know. This tract is dedicated to these few, true individuals. Go to it, my children, and open the can of worms. You have nothing to lose but your mental fetters.

>>>>>[Thus endeth the lesson.]<<<<<
—Bung (11:01:10/3-30-54)

>>>>>[Have you guys read through the file summary? What gives? This board's for shadowrunners, not economy and business majors. Definitions of megacorporate structure? Junk bonds?

Leveraged buyouts? Give me a fragging break. Why do I need to know all this stuff?]<<<<<
—Honker (20:19:42/4-2-54)

>>>>>[Personally, I don't go along with a lot of Neo-A drek, but I agree with them on this one. I know you by rep, Honker, if not by face. Ex-military, right? I heard you did a stint on that "peacemaking" mission to what was left of Pakistan. When you planned ops against the Nuevo-Hindu extremists, did you go in blind? No. You gathered all the intelligence you could on their goals, belief systems, backgrounds, and origins as well as on their military capabilities. "Know thine enemy," right?

So now you're a runner. You run ops against megacorporations. Know thine enemy applies here as well. I'm sure you research security assets at any corp facility you plan on raiding. But doesn't it also make sense to learn as much as possible and use it to your benefit? Who knows, you might find a way to prevent the corp from using all of its security against you. Also, it pays to understand your employer. If you know who's causing trouble for the megacorp hiring you, or who it wants to cause trouble for, you'll understand how your run fits into the bigger picture. That makes you less likely to play patsy and wind up dead.

Sure, plenty of shadowrunners out there like to play ostrich when it comes to megacorp economics and politics. But don't forget the ostrich is extinct.]<<<<<
—Argent (16:11:20/4-7-54)

MEGACORPORATE PRIMER

Most people believe they know what a corporation is and how it works. A corporation is a business; like any business, it makes a product and sells it to consumers for enough money to pay its production expenses and make a profit. However, few people realize that corporations take many forms and have far more complex structures than an average business.

>>>>>[For those of you not up on basic business, I've copped the following file from an introductory business text. It's rudimentary, but it has plenty of ideas in it that'll get your brains firing.]<<<<<
 —SYSephan OPus (17:23:01/3-4-54)

CORPORATIONS

Corporations have existed, virtually unchanged in form, since the mid–19th century. The business organizations that evolved into corporations started as individual proprietorships, in which one individual owned and operated the business. He might hire employees and managers to work for him, but he took ultimate responsibility for every facet of his business operation. No significant distinction existed between the assets of the business and of its owner; the owner paid full personal taxes on any profit his business made. The proprietor also took personal responsibility for any liabilities his business incurred beyond its ability to pay. Legally, creditors could seize the proprietor's house or other assets if the company failed to pay its bills.

As business became more complex, sole proprietorships gave way to partnerships. Operating in a manner similar to sole proprietorships, partnerships allowed multiple partners to pool their funds to operate the business. In addition to a larger pool of capital, partnerships offered the advantage of allowing individuals to specialize in certain facets of running the business. One individual no longer had to do everything, but could safely leave some aspects of the business to his partners. However, partners enjoyed no tax benefits and could still be held fully liable for business losses or other liabilities such as legal judgments against the partnership.

The corporation evolved as a method of sidestepping such liabilities. Corporations arose to combine the financial strength and diversity of several investor-owners (called shareholders) with the flexibility of hired managers, and also provided highly desirable tax breaks and legal protection for business owners.

Consider these two factors one at a time. Most governments tax corporate profits at a considerably lower rate than personal income. For example, the UCAS taxes corporate profits at a flat rate of 10 percent; the highest marginal tax rate for individuals is 48 percent. This 38-percent difference offers corporations a significant financial advantage.

>>>>>[Fragging sickening, isn't it? Ms. Jane Q. Public pays *five times* the tax rate paid by a corp. Just goes to show who and what the government really cares about, doesn't it?]<<<<<
—Thais (02:14:27/3-19-54)

>>>>>[It's not quite that bad. To pay that marginal rate, Jane Q. Public would have to be pulling in something like 115K¥ a year. Lower incomes get taxed at lower rates.]<<<<<
—Collins (17:30:13/3-20-54)

>>>>>[With the right kinds of tax shelters, write-offs, tax amelioration strategies, and good old-fashioned tax fraud, Jane wouldn't have to pay anywhere near the 48 percent marginal rate on her 115K¥. Bank on it.]<<<<<
—Rhodes (19:31:03/3-25-54)

>>>>>[Check out just how many of the megacorps with divisions in UCAS actually paid tax last year. Very few, chummers, very damn few. If you want to talk "good old-fashioned tax fraud," talk to the megacorps.]<<<<<
—Caine (10:13:15/3-26-54)

>>>>>[Why the frag doesn't the IRS *do* something about that, huh?]<<<<<
—Sally Steel (19:55:35/3-26-54)

>>>>>[Listen to one who knows, Sal. I used to work for the IRS in N'Yawk before I came to Seattle, as one of the service's front-line undercover investigators. Want to know why I quit my job and started running the shadows? Because the shadows are safer.]<<<<<
—The Chromed Accountant (22:37:44/3-6-54)

In addition to a markedly lower tax burden, the process of incorporation offers significant legal protection to business owners and managers. Incorporation creates a distinct legal entity, the corporation, that exists completely apart from the individuals who own and/or run it. If the company loses money or goes out of business, the investor/shareholder can lose no more than the amount of his original investment. No one can try to extract from the shareholders any additional money the corporation might happen to owe. The corporation also filters out many other legal unpleasantries, acting as a vital safeguard for the shareholder during the litigation explosion of the 1980s and '90s. The legal realities of incorporation even allow a corporation to go bankrupt without devastating the personal fortunes of board members and major shareholders.

>>>>>[Megacorps don't go out of business.]<<<<<
—Thais (02:31:02/3-19-54)

>>>>>[Not the majors, no. But the attrition among second- and third-tier corporations is astounding, particularly when the majors start feeling their oats. Remember that "corporate reorganization" at Yamatetsu Seattle last year? The shock waves spread throughout the corporate sector. Huge numbers of smaller corps, mainly subsidiaries, but also a few GDIs (God Damned Independents) went under. It looked like the aftermath of a massacre.]<<<<<
—The Chromed Accountant (21:59:09/3-22-54)

>>>>>[Theoretically, when a corp goes under the shareholders lose their investments. That happens to the small shareholders, the people who buy a chunk of the company on the stock market. The major shareholders, usually the board members and a few other interested parties, find it easy to gut a failing company and disappear with the nuyen. Before publicly going bankrupt, they drain the corp of its assets in various legal, quasi-legal, and grotesquely illegal ways. Once the money enters the shareholders' hands, the corp's creditors can't get at it. By the time the company actually declares bankruptcy, it's a shell with no assets worthy of the name.

Of course, if the major investors get caught illegally looting the company and get convicted, the law no longer protects the money. But catching and convicting these white-collar sharks poses two big problems. First, major shareholders can afford to hire major lawyers. And second, the extraterritoriality of multinational corporations makes it difficult to prove commission of a crime, let alone convict the guilty party. The jurisdiction problem turns into a bloody nightmare.]<<<<<
—Legal Beagle (09:06:45/4-1-54)

In summary, the overall advantages of incorporation are as follows:

• Extensive resources: Even taking into account uncertain economic returns, a large corporation usually has the wherewithal to keep up its research and development programs.
• Wide management base: A corporation can hire, retain, and train a wide range of competent managers, both generalists and specialists.
• Wide range of expertise: Its size allows a corporation to cover several different financially profitable areas.
• Social benefits: Corporations provide well-paying jobs for a large number of people, allowing them to maintain a high standard of living.

>>>>>[Frag, does this boy blow smoke, or what? Social benefits? Rewrite that last one to read "Corps *exploit* a large number of people who could otherwise enjoy a hassle-free existence."]<<<<<
—Doobie (16:44:58/3-19-54)

>>>>>[Hoo boy, if corporations are so great why don't *we* incorporate? Shadowrunners Inc., I can see it now . . .]<<<<<
—Bung (14:42:41/3-28-54)

As well as advantages, corporations also have drawbacks, more often for the consumers they serve than for business executives. In general, larger businesses enjoy economies of scale that allow them to make products more efficiently and cheaply than smaller organizations. However, because the larger companies control the market to a greater extent through monopolies, oligopolies, acquisition, and other methods, economy of scale rarely translates into a cost saving for the consumer. In the most extreme cases, corporations grow so large that the upper levels of the executive hierarchy forget that the corp engages in any business aside from guaranteeing its continued existence, growth and profitability. Top management loses sight of the fact that any business exists primarily to provide goods and/or services to the market, and instead bases its decisions on a completely different agenda. This situation offers the greatest potential for abuse of the corporate system.

>>>>>[I think just about every megacorp you can name has already gone *way* past this point.]<<<<<
—Doobie (16:49:32/3-19-54)

Corporations that forget about their market generate profit and cash flow by acquiring, divesting and stripping the husks of other companies and divisions. This kind of activity is meaningless in economic and market terms, because the corps engaged in it generate neither goods nor services of value to the consumer.

>>>>>[There's a lot more dirt later on about acquisitions, mergers, and divestiture. Check the section on **Competition** a couple of files down the line from here. It'll blow your mind.]<<<<<
—Legal Beagle (09:13:20/4-1-54)

CONGLOMERATES

Conglomerates arise from the merger of several independent corporates in different lines of business. The new conglomerate entity must then either organize itself to make one of its component corporations the visible organization, or else create a new public facade under which all its components can operate. For example, when Global Oil merged with UCAS Steel in 2041, both facets of the conglomerate continued to do business under the Global Oil banner. By contrast, when Maranouchi Entertainment and Hatari Computers merged in 2051, the conglomerate became Nihon Enterprises.

>>>>>[What happens when a corp acquires another company in the *same* line of business? Like, it buys out a competitor, either openly or secretly.]<<<<<
—ZeroTolerance (17:42:23/3-17-54)

>>>>>[Yeah, that happens despite the fact that it's illegal in a lot of jurisdictions. Sometimes it happens openly, and the law and public opinion be damned. It gets a lot more disturbing, though, when it happens secretly. Corp A takes over Corp B, and nobody knows it happened. (Maybe Corp A did it through intermediary shell companies, or maybe a mega that owns Corp A buys B and unofficially cedes management control of the new corp to A's board of directors.) Everyone who wasn't in on the deal thinks that A and B are still healthy competitors, but behind the scenes the two corps can go to town with price-fixing. Check out the later file on competition, mergers and buy-outs. I've got more to say there.]<<<<<
—The Chromed Accountant (22:21:06/3-22-54)

MULTINATIONALS

Though many business analysts discuss them as though they have only appeared recently, multinational corporations have existed for a century and a half. Oil companies, with exploration and drilling operations in different countries or even on different continents from their home offices, represent the first real multinationals. For example, the multinational Singer Company was incorporated in 1863.

>>>>>[*1863*, jokers. Ocean travel meant sailing on a wooden ship, and the first transatlantic telegraph cable didn't appear until a few years later. Telephone communication across the Atlantic wouldn't appear for more than 80 years. Nowadays, managers meet in "virtual boardrooms" or use trideoconferencing for realtime communication. But 190 years ago, almost two centuries, the managers of Singer kept their business operating without any of those bells and whistles.]<<<<<
—Sarah B (13:41:10/3-26-54)

>>>>>[Okay, maybe some companies operated in multiple countries, but they weren't *real* multinationals.]<<<<<
—Featherstone (12:36:56/3-27-54)

>>>>>[Depends on your standards, I suppose. Back in the 1980s and 1990s, good old Shell the petrochem giant had more than *800* operating companies in different parts of the world. I'd call that a "real" multinational. (Keep in mind that, compared to what we use today, the communications Shell used in the '80s and '90s weren't much more advanced than the ones Singer used . . .)]<<<<<
  —Sarah B (13:04:15/3-29-54)

In the mid-19th century, multinationals developed because their ability to establish, control, and manage facilities on foreign soil allowed them to circumvent tariffs and other barriers to international business. At various times in the past, most countries required a company to establish an independent local organization before it could do business within a national jurisdiction. Canada enforced this requirement with particular zeal, forcing American companies to set up Canadian subsidiaries such as Apple Canada, Ford Canada, and so on to gain access to a potentially lucrative market.

>>>>>[Check my comments later in this file about autonomous vs. centrally managed divisions or subsidiaries. Plenty of Canadian "branch plants" were centrally managed to a ludicrous degree. Back in the 1990s, if you lived in Vancouver (only 300 klicks or so north of Seattle) and you ordered a mouse (an ancient input device) from Microsoft in Bellevue, Microsoft shipped your rodent up to the HQ of Microsoft Canada in Toronto, 6000+ klicks east of Vancouver. Microsoft Canada then shipped it to you in Vancouver a week or so late. Your mouse cost you Canadian tariffs, plus shipping and handling costs for a 12,000-klick round trip, *plus* the overhead for the Canadian HQ. Stupid.]<<<<<
  —Bure (13:54:04/4-21-54)

Today more multinationals exist than ever before, with a larger average size than in past eras. The largest multinational ever to exist, however, is not a modern-day megacorp. During its heyday in the first decade of the 21st century, Nestle Corp. dwarfed even the mightiest of the later megacorporations. MCT, Ares and Aztechnology, for example, are all less than 80 percent as large as Nestle was four decades ago.

>>>>>[Yeah, well, that's true if you're talking about the sizes that appear in business indexes and other public places. But what's that got to do with reality? Does anybody outside the Mitsuhama boardroom *really* know how big MCT is? The sizes that this guy is talking about refer to the total of all subsidiaries and divisions *known* to be part of the Mitsuhama empire. But how many more companies does MCT *secretly* own that don't show up in the official tally? The comparison is meaningless. Before Nestle imploded in 2008, we *knew* about all of its parts.]<<<<<
  —Collins (17:36:34/3-20-54)

>>>>>[You *think* . . .]<<<<<
  —Caine (10:19:38/3-26-54)

>>>>>[And another thing; size means more than physical extent, number of employees, or even cash flow. These days, information

is power, and the Matrix is the best place to have clout. A corporation can look small, yet control massive amounts of information. It doesn't take much manpower or equipment to regulate the info that passes between and inside these corps. Because their influence comes from pure data and not from monetary credit, they might not record much in the way of cash flow either.]<<<<<
  —Frazier (20:34:09/3-27-54)

The simple definition of a multinational is a corporation or conglomerate that conducts business in multiple countries, with more or less autonomous divisions or subsidiaries handling operations in each nation or region. Most jurisdictions consider each national division an independent corporation for taxation and other legal purposes.

The level of autonomy enjoyed by national divisions varies widely, from nearly 100 percent to virtually none. At the one extreme, regional managers account to corporate headquarters for the profitability of their division, but remain free to decide how to conduct business to maintain that profitability. The management process for such an autonomous division differs little from that of an independent national company. At the other end of the scale, divisional managers must refer every significant decision and many less significant decisions as well to the multinational's headquarters for approval. Not surprisingly, most multinationals fall near the middle of the autonomy scale.

>>>>>[Titles can sometimes give you a clue as to how much autonomy a division has. For example, the head honcho of Hanara Seattle has the title "General Manager," while the big cheese of Kigune UCAS is "President and CEO."]<<<<<
  —Dean (10:44:23/3-19-54)

>>>>>[Not necessarily true. Taking your two examples, Dean, Hanara's GM has a trideoconference with HQ just once every quarter. The rest of the time, he can run his business the way he wants to as long as he keeps making money. The "Prez/CEO" of Kigune UCAS has to get Tokyo headquarters to approve *every* expenditure higher than 100K nuyen. For a big corp, 100K nuyen is petty cash. So job title has nothing to do with the level of autonomy.]<<<<<
  —The Chromed Accountant (10:16:23/3-26-54)

All levels of autonomy have advantages and disadvantages. Greater autonomy allows the divisional manager in the country of operation to make decisions based on firsthand knowledge of local conditions. Because such a manager need not refer decisions up the ladder and incur potential delays, the company remains much more responsive to changing conditions. On the other hand, the autonomous divisional manager may concentrate on his own business without regard to the overall scheme of the multinational corporation. In an extreme case, a divisional manager might make decisions that help his own division while harming the multinational's prospects.

Direct, centralized control ensures that each division plays its part in the corporate grand scheme. Requiring divisional manag-

ers to refer most or all decisions to corporate headquarters eliminates the risk of a "loose cannon" divisional manager pursuing his division's specific goals to the detriment of the overall corporation. On the other hand, the constant reporting and checking demanded by centralized control takes time, and diminishes the overall responsiveness of subsidiary divisions. Also, direct control can give headquarters-based managers with little or no personal experience of foreign business conditions the power to make uninformed or harmful decisions. Though so-called "remote control" management ensures that all divisions work together toward the same goal, it frequently diminishes the profitability and effectiveness of each individual division.

>>>>>[It also takes its toll on divisional managers. Burns them out right quick.]<<<<<
　　—Thor (11:02:17/3-18-54)

>>>>>[Let's talk dirty tricks here. Competitors planning a run or any other operation against a national division should know as much as they can about the target corp's management style, and as much as possible about the people in positions of authority.

Take a largely autonomous division. The local manager has a lot more freedom to react appropriately and quickly when he realizes somebody's taking a run at his operation. (Unless, of course, he's a lame-duck manager. But lame ducks don't get to run autonomous divisions very often.) To make a successful run against a division like this, you need to capitalize on that division's weaknesses.

With a centrally controlled division, where the local manager has to get headquarters approval for all significant actions, the corp or other group that's running the shadow op has a lot more time to do its dirty work before the target can respond. Also, senior management at headquarters might not realize the significance of the threat to its division, and may not respond appropriately. In this case, you can capitalize on the weaknesses of either the local division or central management.]<<<<<
　　—Ronson (14:40:44/3-24-54)

>>>>>[So the corp making the run (or whatever) should lull central management into a false sense of security, right? Make the divisional manager look like he's overreacting, jumping at shadows, going paranoid, whatever.]<<<<<
　　—Markasy (17:52:38/3-25-54)

>>>>>[I helped pull off a run against a centrally managed division where we compromised the division's communication channel with headquarters. The divisional manager screamed bloody blue murder when he first got wind of our operation, demanding that someone in authority respond to the run. We fragged around with the message to make him sound like he was flipping out over something inconsequential. When HQ asked him to explain why he thought matters were so bad, we changed the message to look like a brush-off. He answered them with a set of messages so panicked and hysterical that we didn't need to frag around with them. By the time everyone sorted out who'd really said what, we'd finished our run and beat feet.]<<<<<
　　—Anonymous (00:03:26/4-1-54)

>>>>>[Makes for a good story, but I don't buy it. Most corps have comm channels so secure *nobody* can compromise them. They've got their own communication satellites handling redundantly encrypted message traffic, mages sending notes back and forth via watcher-spirit couriers, private fiber-optic land lines, you name it. *Nobody* can break that kind of channel.]<<<<<
　　—Pentecost (03:15:29/4-1-54)

>>>>>[You can *always* find ways to compromise channels, Pentecost. Software and hardware too secure for you? Bribe one of the comm techs or somebody's secretary. I do it all the time. The "wetware" is always the weakest link in any system.]<<<<<
    —Kip (14:00:22/4-3-54)

>>>>>[I keep hearing rumors that fiber optic channels aren't as secure as everyone wants to believe. Think on that, and pleasant nightmares.]<<<<<
    —Vongole (23:02:03/4-3-54)

MEGACORPORATIONS

No widely accepted definition exists to distinguish a multinational conglomerate from a megacorporation. Every business analyst agrees that the so-called "first tier" corps such as Mitsuhama, Aztechnology, and similar organizations are megacorps, but the second and lower tiers contain considerable variation among individual organizations. For example, though most business analysts consider Kyoto-based Yamatetsu Corporation a megacorp, a small school of thought applies that term according to stricter

criteria, and therefore does not class Yamatetsu in the megacorporate league.

The third-tier companies that sprang from the "merger fever" of the 2030s, such as Chrysler-Nissan, Honda-GM, and Renault-Fiat, do not possess the economic clout of the first– and second–tier firms despite their size and influence. Opinion about the megacorporate status of such companies varies widely among business experts, with most analysts regarding them as too small to be true megacorps.

According to the most common definition, a true megacorporation has a cash flow and degree of world influence roughly equivalent to that of a late 20th century nation-state. Using this definition, twenty five true megacorporations exist today.

>>>>>[This definition makes sense to me. For example, the entire MCT "empire" has an annual cash flow of about 95 *billion* nuyen, several times the GNP of Ireland. Please note that's *cash flow*. The figure for total assets is much higher.]<<<<<
    —The Chromed Accountant (10:25:15/3-26-54)

>>>>>[Where the frag did you get that figure, Chrome? That's *way* above published data.]<<<<<
    —Margo (05:26:21/4-1-54)

>>>>>[The figure above *is* published data, but also short of the true amount. I imagine that some of my one-time colleagues are also curious as to your source of information . . .]<<<<<
    —Mitsuhama Refugee (19:00:28/4-7-54)

EXTRATERRITORIALITY

Everyone has heard of corporate extraterritoriality. Most people understand at least a portion of the consequences set in motion by the landmark Shiawase Decision of 2001, but each individual seems to understand a different portion. To make sense of the contemporary megacorporate business environment, the business student must comprehend the full meaning of corporate extraterritoriality.

HISTORY

A complete understanding of the present can come only from an analysis of the past. The trends that eventually led to the Shiawase Decision had been building for decades before they came to a disastrous head in 1999, in New York City. Taken alone, the individual events that contributed to the crisis seemed neither catastrophic nor particularly unusual. Their simultaneous occurrence, however, added immeasurably to their significance.

As the end of the millennium approached, society began to realize that the developed world could not maintain the level of wealth, security, and continuous growth that had categorized the last half-century. Predictably, special-interest groups began to pressure the government to grant them concessions while the government still had something to concede. As different groups struggled over slices of a shrinking global pie, civil disobedience became a common tactic, particularly among the newly resurgent trade unions. Among the most militant groups was the Teamsters union. In late 1998, the Teamsters' New York local went on strike, interrupting the flow of fresh food into the sprawling megalopolis and virtually paralyzing the city.

At that time, the New York state government employed the largest number of unionized truckers. The Teamsters believed that public protests by 15 million New Yorkers who saw their food vanish off supermarket shelves at a terrifying rate would force the state to renegotiate the truckers' contract. The Teamsters had unfortunately overlooked the fact that the state government did not have the money with which to meet their demands. When the Teamsters' leadership belatedly recognized reality in early 1999, it urged the union's rank-and-file members to accept the state's final contract offer. For various reasons, including refusal to lose face by backing down, the truckers rejected the contract. The strike continued, triggering citywide food riots scant weeks later. Mobs of starving New Yorkers rampaged through the streets, looting and destroying.

Before the Teamsters' strike, Seretech Transport had carried most of New York's vegetables into the city. The transport company's parent corporation, the U.S.-based conglomerate Seretech, enjoyed a high profile and worldwide influence. Seretech had divisions engaged in more than twenty major industries, among them Seretech Medical Research. When a mob on the streets of Staten Island one chill February night saw the blue-and-white Seretech logo on the side of a large, refrigerated truck, they assumed the vehicle was packed with food. Starving and furious, they attacked.

In fact, the truck belonged to Seretech's medical research division and contained highly infectious medical waste. As the courts later ruled in a landmark decision, the limited security forces aboard the Seretech truck acted to protect public well-being as well as their own lives when they defended the vehicle from the attacking mob and called additional security forces.

>>>>>[Taking the long view, I sometimes think a minor epidemic in New York might have been better for everyone than extraterritorial megacorps . . .]<<<<<
　　　—Bromley (17:17:39/3-21-54)

>>>>>[Except for the people who bit it from some bug they caught from the "food truck" they rolled. Face it, extraterritoriality was bound to happen. If the Seretech decision hadn't done it, something else would have.]<<<<<
　　　—Voodoo (05:41:53/4-3-54)

>>>>>[You got *that* one. Read my comments on FutureLand™ later on in this file.]<<<<<
　　　—Mick (09:33:35/4-29-54)

At the outset of the assault, the armed mob far outnumbered Seretech security forces. The flood of angry people blocked the truck with their bodies, trying to roll it over. As reinforcements joined both sides of the conflict, the attempted hijacking of the truck became a rolling firefight. Despite the timely arrival of lightly armed Seretech security vehicles, the truck remained in jeopardy

and the risk of widespread exposure to the infectious agents it contained remained unacceptably high. Battling the mob at every step, the security forces managed to move the truck to a readily defensible Seretech research site across the New Jersey state line in Linden.

Subsequent police interrogation of the security personnel shows that they intended simply to hold off the mob long enough to explain that the truck contained no food. Unfortunately, the mob refused to listen to reason. Throughout the night of February 21 and early morning of February 22, the mob repeatedly tried to storm the Seretech facility's defensive perimeter.

>>>>>[By this time, most of the attackers had probably forgotten about the food. Mobs get a mind of their own; they'll keep trying to overrun anything in their path, even if they no longer know why.]<<<<<
　　　—Socio Pat (05:49:43/3-30-54)

By the time the overworked, exhausted civilian police department appeared on the scene and broke up what had become a siege, 20 Seretech employees lay dead along with ten times that number of civilians. Countless others were wounded on both sides of the conflict.

Because the rolling combat had crossed a state boundary, the Seretech siege seemed to give the federal government a perfect opportunity to crack down on the proliferation of private corporate armies. *The United States v. Seretech Corporation*, charging the corporation with criminal negligence, came swiftly to trial.

>>>>>[Apparently the government wanted to charge Seretech with premeditated murder, to send an even stronger message to the corps. Course, they couldn't have got a conviction on that, and they knew it.]<<<<<
　　　—Legal Beagle (17:08:11/3-18-54)

The initial court case resulted in a conviction, which Seretech's lawyers immediately appealed. In late 1999, less than a year after the incident, the Supreme Court handed down its landmark decision. In a 193-page judgment, the Supreme Court upheld Seretech's right to maintain an armed force for the protection of its personnel and property, and commended the corporation for protecting innocent citizens and honoring its trust to dispose of contaminated materials safely.

>>>>>[According to people I know whose parents were peripherally involved with the case, or knew others who were, *everybody* involved with the prosecution got canned. Maybe "purged" is a better word. The government was *incredibly* pissed, understandably so. Their *cause celebre* got them the opposite result from the one they'd intended.]<<<<<
　　　—Legal Beagle (17:13:01/3-18-54)

The Seretech decision set an important precedent, perfectly understood by the legal staffs of the growing megacorporations. Using the Supreme Court ruling as a basis, corporate lawyers began to challenge civic, state, and even federal restrictions on equipment, training and deployment of corporate security forces. They successfully argued that the Supreme Court had declared private security forces legal and of benefit to the public. Therefore, restrictions limiting the effectiveness of such forces ran contrary to the public interest and should be weakened or removed.

>>>>>[That's an oversimplification of the complex arguments used, but it conveys the general thrust. If anyone wants to learn about the actual legal niceties, you can find several thousand terapulses (that's *billions* of megapulses, for the exponentially challenged) of analysis in various law libraries on the Net.]<<<<<
    —Legal Beagle (17:14:58/3-18-54)

This argument proved remarkably effective in settling court cases. Over the course of two years, courts rolled back or emasculated more and more restrictions on the deployment and activities of corporate security forces. Finding this trend threatening, various branches of government escalated their attempts to bring the corporate armies to heel. Taking a leaf from the corporations' own book, government prosecutors argued their cases based on maximizing the public good. Early in the year 2000, the Supreme Court upheld several important government challenges to corporate autonomy. Apparently, the legal tide had turned against the corporations.

Shiawase Goes to Court
A year later, the landmark Shiawase Decision permanently reversed previous government victories. To carry out vital metallurgical processes such as the smelting of aluminum, the Shiawase Corporation's metallurgical engineering division needed huge amounts of electrical energy. When the plant opened in 1997, it drew its power from the regional utility grid. As government backlashes against perceived corporate excesses grew, the publicly owned and government-run utility grid raised its rates for high-load commercial customers, increasing Shiawase's energy costs by more than 550 percent in less than six months. Recognizing the futility of fighting the utility's price increase directly, the corporation instead approached the Nuclear Regulatory Commission in 1998 and demanded the right to set up a nuclear plant. A corporate-owned power plant would make Shiawase independent of the regional utility grid, saving it untold millions. Appalled at the idea of a private nuclear facility belonging to an independent corporation, the government-run Nuclear Regulatory Commission refused Shiawase permission to establish one. Predictably, Shiawase challenged the decision and carried the case to the Supreme Court.

>>>>>[Supreme Court must've been busy back then.]<<<<<
    —Bung (11:12:57/3-29-54)

>>>>>[You don't know the half of it.]<<<<<
    —Legal Beagle (17:17:13/3-18-54)

Shiawase based its argument on restraint of trade. The corporation's lawyers argued that different facets of the government had tried to prevent Shiawase from continuing in business.

Through the regional utility grid, the government had first raised energy costs to a prohibitive level, then used the Nuclear Regulatory Commission to prevent Shiawase from obtaining cheaper energy. The Supreme Court agreed with the corporation's arguments, and handed down the first of two decisions known as *Nuclear Regulatory Commission v. Shiawase Corporation* in favor of Shiawase. The corporation built its reactor and brought it on-line in late 2000, and immediately declared itself independent of the regional utility grid.

>>>>>[Hold the phone here. The court said go ahead in the summer, and before the end of the year the corp had the reactor up and running? When East Bay MUD in San Francisco decided they needed another reactor, *three years* elapsed between the date of the court decision and the date the new facility went on-line. How could Shiawase turn it around so fast?]<<<<<
    —Lodestone (13:11:38/4-2-54)

>>>>>['Cause the local government participated in the East Bay MUD project.<grin>
    Seriously, it's an interesting discrepancy. Sure, private corporations usually run things much more efficiently than the public sector, but even then it takes a lot longer than six months to build and commission a nuclear plant. A lot of the relevant records disappeared in the Crash of '29, so we'll probably never know the truth. But it looks like Shiawase used a pre-engineered reactor shipped from their Singapore operation. The reactor vessel, the control electronics, and the support engineering were all ready-made.
    Course, they still had to finish the containment building and other structures, a pretty big construction project to pull off in a couple of months. It looks like Shiawase started construction the moment the utility grid started gouging them. The corp put who knows how many millions into the project, knowing full well that the NRC and every other government agency would try to block them. *And* it looks like they kept the project going while the challenge to the NRC ruling went through the courts. Shiawase kept pouring megabucks into a project they might easily have had to scrap if the court ruling didn't go their way.
    Almost makes you think they *knew* something, doesn't it?]<<<<<
    —Harker (04:38:16/4-6-54)

>>>>>[Are you saying Shiawase had the fix in with the Supreme Court?]<<<<<
    —Sydney (10:42:33/4-8-54)

>>>>>[I'm saying it's an interesting thought.]<<<<<
    —Harker (02:52:18/4-17-54)

Shiawase's problems did not end with the commission of the nuclear plant in late 2000. The turn of the century saw the rise of ecological sabotage and environmental terrorism, with nuclear facilities among the primary targets. Shiawase's highly publicized Supreme Court victory attracted enormous attention to the corporation's new reactor, particularly among environmental activists. Within weeks of the plant's opening, various groups began planning acts of "ecotage" against the corporate site.

A special forces team from a group known as TerraFirst!, armed with military-grade weapons, penetrated the nuclear plant's security perimeter and met Shiawase's security forces. The TerraFirst! team packed enough explosives to split the containment building and reactor vessel like eggshells, spreading nuclear material throughout the surrounding area. Fortunately, they never reached the containment building. Shiawase security forces cut down every last member of the heavily armed eco-terrorist group, setting the stage for the second and best-known Shiawase Decision.

>>>>>[Ah, the eco-terrorist's logic. "We believe that nuclear power is bad because it might kill people. So let's kill people to prove it's bad, and then it won't kill people." Huh? Not only are they neo-Luddites, they're fragging certifiable.]<<<<<
—Jan (00:53:15/3-27-54)

Shiawase Decision

Earlier court rulings had allowed Shiawase's private forces to provide all security at the Shiawase nuclear plant. The Nuclear Regulatory Commission had tried to force Shiawase to include local police in their defense personnel, but the Supreme Court struck down this demand as unreasonable. In the aftermath of the widely publicized TerraFirst! incident, the Nuclear Regulatory Commission decided to capitalize on the widespread fear the assault had engendered in the populace. The NRC brought suit against Shiawase for criminal negligence and reckless endangerment, charging that Shiawase's inadequate security had failed to prevent the eco-terrorists from penetrating the nuclear reactor's outer perimeter. The NRC maintained that only sheer luck had allowed corporate security forces to stop the TerraFirst! team before it could release radioactive material across the countryside.

To this day, legal analysts consider the NRC's short-sighted strategy foredoomed to failure. Shiawase countered with evidence that its private security forces could have stopped a raiding force three times the size of the TerraFirst! team. They also proved that the raiders had only penetrated the outer perimeter because restrictions on private security operations had effectively emasculated Shiawase's defensive plans. The corporation's lawyers argued that the conflict between the unarguable requirements of corporate security and the laws of the United States that limited the effectiveness of such security represented an unacceptable

threat to public safety. Because the Shiawase Corporation would not presume to demand that the court alter laws of the land on its behalf, the lawyers maintained that the Shiawase Corporation should no longer be subject to those laws within the boundaries of its private property. The corporation argued for extraterritoriality as the only logical solution to the dilemma.

The NRC argued strenuously against this proposition, but could not stop the inevitable. Shiawase had based its arguments on security and public safety, issues the NRC had first brought into question. After several weeks of deliberation, the Supreme Court in 2001 declared Shiawase and all other major corporations extraterritorial. The most famous of the two *Shiawase Corporation* decisions, the ruling declared corporate property sovereign territory not subject to the jurisdiction of the surrounding nation-state.

>>>>>[This means that corp property in Seattle isn't part of the UCAS. You step into the Renraku Arcology, and you're no longer in the UCAS; you're in "Renraku-land." UCAS laws don't count any more; only Renraku corporate laws matter.]<<<<<
—Zingo (12:31:42/4-10-54)

>>>>>[Extraterritoriality has always been the rule for consulates and embassies, even though a lot of people don't know it. If you go to the British Consulate down on Seneca, the moment you step in the door you're not in the UCAS. You're in the United Kingdom. So if you're in another country and get in trouble with the law, head for the UCAS embassy or consulate. As long as you didn't violate UCAS law, the local yokels can't touch you unless they go through the whole deportation rigmarole.]<<<<<
—Honey (02:37:04/4-13-54)

>>>>>[Honey basically has it right. But until the Shiawase Decision, extraterritoriality only applied to representatives of foreign governments. After the decision, it included the corps. That was new.]<<<<<
—Zingo (12:04:53/4-16-54)

>>>>>[One place set a precedent for partial corp extraterritoriality long before the Shiawase Decision, boys and girls. Remember that little ol' place down in Florida, FutureLand™? Even back in the '70s and '80s, that place got pretty fragging close to extraterritorial. It constituted its own county and had its own police force. (My dad called them future cops when I was a kid; I thought they carried

laser guns.) Only FutureLand™ employees could rent accommodation inside its boundaries. All residents supposedly elected the county council or whatever they called the governing body, but the company proposed the slate of candidates. If you didn't ratify it, you might lose your house or your job. The county council could make and enforce local laws. The way I read it, FutureLand™ was the harbinger of extraterritoriality.]<<<<<
—Mick (15:35:38/4-20-54)

The vast majority of other nation-states, including those considered major players on the world stage, soon enacted laws analogous to the Shiawase Decision. The classes of corporation to which extraterritoriality applies vary from jurisdiction to jurisdiction. For example, in Germany only the largest and most influential megacorps enjoy extraterritorial status. However, most jurisdictions consider the major megacorporations extraterritorial, with a few minor exceptions.

>>>>>[I'd like to point out that though the Shiawase Decision pushed things over the edge regarding extraterritoriality, the Supreme Court didn't make that decision in a vacuum. Shiawase was just the latest of the Supreme Court's many decisions that resolved a question of national law. For example, one of the cases indirectly resolved by the Shiawase Decision involved the murder of an employee of an offshore multinational. The victim was a citizen of the island the company had incorporated itself on. The murderer was a United States citizen, apprehended by corporate security on the corp's grounds. The United States had no extradition treaty with the island, so the corp transported the killer to the island for trial before local U.S. government could react. In defense of its action, the corp claimed that offshore incorporation represented establishment of a legal identity that afforded them the status of a foreign embassy. From this legal disassociation from local jurisdiction, it took only a few simple steps to reach true corporate extraterritoriality.]<<<<<
—Kinnsey (10:25:18/4-22-54)

CONSEQUENCES OF EXTRATERRITORIALITY

The Shiawase Decision meant that any territory a corporation owned came under that corporation's legal jurisdiction rather than that of the surrounding nation-state. Subsequent refinements of the law extended extraterritoriality to apply to land and structures used but not owned by the corporation.

In the first five years after the Shiawase Decision, the Supreme Court recognized extraterritoriality only when the corporation involved owned a particular site and the buildings on it as a freehold. If the corp leased the land, extraterritoriality did not apply. The megacorporations brought their legal assets to bear on this interpretation, however, arguing that foreign embassies and consulates did not need to own land or buildings to be considered distinct jurisdictions. After several bouts of legal wrangling, the corporations won their point. To this day, in the UCAS, many Native American Nations, Japan and most other developed countries, any "continuous and contiguous, recognized and long-term" corporate site or facility is extraterritorial regardless of property and building ownership.

>>>>>[Translation follows. "Continuous and contiguous" means the area involved must be recognizable as a single area distinct from its surroundings. Throw up a fence around a tract of land, or lease an entire floor of an office building, and it's "continuous and contiguous." As long as you can see some kind of intuitively obvious distinction between corp property and surrounding territory, like "the tenth floor as opposed to the ninth floor" or "all the offices that can only be reached via the Gaeatronics lobby," the area qualifies as extraterritorial. A hypothetical Yamatetsu rep who shares a bullpen style open office with reps from other corps couldn't claim her desk is extraterritorial, because you can't see a clear distinction between her territory and everyone else's. It sounds complicated, but the "intuitively obvious" rule makes a good guideline.
"Recognized" means the area must have official and public recognition as corp territory. For example, MCT can't open up a secret office under the name of a local sole proprietorship and then claim extraterritoriality for it. It's not recognized as MCT turf, so it doesn't get those benefits.
"Long-term" means an official lease must exist, signed by a duly authorized officer of the corporation. A couple of court cases tried to hash out exactly how long the lease has to run to qualify, but the corp has to have the lease with the officer's signature. That means a Renraku suit can't stand in the middle of his living room just as Lone Star goons kick down his door and claim his apartment is Renraku corp territory. That's how extraterritoriality works.]<<<<<
—Legal Beagle (17:38:00/3-18-54)

>>>>>[I hope all you runners out there paid attention to that last posting. The information in those few sentences could save your puny lives a few times over.]<<<<<
—Uncle Rex (02:12:26/3-20-54)

>>>>>[As in most cases, use the "maximum drek" rule of thumb. If you're not sure whether or not a particular place qualifies as extraterritorial, assume the ruling that would get you in the maximum drek, and plan accordingly.]<<<<<
—Olympus (16:00:41/3-28-54)

>>>>>["Recognized" isn't as cut and dried as you make it sound, Beagle. What about those corp "zero zones" out along Highway 5? They're not publicly advertised as corp facilities, but you can bet your hoop that if you go over the fence you're in another jurisdiction. As far as I know, "shoot first and frag the questions" isn't the law in Seattle.]<<<<<
—Mary (16:28:19/4-1-54)

>>>>>[Okay, granted. But arguing over that kind of interpretation keeps lawyers rich. I like Olympus' "maximum drek" rule. Keep that in mind, and you can't go far wrong.]<<<<<
—Legal Beagle (14:33:11/4-7-54)

The Shiawase Decision approved extraterritoriality specifically to allow corporations to better protect their assets and operations. In subsequent decades, the application of extraterritoriality has expanded. Today, megacorps use extraterritoriality to continue principles and policies of operation forbidden by various jurisdictions in which they operate, or to prevent local laws from interfering with corporate business practices. For example, UCAS laws allow workers to organize into a union for the purposes of collective bargaining, and employers may not legally fire or harass employees who attempt to organize. In 2038, a group of workers within an Ares Macrotechnology subsidiary attempted to form a union, and Ares management terminated everyone involved. When the fired workers appealed, the courts recognized Ares' right to fire the employees because their action violated the megacorporation's law prohibiting unionization. The attempts at organization took place within Ares facilities, and so fell under corporate jurisdiction. The court ruled that Ares corporate law took precedence over UCAS law in the case.

Megacorporate extraterritoriality applies not only to labor law, but also to criminal law, civil law, and environmental law. For example, the UCAS has strict laws regarding the use of lethal force by a security official or peace officer. These laws hold on the streets of Seattle regardless of the people involved. Within a corporate site or enclave, however, corporate law applies, and UCAS legal restrictions on the use of force go by the board.

>>>>>[Okay, now *this* is the kind of stuff you jokers out there want to read about, am I right? Before you go prancing around inside some corp site, take the time to find out about that site's laws. Corp laws are more or less arbitrary; the corps can change them from location to location. Do security forces have to verbally warn you or fire a warning shot before they shoot to kill? Or can they drop you from ambush? Better know this stuff before you go in, chummer, it could save your rotten little hide.

Also find out how strictly the corp enforces its laws. For example, Yamatetsu Seattle guards officially have to give perpetrators one clearly audible, verbal warning before they fire. In practice, the standard procedure usually sounds more like "*Bam-bam-bam*-FREEZE!" So far, no sec-guard has gotten so much as a reprimand for breaking the corporate law about fair warning.]<<<<<
　　—Coralee (16:54:41/4-13-54)

>>>>>[Fraggin' A, come *on*, Cora. What the frag good does it do finding out about a corp's laws? Like you said, they're arbitrary. That means they can change at *any* time. The normal procedure may be a warning shot before the SMGs open up, but say you and your runners look too tough for the guards to take the risk. So the sec team hoses you down with heavy MGs, then uses mortars to take out the stragglers, all without so much as an "okay-gutterpunks-turn-into-ice." When the "unfortunate incident" comes to light, corp management arbitrarily changes the law retroactively so that they no longer require a warning. The guards are off the hook, and you're rapidly chilling meat. The ugly truth of the matter is that the corps can do whatever the frag they want, whenever the frag they want. Face it.]<<<<<
　　—Vi (00:16:09/4-16-54)

>>>>>[What about the Constitution and the Bill of Rights, huh? No corp can overturn them.]<<<<<
　　—Box (05:04:21/4-17-54)

>>>>>[Okay, Box, the Constitution and Bill of Rights. They apply to everyone in the UCAS, inalienable and all that claptrap, right? Okay. So say you hop a semiballistic and fly over to London, England. Do the Constitution and Bill of Rights apply to you as you're walking the streets of Merry Olde England? Of course not. You're not in the UCAS any more. Now let's say you give the semiballistic a miss, and instead sashay into the Renraku Arcology shopping mall. Do the Constitution and Bill of Rights apply to you? *No*, you slot, you're not in the UCAS any more. The moment you stepped onto Renraku turf, you effectively left the country.

Read my lips, Box, and any other congenital idiots out there. *Corp territory is another fragging country.* Like Vi said, face it.]<<<<<
　　—Dr. Demento (09:41:42/4-19-54)

>>>>>[That's why shadowrunners don't shop the Arcology.]<<<<<
　　—Bung (16:00:02/4-11-54)

>>>>>[For people who wonder where to shop safely, most normal malls don't count as extraterritorial corporate turf even though corporations own them, because most malls don't meet Legal Beagle's requirements of continuity and contiguity. Westlake Center, Southcenter and the rest aren't extraterritorial. The Renraku Arcology Grand Arcade *is* extraterritorial, because it's inside the arcology. Get it?]<<<<<
　　—VickiD (17:24:29/4-14-54)

Criminal Offenses

Many trideo shows and simsense programs involve corporate employees committing a crime outside corporate territory, then returning to the corporation and claiming protection from the outside law. According to this scenario, the guilty party sits comfortably in his office as the Lone Star detectives stand impotently outside the facility gate. Unfortunately, this fictional portrayal carries considerable truth. Peace officers or security officers from a different corporation have no jurisdiction on corporate territory. They cannot arrest a suspect, or even question him against his will. The agency wishing to question or arrest a suspect must officially apply for an extradition order from corporate management, just as they might apply to a foreign government. Whether or not management grants the order depends on many factors, including whether or not the alleged offense is considered illegal in the jurisdiction of the offender's corporation. In most cases, the agency or body requesting extradition must prove to the satisfaction of corporate management that the suspect has in fact committed the crime, or at least that the evidence warrants a trial. However, the actual decision remains up to the management of the offender's corporation. If it decides against extradition, outside law enforcement may not appeal.

>>>>>[Not exactly true. This happens if a national government or representative thereof, like Lone Star acting as a police agency, requests extradition. If another corp demands extradition, it can appeal the decision to the Corporate Court in Zurich-Orbital. (See **Corporate Court**, p. 96 of the **Zurich-Orbital** file.) Of course, Lone Star might pull off this kind of extradition if it intends to try the suspect under its own corporate laws instead of under Seattle

or UCAS laws. Oh, the complexity when the law enforcement agency is also a corp in its own right.]<<<<<
—Legal Beagle (17:26:32/3-18-54)

>>>>>[If a corp decides to protect a perp, nobody can do anything about it. You can wait for the slime to step off corp property back into your jurisdiction, but he won't do that unless he's really stupid. Or (shhh, I didn't say this) you can pull a snatch. Or you can kick up such a fuss that the corp caves in to the pressure of bad press. In this case, they usually "vanish" the perp rather than handing him over to you anyway. Charming set of options, ain't it?]<<<<<
—SPD (23:34:08/3-21-54)

>>>>>[SPD's right; corps drag their heels or totally ignore requests for extradition from governments or law-enforcement agencies. But when another corp demands it, they usually extradite pretty quick. Not doing so can lead to some messy corp wars. (Okay, okay, not full-on corp war, but at least border skirmishes.) Something like that happened a couple of years back, when a nutso working for Renraku greased a suit at Yamatetsu. Yamatetsu was new kid on the block at the time, nowhere near as tough as they are now. The killer ducked into the arcology and wouldn't come out. Yamatetsu asked nicely for Renraku to turn him over, but Renraku was having a bad fiscal year and told Yamatetsu to drek in a pot. Yamatetsu considered appealing to the Corporate Court, but that would have taken months and cost millions. Renraku also had a lock on the court at the time, so Yamatetsu decided on an alternate plan. Yamatetsu's veep, a real cold bugger called Barnard or something like that, hired a scroffy bunch of runners to extract the killer. The run got blown and the runners got geeked. Barnard covered himself with plausible deniability, but I'm sure Renraku suspected.

So Barnard hired another shadow team, this time to "expend Renraku assets." In other words, sabotage, mayhem, mess 'em up a little. That run went just fine. Barnard officially expressed his dismay to Renraku about the "random violence" the corp suffered, but remarked that such incidents were bound to happen when corporations strayed from civilized behavior. Translation: you keep the killer, I mess you up.

After a couple of rounds of escalating retaliatory strikes, Renraku head office in Tokyo realized the arcology had more to lose than Yamatetsu Seattle. They ordered the killer handed over to Barnard and transferred the arcology general manager to the experimental arcology in Antarctica. Barnard trideoed the killer's trial, conviction, and execution and sent the chip to the Renraku head honchos just to prove he did everything by the numbers.]<<<<<
—Raleigh (17:47:32/4-7-54)

LIMITS TO EXTRATERRITORIALITY

In the decades immediately after the Shiawase Decision, some megacorporations used extraterritoriality to protect egregious examples of environmental mismanagement. For example, several corporations used established corporate facilities to store hazardous wastes under conditions that contravened all national and international environmental guidelines. When governmental agencies tried to enforce responsible environmental stewardship, the corps involved claimed that because the waste dumps existed on corporate property, they fell within corporate rather than national legal jurisdiction.

Strictly interpreted, the law supported the corporate position. However, the Supreme Court of the United States and equivalent bodies in other countries recognized the need for some provision to protect the environment from shortsighted corporate behavior. With this in mind, the Supreme Court amended the extraterritoriality provisions in 2023. The amendments defined the limits of "territory" for the purposes of determining extraterritoriality. According to these amendments, territory owned by a corporation extended down into the earth in a cone traced out by connecting each point on the territory's boundary with the center of the earth. It also extended upward from the earth's surface along these lines to an altitude of 1,200 meters. Through these specific guidelines, the amendment set limits to the territory a corporation could claim. Legally, a corporation may take any action consistent with its own laws as long as the consequences of its actions remain limited to its conical slice of the globe or atmosphere. Any action whose consequences extend beyond the cone becomes subject to local jurisdiction.

Local and national governments used this argument with great effectiveness throughout the 2020s. Several corporations had buried toxic waste on their property without adequate containment, allowing hazardous materials to spread into groundwater. The moment the contaminated groundwater spread beyond the corporation's conical slice, that corporation faced prosecution under the surrounding nation's environmental laws. The same principles applied to atmospheric pollution, and the offending corps paid hefty prices for cleanup. The territorial amendments of 2023 allowed national governments the limited control over corporate action that they continue to enjoy.

>>>>>[Not much to crow about, but it's sure as frag better than nothing.]<<<<<
—Hard Green (10:01:01/3-23-54)

>>>>>[The principle's just an extension of the old axiom, "Your right to throw a punch ends where my nose begins." A corp can drek in its own nest as much as it likes without suffering legal consequences. But when that drek spreads into *my* nest, then the corp can get nailed. Sounds reasonable to me.]<<<<<
—Simone (03:02:51/3-24-54)

>>>>>[It is *not* reasonable. The Earth is One, a single, interdependent living system. It is Gaia. The pollution and desecration of any part of Gaia spreads to all parts of the system, and perverts our relationship with Gaia-Mother. We must not tolerate desecration of our home. Allowing corporations or anyone else to poison and corrupt "their" portion of the world (as if anyone can own any portion of Gaia!) is wrong-headed, and *must stop.*]<<<<<
—Crystale (09:10:42/4-2-54)

MONOBE ORGANIZATION

MONOBE BIOTECH

| VANTAGE PARTNERS | WEAPONS WORLD INC. | MONOBE WORLD ENTERPRISES | UCAS COMPUSTAT | CHIPS'N'TECH |

| MONOBE UCAS | MONOBE JAPAN | MONOBE UK | MONOBE PAN EUROPE |

>>>>>[So why don't you visit all the corp HQs, Crystale, and tell them that? I'm sure that once you explain it clearly to them, they'll recognize the error of their ways and start living in peace and harmony. Yeah, that's *exactly* what they'll do.]<<<<<
    —Hersh (13:41:46/4-4-54)

>>>>>[I agree with Crystale in principle. But in this case, there's a *big* fragging gap between principle and practice.]<<<<<
    —Piers (23:31:35/4-15-54)

CORPORATE STRUCTURE

All corporations have a hierarchical structure, with power flowing from the top down. After various abortive experiments with non-hierarchical concepts such as matrix management in the 1970s and 1980s, and again in the 2010s, corporations returned to categorical and codified reporting channels and chains of command. In the vast majority of cases, the typical megacorporation has a central "umbrella" corporation that oversees and controls the operation of various subsidiary corporations. Each of these in turn comprises several divisions, which it controls.

As an example, the accompanying illustrations show a portion of the corporate structure of Monobe Corp, a "double-A" megacorporation. Note that this sketch represents only a minor portion of the Monobe business empire.

The umbrella corporation, Monobe International, owns more than 20 subsidiary corporations. Among these is Monobe Biotechnical, the portion of the corporation most familiar to residents of Seattle.

>>>>>[Wait a tick. Monobe owns Fabrique Nationale? The Belgian arms manufacturer?]<<<<<
    —Tev (12:18:07/3-29-54)

>>>>>[FN. That's Fabrique Nationale, alright.]<<<<<
    —Debbie (21:01:32/4-1-54)

The subsidiary Monobe Biotechnical is an international conglomerate in its own right, owning at least ten subsidiary corporations. (A section of Monobe Biotech's overall operation is shown in the second organizational chart.) Monobe Biotechnical Inc. owns the management company Monobe World Enterprises Inc., which in turn owns such well-known national and regional divisions of Monobe Biotechnical as Monobe UCAS, Monobe Japan, and so on. Each of these divisions also owns multiple subsidiary corporations.

>>>>>[For example, Monobe UCAS owns and operates Monobe Seattle, which in turn owns and operates subsidiaries like Designer Genes Inc.]<<<<<
    —Martigan (21:42:20/4-1-54)

This simplified discussion illustrates the basic principles of corporate structure. The reality becomes much more complex, taking into account additional subsidiaries that each frequently own still more subsidiaries.

>>>>>[I can't believe how complicated this thing is. How many companies does the outfit at the top of the pyramid own? Hundreds? Thousands? Frag, this is scary.]<<<<<
    —Luke (00:03:01/4-2-54)

>>>>>[That's why they call them *mega*corps, Luke. But yes, it *is* complex, and scary. It's also the way our world works.]<<<<<
    —The Chromed Accountant (21:26:41/4-6-54)

>>>>>[The file calls Monobe World Enterprises Inc. a "management company." What's that mean?]<<<<<
    —HPJ (23:41:41/4-9-54)

>>>>>[A management company works kind of like a holding company and kind of like a shell company. It doesn't do any business of its own. Monobe World Enterprises Inc. doesn't buy, sell or produce anything. It just manages the various Monobe regional/national divisions, and gets revenue funneled up the pyramid from those divisions. Theoretically, it's "selling" management expertise to those divisions. In practice it collects, invests, disburses, and sometimes launders money.]<<<<<
    —The Chromed Accountant (19:52:30/4-10-54)

>>>>>[The line between bad crime and good business really starts to blur, doesn't it?]<<<<<
—Caine (20:34:23/4-11-54)

OWNERSHIP

Shareholders, or stockholders, own corporations. As the term implies, a shareholder owns a share of the corporation. The corporation's board issues the shares, under the restrictions and provisions of its charter. The nature of these provisions depends on the jurisdiction in which the organization originally incorporated. The charter specifies how many shares the corporation can issue, and frequently which individuals or organizations may purchase them.

When a shareholder buys a share in a corporation, the money he pays becomes part of the corporation's operating funds when the corporation first issues the shares for sale. Public corporations, whose stock can be publicly traded, have given rise to a booming secondary market on which the shareholding individual or organization can sell his shares for the current market value at any time. The sale price of stocks sold on the secondary market goes to the seller of the stocks, not to the corporation that initially issued them. The international stock market exists to facilitate such secondary trade.

>>>>>[Check out the next file, **Doing Business**, for some real Neo-A blather about the stock market.]<<<<<
—SYSephan OPus (18:01:35/3-4-54)

As noted earlier, a corporation exists separately from its shareholders. Property acquired by the corporation belongs to the corporation rather than the shareholders, and the shareholders are not liable for corporate debts. If the corporation goes bankrupt, creditors cannot attempt to recoup lost funds from the assets of individual shareholders. A shareholder may lose only the sum of his or her initial investment.

The shareholders who own the corporation control it through voting privileges that the shares confer. In general, each so-called "common" share of a corporation carries one vote. At each annual meeting and at other special or general meetings throughout the year, shareholders exercise their voting rights as owners to control the destiny of "their" corporation.

>>>>>[That's a great theory. I believe in it about as much as I believe in the Easter fragging Bunny.]<<<<<
—Lukaas (17:17:03/3-21-54)

>>>>>[That shows how little you know about it, Lukaas. Believe it or not, that's *precisely* how it works. Everyone who owns shares in Renraku, for example, gets to attend the corp's annual general meeting and vote on the makeup of the board of directors. And the board runs the corp. Don't like the way Renraku handles things? Vote the board out of their jobs and replace them with people who share your viewpoint. Of course, during its corporate "life" Renraku has issued seven *million* shares. Each of those gets one vote at any meeting. And four million of them just happen to belong to the thirteen men and women currently sitting on the Renraku board of directors. So even if you and everyone else who owns a single Renraku share show up and cast your vote against the current board, they've already voted you down.

That's how corporate control works, cobber. One share means one vote, so the guys buying more shares own more votes.]<<<<<
—The Chromed Accountant (20:29:46/3-24-54)

>>>>>[Ah, plutocracy in action.]<<<<<
—Bung (23:41:6/3-24-54)

>>>>>[Mark well the key points above, my friends. The person or group who owns or otherwise controls the most shares controls the corp. You don't have to own the whole thing to have absolute control over it. You need to control a majority of shares and their votes. If you're willing to settle for a strong influence over corporate policy rather than absolute control, you can get by with a lot fewer shares. So, the corollary of this idea is . . . ?

I leave that little mental exercise for the reader.]<<<<<
—Arioch (17:39:09/4-12-54)

>>>>>[I get your drift. Prevent any individual or bloc from owning or controlling a majority of shares, or stop them from exercising their votes and you can keep them from controlling the corp. Right?]<<<<<
—Grendel (00:02:01/4-14-54)

>>>>>[A big shiny gold star for the good Mr. Grendel.]<<<<<
—Arioch (09:31:28/4-13-54)

>>>>>[So everyone who owns shares in a corp and wants to exercise their votes shows up at the meeting, eh? What an incredibly good time to have a semiballistic tragically crash on the building. Or have a free toxic hearth spirit manifest and trash the place. Or whatever.]<<<<<
—Borg (15:28:09/4-19-54)

>>>>>[That's happened in the past. That's why security at shareholders' meetings gets extreme. Magical, physical, Matrix (in case someone wants to turn on the computerized Halon fire extinguishers and asphyxiate everyone), you name it. Security at the annual meetings of a big corp gets tighter than you'll find at international summits.]<<<<<
—Hangfire (02:48:01/4-23-54)

>>>>>[Echo that. To get into the building, you've got to walk through chem-sniffers and metal detectors; undergo astral scrutiny by mages and shamans; hand over all weapons, talismans, fetishes and other gizmos; have your cyberlimbs "restrained". . . It's ugly.]<<<<<
—Morris (21:53:39/4-23-54)

>>>>>[What about once you're inside? What's to stop a mage on the board of directors nailing somebody, or casting a spell to make sure everyone present votes the way he wants them to?]<<<<<
—Tenmace (22:27:08/4-23-54)

>>>>>[To start with, hermetic circles and medicine lodges often protect the board members from magical assassins in the audience. Also, the board usually hires a few mages from an independent security corp to assense the place astrally throughout the meeting. These guys respond right quick to magical threats from any direction. The magical security group usually also summons a few elementals or spirits to kick the drek out of anyone who tries anything magical. As for magical influence over the attendees at the meeting, that trick usually poses too much of a risk to bother. Odds are that at least one drek-hot hermetic or shaman not involved in the scam will be present, and he might easily report it or stop it.]<<<<<
—Fisk (06:47:24/4-24-54)

>>>>>[Of course, none of these precautions prevent magical (or other) influence of individuals *before* they attend the meeting. Ritual magic provides an awfully good incentive for a major shareholder to vote the management party line.]<<<<<
—Claude (15:23:04/4-24-54)

>>>>>[That comes down to personal security, doesn't it? And that's outside the purview of this discussion. So take it elsewhere, boys and girls.]<<<<<
—Mel (03:29:51/4-25-54)

>>>>>[All this magical security sounds just wiz, but they've got to watch that kind of stuff at Saeder-Krupp shareholders' meetings. Unless the owner and chairman of the corp, the dragon Lofwyr, doesn't mind showing up in his true form. (Must be a large meeting room.)]<<<<<
—Tolly (11:39:57/4-25-54)

>>>>>[Sometimes magical security gets a little lax at the smaller corps. Remember that weirdo Kent-based outfit, Stuffwerks? One of the board members turned out to be a free spirit, an anima who'd bought up enough shares to vote herself in as a director. Magical security didn't point her out as anything but a very pneumatic blonde.]<<<<<
—Adkison (09:32:59/4-27-54)

Voting by Proxy

Every shareholder has the right to attend every official shareholders' meeting that a corporation holds. If a shareholder wants to exercise the voting power of his or her stock, he or she must attend these meetings.

Of course, the vast majority of corporate shareholders own such small stakes in the company that paying the money or making other efforts required to attend shareholders' meetings may not be worth their while. On the other hand, requiring them to pay such money or make such efforts in order to exercise their legal rights effectively disenfranchises them. Because corporate law throughout the world legally requires all stockholders to be able to vote easily, corporations began the practice of voting by proxy.

A proxy is a power of attorney given by a shareholder to another individual, allowing that person to vote for the shareholder at a corporate meeting. Depending on the corporate jurisdiction involved, the proxy holder need not necessarily also be a shareholder in the corporation. At the meeting for which the proxy is granted, the proxy holder casts votes for the absent shareholder, in addition to his own votes if he also owns shares. A proxy usually lasts for one meeting as well as any adjournments, during which the proxy holder may vote with the full weight of his own shares plus the weight of all shares for which he holds proxies.

In all jurisdictions, the corporate management of public companies must solicit proxies from shareholders. Most shareholders gladly sign over their proxies to management, giving corporate management control over a vast number of votes. If a particular shareholder plans to attend a meeting, he does not sign over his proxy to management. If he disagrees with ongoing management practices, he may issue his proxies to a nominee he trusts to vote in a particular manner, though the law does not require a proxy to vote according to the shareholder's preference. At most corporate meetings, however, management controls enough votes through personal stock holdings and legal proxies to vote through any and all resolutions.

>>>>>[Here we get into so-called "proxy fights." For example, say corp management personally owns 40 percent of all voting shares and a rival corporation trying for a takeover also owns 40 percent of all shares. The faction with the most votes can put its own people on the board of directors and run the corp its way. So both factions scramble for proxies. The two groups account for 80 percent of the corp's outstanding shares, leaving 20 percent owned by spirits know who. Some belong to minor shareholders you know, Ma and Pa Kettle of Puyallup who've owned five shares for the past 30 years. Each individual minor investor might own only a handful of shares, but the total amount might add up to 10 percent of the outstanding shares and the corresponding 10 percent of the vote. That's enough to give one faction or the other 50 percent of the vote and total control of the company. Now, sure as frag Ma and Pa Kettle don't plan on hopping the suborbital over to Renraku's Tokyo headquarters just to vote their five shares. No, they'll give their proxy to someone. And you can bet your assets both factions'll troll for it. They might sweeten the deal, paying some special "token of esteem" for the right to cast the Kettles' proxy. Or each faction might try to scare them, telling them how bad things could get if the other guy gets their proxies. If they pull tactics like that for Ma and Pa Kettle, just imagine how enthusiastic things get when an investor with a significant number of shares can't attend the annual meeting . . .]<<<<<
—The Chromed Accountant (20:37:34/3-24-54)

>>>>>[If something important is coming up and the corporate management suspects it won't have enough votes to control everything, the dirty tricks reach an amazing level. Corps or their rivals steal shares (physically or electronically), forge proxies, deck into the corp's and securities commission's computers to "adjust" the numbers of shares held by different factions—whatever it takes. This kind of thing gets really vicious when one corp tries to

take over another. A lot of this kind of drek happened a couple months back, when Ares tried to take over Highstar Incorporated after the Shadows debacle.]<<<<<
—Lotus (22:14:57/3-24-54)

>>>>>[So that's what went down! Some chummers and me took a job from an MCT Johnson to do close cover on a courier carrying an optical chip to some boardroom downtown. Couldn't figure it at the time, but now I think I get it.]<<<<<
—Harkness (05:00:11/3-27-54)

>>>>>[The chip probably contained a proxy or proxies that MCT needed to block the Ares takeover of its subsidiary, Highstar. The MCT suits didn't want to transfer the proxies electronically, in case somebody subverted the computer. Or maybe they just thought someone might monitor it and they didn't want Ares to know how many proxies they'd solicited. Safer to do it physically, particularly with a bit of shadow muscle riding close cover.]<<<<<
—The Chromed Accountant (12:03:41/4-1-54)

none at all and have restrictions on selling. However, they have better voting rights than those normal shares. For example, each share of normal common stock gives you one vote. Each share of special stock gives you *ten* votes. The special issue also includes a provision that lets you exchange one special share for one common share.

Most shareholders buy corporate shares as financial investments and don't give a flying frag about voting rights. They look at the new shares, see the lower (or nonexistent) dividend, and swap them one-for-one for normal shares. Meanwhile, corporate management hangs on to their special shares. So among the rank-and-file shareholders, most of whom swapped their special shares for common shares, each person now has twice as many votes as they had before. They have one for each share they originally held, plus one for each new share they got in the trade. However, each person among corp management now has *eleven times* as many shares as before: one for each share they originally held, plus ten for each special share they got. Voting control of the company just shifted big-time in favor of management.]<<<<<
— Keynesian Kid (10:22:45/4-13-54)

>>>>>[And here I was after thinkin' that this corporate maneuvering didn't affect me on the streets.]<<<<<
—Sinead (03:17:10/4-2-54)

>>>>>[Like the Neo-A slag who wrote the intro file said, it *all* affects you. It affects every last one of you reading this. The only difference is whether or not you understand that.]<<<<<
—Argent (02:00:10/4-7-54)

>>>>>[If management thinks it may need complete voting control, it can get that control in perfectly legal ways. Here's a good one.

The board issues special shares and distributes them to all current shareholders. For each normal share you currently hold, you get one special share. As investments, these special shares give the holder a lot less of a profit; they pay smaller dividends or

>>>>>[For those of you who care, this scam is called "dual class recapitalization," and corps use it to defend against corporate takeovers.]<<<<<
—Dent (23:53:11/4-14-54)

>>>>>[I don't care, and I don't understand why anyone reading this board *would* care. What self-respecting shadowrunner owns megacorp stock?]<<<<<
—Lol (11:41:33/4-15-54)

>>>>>[*I* own megacorp stock, Lol ol' scag, and I have no trouble looking at myself in a mirror. I own one nominal share in every megacorp that even vaguely interests me: Ares, MCT, Renraku, Aztechnology, Saeder-Krupp, Yamatetsu, even Gaiatronics. That way, I get all the annual and special shareholder reports, information circulars, announcements on new stock offerings, all that drek.

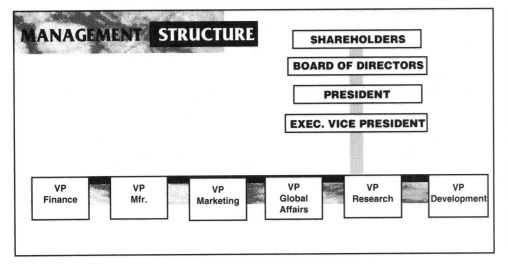

MANAGEMENT STRUCTURE

SHAREHOLDERS

BOARD OF DIRECTORS

PRESIDENT

EXEC. VICE PRESIDENT

| VP Finance | VP Mfr. | VP Marketing | VP Global Affairs | VP Research | VP Development |

the frag-up some months back when a Highstar exec veep tried to squeeze a private recording outfit called Caravan, Ares got its hands on a drekload of Highstar shares. I don't know how Ares managed this, and I don't want to know. I can only say that as dirty tricks and black ops go, Ares made moves about as dirty and black as they come.

Anyway, Ares tried for a total take-over in a big proxy battle. They didn't make it, but they put several of their trained monkeys on the Highstar board of directors. They don't control the board, but they have enough clout to make things unpleasant for the MCT interests.]<<<<<
—Torpedo (11:53:20/4-15-54)

My mail lets me keep an eye on what the corps are up to without any effort. (Well, really what they *claim* they're up to, but that's interesting on its own.) Also, as a shareholder I have the inalienable right to show up at any shareholders' meeting. For a grand total investment of a couple thousand nuyen, it's more than worth it, *omae*.]<<<<<
—Tuo (06:35:00/4-17-54)

>>>>>[If you turned up at one of those meetings, corp security would blow your head off.]<<<<<
—Rocker (08:41:32/4-17-54)

>>>>>[Well, yeah . . .]<<<<<
—Tuo (04:59:38/4-1   9-54)

MANAGEMENT

The accompanying illustration shows a simplified organizational chart for a hypothetical corporation. Note the body of shareholders that wields the highest authority.

Board of Directors

Elected by the shareholders, the board of directors acts as their trustee in running the corporation. At any annual shareholders' meeting, the shareholders can vote the entire board or any board member out of office and replace them with other parties.
>>>>>[Theoretically. In practice, board members usually own or control such big voting blocks that no one can oust them.]<<<<<
—Converse (11:22:04/3-18-54)

>>>>>[Lots of interesting drek can go down among corp board members. Most people mistakenly think that the board of directors always acts as a monolithic unit ("the board says this"). A lot of the time, though, it doesn't shake out that way. Corporate boards can get into rivalries and politicking like you've never seen before. For example, in an earlier post someone mentioned the Shadows frag-up and the attempted takeover of Highstar Incorporated. Up until recently, MCT owned and operated Highstar as a subsidiary company. That means that Mitsuhama or people it controls owned a majority voting block of Highstar shares. After

>>>>>[It gets more interesting than that. The Highstar board comprises thirteen people. Of that thirteen, six are hardcore Mitsuhama types or people that MCT has something real heavy on. Another six are Ares people. The chairman of the board is (drum roll, please) Martha Grimes, veep marketing for Renraku! And how she got there makes quite a story.

Officially, no one admits anything, but I'm telling you chip truth. About two years back, a second-tier Korean outfit by the name of Eastern Tiger Corporation tried to take over Highstar. At the time, MCT Seattle had overcommitted itself to a bunch of other projects, and couldn't transfer enough assets to protect Highstar from Eastern Tiger. Because they couldn't mount the takeover defense themselves, MCT tapped Renraku as a so-called "white knight." MCT let Renraku buy up a major chunk of Highstar stock and some selected corporate assets, based on a gentleman's agreement that Renraku would sell them back to MCT at favorable prices once the takeover threat had blown over. With Renraku in the picture, Eastern Tiger backed *way* off and ended the takeover attempt.

Once Eastern Tiger had slunk off home, Renraku conveniently forgot they'd ever agreed to sell back the shares and other assets to MCT. They claimed they'd bought the shares and assets fair and square and had no obligation to sell them back. Naturally, MCT appealed to the Corporate Court. When the court started investigating, however, they found no recorded contracts or binding agreements between MCT and Renraku that could force Renraku to sell the assets back. MCT Seattle's president, Toshikazu Nakamura, swore up and down that he *had* signed and recorded contracts with Renraku, but Corp Court investigators found nothing in either corp's computer systems. Either Nakamura never executed any binding agreements (a really fragging stupid move) or Renraku sent some deckers into MCT Seattle's system to obliterate all records of those agreements. We'll never know for sure. Shipped back to Japan in disgrace, Nakamura supposedly committed ritual suicide from shame. Shot himself in the back of the head. Twice. After beating the drek out of himself.

Anyhow, with the assets they bought from the late, unlamented Toshikazu Nakamura, Renraku had enough clout to elect Martha Grimes chairman of Highstar's board. As such, she holds the swing vote. Most of the time, the six MCT puppets vote one way and the six Ares puppets vote the other. Grimes then breaks the deadlock, casting her vote for whatever outcome best suits good old Renraku. Nice, unified, monolithic board of directors, *neh*?]<<<<<
—Vickers (13:22:06/4-24-54)

>>>>>[You couldn't pay me enough to be in Grimes' shoes. Once she blocks something that means enough to one or both of the other corps, somebody's going to ice her. I'd lay money on it.]<<<<<
—Armstrong (19:50:34/4-27-54)

>>>>>[Grimes has herself covered nine ways to Sunday. First she's got Renraku security; not the local yokels, but some hard men brought in from HQ in Japan. She also has a Knight Errant close-cover team, including two combat mages on round-the-clock duty. Plus she hired some talent from the shadows. Nobody, but nobody, can take her down.]<<<<<
—Baie (13:13:54/4-29-54)

>>>>>[A couple of Red Samurai plus a KE platoon makes for tough opposition. I know the shadow talent the Johnsons at Renraku hired, and they're all top-drawer people. But if somebody wants Grimes dead bad enough, they're going to make her dead. God Almighty couldn't stop them. Trust me on this.]<<<<<
—Green Ripper (12:28:58/4-30-54)

>>>>>[For those of you unfamiliar with the Green Ripper, the man is arguably the best honorable hatchet man in the biz today. The name's a bastardization of "Grim Reaper" he copped from a 1970s-vintage novel. Hey, Rip, why don't *you* bid on the Martha Grimes contract?]<<<<<
—Lizard (03:34:36/5-1-54)

>>>>>[Neither MCT nor Ares wants to pay my tab.]<<<<<
—Green Ripper (12:02:29/5-1-54)

>>>>>[Am I prescient, or what? Martha S. Grimes, VP Marketing of Renraku Seattle, bought the farm when her semiballistic flight to Tokyo went down just short of Narita airport. In addition to Grimes and the 17 members of her personal security party, the SB carried 109 passengers plus a flight and cabin crew of ten. No survivors.]<<<<<
—Armstrong (14:44:46/5-10-54)

>>>>>[Somebody took out 119 innocents just to grease Grimes?]<<<<<
—Victoria (15:04:32/5-10-54)

>>>>>[Why not? The assassin probably figured he'd have to penetrate less security to sabotage a Japan-bound semiballistic than to get a clean shot at Grimes and live to tell about it.]<<<<<
—Green Ripper (13:12:41/5-11-54)

>>>>>[That makes no sense. What do MCT or Ares gain by scragging Grimes? Renraku still has the assets that Grimes controlled, right? So the board calls a special shareholders' meeting, Renraku plops in a new sacrificial victim in place of the late, lamented Grimes, and goes on with biz as usual. I think the crash that killed Grimes was an accident, or else meant to get someone else.]<<<<<
—Harlan (01:52:05/5-17-54)

>>>>>[What if I told you that Renraku lost one of its major assets about the same time the SB flamed down? A Renraku research facility on a floating island off Matsushima Bay went up in a "tragic and mysterious fire" that killed 98 percent of the facility's highly trained staff.]<<<<<
—Kip (06:31:00/5-17-54)

>>>>>[Oh, frag . . .]<<<<<
—Harlan (14:59:41/5-17-54)

>>>>>[That's how things work in the wonderful world of megacorporations, boys and girls.]<<<<<
—Deb (03:41:42/5-19-54)

>>>>>[No, that's how things *can* work. Taking out a semiballistic and a research facility, with a total death toll around 450, is not exactly biz as usual. The corps generally keep the mayhem at a lower, more personal level.]<<<<<
—The Chromed Accountant (13:07:09/5-21-54)

>>>>>[So Ares and/or MCT eliminated some major Renraku assets to get rid of Renraku influence on the Highstar Incorporated board. Should we watch for Renraku reprisals? Corp war?]<<<<<
—Bingo (08:09:37/5-22-54)

>>>>>[Fortunately, it takes more than that to start a corp war. . .I think. I know it sounds weird, but the megacorps stick to their perverted principles more consistently than most individuals ever do. A corp only takes actions that have some percentage in it for them. At the moment, reprisals don't seem to have any percentage for Renraku. To quote an old chummer of mine, "Revenge don't count no beans."]<<<<<
—TS (20:19:30/5-22-54)

Corporate Officers

Corporate officers such as the president or chief executive officer (CEO), chief financial officer (CFO), chief operating officer (COO), secretary, and so on handle day-to-day business operations. Depending on the bylaws of the individual corporation, certain officers are specifically appointed and dismissed by the board of directors. This provision usually applies to the president and the secretary. Other officers usually owe their positions to the president/CEO, who may also dismiss them.

The board of directors appoints the president/CEO, who reports to them. Through the board, the president/CEO also reports to the corporation's shareholders.

JANET AULISIO

>>>>>[Pay attention to this point, folks. Down here on the street, most of us see a megacorp prez as one short step down from Great Ghu himself. National governments run at his beck and call, and he kowtows to nobody. Not true, chummers. He owes his job to the board of directors, and they can introduce him to the street at any time. If the majority of the board votes to replace the prez, that's it. He's gone, toast, history.]<<<<<
  —Roberts (02:33:45/3-29-54)

>>>>>[True, but a board doesn't oust a president lightly. The smoothest of transitions between corporate presidents makes national succession after an assassination look seamless by comparison. The outgoing prez almost always crams management with suits loyal to him. Instead of dealing with upper management loyal to his fired predecessor, the new prez tries to oust this "old guard" and replace them with his own cronies. Predictably, the old guard resists any attempt to oust them, aided by their own supporters, sycophants, and toadies further down the hierarchy. The old guard may have unbreakable contracts, or they may know

where the bodies are buried. They might even control significant share voting blocks, making them a threat to the board that ousted the old prez. Canning a president usually brings on wholesale bloodletting in the executive offices. With that kind of disruption to look forward to, any sane board thinks long and hard before taking such a drastic step.]<<<<<
  —Diva (16:05:06/4-2-54)

>>>>>[Yes and no. It depends on why they give the prez the boot. If he's incompetent, his senior management probably knows it and will have cut themselves loose from him long ago. Ten to one they won't cause trouble when he goes.
  Things get nastier if the board gains some benefit by making the prez look bad. For example, the board might force the prez to initiate a new policy or business initiative that goes disastrously wrong. To maintain shareholder confidence and keep the corp's roster of investment bankers happy, they may use the prez as a scapegoat. He gets sacrificed on the altar of public relations, and the corp keeps getting the money it needs. Intelligent execs

If the firing results from a shakeup of the board, things can go flat-out crazy. For example, let's say Ares had filled seven of the seats on Highstar's 13-member board instead of six. Once they had a majority, you can bet your hoop they'd replace the prez/CEO appointed by the previous MCT-dominated board with someone they owned. In this scenario, the current prez may not be a lame duck or a sacrificial lamb (ooh, animal analogies!). That means a severe shakeup in the upper ranks, with the "outplacement" of lots of suits. These guys usually land jobs with the competition, limited only by the anti-competition clauses in their contracts and the militancy of their former employer's legal team.]<<<<<
—Laurence (16:29:17/4-26-54)

>>>>>[Of course, "outplacing" the prez and other suits poses other risks to the board. Picture a bunch of high-powered executives that know more or less everything about how the corp does business. They have every reason in the world to use that knowledge against the board that canned them. Trust me, the biggest golden handshake or separation bonus in the world won't salve a bruised ego. Supposedly, the canned officers' employment contracts make it illegal for the slots to scuttle over to another corp. But those contracts aren't always enforceable. Nothing can stop a disgruntled, newly redundant exec from leaking sensitive information to a contact at a rival corporation. So firing people lands the board in a scary situation, no matter how you look at it.]<<<<<
—Nilsen (03:06:59/4-28-54)

>>>>>[What difference does it make to us, *omae*? Sweet frag all, that's how much.]<<<<<
—Mace (04:51:54/4-28-54)

>>>>>["Sweet frag all" is about how much you understand what we're talking about here, Mace old chummer. If you'd actually read the preceding posts rather than ignoring them because they didn't include any pictures, you might figure out a number of ways this info can affect your miserable little life. Allow me to enumerate.

A new board can either remove the president appointed by the old board or bring him under their control. They might do this through direct threats to the president or to his family. Or they might try blackmail, dredging up something damaging from his past and threatening to publicize it. A third choice might be magical or chemical influence (brainwashing and all its nasty kin). To do this kind of dirty work, the board might want to hire a few "unattributable assets," such as shadowrunners. As for the president, he knows all about such unpleasant possibilities. Think he might hire shadowrunners to protect him and his loved ones? Just maybe.

Let's talk about fired executives. If the board doesn't trust legal niceties like non-competition clauses, they might decide to eliminate the executives rather than fire them. After all, dead men tell no tales. Or they may brainwipe them, or hold them hostage until the information they have gets to be old news. They might also decide to use threats and intimidation against the execs or against their families and friends. Once again, the board will hire shadowrunners for the job. The execs at risk might also hire shadowrunners to keep them alive and healthy.

would see this power play coming a long time off and distance themselves from the doomed prez. (Not much comes as a surprise in the executive suite.) Executive upheaval tends to occur among the execs too dumb or too trusting to take precautions, and they're no loss.

Get it now, bimble-brain? This info can get you good-paying work. Seems like a pretty good reason to pay attention.]<<<<<
—Pittman (17:01:07/5-16-54)

CORPORATE CONNECTIONS

In addition to those divisions and subsidiaries included in its organizational chart, a megacorporation's control and influence can extend far beyond its integral divisions through its legal connections to strategic partnerships and/or joint ventures.

>>>>>[Want to hear about corp "influence?" A chummer of my father served on the board of a small software development corp in Kent. Apparently Fuchi took an interest in their work. One day Dad's chummer got a polite e-mail from a Fuchi suit, informing him that the suit had bought a dozen or so company shares and would show up at the next shareholders' meeting in a day or two. Mind you, a dozen shares legally amounted to drek-all against the total shares. So the next night this chromed-up street monster shows up at dad's chummer's house. Doesn't do anything physical, just casually mentions that he knows where the guy's wife works and where their kids go to school. Then he hands over a hardcopy letter from the suit at Fuchi, explaining in detail how he wants dad's chummer to run the shareholders' meeting. The suit lays out who to nominate and vote for to fill a spot on the board, that kind of thing. He finishes by saying that he can't make the meeting after all, but he'll send his proxy with the street monster.

Needless to say, dad's chummer did every little thing the Fuchi suit wanted.

That's megacorp influence. And that's also another way runners get drawn into corporate maneuvering. Ten to one the chromed-up street monster was anything but an official Fuchi employee. They hired him out of the shadows for this gig. Bet on it.]<<<<<
—Ranger (11:28:16/3-27-54)

Strategic Partnerships and Joint Ventures

Instead of purchasing a company outright and converting it into a subsidiary, a corporation may initiate a joint venture or strategic partnership with another company. Such joint ventures sometimes serve as the prelude to a merger or acquisition. At other times the two organizations may work together until they achieve a specific goal. Often, the two organizations involved in a joint venture may differ greatly in size. For example, two world-girdling megacorporations may sign a strategic alliance, or a megacorporation may strike a deal with a much smaller company.

>>>>>[If that happens, the smaller one is as much under the big one's thumb as if the megacorp took direct control. Believe it.]<<<<<
—Dodd (11:21:05/3-27-54)

>>>>>[I did some bodyguard work a while back for the owner of a local software developer. The corp was privately owned, meaning the shares didn't get traded on the stock market. My Johnson, a guy called Bauhaus, owned something like 80 percent of the outfit. This little corp had done some serious research into expert

systems and AI, and had made some breakthroughs that had the bigger research labs drooling.

Needless to say, Fuchi got interested. They approached Bauhaus and proposed a joint venture. Bauhaus needed an infusion of capital to keep his research going, and Fuchi looked like a good source of investment funds. The Fuchi suits promised him they'd keep their hands off the day-to-day running of his business if he gave them an equity position in his company. In other words, he had to sell them 49 percent of the company's shares in order to get Fuchi's money.

A little reluctantly, Bauhaus took the deal. Fuchi offered him a good price for his shares, and he personally became very rich. The corp also poured research and development money into his company, but Bauhaus felt a little antsy about the indirect influence that money gave them. After a little while, Fuchi pressured some of the other private shareholders to sell them more shares in the company. As soon as they had a controlling 51 percent, they squeezed Bauhaus out of company operations. Eventually they bought him out, lock, stock and barrel. The guy grossed a total of 20 million-plus nuyen, but he's still bitter about losing his company to a bunch of megasuits.]<<<<<
—Dean (13:28:41/4-2-54)

>>>>>[If you get into bed with an elephant, watch out when it rolls over.]<<<<<
—Sun Tzu II (03:42:45/4-5-54)

>>>>>[So now we know all about legal and aboveboard ownership of other companies. But how many corps actually do it that way? Pretty fragging few, I figure.]<<<<<
—Vernal (11:39:27/4-7-54)

>>>>>[You might be surprised. The only laws that really affect a corp come down from the Corporate Court, so keeping ownership or control a secret doesn't often gain a corp any legal advantage. In fact, secret ownership poses a thorny set of problems. A secretly owned subsidiary with legal independence can't dodge taxes by funneling all revenues to its parent disguised as "cost of goods and services."]<<<<<
—Wolfe (21:05:06/4-9-54)

>>>>>[Maybe. But corps keep all kinds of secrets for all kinds of reasons. The corps are always jockeying for power. Sometimes it pays to have control over an asset that nobody knows about.]<<<<<
—The Chromed Accountant (12:27:41/4-10-54)

>>>>>[That's probably the scariest thing about the megacorporate world. When street ops like you and me think of an ace in the hole, we usually mean a hold-out pistol in the boot. When the megacorps think of an ace in the hole, they mean a couple of fragging multi-million nuyen corporations. I'm out of my depth.]<<<<<
—Cam (21:58:44/4-13-54)

DOING BUSINESS

From your itsy mom'n'pop corner grocery to fragging Mitsuhama, corporations do biz to make money. Never mind the corporate drek about "fiduciary responsibilities to shareholders and employees," "responsibility to the environment," or "historical and social mandate." Corporations came into being solely to let capitalists make piles of money more efficiently with less personal risk. Strictly defined, "capitalist" means people with capital, or money. Stuffed to bursting with greedy little capitalists, a corporation is a legal mechanism behind which its shareholders, officers, and managers can hide. Protected from creditors and other forms of legal unpleasantness, they rake in the dough and line their pockets at other people's expense. Corps make buckets of nuyen, sometimes in legal and obvious ways and sometimes in ways so subtle and sneaky that law enforcement has not a prayer of catching them.

>>>>>[We hereby officially come to the Neo-Anarchist blather. As always, Shadowland does not guarantee the accuracy or completeness of what you are about to read and all that legal drek. Go to it.]<<<<<
    —SYSephan OPus (17:59:19/3-4-54)

MARKETING

Marketing is a corp's most obvious legal moneymaking tool. Marketing means providing a good or a service to consumers who willingly pay to acquire it. Consumers range from end-users like the street op who buys heat from Ares Arms, to another corp like Yamatetsu, which buys much of its security electronics from Fuchi's shadow facilities.

>>>>>[Hold on just a tick. "Shadow" facilities?]<<<<<
    —Lacey (13:42:19/3-18-54)

>>>>>[If you don't know, you don't *want* to know.]<<<<<
    —Mouser (21:48:53/3-19-54)

>>>>>[Shadow facilities are companies a corp owns indirectly. Fuchi's shadow facilities are actually run by VST Electronics Inc., a private corp based in Redmond. Fuchi owns VST, but through so many intermediaries and shell companies you could never prove it.]<<<<<
    —Nuyen Nick (15:51:02/3-24-54)

>>>>>[Get off that one. VST has nothing to do with Fuchi, never has, never will. Aztechnology pulls the strings and pays the bills.]<<<<<
    —April (21:45:29/3-27-54)

>>>>>[Forget that crosstalk. The Big A does all that security stuff in-house.]<<<<<
    —Mercedes (20:40:20/3-29-54)

>>>>>[Not all.]<<<<<
    —Pyramid Watcher (03:21:37/4-4-54)

The consumer might also be another division within the same corporation. For example, the Ares entertainment combine hires Knight Errant, an Ares subsidiary, to protect a senior veep against assassins. The consumer's identity doesn't matter in the long run, because the marketing process rarely ends after one step. In manufacturing and other industries, half a dozen or more steps often occur between the actual creation of a good and its arrival in the sweaty hands of the ultimate user.

For example, take the optical chip you plugged into your simsense deck last night. The chip-blank probably came from Crystal Optics Incorporated, a Singapore manufacturer owned by Ares Macrotechnology. Fuchi MicroLith buys chip-blanks in bulk from the Singapore outfit and does the micro-etching and such that changes the blank from an undifferentiated crystal of contaminated silicon into an actual optical chip. MicroLith sells the etched chips to LifeScape, part of the Ares entertainment combine, which "burns" the simsense software into them. Then they get dumped into distribution. MegaMedia handles preliminary distribution, sending the chips off to a regional distributor like Optical Dreams. These guys turn around and sell them to a retailer like Chips 'n' Things, who finally peddles them to chippies on the street. Each step of the process adds value to the product through micro-etching, software, advertising, packaging, and point-of-sale distribution. At each step, the corporate entity involved takes its cut. That's why street prices for the latest Nicky Saitoh simsense chip run around 350 nuyen even though a single nuyen buys more than 100 chip-blanks.

>>>>>[*Honto*? A 350,000 percent markup? That's obscene.]<<<<<
    —Marjorie Morningstar (16:43:04/3-21-54)

>>>>>[Got an idea, Marj. Drop by my place later and I'll give ya a couple hundred chip-blanks, free of charge. Somebody got sloppy labeling some crates in a yak warehouse, and I'm swimming in the things. You go out and run off your own Nick Saitoh simsense chips and sell' em on the street. Take the 350¥ a pop, keep it yourself. What? You don't have the hardware to program the blanks? Don't have access to Saitoh? Don't have the hardware to make those ever-so-neat, full-color packages? Don't have meganuyen for ads? Can't get anyone to take you seriously on the street? Can't do any of those things the manufacturing and distribution channel does?
    Guess the big markup makes sense, doesn't it?]<<<<<
    —Shag (21:46:04/3-28-54)

>>>>>[You think *that* markup's bad, how about BTLs? A beetle uses the same 100-for-a-nuyen chip-blank, but sells on the street for a *lot* more than Nicky puppy Saitoh.]<<<<<
    —Blaine (05:37:51/4-2-54)

>>>>>[Partly to compensate everyone for the risks of selling something illegal. No one wants to risk a jail term unless the payoff's well worth it.]<<<<<
    —Raiko (02:50:42/4-4-54)

>>>>>[So you chose the high-margin career of shadowrunner for the salary, I take it.]<<<<<
    —Bung (05:55:10/4-4-54)

>>>>>[Something else interesting here, jokers. Think about what happens when the distributor and the retailer are actually the same corp under different names, or owned by the same corp. For each step in the process that it owns, the corp doesn't have to pay a mark-up to someone else. Theoretically, it should pass its savings on to the consumer, but how often does that happen? And what if the same corp also owns the manufacturing end?]<<<<<
    —White (08:14:52/4-14-54)

>>>>>[Megacorps do that all the time, *omae*. Our friendly neighborhood Neo-A even discusses it somewhere else in these files under tax amelioration strategies (read "tax fraud").]<<<<<
    —Marcus (23:01:42/4-16-54)

>>>>>[Ever notice how every time some law enforcement agency or government starts bagging on about the "BTL problem," the entertainment megacorps all put on their holier-than-thou faces and claim they have nothing to do with it? Think through the number of beetles actually on the street. BTL ain't the basement-workshop kind of trade the megacorps want us to think it is, chummerinos. Illegal chips are a high-volume, high cash-flow biz. Who's big enough to handle it? The yaks, maybe. Some Seoulpa Rings, but not many. Tir Tairngire's "crime corps" possibly, but I doubt it. Doesn't quite jell with the "back to the trees" philosophy. Eliminate these (relatively) small fry, and that leaves the entertainment megacorps. They keep claiming that the beetle trade cuts into their legitimate simsense sales and costs them big nuyen every year, yet they do nothing to stop that erosion of their profits. They just sit there. No way would the megacorps not put a stop to something that costs them big.
    So the BTL trade can't possibly cost them anything. The corps don't stop the beetle trade because it puts more money into their coffers than it takes out of their legitimate simsense market. Makes sense, *neh*?]<<<<<
    —Dada Pierre (22:53:13/4-20-54)

>>>>>[Only to a paranoid conspiracy addict.]<<<<<
    —Vambrace (01:11:15/4-21-54)

>>>>>[No, the theory makes a lot of sense. Just try proving that theory to anyone's satisfaction. I may dig into this.]<<<<<
    —Tad (03:28:50/4-23-54)

>>>>>["Digging into" something like that won't get you conclu-sive evidence, it'll just get you dead. Count on it, *omae*.]<<<<<
—Touchstone (17:09:39/4-27-54)

AVOIDING THE MARKET

According to conventional wisdom, to stay in business a corp must provide a service or a good for which people are willing to pay, and must add value to everything they put on the market. Of course, practice can work plenty different from theory. Back in the 1980s and even before, the major corporations that eventually became the megacorps discovered ways to make money without risking the vicissitudes of the market.

Late in the twentieth century, companies discovered that corporate takeovers could let them rake in huge sums of money. Corporate raiders took over other companies, stripped them of key assets, reorganized them, and then hawked their component parts to other corps. Through this kind of skullduggery, they could generate huge cash flows without having to produce and market goods or services. This kind of so-called "churning" reached a peak in 2029, then dropped to almost zero after the Crash. However, it's started up again during the past decade.

After studying some of these churning activities pretty closely, it's staggering to realize how much money a corp can make doing absolutely nothing productive. For example, just last year Ares took over Syntronic Biotech, an Atlanta-based company that Saeder-Krupp had divested. Ares brought in its new management team, and they performed a management buy-out. (I'll have more to say about MBOs in a later file.) The management team bought up all outstanding Syntronic shares and took the corporation private, off the stock market. During the buy-out, the managers paid shareholders 175 nuyen per share. With the stock valued at 130 nuyen per share, the 45-nuyen mark-up looked like a princely offer. Six months later, the managers went public with Syntronics and started selling stock on the open market. The initial offering price shot up to 293 nuyen per share, and rich investors snapped them up almost instantly.

What happened to Syntronics in the six-month interim to raise the stock's value from 130 nuyen to almost 300 nuyen? Sweet frag all. During those six months, Syntronics signed no new contracts. It spent no money on research and development. It neither hired nor fired employees. In other words, the company valued at 300 nuyen per share had not changed from the one valued at 130 nuyen per share half a year earlier. In fact, logic suggests that it should have lost value. A high-tech firm that did no R&D to keep up as the cutting edge moved six months ahead of it must have lost a fragging lot of ground and potential market share during the half-year gap. Apparently, the company in-creased in value simply because it suffered a management buy-out. As soon as the management team that bought out the company had taken Syntronics public again, they took the money and ran. Most likely they pulled the same trick with another undistinguished company, making themselves even more hid-eously wealthy in the process.

>>>>>[As an interesting little addendum to this story, let's look at some figures. The original shareholders of Syntronics got paid 175¥ for stock worth 130¥ on the open market. They made 45¥ per share, or about a 26 percent profit. The management team bought shares at 175¥, then sold them six months later at 293¥. They made a profit of 118¥ per share, or 40 percent.

Rich though they were to begin with, the managers couldn't acquire Syntronics' 270,000 or so outstanding shares with just their own credit. So off they trooped to investment bankers, the people who provide capital in this kind of case. Predictably, the bankers wanted something in return for their generosity. I happen to know that the bankers and managers split the profit on taking Syntronics public, so both groups realized a 59¥ profit per share. 270,000 shares changed hands, so the managers as a group cleared 15,930,000¥. So did the bankers. Everybody made money, but supposedly that's impossible. Where did all that profit come from? These buyouts work like the economic equivalent of a perpetual motion machine.]<<<<<
—The Chromed Accountant (10:52:53/4-2-54)

>>>>>[The profit came from interest charged by the bankers to other clients, and from tax breaks given to the corp by the UCAS government. In other words, it came from every UCAS citizen in the form of increased taxes or decreased social services. Ain't capitalism grand?]<<<<<
—The Neon Antichrist (10:40:48/4-3-54)

>>>>>[Not from me, *'mano*. I ain't paid taxes since 2046, and I'm fragging proud of it.]<<<<<
—Timbale (13:35:45/4-3-54)

>>>>>[Well, whoopie drek for you, Timbale. The issue isn't whether individual slags like you manage to dodge the bullet. The principle of the thing matters, you slot. All the money taken in by the investment bankers, managers, stockholders, and so forth comes from taxpayers. The government takes money out of its citizens' hands and disburses it to corps and capitalists without letting those citizens choose what happens to their money. That's coercion. Neo-Anarchists are staunchly opposed to exactly that kind of drek.]<<<<<
—Chaos Lord (00:41:59/4-7-54)

>>>>>[By that rationale, no government can justify any expendi-ture because no program or initiative exists to which all citizens will agree. Coercion in some form is necessary to the continuance of orderly government and conducive to the health and welfare of the citizenry. As I shall explain later, the current climate of corporate acquisitions and mergers is equally necessary.]<<<<<
—Pirate (11:13:51/4-9-54)

>>>>>[For those who don't know, Pirate is actually Sir Geoffrey Barthwaite, elf, snotty Brit, and corporate raider *extraordinaire*.]<<<<<
—Skeleton Hunter (18:51:23/4-10-54)

>>>>>[Back up a few posts here. The Chromed Accountant asks where all the profit came from, and people go ballistic over government coercion. Simple answer, folks; it came from the slots

who paid 293¥ for Syntronics stock. No mystery at all. You guys get so hung up on principle that you ignore reality.]<<<<<
    —Godot (21:13:50/4-10-54)

>>>>>[Hey, Godot, where you been, man?]<<<<<
    —Bung (23:56:11/4-11-54)

PUBLIC RIVALS, PRIVATE DEALS

As with most developed countries, the UCAS economy works on the rule of the market, also known as *laissez faire* capitalism and free enterprise. In principle, the balance of supply and demand on the open market determines both prices and the success or failure of individual corporations. From all competing products on the market, consumers select those individual products that meet their specific and personal definition of "best price for value."

In their fight for market share and the revenue it brings, competitors offer products either at a lower price than those already on the market, or with more real or perceived value. If a product offers a better price for its value, the market moves toward that competitive product. As competing manufacturers or service providers lower their prices and/or increase their products' perceived value, the market matures. Those companies that best determine and provide what consumers want eventually succeed, and the consumer enjoys high-value goods and services produced at low cost.

Of course, market theory assumes that competition actually exists in the marketplace. Without competition, a company has no incentive to increase value or decrease price. If the good or service in question is vital, the consumer ends up paying whatever outrageous price the provider asks, or else does without. For example, if only one car manufacturer existed in the world, you

>>>>>[Of course, value means different things to different people. Your corp suit who buys a low-quality Fellini-Med breather for a vastly inflated price still gets the optimum price-value balance, because the Fellini-Med logo matters to a superficial slot like her.]<<<<<
    —Fraser (12:28:10/3-30-93)

According to free market theory, overpriced products that don't provide enough value for consumers to lay out their hard-earned credit will fail, as purchasers instead choose those products that give them the value they want. Every buying decision becomes a cost-benefit analysis, where the consumer compares the benefit/value of a good to its cost. Advertising represents an attempt to add value to products by playing on public perceptions. If advertising can make potential customers see a particular product as trendy or fashionable, that belief becomes a benefit that purchasers take into account when deciding what to buy.

could either pay whatever they asked for any shoddy product they wanted to push on you, or do without a car entirely. Some choice, eh, chummer?

Because only competition can save the consumer from getting royally gouged, all developed countries have laws designed to maintain the competition necessary for a free market. Such laws can take the form of antitrust legislation, antimonopoly rules, and similar statutes intended to prevent a single provider from holding an unbreakable monopoly on any universally necessary good or service.

>>>>>[In the last century, the biggest example of monopoly-busting was the breakup of AT&T and the subsequent deregulation of the telecom system. The U.S. government decided that AT&T dominated too much of the telecom market, and legally forced the corp to break up into lots of "Baby Bells."]<<<<<
    —The Chromed Accountant (22:12:54/3-2-54)

>>>>>[So what? Back then the government still had the clout to tell a corp what to do. Can you imagine today's UCAS government walking up to the office of the president in the Mitsuhama Tower in Tokyo and saying, "Excuse me, sir, but we believe you've got a monopoly over thus-and-so market. If it's not too much trouble, we'd like you to stop. Yeah, right.]<<<<<
—Zonker (13:15:04/3-4-54)

>>>>>[Okay, so breaking up a megacorp doesn't work these days. But different national governments can still dictate to corporations in various ways. In Tir Tairngire and some of the NAN countries, outside corps can only operate if they have a government charter. If one of those governments decides that MCT, for example, holds a damaging monopoly, it can threaten to pull MCT's charter and send them packing unless the corp changes the way it does business. Same thing in Aztlan, though I've heard that sometimes key execs disappear along with the charter.

In more free and easy jurisdictions like UCAS where corps don't need a government charter to operate, the government can still levy fines or refuse to conduct business with the corp involved until it cleans up its act. Imagine how big a slap in the face the Seattle Metroplex government could give Lone Star by threatening to pull its contract and hire Knight Errant to handle civic law enforcement. That's a pretty big club to hold over a corp.]<<<<<
—Smoke (13:28:09/3-7-54)

>>>>>[Go back to the AT&T breakup and take a look at why the government suddenly decided AT&T had gotten too big. Other corps wanted into the telephone business, but AT&T kept blocking their entry into the market. That really slotted off the competitors. So in the finest old American tradition, they went whining and sniveling to the government. By pulling in markers and promising campaign donations, the corps got a lot of the pols behind them. The pols realized they'd get lots of votes for nailing AT&T; they could bravely cut down the Big Bad Corporation oppressing the little guy, and all that drek. So the government acted and AT&T went down. Its collapse made space for half a dozen Big Bad Corps to oppress the little guy, but that's often the way it works. That kind of thing still happens. Corps still use anti-trust legislation as a weapon against their rivals.]<<<<<
—Mac E. Vallian (01:33:38/4-10-54)

PRICE FIXING

Within the UCAS, various laws on the books prevent corps from getting and keeping a monopoly (from "mono," for "one," meaning they're the only kid on their particular block). Less well-known laws also exist against duopolies, where two companies control an entire market, and oligopolies, where a group of conspirators controls a market.

Monopolies pose an obvious problem to the consumer. The other two "opolies" may look less dangerous, but they can gouge you just as hard through the fine tradition called price fixing. In a duopoly or oligopoly, the participants pretend to compete while cooperating behind the scenes. They're on the horn to each other constantly, arranging to keep their prices the same or close enough not to matter. Instead of undercutting the others to grab their market shares, all the corps involved agree to share the market "pie" more or less evenly.

Okay, I can hear you asking what's in it for the corps. Couldn't a single corp pocket more credit if it undercut the others without warning and scooped all their clients? Not really.

In the short run, the corp might gain something. However, the other corps would respond by actually competing with each other, and that costs money. If you're truly competing rather than pretending to compete, you have to pay research and development costs to improve your product, fund market research to find out what the buyers really want, advertise to convince them that they want what you're offering, pay for competitive research to find out what the other corps are doing and planning . . . y o u get the idea.

>>>>>[Plus, if you've just slotted around with one or more megacorps, they might express their displeasure with you directly. Assassination of directors remains a favorite tactic, as does "involuntary downsizing of an asset." That's corporatese for the destruction of facilities.]<<<<<
—Tenmace (15:54:31/3-27-54)

>>>>>[Good contract opportunities come up for runners when this kind of drek flies. The corps want "unattributable assets" like shadowrunners to pull their raids.]<<<<<
—Vogon (23:31:44/3-29-54)

>>>>>[Unattributable and expendable assets. Trust me. Before I left the corporate environment, I hired enough of them.]<<<<<
—Hangfire (02:09:43/4-1-54)

>>>>>[As one of your erstwhile employees, frag you very much.]<<<<<
—Tomtom (14:00:51/4-8-54)

Rather than paying the costs of true competition, members of a price-fixing oligopoly prefer to count on a stable, controllable income stream. In other words, they'd rather have a free slice of the pie than pay the cost of a grab at the whole thing. The facade of competition allows them to slowly raise their prices in synch, sadly claiming that the increase reflects the cost of research, development, and product improvement that none of them are actually spending money on. Because it eliminates the natural checks and balances of a free market economy, price fixing is anathema to all developed nations. All national governments have passed various laws and regulations against such conduct.

>>>>>[Which those governments may or may not enforce, depending on the power of the corps involved or the dirt they have on the regulatory agencies. Sound cynical? Just remember that price-fixing scandal a couple of years ago in CAS. The regulatory agency figured out that a consortium of pharmaceutical firms had artificially jacked up the prices of the immunosuppressants used in implant surgery (*big* business, multibillion nuyen). With fanfares and three-ring circuses, the agency charged all the corps involved, then backed off and let everything fade away. Tell ya why,

chummers. The corps hired me and other runners to dig up all the dirt we could get on the members of the regulatory agency pressing the charges. Predictably, they told none of us the whole story, or even that other runners were on the job. I know because I did some fixing on the side at the time, and in my fixer persona I brokered the contracts for several runners involved.

Anyway, we found some deep darks that the director of the agency wanted to keep secret. The corps put pressure on her, and she declared that "further investigation into the price fixing had disclosed insufficient evidence to proceed with the case." So that was that.]<<<<<
—Ma Hell (11:16:42/4-12-54)

Because price fixing is illegal in most jurisdictions with varying penalties for conviction, corporations involved go to extreme lengths to hide it. Regulatory agencies often find it difficult to prove price fixing, and may resort to underhanded tactics to get evidence. Recently, most successful convictions have come from evidence provided by less-than-brightly-illuminated sources.

>>>>>[Yes, folks, shadowrunners. A chummer of mine in CalFree made a run on a SanFran-based subsidiary of Fuchi and stumbled over some documentary evidence of a price-fixing scam. As well as scooping what she'd crashed into the system to get, she took the evidence and e-mailed it to the local antitrust taskforce. Apparently, the biz-cops didn't care where the evidence came from as long as they had something solid. They pressed charges, convicted the corps involved, gave my chummer a finder's fee and buried her involvement in the whole thing.]<<<<<
—Borodin (16:35:23/4-1-54)

>>>>>[Are you talking about Valerie Stupnikov? If so, they didn't bury her involvement deeply enough. She took three rounds to the brain last week in Gilroy, and everything about it looks like a Fuchi assassination. Moral of the story: corps have long memories and no sense of humor.]<<<<<
—Yuri (04:05:38/5-27-54)

In order to pull off a price – fixing scam, the participants have to trust each other to at least a limited degree. Needless to say, trust doesn't come easy to megacorps. The emergence of the truly massive extraterritorial conglomerates between 2010 and 2020 eliminated this problem by giving the old game a new twist; a single megacorp actually owns all the participants. (Secretly, of course, and indirectly.)

The so-called subcorps appear independent on the surface, and often engage in heated and vituperative public rivalry. Each advertises heavily, promoting its own products and denigrating its "competitors" in an effort to keep the buying public from suspecting any shady dealings. Behind all this supposedly healthy competition, the subcorps play the price fixing game for all it's worth. They orchestrate the competition, designing it to give each company an excuse to raise its prices. The extra charge supposedly pays for "product enhancements" that don't occur. After all, how much does it really cost to stick a "New & Improved!" label

on the same old drek? If the subcorps and the owner bury the connection between them well enough, this kind of scam can last for years or decades. The hideously high profit margins make price-fixing damn near irresistible for the nuyen-hungry corps.

>>>>>[This goes a long way back, but the "Soda Wars" of the 1980s and '90s came from this kind of scam. The same conglomerate owned two of the major players, through about five levels of "blind" and shell companies. Sneaky little slots.]<<<<<
—Lane (13:05:45/3-25-54)

>>>>>[Absolute paranoid nonsense.]<<<<<
—The Chromed Accountant (12:59:08/3-28-54)

In addition to trust among thieves, price-fixing schemes pose other problems. For example, other megacorps might take an interest in penetrating the controlled market. Instead of trying to break in through normal business means, would-be competitors can simply dig up the connection between the putatively independent subcorps and deliver that knowledge to the appropriate regulatory agencies. When megacorps go looking for drek like that, they tend to find it; after all, megacorps have a lot more resources at their disposal than any government agency. Once they've done their dirty work, they simply sit back and wait for the agencies to put an end to the scam. To prevent this from happening, the corp running such a scam frequently pays other corps a cut of the profits to keep them quiet.

>>>>>[A middle ground also exists between independents who form a price-fixing cartel and subcorps of a single multinational pretending to compete. Some of the rival subcorps might not know the same megacorp owns them.]<<<<<
—Swamp (11:41:55/4-10-54)

>>>>>[This kind of scam brings up lots of opportunities for shadowrunners on all sides. Dig up hidden connections or make sure connections stay buried. Encourage or eliminate independent investigators. Leak stuff to the media or keep the media distracted. Lots of work out there if you know where to look for it, chummers.]<<<<<
—Harley D (17:06:51/4-18-54)

>>>>>[And if you don't mind working for the slots doing the hiring.]<<<<<
—Lake (11:40:52/4-21-54)

>>>>>[Oh, come off that drek, Lake. Does it matter who's issuing the credit? Everybody works for everybody in the shadows. The corp you ran that big score against last year subsidizes your lifestyle this year. If you want to live out of the light, scruples about working for "the bad guys" get to be an expensive luxury.]<<<<<
—Blaze (20:42:11/4-29-54)

>>>>>[Will wonders never cease? An ethical shadowrunner . . .]<<<<<
—Pirate (17:23:21/5-1-54)

>>>>>[They exist. They just ain't common.]<<<<<
—Ryker (23:44:00/5-1-54)

RAIDING THE PIGGY BANK

Like every other business in the world, megacorporations need money to fund ongoing operations and pay for expansion or development. A well-managed corp can usually finance itself from its ongoing cash flow without the need for additional fundraising. Particularly profitable corps can sometimes finance major acquisitions or developments from cash flow as well.

Trideo programs love to show the steely eyed corp exec calling up the Zurich-Orbital Gemeinschaft Bank and ordering the credit transferred to buy a competitive corp lock, stock, and balance sheet. As usual, real-life big money moves get a little more mundane. Sure, megacorps have deposits in the Z-O bank that look astronomical in comparison to personal net worths. However, the cost of even the smallest corporation usually runs much too high for the megacorp to make the purchase out of operating reserves. Even if a megacorp had that much money kicking around, why the frag would they stuff it into the Z-O bank? Unlike the banks most of us think of, the Z-O Gemeinschaft Bank doesn't pay interest. In fact, it withholds a percentage of all deposits to pay for the bank's security and other services.

>>>>>[Just like your typical Swiss bank.]<<<<<
—Vitas (12:02:45/3-13-54)

Any intelligent management team invests its money where it generates a return. And anyone in a megacorp's management suite or boardroom has considerable intelligence. If they didn't, they'd never survive the infighting.

>>>>>[Ever notice that a lot of lousy trideo and simsense shows portray megacorp bosses as dumb thugs? Rich dumb thugs, but still dumb. Realistic? Not at all. The level of political infighting in your typical corp makes a Machiavellian government look like a garden party. Could Governor Schultz have made it to her present position without serious smarts? No. How about the prez of a corp with a greater net worth than the entire Seattle Metroplex? No. High-level corp suits have brains, chummers, and they excel at what they do. Don't ever lose sight of that fact.]<<<<<
—Friday (12:20:26/3-14-54)

>>>>>[Unless they didn't have to claw and fight their way to the top. What about that Villiers slot who owns one-third of Fuchi? He didn't earn his position, he inherited it. Having the right parents doesn't make you smart, cobber.]<<<<<
—Bongo (10:49:52/3-15-54)

>>>>>[Wrong. I'd argue Richard Villiers has had to be smarter than most corporate climbers. Sure, he inherited control of a large portion of the Villiers corporate holdings (his brother Martin gaining the rest), but Richard used the leverage of the Villiers assets to create Fuchi. Without the Villiers piece of the pie, the Nakatomi and Yamana assets at Fuchi would have devoured

themselves within a few years. And, by Christ, he's kept control of his one-third of Fuchi. The two other factions would love to see him gone, through bankruptcy or preferably in a box. But he's still there. That alone makes Villiers one smart slot. Bet your assets on that one, *omae.*]<<<<<
—Friday (13:04:18/3-15-54)

When a megacorp wants to play with money, whether to buy out a competitor or supplier or add a new arm to its world-girdling corporate structure, it does more than transfer credit from the central corporate bank. A large enough corp might generate the necessary credit by redirecting funds within its various divisions. It might cut corners here, delay payments there, renegotiate interdivisional loans and other agreements, and other such drek. Considering the vast sums of credit flowing through even a modest megacorp, saving a fraction of one percent can add up to huge sums. However, this kind of fiscal shell game won't net the corp enough current credit for most major transactions. The management team must find another way to generate money. Most commonly, corps raise additional funds through stock issues or so-called debt financing.

STOCK ISSUES

As most people know, stock (or shares) in a company represents partial ownership of that company. The individuals who own stock in a corp, called shareholders, legally own that corporation. Of course, an individual's percentage of ownership determines the amount of control he can exert over the actions of his corporation. If shareholders own few shares in comparison to the total number issued, they don't have much control.

When a corporation forms or undergoes significant enough changes to warrant a new charter, the charter of incorporation specifies how many shares that corporation can issue. The corp issues most of these shares when it starts up, to fund its initial operation. For example, a new corp might issue 100,000 shares with a par value (list price) of 100 nuyen. Assuming the corp sells all these shares, it receives 10,000,000 nuyen from the stock offering (minus brokerage fees and such, of course). The actual process of putting out a stock offering gets more complex than my simple little explanation, but nobody reading this board gives a flying frag about financial intricacies.

>>>>>[Remember what the previous file said about corp stock. Once shares get out on the so-called "secondary market" where slags like us buy and sell them, share value need not have any connection to the par value at which the corp first issued them. If people think the stock makes a good investment, paying dividends or increasing in value, that stock can trade at many times its par value. And vice versa, of course. Depending on how well the corp's doing, share prices can vary wildly.]<<<<<
—The Chromed Accountant (12:34:10/3-21-54)

Once a corp issues all the stock its charter allows, it can't fund itself by this method any more. So predictably, a corp issues all its authorized stock only if it desperately needs all the money those shares will net. In general, corp management prefers to hold back some of the authorized shares for later issues, when the corp may need another infusion of funding.

>>>>>[Okay, concrete example. When Ares bought Syntronics, that Atlanta-based corp that Saeder-Krupp sloughed off awhile back, it didn't have enough credit in current accounts to make the purchase. The Ares-Atlanta division had a bunch of authorized stock it hadn't issued yet, so it made a targeted stock offering to a bunch of CAS-based investment firms. The offering netted Ares-Atlanta enough current credit to snap up Syntronics.]<<<<<
   —Vic (13:17:29/4-1-54)

>>>>>[If a corp makes a stock offering, that means it needs current credit to buy something, cover a big debt or loss, or fight off a rival's move against it. Even if you don't give two frags about the stock market, keeping an eye on the market news can give you a feel for what's going down with the corps. You watch close enough, you can tell who's expanding, who's weak, who's ripe for a takeover, who's flexing their muscles, and so on. Believe me, the more you know about the corp that hired you or the one you're making a run against, the better chance you have of coming out of the biz with all parts still attached.]<<<<<
   —Blaze (21:51:20/4-2-54)

The market reports on the Matrix include listings like YAM-CF A and ARES-UCAS U. In English, those two listings translate as Yamatetsu CalFree, Series A and Ares UCAS, Series U. The final letters allow the corp to distinguish between different series of shares it issued at different times. Start-up shares get tagged as one series, and shares issued when the corp wants to buy another company get called something different.

DIVIDENDS

Because shareholders officially own a corp, some of that corp's profit finds its way into the owners' pockets as dividends. If a corp has a good year, it splits up a portion of the profits it made and divvies the nuyen up among its shareholders. The corp retains the rest of the profits to fund expansion, acquisitions, and all that drek. Dividends are expressed in terms of a given sum per share. For example, Yamatetsu's CalFree operation issued a whopping great dividend of 1 nuyen per share outstanding; not a bad return, considering the shares were trading at only 5 nuyen per share at the time.

>>>>>[A 20-percent return on your investment if you happened to pick up your shares at 5 nuyen. Predictably, the price of shares shot up after the dividend became public knowledge. Exactly the outcome Yamatetsu wanted.]<<<<<
   —John Maynard (13:39:08/3-19-54)

Dividends announce to the marketplace that a corp is turning a profit. If the business community shows its confidence in a corp by generating a healthy trading price for that corp's shares, the corp has a much easier time raising money when it needs to. It can guarantee the sale of any new shares it issues, banks will loan it money at preferential rates, and so on.

>>>>>[That's why corps protect their public image so well. And why other corps often go to great lengths to trash the image of a competitor.]<<<<<
   —Vache (23:41:41/3-21-54)

Of course, a solid record of paying dividends each year also has a negative side. As long as the corp keeps up the record, it impresses the sweet drek out of everyone. However, the first time the corp breaks its implied promise to keep paying the shareholders dividends, it can run full tilt into a nasty public-opinion backlash.

>>>>>[We're runners, not fragging stockbrokers. Why should we care about this drek?]<<<<<
   —Roach (14:03:47/3-29-54)

>>>>>[Don't know about you, chummer, but I like to know the ins and outs of the medium I get paid in.]<<<<<
   —Loran (18:43:41/3-29-54)

>>>>>[You get paid in fragging corporate stock? What's wrong with good, old-fashioned certified credsticks, huh?]<<<<<
   —Zilch (21:06:14/3-29-54)

>>>>>[Nothing's wrong with credsticks . . . sometimes. But the Johnson hiring you may not always want to go the cert-credstick route. From the street end, a certified stick is untraceable; it's pure credit, with no identification. But acquiring or creating the credstick gets to be a different story. The Johnson who gives you the stick can be linked to the payment, even though you can't.
   So who cares, as long as no link exists between you and him? He does, chummer. If someone traces the transaction from his end, they might find out he issued a certain amount of credit in the form of a certified stick. That might make people ask uncomfortable questions. After all, most people never need to use a certified credstick. A standard stick with an ident trace on it works fine for any legitimate transaction. So sometimes the Johnson finds it easier to pay you by transferring some corporate stock from his corp or another one to a blind account, or just by giving you a briefcase full of share certificates.]<<<<<
   —Loran (17:56:34/4-1-54)

>>>>>[Or sometimes you're the Johnson. Maybe you're fixing, or subcontracting out a job. Or maybe you just need to hire a combat mage or a triggerman. Don't know about you, *omae*, but I don't want to visit a bank and transfer credit to a certified credstick when I set up a run. Better to transfer something physical that no one can trace.]<<<<<
   —Argent (18:36:15/4-4-54)

>>>>>[What about cash?]<<<<<
   —Lucy K (21:09:09/4-4-54)

>>>>>[If you know everything's going to go down within one country, maybe. CAS dollars in Atlanta, hard-currency nuyen in Seattle. But the way the world works now, how often does that

happen? Frag, the decker I usually work with operates out of San Francisco. The slag who gets me heavy-duty decryption or encryption lives in fragging Hong Kong. How do I pay them? Corporate scrip? Right. It may be international, but it carries too many disadvantages. And the restrictions on shipping hard currency into and out of countries make cash payment a nightmare, even without taking into account fluctuating exchange rates.]<<<<<
—Argent (19:04:27/4-5-54)

>>>>>[Argent and his (rebuilt) Wrecking Crew aren't the only ones around the plex who like their pay in corporate stock. Once upon a time only a few people did it, but more and more Johnsons pay that way as people figure out the benefits. For example, stocks represent a slick performance bonus that doesn't cost the Johnson who hired you one bean but can really line your pockets. Let's say your run stands to benefit the hiring corp significantly enough to raise its share prices. And let's say that when you sign on for the run, you get 10,000 shares currently trading at 1¥ a share as a "binder." If you pull off the run, the share price jumps to 2¥ a share. Suddenly your 10,000-nuyen binder nets you 20,000 nuyen. You get an extra 10K for a job well done, and the market foots the bill. Elegant.]<<<<<
—Nagel (21:45:15/4-9-54)

>>>>>[Of course, if a Yamatetsu Johnson pays you in Yamatetsu shares, he's given you a personal incentive to protect your investment at least long enough to unload it. In this case, "protecting your investment" means not doing anything that might cause the share prices to drop. For example, making a "return engagement" run against Yamatetsu in the near future might not look like an attractive proposition. That's elegant too.]<<<<<
—Plessey (23:30:31/4-9-54)

>>>>>[Paying with stock just gives the corps another way to subvert the shadow community. They'll do anything to control what threatens them.]<<<<<
—The Neon Antichrist (03:57:31/4-11-54)

>>>>>[The corps don't need to "subvert" us when they pay us. Nemeses, patrons, reasons for existing, they're all the same, *neh*? We have to play their game anyway. Why not make a little more scratch by playing it efficiently?]<<<<<
—CySky (18:17:53/4-13-54)

>>>>>[Ever notice something really interesting? The infrastructure necessary to schlep stock from owner to owner untraceably by stepping around all kinds of corporate and civil laws is much more dependable than that necessary to transfer pure credit the same way. Another reason to pay in stock. Also another indication of the ways in which the world works for the convenience of business instead of for the private citizen.]<<<<<
—Jean (23:49:44/4-16-54)

DEBT AND EQUITY FINANCING

When you buy stock in a corp, you own a piece of the company. Should it close down or go bankrupt, you and all other shareholders have a legal right to a chunk of any assets left over after debts, proportional to the number of shares you hold in comparison to all shares outstanding. This deal sounds good, but nets you sweet frag-all because the debts swallow everything that the major shareholders couldn't loot. As a rule of thumb, if you own shares in a company that goes out of business, the share certificates are worth more as buttwipe than as financial instruments. In the case of a management buy-out, the corporation might offer to buy your shares back. However, it has no legal obligation to do so. Raising money through buying back shares is called equity financing, because the sellers own equity in the company.

Debt financing differs from equity financing more in principle than in practice. When using debt financing to raise funds, a corp issues bonds or debentures instead of stock. A bond represents a loan that the holder has made to the corporation, and legally obligates the corporation to pay that loan back with interest.

Bonds differ from stocks in that the bond certificate has a maturity date. The issuing corporation commits to buying the bond back from whoever owns it on that date, paying the full face value of the certificate. In the interim, the corporation pays the current bondholder a specified amount of interest quarterly, annually, biannually, or with whatever frequency the corp specifies when issuing the bonds. Corps can pay out this interest in various ways, but the details don't matter as much as the fact that the corp legally owes interest.

As with stocks, a healthy secondary market exists for corporate bonds. People buy and sell them at varying prices, depending on the fiscal health of the issuing corporation. In general, bonds sell at a premium (more than their face value) to reflect the fact that they pay their holder interest until they mature. As the maturity date nears, the premium decreases because the interest shrinks, drawing the trading price closer to the bond's face value.

As investments, bonds carry the same risks as stock. Prices can fluctuate wildly, and you can lose a bundle if you sell at a bad time. You can also lose your entire investment if the company goes out of business or otherwise defaults on its obligations. On the up side, bondholders can make capital gains as the selling price of their bonds increases and can also earn income from the bond interest.

>>>>>[More to the point for runners, bonds sometimes make a better medium of payment than corporate shares. Because shares represent ownership in the corporation and usually carry voting rights, stock ownership normally has to be registered somehow. Not so certain bonds, called "bearer bonds." These babies carry no way to trace ownership. If you pick one of these up on the sidewalk, it's yours and nobody can prove different. Of course, if you want to collect interest from a bearer bond you have to tell the company where to deposit the money, but that problem's easy to get around. Lots of people I know get paid in bearer bonds for shadow work.]<<<<<
—Firedrake (11:30:26/3-24-54)

>>>>>[Bearer bonds are the closest thing a lot of countries have to hard currency. Most banks and corporate vaults don't contain money any more. Their "money" amounts to digital data stored on a computer network. If you want to steal something with a good old-fashioned bank heist, swipe bearer bonds.]<<<<<
—Thunderbolt (06:32:14/3-26-54)

>>>>>[Yeah, but bearer bonds also have the same kind of protection that hard currency had when it meant something economically. Safes, alarms, armed guards, magical protection for large enough sums, you name it. You'd find it easier to waltz into some corp's computing system, dodge the ice, and flip a few bits here and there to transfer a large chunk of electronic credit into your account than to crack a physical vault in the heart of the Yamatetsu building.]<<<<<
—FastJack (14:27:14/3-29-54)

>>>>>[Ah, but think of the satisfaction . . .]<<<<<
—Dog Soldier (21:04:16/4-3-54)

>>>>>[All kinds of different bonds float around out there, chummers. Convertible, extendible, retractable, and so on and so forth. You can convert some bonds into common shares in the corp. Some the corporation can buy back before the maturity date. And so on, and so forth. Bonds can get pretty fragging compli-

cated. If you want to hang on to any bonds as a long-term investment, or even (perish the thought) a retirement fund, I strongly suggest you read up on this drek.]<<<<<
—Nuyen Nick (23:42:26/4-5-54)

>>>>>[Yes, well, most of us just want the nuyen. Bonds make it easier to launder payments from various Johnsons. Personally, I hang onto corporate bonds just long enough to set up a good deal and sell the peckers.]<<<<<
—Vatjob (08:59:12/4-6-54)

Junk Bonds

The 1980s and '90s saw the appearance of a new type of corporate bond. Officially classified as "high-yield" bonds, most people called them "junk bonds." Junk bonds are debentures issued by unstable corporations unlikely to still exist when the bonds mature.

For example, if you buy a bond issued by Ares Macrotechnology, the odds are pretty fragging good that the corp will still exist a couple of years down the road when the bond matures. Megacorps don't go out of business, so bondholders can expect payment when due. A bond issued by a smaller corp like Keane Incorporated, an outfit limited to the Seattle metroplex area, might tell a different story. Though Keane has significant local clout, it's a small fish in a very big pond compared to some of the big names in the global military/industrial/entertainment complex. Compared to a giant like Ares, Keane Inc. has much less certain prospects of surviving and prospering long enough to redeem the seven-year bonds it issued this January.

>>>>>[Bulldrek. Shiawase owns Keane. It's a stable outfit.]<<<<<
—Link (12:18:24/3-7-54)

>>>>>[Only as long as Shiawase wants to keep it stable, boyo. Just because one of the big boys owns a small corp doesn't mean the owning corp wants to pour money into a losing concern just to keep it going. If Keane gets into trouble, Shiawase management might let it go under. Who knows, they might need the tax write-off or something. Or a rival corp might raid the Shiawase empire, and Shiawase could tube Keane as part of its defense. Lots of possibilities could frag up Keane.]<<<<<
—Keynesian Kid (21:29:23/3-15-54)

If the Ares Macrotechnology and the Keane bond offer the same rate of interest, no sane investor would consider the Keane debenture. Therefore, if a less stable corp wants anyone to buy its bonds, it offers a higher interest rate to compensate for the greater risk that the company may fold before paying off the bond. The higher the chance that the company might go under, the higher the yield it offers to get people to take it seriously. The combination of high yield plus low odds of collecting it makes these risky bonds financial junk, hence the name "junk bond." In the 1980s and early '90s, some corps issuing bonds had so little stability that they couldn't hope to last a couple of months, let alone until their bonds matured. Investing in any of these bonds carried so many risks that no investor with the brains of a turnip should have bought the

things. However, in plenty of cases the staggeringly high yields overcame common sense. Quite a few major investors sank a lot of money into junk bonds.

The following example gives a picture of the way junk bonds work for those who get lucky. To simplify things, assume a rate of return around 10 percent for "blue-chip" bonds from stable corps. Estimate the yield of your average junk bond at 20 percent. Also assume that 2 percent or so of the companies issuing the junk bonds sink without a trace within a year of issue. Using these figures, if you invest 1 million nuyen in blue-chip bonds, at the end of one year you walk away with 1.1 million nuyen.

Say you invest that same 1 million nuyen in 20-percent-yield junk bonds from 100 smaller corps, putting 10,000 nuyen in each corp. Two of those 100 corps go under within the year, costing you 20,000 nuyen. However, you get a 20-percent return on the remaining 980,000 nuyen, for a total profit of 196,000 nuyen. After one year, you walk away with 1,176,000 nuyen. Even with the 2 percent default rate, you've made an extra 76K nuyen by investing in the junks instead of the blue-chip bonds.

>>>>>[Even blue-chip corps sometimes default on their bonds. The default rate for AAA-rated bonds runs at about 0.25 percent, closer to 3 percent for junk bonds.]<<<<<
—Keynesian Kid (13:20:17/3-21-54)

>>>>>[If you use real figures, not the fake ones this Neo-A slot used, the difference between junk and investment-rated bonds gets a lot smaller. The yield on investment-rated paper averages close to 15 percent, but junks don't go much over 20 percent.]<<<<<
—Hogarth (21:52:42/3-21-54)

>>>>>[But the principle remains the same, and investors rich enough to play on the international market can invest much more than a piddling million.]<<<<<
—Keynesian Kid (10:32:31/3-22-54)

>>>>>[So why does it matter, anyway?]<<<<<
—Laker Girl (21:09:37/3-27-54)

>>>>>[It matters because junk bonds tend to force out good bonds. Only the most cautious investor puts money into stable corps when junks offer a better return. That means that the stable corps can't raise the money they need for expansion, acquisition, or whatever through bond issues unless they raise their own yield rates to offer a better deal than the junks. But the stable corps already offered the highest rates they could justify based on their business position. If they raise those yields to compete with the junks, they're paying out more money than they can afford. That puts otherwise-stable corps at a higher risk of going out of business. Meanwhile, the companies that normally float junk bonds have to raise *their* yields higher to stay more desirable than the stable corps. Each rise in yield increases their chances of defaulting. Higher junk yields force the stable corps to raise their own yields once again, starting a spiral of increasing interest rates.

Yields can only spiral so high before the businesses involved can't maintain them any more. Then you get "junk bond crash," where a whole lot of corps go belly-up at the same time. I'm talking a lot more than the 3 percent default rate the Keynesian Kid suggested; 50 percent or more may go under.]<<<<<
—The Chromed Accountant (13:36:40/3-29-54)

>>>>>[So a bunch of corps buy the farm. So fragging what? Good riddance, I say.]<<<<<
—Lucinda (21:23:06/3-29-54)

>>>>>[And your source of income also buys the farm. Have you been paying attention?]<<<<<
— Caine (22:12:09/3-29-54)

>>>>>[Hate to break it to you, chummer, but financial institutions like banks and insurance companies tend to invest in junk bonds. As of this minute, major financial institutions own close to 85 percent of all the junk bonds out there. If we have another junk bond crash like the one in the late 1980s or in 2045, a bunch of banks go belly-up. The economy gets drek-kicked. People lose their savings and their homes. How'd you like it if next time you slot your credstick, the reader comes back with the dreaded "insufficient funds" message? I think we're in another upward spiral. The next junk bond crash could happen at any time.]<<<<<
—The Chromed Accountant (15:42:59/4-1-54)

>>>>>[Oh, just fragging charming ...]<<<<<
—Piers (18:35:19/4-1-54)

Smaller corps go the junk bond route because it lets them raise large sums of money in a real hurry, letting a small company metastasize into a big company overnight. As technology and society advance, the changes cause rampant uncertainty in the business community. Uncertainty makes a perfect climate for acquisitions and mergers, both of which take mucho nuyen. A small corp can double its size in no time by staging a hostile takeover of a rival or a corp in a different line of business. Junk bonds raise lots of cash fast, fueling the takeover fever. (I'll talk more about takeovers in a later file called **Competition** [p. 63]. Watch for it, boys and girls.)

STOCK MARKET GAMES
Even today, the words "stock market" conjure up images of the vast trading floor at some frantically busy stock exchange where sweaty and exhausted traders scream at each other as they hash out deals from opposite sides. Unfortunately, that kind of stock market went out before the end of the last century. Fast-developing computer tech sounded the death knell of the trading floor a decade or more before it actually vanished. Nowadays, all trading of stocks and bonds occurs electronically and almost instantaneously through the Matrix.

Virtual Exchanges
In some parts of the global Matrix, virtual meeting places serve most of the functions of the old-style physical stock exchange. Professional traders swapping securities owned by others or individuals making their own deals can "meet" in the virtual reality of the net to buy or sell securities or to exchange credit. The virtual exchanges make good places to clinch deals without needing to tap a specific buyer or seller. However, recent figures indicate that only 38 percent of all security trading goes on in these virtual exchanges. Most trades happen privately. Individual buyers and sellers meet either virtually or physically as circumstances allow, to exchange securities and payment. Obviously, these private deals only happen when and if buyer and seller both know of each other's existence and willingness to deal.

>>>>>[Visual details vary from one virtual exchange to another, sometimes even from month to month within the same exchange. The Hong Kong virtual exchange looks like the old-time crowded trading floor. The New York exchange comes across as the biggest fragging computer room you've ever imagined (a frightening place for the uninitiated). And the Central Exchange in Zurich-Orbital that the corporations use is literally indescribable.

Only one thing stays consistent; unless you know how an exchange works, they'll rip you off big time. Nobody outright robs you, of course. As far as that goes, the places are safe as houses. After all, why should anyone rob you straight out when they have so many more subtle ways to stiff you?

You may be a big-time wheeler-dealer on your own turf, able to squeeze that last nuyen out of any fixer or fence. Compared to the professionals who hang out in the exchanges and trade billions of nuyen worth of securities every day, you're *nothing*, chummer. They can hook you, clean you, fillet you, and fry you before you know whazzappenin. And they do it so smoothly that you'll thank them for the experience. Assuming they pay attention to you, of course. No trader with a terabuck daily quota will give you the time of day if you just want to sell a piddling 2,000 shares of Ares Series C.]<<<<<
—Majendie (14:48:52/4-2-54)

>>>>>[You said the virtual exchanges are safe. What do you mean?]<<<<<
—Tom Thumb (21:49:32/4-4-54)

>>>>>[At any virtual exchange worthy of the name, Matrix security is tighter than a devil rat's hind end. Just about anybody can come and go as long as they use a deck with a nice, legal ident signature in the chips (or a good fake one). Heavy-duty ice trashes anyone who does something they shouldn't. As well as the ice, the exchange usually hires a few console cowboys and loads them up with the hottest combat utilities money can buy. Those guys make short work of anyone who gets unruly.]<<<<<
—Majendie (15:01:46/4-5-54)

>>>>>[You're talking about the official exchanges. The yakuza run several of their own, as do some of the Seoulpa Rings. A few floating "shadow exchanges" also exist. Like so much in the

shadows, no one knows exactly what to expect at places like these. The first time you visit one, it might not seem any different from a legitimate operation. Go back two weeks later, though, and you may find an ugly scene.]<<<<<
—Harmony (14:56:22/4-12-54)

>>>>>[Actually, knowing where to find one of the so-called "shadow exchanges" can give you an advantage. Say someone starts dumping bucketloads of Ares stock. That means something's about to happen to Ares that'll lower their trading value. The stocks get traded on the shadow exchange at less than true trading value, but Ares takes longer to tip to what's happening than if the trading had occurred on an open exchange.]<<<<<
—The Big Seat (02:12:51/4-13-54)

>>>>>[Predictably, national governments and the corps that run the legitimate exchanges both want to shut down the shadow exchanges. A legitimate virtual exchange takes a tiny percentage of the credit that changes hands in any transaction, about 0.001 percent. (Sure adds up when the exchange trades billions of nuyen daily.) The corp running the exchange considers this percentage a service fee for providing a nice, safe place to do business. The national government that has jurisdiction at a legit exchange also withholds any appropriate taxes on each transaction. (Granted, jurisdiction keeps getting more and more meaningless, but it still occasionally counts for something.) Neither happens at a shadow exchange, so each transaction that goes down in the shadows represents lost revenue to corp and government.]<<<<<
—Skip (15:00:10/4-14-54)

Brokerage Firms

Okay, boys and girls, I know what you're thinking. Virtual exchanges can track the transactions because the shares being traded exist as digital bits. But share and bond certificates that prove ownership are physical objects. How can you exchange those in a virtual meeting through the Matrix?

People get around that problem in many ways, including going through a brokerage firm. I use the term "brokerage firm" in its widest possible application. That includes an outfit specifically incorporated to trade in securities like Woods-Gordon, a bank with a securities department, or a corp of some kind that has a securities department. Even a good department store might qualify, if it has personnel who handle securities. No matter what form it actually takes, the idea behind it stays the same.

If as a legitimate investor (yeah, right) you decide to buy Ares Macrotechnology stock, you contact a brokerage firm. Use the vidphone, "visit" them virtually, or go see them in the meat and tell the sales rep you want X number of shares of Ares Series D at market price. You transfer your credit and the firm's broker makes the deal.

Of course, she doesn't hand over the share certificates unless you demand it (and then bully the company into giving you what you want). Assuming the certificates exist and assuming the company has them, it keeps them somewhere in the bowels of its corporate office. For all you know, the share certificates stay in the Ares vault. Or they may never have physically existed at all. In this

kind of transaction, only the record of ownership changes. Once you buy stock, you become the official owner of shares numbered XXX through YYY. If at a later date you sell them through a broker, the transaction stays entirely electronic. The ownership record changes so that you no longer own the shares. Instead, they officially belong to the slag you sold them to. Simple, *neh*? Works just like the transfer of electronic credit.

If someone gives you a briefcase full of share certificates as a payment for a run and you want to convert those oh-so-pretty embossed pieces of paper into credit that can actually buy your friends a round of drinks, you have a couple of options.

First, you can do everything legal and aboveboard. Take the shares physically into the office of a brokerage house and put them on deposit. UCAS law forbids brokerage firms to ask where you got them, and so do plenty of other jurisdictions. Once the brokerage house has the physical certificates, you can trade the damn things on the market like any legit investor. However, to deal legally with a brokerage firm anywhere in the UCAS, CAS, CalFree, most of the NAN states, and even the Tir, you need a SIN. (Without one, the government can't tax you. Big no-no, chummers.)

>>>>>[Here's where simplification gets dangerous. People have hinted that different types of bonds exist. With so-called bearer bonds, physical possession equals ownership. If they're in my hand, they're mine. But with some bonds and shares, ownership gets recorded at an office of the issuing corporation. You might have the physical certificates, but if the official record says they belong to Governor Schultz, the bonds are hers and you're in deep drek. Make sure you know exactly what kind of bonds or shares you get in payment. If they're not bearer bonds, then by god make sure your Johnson changes the official record of ownership. And remember, if you ever want to sell those bonds legally, you have to prove your identity as the officially recorded owner. Keep that in mind if you have the bonds recorded under an alias and make that alias pretty damn watertight.]<<<<<
    —Loree (15:57:45/4-2-54)

>>>>>[Even with bearer bonds, you can still get in deep frag. Where'd the scag who gave them to you get them, huh? If he or someone else stole them from a brokerage firm vault, the serial numbers are on record. Try selling those puppies legally and you'll get nabbed for trafficking in stolen goods. Or worse.]<<<<<
    —Sergei (00:16:08/4-6-54)

>>>>>[I thought bearer bonds worked like cash. If you have them, you own them.]<<<<<
    —Talbot (04:21:59/4-6-54)

>>>>>[Try this analogy. Someone gives you a Confederate ten-dollar bill. Technically, that bill is legal tender anywhere in the CAS regardless of where you got it and how you came to own it. But suppose someone stole that bill from some obsessive old scut who kept an exact record of the serial number of each bill in his possession. When he got robbed he gave his list to the cops, who disseminated it all over town. So when you try to spend your bill, the shopkeeper compares the serial number to the list. He sees that it was stolen and calls the cops, and you get nailed for trafficking in stolen goods. (Okay, probably not for a $10 bill; make it a $1,000 bill.)

Usually, money's finders-keepers . . . but exceptions do exist. Same with bearer bonds.]<<<<<
    —The Chromed Accountant (13:33:34/4-7-54)

>>>>>[Um . . . anyone out there know how to search records of stock ownership . . .?]<<<<<
    —Suki (04:10:34/4-9-54)

>>>>>[Some Johnson paid you with a case full of stock and you're getting nervous, huh, Suki?]<<<<<
    —West (04:13:23/4-9-54)

>>>>>[Shut up, fragface.]<<<<<
    —Suki (04:13:58/4-9-54)

>>>>>[Brokerage firms are like banks. They have tough computer security, Suki old scag. We're talking black ice, probably Red-5 and up for the key datastores. I don't know about the virtual exchanges, but I'd guess at least Red-6. You're looking at a tough hack.]<<<<<
    —Red Wraith (09:42:15/4-9-54)

If you've acquired some security certificates and prefer to avoid official involvement, you can fence the damn things. Sell them to a fixer, another runner, or whoever wants to deal with the legal niceties you prefer to sidestep. As with any kind of property, fencing certificates costs you big. Expect to net about 20 percent of the market price for bearer bonds; for anything with an official record, less than one percent of the market rate.

>>>>>[That 20 percent only applies if you've got a good fence. Ten percent sounds more like it, chummers.]<<<<<
    —Vivian (21:04:41/4-1-54)

>>>>>[The best fence for securities is a stockbroker interested in doing a little something under the table.]<<<<<
    —Maurice (23:22:53/4-1-54)

>>>>>[Can you sell them through a shadow exchange?]<<<<<
    —Kip (05:32:56/4-3-54)

>>>>>[You might pull off a deal, but you still have to make the physical exchange. Remember, you only make money when you've got the certificates in your mitts. You can bet that someone in the shadow exchange listened in when you arranged the deal. (Shadow exchanges are that kind of place.) That makes your meet vulnerable to compromise by several big guys with heavy ordnance, ready to relieve you of the share certificates and the buyer of his certified credstick. Risky.]<<<<<
    —Maurice (00:01:43/4-6-54)

Investment Services

In most cases, "investment services" is just a pretty euphemism for crooks. You want my advice, stay away from these jokers.

An investment service works like a cross between a brokerage firm and a bank. You hand over your money (or shares or whatever) to them, along with legal power of attorney. In turn they invest your credit, trade on the market, buy and sell, or otherwise wheel and deal to make your money grow.

At least they try. Most of the investment services I know are incompetents or thieves. Take your pick. A few do a real fine job, such as the Zurich-Orbital-based Caspar & Associates, who handle Samantha Villiers' investments. (Yes, *that* Samantha Villiers, ex-wife of the Richard Villiers who owns about one-third of Fuchi!) Caspar & Associates has made Sam Villiers even more excrementally rich than she used to be. But Joe Public (or Joe Shadowrunner) can't get a foot in their door. Forget it, chummers. They won't even return your calls if your net worth amounts to less than a billion nuyen. Just a poor shadowrunner, not rolling in cred? Handle your own investments unless you know something the rest of us don't. Or unless you don't care how rich your "investment consultants" get at your expense.

>>>>>[Ooh, cynical.]<<<<<
　　　—Bung (16:31:11/3-13-54)

>>>>>[But accurate.]<<<<<
　　　—The Chromed Accountant (12:38:21/4-1-54)

>>>>>[Hey man, I don't got the time to watch stocks and bonds. So how's a guy like me s'posed to play the game? My investment guy's making me rich while I do what I do best, that's how.]<<<<<
　　　—Timex (03:15:56/4-2-54)

>>>>>[And if you believe that, I've got a piece of Florida farmland you might want to buy.]<<<<<
　　　—Whiley (08:46:19/4-2-54)

Stock Prices

To make our lives a little easier, from here on in use the word "stocks" to refer to both stocks and bonds. If you want to know about stock prices, log onto one of the market-tracking services available on the Matrix sometime and watch how they fluctuate. Depending on circumstances, the market price of a particular stock can fluctuate hundreds of nuyen within a few seconds. It might plunge into a trough, soar to a peak, or drop off the market entirely.

Freaks you out at first glance, but it has a logic to it.

Like goods and services, stock prices depend on supply and demand. If lots of prospective investors scrap over a few desirable shares, the price goes up. If lots of people want to dump a stock but can't find many buyers, the price drops like a paralyzed pigeon. In this case, the commodity subject to the laws of supply and demand is the value that investors perceive in a particular stock.

Perceived investor value can come from either the underlying stability of the corporation that issued the stock or from potential short-term profit. If the issuing corp keeps reporting profits every fiscal year, never defaults on loans and always pays its dividends, that stability represents value to investors. For example, if you bought stock in Yamatetsu-Seattle three years ago, the corp's growth and improvement in the marketplace would have more than quadrupled your money. As for potential short-term profit, rapid changes in the price of a so-called "volatile" stock can potentially make a lucky investor a bucket o' nuyen in a very short time.

>>>>>[Okay, that works if the price is going up. Buy low, sell high, I get that. But what if the stock price drops? How can I make money on that?]<<<<<
　　　—Magritte (16:48:49/3-15-54)

>>>>>[Ah, the wonders of capitalism. A technique called "selling short" can make you money on a dropping stock. This explanation is way oversimplified, but here goes. You sell shares you don't own at the current market price by "borrowing" them from a brokerage firm, on the understanding that you'll buy the actual shares later. You still sell high and buy low, Magritte, but the time order's different.

Take a fictional example. Drekware stock currently trades at 2 nuyen, but I think the corp's headed for the dumper. So I sell short 10,000 borrowed shares, making 20,000 nuyen. When Drekware stock drops to 1 nuyen, I buy the 10K shares I borrowed for a total cost of 10,000 nuyen and pocket the remaining 10,000 nuyen difference. Nice, huh?

But if I'm dead wrong and Drekware stock goes up, I can be in deep drek. Say I sell short 10K shares of stock at 2 nuyen, grossing 20K nuyen. Then Drekware announces it's found a cure for death or taxes or something, and the market pushes Drekware's price up to 10 nuyen per share. Uh-oh, I have to buy back the 10K shares I borrowed. At 10 nuyen a pop, I'm out a whopping 100,000 nuyen! All told, I lose 80,000 nuyen. Not exactly soybeans.

So don't play out of your league, chummers. You can make a packet selling short, but that technique poses more risks than a straightforward stock buy, and only experts should try it. If you buy stock and it goes off the market, you can't lose more than the amount you initially invested. I pay 100 nuyen for stock that no longer exists, I lose 100 nuyen, right? But if you sell short, there's no limit to how much you can lose. In the example above, I lost 80K nuyen. Suppose Drekware shot up to 20 nuyen a share? Or 100, or 500¥? If it hit 500 nuyen a share, filling my order would have cost me *5 million nuyen*, for a total loss of 4,980,000 nuyen. Can you say ouch?]<<<<<
— Keynesian Kid (05:02:43/3-20-54)

>>>>>[Selling short occurs often with insider trading. Individuals know that a company is heading for fiscal or physical damage and that therefore their stock will drop. Someone may have tipped them off about a run, or they're sponsoring one themselves, and so on. You get the drift.]<<<<<
—The Big Seat (02:39:12/4-13-54)

Sometimes investors jump on a particular stock and push it into a meteoric rise. This kind of fiscal high jump occurs not because of any fundamental strength on the part of the issuing company, but simply because investors expected such a rise.

Yes, my children, the stock market often acts like a self-fulfilling prophecy. A few market gurus predict that a certain stock will increase in price, so they buy tons of it. Others see the gurus buying up that stock, figure they know something, and buy it themselves. Shares go up even higher, encouraging yet more people to buy the stock. Up it goes, until it hits a limit.

At some point, the share price flies so high above the value the stock should have, based on the fundamental strengths and weaknesses of the issuing company, that something's got to give. The ability to judge that point to a nicety separates a good market-player from a hack. Just before the stock reaches its highest point, the market gurus unload their shares and take their profit. The stock may rise a few more nuyen, but quite often the profit-taking alone stops the price in its tracks. With the price rise slowing and the gurus unloading, the less savvy investors begin to sense the end of the gravy train. So they start to sell as well. Soon everybody wants to sell, a situation that drives the share price down (sometimes even faster than it went up). People madly try to unload their holdings, but can't find many buyers. Potential purchasers see the writing on the wall and say no thank you; they don't want to buy losing stock, and the price plummets merrily down. That's what causes the ballistic rise and fall of stock prices, boys and girls. Sometimes this process takes a couple of days from start to finish; in a highly volatile market, it only takes a couple of hours.

>>>>>[With the Expert System trading networks some financial institutions use, that can make decisions and issue transactions in milliseconds, the whole cycle can take a couple of minutes. It happens so fast that only the most conscientious market-watcher even notices the peak. In that couple of minutes people can make or lose millions or billions of nuyen.]<<<<<
—The Chromed Accountant (09:28:12/ 3-23-54)

>>>>>[It used to be worse. Computer systems triggered at least one crash in the past, and nearly brought on a couple of others. For a while they were all but outlawed, until the exchanges imposed transaction limits (X number of transactions in Y time interval) to calm things down. It can still get rough, but the market generally stays smoother now.]<<<<<
—The Big Chair (02-43-02/4-13-54)

The gurus who anticipated (or prompted) the price rise make the most money. They bought in at the bottom and sold just short of the peak. Other investors who jumped on the bandwagon fast and bought at the bottom but unloaded their shares a little more slowly can still make a packet, even if they sell their shares as the price is on its way down. Most unsophisticated investors don't really understand how the market works, so they buy in halfway up and don't manage to unload until the shares have crashed all the way to the bottom. Those poor working stiffs take a real bath.

Remember this lesson, cobbers. Sometimes, the simple fact that major investors buy into a stock can increase its price. That means that these investors can "make a market." By buying large volumes of a stock, they can force the price up; by selling large volumes, they can force the price down. Either way, the major investors have total control.

>>>>>[Remember the old joke about the high powered suit on the phone to his stockbrokers all over the world? "New York? Sell. Chicago? Sell. London? Sell. Tokyo? *Buy!!*" The market works that way sometimes. Force the price of a stock down by selling, then buy it back at a lower price and make a fast packet. Assuming you have enough influence to affect the market, of course.]<<<<<
—Randolph (13:37:35/3-21-54)

And this, my children, is one way in which the corporations truly compete. They force undesirable changes in each others' share prices. Say that Ares Europa needs money to buy out a major hydroelectric project on the Danube River, and plans to raise the funds by making a new stock offering. Say Fuchi knows this, knows the timing, and would purely love to frag things up for Ares. Through many, many intermediaries, Fuchi happens to own a whack of Ares Europa stock, but not enough to give them voting control. So instead, a day or so before Ares Europa announces its new stock offering, Fuchi starts dumping all its Ares Europa stock at slightly below market price. If Fuchi dumps enough stock volume and uses its intermediaries to make it look as though a lot of different people are unloading Ares Europa shares, the market reacts by pushing down the price of that stock. This drop diminishes investor confidence in the corp. In this kind of environment, Ares Europa stands to get frag-all from its new stock issue. To make the scam even sweeter, after the market pushes the price way down, Fuchi will buy back the stock it originally sold. Lucky ol' Fuchi gets to make money while jacking with a rival.

>>>>>[The market isn't dumb (at least, not always). If investors can tell that Fuchi is selling all the Ares Europa stock, the market will recognize the power play going down and won't react as strongly.]<<<<<
—Varithien (08:09:54/3-29-54)

>>>>>[It can work with price rises, too. Let's say that Ares Europa is planning a hostile takeover of Germany-based Microlux Corporation and quietly starts buying up shares. Fuchi gets wind of it and decides to risk a little money to drek in Ares' pool. Fuchi starts buying Microlux shares, but not quietly. No, they make all kinds of public sound and fury about it. The market reacts by pushing Microlux stock prices into the stratosphere, making it extremely expensive for Ares Europa to acquire control. Fuchi might make money on this scam too, because it can unload the Microlux shares it bought at a much higher price than it paid for them. It might even sell them to Ares Europa! Delicious irony, *neh*?]<<<<<
    —Jan (19:09:58/3-31-54)

>>>>>[Corps keep their strategic plans *very* close to the old vest to avoid exactly that kind of drek. If your rivals know what you're planning, they can find many, many ways to drek on you.]<<<<<
    —KHB (10:01:04/4-2-54)

>>>>>[Why should we care about this? We're never going to have the financial clout to pull any of these scams.]<<<<<
    —Ramp (19:08:02/4-4-54)

>>>>>[Granted. But hey, chummer, it sure helps to understand this crap. It might give you some clue as to why your next Johnson is hot and bothered enough to pay good nuyen to hire shadowrunners. If you know the whys and the wherefores that no self-respecting Johnson ever levels with you about, you might stand a better chance of predicting and avoiding any unpleasant consequences of taking on a run.]<<<<<
    —Hangfire (10:09:36/4-5-54)

>>>>>[Echo that one. All the time I hear about runners who work totally blind. They take a Johnson's credit, concentrate on the run, and don't bother to figure out how the run fits into the rest of reality. They could give a frag why the Johnson needs the job done, whose toes it's going to tread on, or any of that. Who needs it, right? And then they howl when the Johnson double-crosses them. Suddenly the "low-level suit" they greased turns out to be a Renraku senior veep, and they've got a Red Samurai payback team on their trail. If you don't do your homework and figure out what's behind the run, you deserve every bit of nasty drek you get.]<<<<<
    —Argent (23:47:37/4-7-54)

Of course, corps can also jack with a rival's share prices by changing the public perception of a corp's fundamental value and stability. To maintain investor confidence, corporations play an ongoing public relations game. They constantly use the media to trumpet their latest record-breaking quarterly revenue. In effect, "Yamatetsu breaks last year's sales records" translates to "Yamatetsu shares can make you big nuyen." The investment community reacts immediately to business news and developments, both positive and negative. If a company posts record earnings or announces a new whiz-bang product, share prices generally rise. If a company frags up badly, loses money, or otherwise drops the ball, share prices tend to decline. Needless to say, corps have an incredible incentive to manipulate the media so that it tells only the stories they want disseminated.

>>>>>[Because seven megacorps directly or indirectly own 95 percent of the world's news media, such manipulation is null sheen for them. For example, MCT owns ABS lock, stock and barrel through a couple of holding companies. Not likely any ABS news broadcast'll portray MCT activities in a bad light.]<<<<<
    —Zee (10:28:45/3-22-54)

>>>>>[Too simplistic by half. Maybe ABS won't bite the hand that owns it by spotlighting MCT's latest frag-up, but you can bet your assets NBS will. Fuchi owns them indirectly, and Fuchi would *love* to break nasty stories about its rival. The only kind of story the media as a whole suppresses is one that paints the entire megacorporate community as villains.]<<<<<
    —Toshi (00:10:31/3-23-54)

>>>>>[Thank god for the pirates and the independents! We kowtow to no corps, we pursue no hidden agendas. We just give you the truth right in your face.]<<<<<
    —Turner (02:40:17/3-23-54)

>>>>>[For as long as the corps consider you unworthy of the effort involved in squashing you, Turner old chummer.]<<<<<
    —Zack (10:35:57/3-23-54)

>>>>>[Setting up even the smallest pirate station costs mucho dinero, doesn't it? Keeping it on the air and in the shadows has got to cost even more. That raises an interesting question . . . which corps are secretly funding the pirates and the independents?]<<<<<
    —Pentecost (11:06:01/3-25-54)

>>>>>[Bad news travels fast and plays hell with the market. Remember last year when UCAStrak's Seattle-to-SanFran maglev-bullet train had that "mishap" with 157 fatalities? UCAStrak tried to cover it up, but of course the word got out. How can you hide a train crash? Within an hour, UCAStrak stock dropped 32 percent. In an attempt at damage control, the corp tried to blame the whole thing on a Tir-based ecotage group. They claimed the dandelion-eaters booby-trapped the track. Some independents tried to hold UCAStrak accountable for shoddy security, but most people bought into that story and the stock started to rise again. Then Marla Thorpe, an independent shadowsnoop, dug up proof that shoddy maintenance by UCAStrak caused the crash. She publicly accused the corp of criminal negligence leading to loss of life, and share prices dropped like a rock. If Shiawase hadn't bought it out through their subsidiary, Ressha Corporation, UCAStrak would have gone belly-up.]<<<<<
    —Toomre (14:49:10/3-29-54)

>>>>>[Want to hear something real twisted? Buzz in the shadows says Marla Thorpe is on the Shiawase payroll and that her "evidence" of negligence was pure jetwash. The same buzz says a Shiawase-hired shadow team fixed the track to make the bullet train crash. Apparently Shiawase wanted UCAStrak, but didn't

Almost as common a tactic among the corps as spreading the good word about themselves is spreading the bad word about a rival. Because perception rather than reality drives the market, negative publicity need not be true. Frequently a corp publicizes a damaging rumor about a rival to drive that rival's share prices down. When the truth eventually comes out, the rival's stock begins to head back to its previous level (or close enough for government work). However, the rumor-mongering corp only cares about the short term. During the temporary drop in the rival's share prices, the other corp can buy up enough stock to either gain control or stack the rival corp's board with its own representatives. This kind of dirty pool makes an excellent prelude to a hostile takeover. Also, if a corp knows its rival plans to announce a new stock offering, it may spread nasty tales just to drek things up in the market.

>>>>>[Chummers, any shadowsnoop has got to know of and watch out for this scam. An old contact tells you something dirty's going on with Corp A, so you look into it. You find evidence and file your story, making Corp A look dirty as hell. Later, you find out that your old contact works for Corp B, and that Corp B manufactured the "evidence" you publicized. Get used as a tool by the corps even once, and your rep goes in the dumper.]<<<<<
—Turner (02:47:56/3-23-54)

>>>>>[As others have said before me, corps playing this game make lots of work for shadowrunners. After all, somebody has to spread the rumors or manufacture and plant the evidence. The corp getting hit by this scam needs to dig up proof that it is a scam, or eliminate the people trying to pull it before they can finish the job.

Also, this kind of dirt looks a lot more convincing if more than just rumor and manufactured evidence backs it up. Let's say Corp A wants the market to think that Corp B's stuffers contain toxic waste. Rather than just spreading rumors, Corp A might actually hire a shadow team to slip into the stuffer factory late one night and dump something unpleasant into a vat. Thanks to the shadow op, a batch of those stuffers actually does contain toxic waste. When the news breaks, independent verification can prove that the stuffers are drekky. There goes Corp B's rep, straight down the sewer pipe.]<<<<<
—Royston (23:11:37/3-31-54)

>>>>>[This kind of drek happens all the time, but not always between different corps. Sometimes one division or faction goes up against another division within the same corp. Some kind of power play goes on between different board members or veeps or whatever, jockeying for position and trying to grab bigger slices of the corp pie. Or someone tries to drekcan a rival, or some other kind of dirty work.

Take Fuchi, for example. The Villiers, Nakatomi, and Yamana families jointly own the corp. The rivalry heats up most often between Villiers and the Japanese interests, but on occasion the Nakatomis and Yamanas trash each other with equal gusto. Two years back, the Nakatomi-controlled Fuchi Microengineering Division announced a major breakthrough in "growing" specialized

want to pay the going market rate for the shares. Much better to drive the stock down and buy at fire-sale prices, and who cares if 150+ people get geeked in the process?]<<<<<
—Fox (01:05:56/3-31-54)

>>>>>[And that, Fox old pal, is disinformation spread by Renraku to trash Shiawase's public image. Talk about twisted . . .]<<<<<
—Moonglum (22:42:19/4-2-54)

crystals in the microgravity of their orbital lab. The announcement claimed that the first shipment of the new crystals would soon reach Earth for release on the market. Microelectronic manufacturers around the world fell all over themselves to place advance orders. Almost overnight, Fuchi Microengineering shares went up 450 percent.

Then a rumor spread around the world's markets discrediting Fuchi Micro's announcement. According to the rumor, the procedure had serious problems and the crystals fell so far short of specifications that Fuchi Micro couldn't fill the advance orders for eight to ten months. All the companies who'd placed those advance orders started hounding Fuchi Micro to get their deposits back. Fuchi Micro stock dropped like a brick, to way below the price it had before the first announcement.

At that point, the Yamanas made their move. After driving down the stock by planting the "crystals-are-bad" rumor, they snapped up as many Fuchi Micro shares as they could lay claws on at the low price. They had to do it quick, before the market caught them buying and pushed the stock back up again. They also had to pull it off before the Nakatomis could react and block the move. They came damned close to gaining control of one of the Nakatomis' major assets; if not for the "unfortunate" crash of the Chiba virtual stock exchange in the middle of trading, they'd have done it.

As it was, the Nakatomis barely managed to keep control of Fuchi Microengineering. They exposed the rumor, and share prices soared back up. The Yamanas unloaded most of the shares they'd bought, turning a tidy profit in the process. To this day, nobody knows exactly who the Nakatomis hired to crash the Chiba exchange.]<<<<<
—Mosfet (21:19:08/4-4-54)

>>>>>[Buzz I hear says FastJack did the job. Who else could have pulled it off?]<<<<<
—Jean-Claude (16:01:42/4-6-54)

>>>>>[Not me, chummer, but thanks for the ego stroke.]<<<<<
—FastJack (19:02:13/4-6-54)

>>>>>[I hear the Nakatomis borrowed a novahot decker from the Villiers' camp to do the job . . . and now they owe Richard Villiers big-time.]<<<<<
—Rat (00:01:06/4-10-54)

>>>>>[Here's a quick brain-dump of other ways to trash a rival's share prices. Corps tend to hire shadow ops to pull this stuff off:
• Extraction or elimination of a vital employee (senior manager, research scientist, and so on).
• Elimination of a board member.
• Destruction of physical assets ("go blow up that lab").
• Publicizing proof of illegal/immoral/unethical/disgusting activity. ("Proof" also includes convincing lies.)
• Publicizing proof of shadow activity against a third party (Corp A hires runners to dig up proof that Corp B is doing the dirty to Corp C, assuming that Corp C will take action against Corp B).
• Publicizing evidence that corp management is skimming off the top or lying to the shareholders to avoid paying dividends.

• Publicizing proof that a product is dangerous or otherwise substandard.
• Interfering with the production or distribution of a good or service (shut down an assembly line, stop the shipment of microgravity-grown crystals from making it to the market, and so on).

I'm sure anyone with half a brain can come up with a lot more than the ops on my list. When corps get going with this kind of game, shadowrunners get involved one way or another.]<<<<<
—Tanner (19:12:15/4-17-54)

CORPORATE SCRIP

Unless you've lived under a rock for the past couple of decades, you know that a lot of megacorps issue their own currency, referred to as corporate scrip. Corps frequently pay their employees in corporate scrip, and sometimes conduct all interdepartmental and interdivisional transactions with it as well. Some corps use electronic-based credit, and others print hard currency. However, corporate hard currency has few uses because it has no worth outside of the issuing corporation. For outside-the-corp transactions, most corps prefer to use corp credsticks or the equivalent.

Corps issue scrip rather than conducting in-house transactions in so-called "real" money because scrip has become real in a key sense. It works pretty much like the currency issued by a national government. In today's world, money is as money does, and corporate scrip does just fine within certain restrictions.

Corps love to pay their wageslaves in scrip. Of course, the employee can only spend his corp scrip at a corp shop, where he buys the goods and services he needs from the corp. Essentially, the corp pays its employee with goods and services that the corp itself provides at a price the corp controls. If said wageslave steps off corporate territory and tries to buy a bottle of synthahol at a corner grocery using scrip, the shopkeeper won't take it any more than he'd take Polish zlotys. Like any national currency, corp scrip has no value outside the "country of issue." In this case, it buys nothing outside the issuing corp's extraterritorial domain.

>>>>>[What a horrible, money-grubbing, capitalistic-pig-dog thing to do. Why don't we all just sell our souls to the corps now and save them the trouble? I'm getting my gun!]<<<<<
—Caine (01:22:34/3-22-54)

So the poor wageslave trundles back to his corp facility and buys his bottle of synthbooze corp equivalent of the PX, paying whatever price in corp scrip the store feels like charging. How does this benefit the corp? Say it sells all its goods and services to employees at twice the cost of manufacturing or providing them. When employees buy those goods and services with scrip, the corp has effectively reduced their buying power by half of their salary's face value. This practice helps the corp retain the hard currency it needs to pay outside suppliers. It can also use hard currency reserves to take over new assets, such as irritating competitors. The employee seems to benefit as well because the corp stores offer goods and services to employees at a discount compared to their street prices. On the street, the markup might amount to three times cost of manufacture instead of double.

However, the corp wageslave can buy only what the corp feels like offering him.

>>>>>[I've heard of corps that pull this fast one well enough to leave employees no better off than when they started. The corp more or less gets free labor.]<<<<<
—En (04:12:09/3-23-54)

>>>>>[It's also a hell of a great way to keep an employee from skipping to a competitor or quitting. Say you work for MCT for 20 years and build up a huge nest egg of savings, all in MCT scrip. If you quit working for the corp, your life's savings become more or less worthless. Elegant, *neh*?]<<<<<
—Laika (14:34:28/3-25-54)

>>>>>[Hey, what about restraint of trade laws and all that drek?]<<<<<
—Siskel (17:58:04/3-26-54)

>>>>>[Hello? Anybody in there? Geez, chummer, ain't you been paying attention? Corps are extraterritorial. The only restraint of trade laws applicable to them are the ones they make, and they don't make any.]<<<<<
—Dalt (16:35:19/3-17-54)

When the first corps started paying in their own scrip back in the 20-teens, they put no restrictions on its use aside from making it legal tender only in each corp's stores. In other words, anyone could legally spend MCT scrip in MCT stores, whether they worked for the corp or not. Predictably, a secondary market in scrip quickly developed outside the corps, setting the stage for a whopping change in corp payment policies.

To show you how it worked, let's assume I'm a good little corp wageslave working for MCT who gets paid in hard-currency scrip. I'm supposed to spend my corp bills and coins only at corp stores, but I don't want to do that. So I wander off MCT territory and stop in at an independent neighborhood store. I strike a deal with the store owner to spend my scrip in his establishment, buy the non-MCT goods that I want, and walk away a happy customer. The store owner now has a whack of MCT scrip. He janders over to an MCT store where it's legal tender and spends it.

>>>>>[Assuming he could get onto MCT property.]<<<<<
—Harvard (14:24:36/3-21-54)

Of course, the corps didn't have this situation in mind when they started paying in scrip. The secondary market gave wageslaves far too much independence. They fixed the problem by putting a rider on the use of scrip, restricting use of corp currency to that corp's employees. Any non-employee attempting to spend corporate scrip violated corporate law; mere possession of corporate scrip by a non-employee became illegal.

>>>>>[Don't anybody try to claim this kind of law is unconstitutional or any such drek. It's corporate law, chummers. As extraterritorial entities, the corps can enforce whatever laws they like on their own turf. And corporate stores definitely qualify as corp turf.]<<<<<
—Abel (02:52:28/3-20-54)

Welcome to the legal reality of 2054, chummers. If you physically or virtually enter a corporate store or otherwise place an order for goods and services and pay for them with scrip, you have to prove your status as a bona fide employee of that corp. Period. If you have no proof, or no proof the corp considers adequate, you've broken corp felony law. Needless to say, you're in really deep drek.

>>>>>[Ha, *gotcha!* You say "physically or virtually," but that doesn't make sense. Say I'm sitting on the floor of my squat, well outside MCT corporate territory, and I try to make a scrip-paid deal with a corporate store or supplier. I show them faked proof that I'm a wageslave, and they detect the forgery. *How can I be within corporate jurisdiction?* My meat body's nowhere near corp turf.]<<<<<
—Zacheriah (01:26:07/3-29-54)

>>>>>[<*deep sigh*> Law in the Matrix age gets so complicated.
Listen up, bud. In the early days of "telepresence," people used limited virtual reality to work remote machinery and waldos. Apparently, some guy died while linked to remote equipment a couple of klicks under the ocean, and a huge legal hassle ensued over where he "was" when he died. Was he sitting in a cradle in Santa Monica, or was he a couple of klicks down in the Pacific? They wrangled for months over where he had really existed at the time of death. (If that makes any sense.) Anyway, the courts decided he was really under the fragging ocean. That ruling set the precedent that the location of your consciousness rather than your meat body determines jurisdiction. So in the Matrix, where a decker "is" refers to his icon's location in the net, *not* the place his meat body happens to be squatting. So Zack, if you enter an MCT virtual store, you're legally in their jurisdiction.]<<<<<
—Legal Beagle (06:10:19/3-29-54)

>>>>>[So extraterritoriality extends to Matrix "territory" as well as physical turf?]<<<<<
—Zacheriah (02:11:28/4-1-54)

>>>>>[Usually. <*deeper sigh*> Like I said, the law gets complex. Somebody said it best in an earlier file; use the "maximum drek" rule and you can't go wrong.]<<<<<
—Legal Beagle (07:14:38/4-3-54)

Though the new restriction decreased the use of corporate scrip outside the issuing corporation, it didn't stop the practice. To this day, determined people can find ways around the "employee-only" laws, from forged corporate IDs to accomplices who work for the corp in question. Of course, the accomplice route carries its own extra little price. Say I've acquired some Fuchi corporate scrip through some shadowy channel, with which I want to acquire cyberdeck components at a corporate discount. I funnel the scrip to a chummer who works for Fuchi; he makes the purchases and

passes the hardware on to me. Because accepting corporate scrip from a non-employee is just as illegal as my having it, my chummer's taking a chance. If Fuchi internal security uses an audit or other shady technique to find out where he got the scrip, he's hosed big-time. So unless he already owes me, I'm stuck compensating him for his risk. That costs me extra.

>>>>>[You've also got to trust the sucker (or else have something pretty heavy-duty on him). By ratting you out, he can earn brownie points with his employer. He makes the purchase, or pretends to, then sics the corp cops on you when you pick up the hardware.]<<<<<
—Timestamp (15:23:04/3-19-54)

>>>>>[Look, slot, nobody said this drek was easy or safe.]<<<<<
—Hangfire (21:15:18/3-25-54)

Of course, people do take the risks associated with dealing in corporate scrip. Most cities with a major corporate presence have a booming corporate scrip market. Though trading in scrip outside the issuing corp violates corporate law, no national body of criminal or civil law prohibits it. As long as the misuse of corporate scrip takes place outside corporate jurisdiction, no laws exist to stop it. Legally speaking, corp scrip markets are safe if they exist outside corp turf.

>>>>>[In places like Brazil, national governments encourage trading in corp scrip just to slot off the corps.]<<<<<
—Aardvark (11:04:37/4-1-54)

>>>>>[It may be legal according to UCAS or Seattle Metroplex law to openly buy and sell corp scrip, but it's also stupid. Every few months, a new epidemic of deaths rears its ugly head among scrip-traders who don't pay enough attention to security. The corps like to send a message by geeking a bunch of people every now and again. They can't stamp out the trade that way, but they do keep the money markets fairly deep in the shadows.]<<<<<
—Gort (16:41:24/4-2-54)

>>>>>[As a public service, the local Neo-Anarchist community runs an on-line money market in one of Shadowland's "conference rooms." For obvious reasons, the actual room changes. Stop in and see us sometime.]<<<<<
—Captain Chaos (23:49:05/4-4-54)

>>>>>[What kind of exchange rate could I get for Yamatetsu Seattle scrip?]<<<<<
—Jake (08:42:28/4-6-54)

>>>>>[Well, child, it varies depending on the supply and demand. According to the last tick, one yen of Yamatetsu scrip is worth 1.86 nuyen. That's up 0.04 nuyen from yesterday, by the by.]<<<<<
—Captain Chaos (22:41:40/4-6-54)

>>>>>[Is that the official bank rate, or what?]<<<<<
—Jake (04:19:19/4-7-54)

>>>>>[Give your head a shake, child. No bank deals in scrip. Banks have to do business with the corps, and you don't want to slot off a business partner that can eat you for lunch. No, this is all shadow-trade. By the by, Yamatetsu scrip is up to 2.63 nuyen. Should have bought yesterday and turned a profit.]<<<<<
—Captain Chaos (00:05:43/4-8-54)

>>>>>[A warning to newcomers to Seattle. I don't know how things work in your burg, but don't flash around corp scrip that you're not entitled to in this neck of the woods. Last time I visited Sao Paolo, I saw some scroffy squatter-type in a corner store buying a pack of smokes with Aztechnology scrip, without giving it a second thought. Try that here and you'll likely get a knock on your door from some Azzie security assets who'll mess with your physiognomy until you give them any more scrip you happen to have and tell them precisely where you got every last peso of it.]<<<<<
—Argent (21:05:59/4-10-54)

>>>>>[How "hard" is corporate scrip as a currency?]<<<<<
—Digit (03:21:08/4-12-54)

>>>>>[How hard is any currency? Scrip from a major megacorp is probably harder than most national currencies, for what little that's worth. Frag, the hardest currency in the world at the moment is probably the New York City subway token.]<<<<<
—Keynesian Kid (07:34:42/4-15-54)

ADDITIONAL CASH COWS

Aside from cheating their employees, playing stock market poker, or actually selling a product or service, corps have plenty of other ways to make money. Bank loans and arbitrage are two of the most common corporate get-rich strategies.

Loans

Bank loans can always fill a megacorp's need for a short-term financial shot in the arm. The world's largest independent banks, such as BankAmerica, PanEuropa, Barclay's, and so on, make most of their revenue raking in interest on corporate loans. These banks offer widely varying interest rates, depending on such factors as the size and stability of the borrowing corp, how much collateral the corp hands over, and the term of the loan.

>>>>>[In all but the weirdest cases, corps can borrow money at much better rates than thee or me, chummbag. Most corps get to borrow at the prime rate, currently running at around 8.22 percent. Best case, an individual usually gets prime plus one. That adds up to more than 9 percent.]<<<<<
—Lou (15:55:09/3-21-54)

>>>>>[No one I know qualifies as a good enough credit risk to get even prime plus one. Then again, nobody I know has a SIN. That kind of puts them out of the market for a bank loan anyway.]<<<<<
—Timmons (09:10:57/3-26-54)

>>>>>[Sounds strange, doesn't it? A megacorporation trundles off to a bank, probably much less rich than itself in the grand scheme of things, to borrow money. But by the nature of their business, banks always have available credit to lend. A corp may have a net worth and cash flow orders of greater magnitude, but it can't use any of that stupendous fortune. If it could, the corp wouldn't go shopping for a loan in the first place.]<<<<<
   —The Chromed Accountant (13:37:19/3-29-54)

>>>>>[To show how fast the pace of modern business has gotten, here's a little gem for you trivia buffs out there. A century or so ago, a short-term loan had to be paid back within 30 days. Want to guess the length of a short-term loan nowadays? *Ten seconds.*
   That's right. "I'll borrow a billion nuyen at 00:00:00/1-1-54 and pay it back at 00:00:10/1-1-54, 'kay?" In spite of crazy terms like that, more and more corps take short-term loans. Go figure.]<<<<<
   —Knocker (21:04:40/3-31-54)

>>>>>[What the frag can you do in ten seconds? Lessee, I could skip on the loan and get about 800 meters out of town on my Blitzen with the throttle wide open. Or hey, I might get almost 15 klicks on a semiballistic. Endless possibilities . . .]<<<<<
   —Bung (04:16:45/4-2-54)

>>>>>[Under the right conditions, I can take a billion for ten seconds and make enough profit to retire on my very own island, complete with broad-chested, tight-bunned sex slaves.
   How? Through arbitrage, discussed later in this file. (Of course, I personally couldn't get a billion-nuyen loaner for ten nanoseconds. Ah, the futility of dreams . . .)]<<<<<
   —Cynthia (19:06:10/4-6-54)

>>>>>[When you hire those sex slaves, Cyn, kindly accept my job application.]<<<<<
   —Scuz (14:52:51/4-7-54)

>>>>>[<Grin>]<<<<<
   —Cynthia (21:20:31/4-9-54)

Of course, the Zurich-Orbital Gemeinschaft Bank issues the majority of loans to megacorporations. As its name implies, the Gemeinschaft Bank resides in the Zurich-Orbital habitat in low Earth orbit. The corps' favorite bank just happens to lie cheek by jowl with the infamous Corporate Court. (To scope out the dirt on that lovely organization, take a gander at the **Zurich-Orbital** Habitat file [p. 87].)

>>>>>[Zurich-Orbital also houses the "retirement villas" of some of the highest of the high corp muckamucks. These guys are all getting a little long in the tooth, and heard somewhere that microgravity can significantly extend your lifespan. Lucky them, they can pay to go live in it.]<<<<<
   —Leapset (16:29:16/3-28-54)

>>>>>[I've heard rumors about that. Is it true?]<<<<<
   —Rah (01:02:04/4-2-54)

>>>>>[Sure. A few of the richest and oldest muckamucks live in Z-O (all humans, by the way). They've stopped taking an active part in the management of their corps, instead acting as the biz equivalent of "President-for-Life." Of course, they've all got to be richer than snot to live comfortably in an environment where cubic volume is at a premium. Everything on Zurich-Orbital, including air, gets shipped up the gravity well from Earth or the Moon. That means residents pay through the nose for it.
   And yes, microgravity extends lifespan . . . in rats and other experimental animals. In humans or metahumans, who the hell knows? People have lived full-time in orbital habitats for less than 20 years. We can't tell anything from barely two decades of observation. A couple of the corp slags living in Z-O are pushing 95, but some people live longer than that on Earth. A couple of would-be Methuselahs have died, one at 81 and the other at 92. So can people like 87-year-old Eiji Yakamura, *eminence grise* of Mitsuhama, expect to be alive and kicking at the ripe old age of 120+? The jury's out. Everyone up there has already lived most of their lives under one grav, so they must have suffered damage that microgravity can't cure. It might slow down further deterioration, but even that's a maybe.]<<<<<
   —Doc Dicer (20:10:43/4-5-54)

>>>>>[Humans only? A nice little racist enclave?]<<<<<
   —Dara (02:44:05/4-7-54)

>>>>>[Not necessarily. The few dwarfs in the corporate upper ranks aren't old enough yet to worry about micrograv and extended lifespans. After all, the oldest dwarf's only 42. Lots more elves have reached the top of the corp ladder, particularly in the Tír, but they're pretty young, too. Why exile yourself to Z-O at middle age or younger?
   As for trolls and orks, pretty few get to the upper corp ranks. I hate to say this, but they tend not to have an overabundance of intelligence or couth. Also, they have limited life spans. Ever notice how few senior suits are under age 55? It takes time to work your way into the top fraction of the corp pyramid. Sad to say, orks and trolls don't have that much time. So I wouldn't describe Z-O as racist, unless you also consider reality racist.]<<<<<
   —Derek (04:19:49/4-10-54)

>>>>>[Well argued. We all know the *real* reason why elves don't bother with Z-O, don't we, hm?]<<<<<
   —Lotus Eater (17:46:50/4-11-54)

Publicly, the Gemeinschaft Bank claims status as an independent entity under the protection of, but separate from, the Corporate Court. In fact, it acts as a tool of the Corporate Court, which dictates its every action.

>>>>>[Ah, now the true Neo-A rant comes out.]<<<<<
   —Bung (16:44:55/4-2-54)

A consortium of the largest megacorporations owns the Gemeinschaft Bank. These same corps sit on the Corporate Court. The court elects the bank's board of directors through a court-designated working committee, and each board member sits for a term of nine years. Provisions exist to oust a board member before the end of his or her term, but impeachment takes a damned near unanimous vote. Not surprisingly, unanimity is a rare commodity among the members of the Corp Court.

>>>>>[Why bother with ousters? It's much easier to arrange an "unfortunate accident" for the unwanted board member.]<<<<<
—Madrid (05:13:29/3-14-54)

>>>>>[That hasn't happened since 2046.]<<<<<
—Hangfire (01:45:42/3-15-54)

>>>>>[Oh?]<<<<<
—Madrid (04:53:34/3-15-54)

>>>>>[Remember when Z-O bank muckymuck Sol Weinstein's personal shuttle burned up on re-entry, leaving a hole on the bank's board of directors? Buzz in Europe says someone hired Madrid for that sanction.]<<<<<
—Nightstorm (10:18:10/3-18-54)

>>>>>[Get real. Madrid spread that buzz to boost her rep. Don't deny it, Madrid you slot, we go back too far.]<<<<<
—Nevchenko (20:04:19/3-18-54)

The megacorps' control over the Z-O Gemeinschaft Bank board creates the interesting situation in which the corps can make loans to themselves. Needless to say, most loans get swift, unconditional approval.

>>>>>[Before anyone thinks of trying to hop a shuttle or something real dumb, Z-O has no hard currency, share certificates, or any other drek like that. The trip ain't worth the risk.]<<<<<
—Cold Breath of Reality (21:04:41/3-15-54)

>>>>>[I saw some low-budget trideo show in England where a gang of "noble thieves" cracked a Z-O vault and took off with umpty-gazillion kilos of fragging gold bullion. Pure bulldrek, at least twice over.

First off, Z-O stores no bullion in its vaults. How could it, considering the density of gold and the staggering cost of lifting a single kilogram into orbit? Second, the trid show had the thieves stow away aboard a corp shuttle. Oh, su-u-u-re. The corps know each shuttle's payload, including crew, right down to the gram. A bunch of extra bodies, not to mention the gold bullion, makes for a helluva lot of extra weight. No way can anyone rip off a Z-O vault, chummers. Forget about it. Zurich-Orbital has nothing to steal. The actual valuables that back up the Z-O Gemeinschaft's deposits lie in corp vaults all over god's green Earth. The Z-O component of the bank is just a huge, honking computer system that tracks credits and debits in terms of bits and bytes.]<<<<<
—Robin (05:31:42/3-19-54)

>>>>>[Thinking of decking your way in and diddling a few of those bits and bytes? Think twice if you value your synapses. The Z-O computer has the toughest security anywhere on or off planet, at least Red-10. Somebody once said Red-13, but I don't think the benchmarks stay accurate that high. But then, they don't need to. Z-O has cascading black ice, Pueblo-style "party ice," all the wiz stuff you'd go a long way to avoid.

Also, unless you can get your mitts on your own shuttle, you've got to make the link from the ground. That means taking into account a time lag that lasts anywhere from 10 milliseconds to more than 400 milliseconds, depending on the geometry of the satellite link-up. That wait degrades your performance something fierce.

Finally, not many satellite uplinks to Z-O exist. The corps prefer it that way. The ones that do exist have heavy shielding, so good fragging luck finding one. Once you find it, you have to get past the heavy-duty security surrounding the uplink access node. Brain-fry, anyone?

Chummers, if you want to commit suicide, then have someone put a bullet in your head. Either way you die, but at least a bullet won't toast your deck.]<<<<<
—Red Wraith (05:33:41/3-19-54)

>>>>>[I heard some decker cracked into Z-O and lived to tell the tale.]<<<<<
—Harbinger (19:42:49/3-20-54)

>>>>>[I heard the same story, but she didn't touch the bank's systems. Just hit some corp bulletin board and pulled out. No one knows why.]<<<<<
—Markie (10:25:56/3-24-54)

>>>>>[Some people say she got that far because the Corporate Court spotted her coming and wanted her to get into the BBS. Chew on that thought.]<<<<<
　　　—Vevayne (07:32:42/3-28-54)

Arbitrage

This fancy term refers to the practice of making money based on exchange rates between different currencies. Even with today's almost instant communication, different money markets sometimes offer different exchange rates. Though these tiny fluctuations don't last long, anyone able to put enough money quickly through the transaction can clear a phenomenal profit in a couple of seconds. Not surprisingly, megacorps have entire arbitrage departments dedicated to moving meganuyen fast enough to make this kind of killing.

Take a hypothetical case, using numbers much larger than existing differences. Suppose the Tokyo money market offers an exchange rate of 1 nuyen to £0.50 (that's British pounds for the currency challenged). Simultaneously, the Z-O Gemeinschaft Bank offers an exchange rate of 1 nuyen to £0.51 because it's heard rumblings of an impending shakeup in the British economy. MCT's arbitrage department notices the momentary discrepancy and decides to capitalize on it. Before the Tokyo market can react, MCT buys a billion nuyen worth of pounds from the Z-O corporate bank, giving them £510,000,000. They then sell those £510,000,000 to the Tokyo money market, which pays for them at its going exchange rate with 1,020,000,000 nuyen. That makes back MCT's original one billion outlay, plus another 20 million nuyen. In the couple of milliseconds it takes to process the transactions, MCT nets a cool 20 million nuyen in profit. Not a bad return on its investment.

Of course, the difference in exchange rates usually runs to tinier fractions, such as £0.50 to £0.5000001. But if a corp puts meganuyen through this kind of transaction often enough, it can rake big-time.

The above transaction, called "two-corner," represents the simplest form of arbitrage. "Three-corner" arbitrage makes an even bigger profit. That kind of money game plays with three currencies. For example, a corp buys pounds with nuyen, converts the pounds into CAS dollars, then buys back nuyen with the dollars. Three-corner arbitrage makes it easier to find discrepancies in exchange rates, giving the corp extra chances to clean up.

Currency also has a futures market, but I won't bore you with the details. Suffice it to say that if you've got lots of money, arbitrage lets you make lots more. The megacorps do it all the time.

>>>>>[This is another fragging example of those churning activities people babbled about earlier. Once again, corps make money without doing anything productive. They also screw the average citizen, because their profit actually comes from inflation in the currencies they buy and sell. Once again, corps extract money from the pockets of the world's citizens without their approval or knowledge.]<<<<<
　　　—The Neon Antichrist (11:25:23/4-17-54)

>>>>>[In the example above, MCT sold its pounds before the Tokyo market could react. Reaction time becomes the key part of the game, so MCT has an interest in making sure the Tokyo money market can't react instantly to the corp's moves. How many recent "random glitches" in the financial networks happened because corporate assets tried to make the swindle game easier for their arbitrage departments?]<<<<<
　　　—Memnos (23:45:46/4-19-54)

>>>>>[Some Johnson hired me last month to insert a tailored virus into the Singapore banking system. At the time I couldn't figure out what benefit the Johnson hoped to gain. Now I think I understand. Singapore has a big money market, doesn't it?]<<<<<
　　　—ZeroSum (02:09:18/4-22-54)

>>>>>[ZeroSum, you just as likely got hired to frag up a rival corp's arbitrage coup as to facilitate one. This kind of drek goes down all the time.]<<<<<
　　　—Nuyen Nick (10:03:32/4-22-54)

>>>>>[Hey, ZeroSum old chummer, I think I've been hired to find *you*. Maybe we should talk off-line.]<<<<<
　　　—Barnet (13:13:11/4-22-54)

TAXATION AND REPORTING

Death and taxes, chummer. Supposedly, death and taxes are the only two certainties in the universe. The corps haven't managed to sleaze death yet, but they've made sleazing taxes a fragging art form. In theory, corps pay taxes and report on their finances to shareholders and local governments. In practice . . .

TAXES

On the face of it, corp extraterritoriality doesn't relieve them of their obligation to pay taxes to the nations in which they do business. The UCAS, CAS, CalFree, and most of the NAN states legally require corps to pay some percentage of annual profits to the national government. Tax rates vary from nation to nation, depending on many factors. However, in most cases corps pay far lower tax rates on their astronomical profits than most private citizens pay on their meager incomes. For example, a corp operating in CAS pays a flat 10 percent on profits, whereas an individual pays 21.5 percent of his income in taxes. CAS recently switched from an incremental tax paradigm to a straight one for private citizens, raising an already nasty individual tax bite. The corps, however, coast along at their comfy 10-percent rate.

Authorities worldwide define "profit" as revenue minus cost of sales. That cost includes such items as the cost of the goods being sold, distribution costs, and so on. Even using this simple definition, corps can easily jack with the tax laws by using corporate structure and legal loopholes to play games with financial reporting.

For example, Yamatetsu Seattle doesn't manufacture the wizzer hardware it sells on the local market. Instead, it buys from Yamatetsu PacRim, headquartered in Honolulu in the independent Kingdom of Hawaii. Logically, Yamatetsu buys goods from itself.

However, in legal terms the distinct corporation known as Yamatetsu Seattle, Inc. buys goods from the independent corp Yamatetsu PacRim. So Y-PacRim charges Y-Seattle whatever the frag it likes for the goods it ships them. Because it's actually part of the same organization, Y-Seattle pays the price gladly. Y-PacRim can change its prices whenever it wants to without warning, counting on Y-Seattle to pay whatever Y-PacRim asks.

Look crazy? Look closer. Say Y-Seattle is just raking, selling more hardware than ever before and turning a huge profit. Legally, it owes a percentage of that whacking profit to the Seattle Metroplex and a little more to the UCAS government. But Yamatetsu prefers to pay as few taxes as possible. So Y-PacRim jacks up the price on its next shipment of gewgaws to Y-Seattle. Y-Seattle pays the skyrocketing tab without a whimper ... and bingo, there goes the profit. Geez, Mr. Taxman, the cost of goods just shot through the roof. Y-Seattle may look like the loser, but Yamatetsu the megacorp gains big because it doesn't have to pay gelt to the government. Better yet, Y-PacRim pays no tax to Hawaii on its whopping profit because Y-AmerAsia increases the "service charge" for the management services it provides to Y-PacRim. And so it goes on up the corporate line.

Of course, both the UCAS and Metroplex governments fume like crazy about losing the revenue they should rightfully receive, but they can do frag-all about it. How about forcing Y-PacRim to keep their prices down? No go, chummer. Y-PacRim is an organization incorporated in a sovereign state that owes no allegiance to UCAS. As for forcing Y-Seattle not to pay those raised prices, forget it. The government can't enforce that kind of restriction.

>>>>>[Why not force Y-Seattle to buy the goods from another, lower-priced supplier?]<<<<<
—Binky (13:05:44/3-29-54)

>>>>>[Because Y-Seattle says, "In our considered opinion, Y-PacRim provides the only goods worth buying. Butt out of our business." The government can't do anything about that. Trust me on this one. Before I came to Seattle, I did that drek for a living.]<<<<<
—The Chromed Accountant (14:42:01/3-31-54)

Other factors such as tax breaks for capital investment, depreciation, and so on add to the complexity of tax laws and offer the corps more loopholes through which to squirrel away money. Of the ten or so megacorps operating in Seattle, only three paid so much as one nuyen in taxes to the Metroplex government in 2053.

>>>>>[*What??!?*]<<<<<
—Zoot (18:09:54/3-26-54)

>>>>>[Welcome to the wonderful world of tax evasion.]<<<<<
—The Chromed Accountant (13:04:27/4-6-54)

Reporting
In almost all national jurisdictions including UCAS, corporations operating within a given country must file various monthly, quarterly, and annual public reports. These reports supposedly detail the corp's financial dealings, concentrating on revenues and expenses. From the figures in these reports, the government determines the amount of tax the corp should pay.

>>>>>[Here's something you might not know. Under UCAS freedom of information laws, anyone can review the quarterly and annual reports of any public corporation operating in the UCAS. Of course, they're not just lying around open on the Matrix where anyone can take a boo at them at any time. You have to approach the Securities & Exchange Commission and file a request for the specific reports you're interested in. Once they've processed, lost, delayed, rerouted, re-lost, and reprocessed your application, you get your choice of electronic or hard-copy of the reports you requested.
One caveat; you've got to provide a SIN when you apply.]<<<<<
—Keynesian Kid (10:31:12/3-24-54)

>>>>>[Yeah, but the SEC doesn't check the SIN real stringently (to make sure it doesn't belong to a stiff, for example).]<<<<<
—Raiko (01:18:09/3-26-54)

>>>>>[During my days as an IRS lackey, someone penetrated the SEC computer system and put various watchdog programs on the report tracking subsystems. Any time a freedom-of-information request for disclosure came in for the monitored files, the watchdog recorded the SIN of the person making the request and fired it off in a data packet. We never did manage to track the packets to their destination, but I can make an educated guess. Ten to one the corps know almost instantly whenever anyone tries to access their quarterly or annual records. Be warned.]<<<<<
—The Chromed Accountant (14:34:53/4-6-54)

>>>>>[Why bother with the freedom of information/SEC route? Public corporations issue annual reports to all their shareholders. Those annual reports include balance sheets, statements of earnings and retained earnings, statements of change of financial position, all that wizzer stuff. It's worth owning a share in every corp that interests you just to get a copy of the annual report.]<<<<<
—Gordo (10:25:46/4-8-54)

>>>>>[If you believe a single fragging word that a corp publishes . . .]<<<<<
—Ripper (19:23:41/4-8-54)

To get around corp extraterritoriality to enforce tax and reporting laws, national governments play a wiz little game with an abstruse point of international law. In the simplest terms, a national government deems any revenue a corporation makes while operating within that nation part of the national economy. By definition, extraterritoriality does not apply to a national economy, and so it falls within the government's jurisdiction. Ergo, national tax and reporting laws apply to corp profits.

(Wonderful, isn't it? Next, lawyers will legislate how many angels can dance on the head of a pin without a permit.)

In the UCAS, a corp that fails to file the required reports or pay appropriate taxes must pay government fines. If the corp fails to pay those fines, the government can slap punitive tariffs on goods the corp ships into the country. Theoretically, the government can even intercept and impound shipments until the corps pay the tariffs and any outstanding fines. In practice, this strong-arm tactic gets pretty tricky. Most corp shipments go directly from corp territory in one jurisdiction to corp territory in another; for example, from Yamatetsu-PacRim's extraterritorial turf in Hawaii to Yamatetsu-Seattle's extraterritorial heliport atop the Yamatetsu building. However, at some point the carrier of the shipment must travel through UCAS jurisdiction. For example, it may travel through UCAS airspace outside the territory claimed by the corp involved. As long as the shipment remains in UCAS jurisdiction, the government can demand that the carrier land or even force it down.

>>>>>[A couple of times in the past when the corps decided to test their freedom of action, the Metroplex Guard ordered its air units to force down corp flights through plex airspace.]<<<<<
—SPD (08:14:55/4-15-54)

>>>>>[I remember that. Scary times, chummers. Once or twice they even exchanged shots, though the corps claimed after the fact that their security teams acted without official sanction. Or they maintained that "a person or persons unknown" committed the violence, and the poor, innocent corp had nothing to do with it.]<<<<<
—Cisco (13:09:59/4-15-54)

>>>>>[It got really scary when that Aztechnology long-haul dirigible supposedly crashed in Puget Sound back in 2042. That fragger didn't crash, it got splashed by a couple of Metroplex Guard fighters when it didn't follow orders. Tensions ran high for a few months after that.]<<<<<
—Rolf (23:31:29/4-17-54)

>>>>>[I don't think anybody felt more surprised than the governor when the Big A backed down.]<<<<<
—Pyramid Watcher (21:50:19/4-21-54)

To everyone's relief, the days of direct corp disobedience to government requirements seem to have ended. In general, the corps have decided to minimize taxes more easily, cheaply, and safely by falsifying the reports they give to the government and then willingly paying the tax required by those fake reports. The IRS and other equivalent agencies know that the reports they receive are tissues of lies, but knowing and proving remain two different things. Jurisdictional issues raised by extraterritoriality make it incredibly difficult for a government investigator to find proof that a corp has falsified its reports. The investigator may subpoena supporting documents or files in the hope of finding some discrepancy between the figures they show and the official data, but the corp can falsify supporting files as easily as it jiggered the official report.

In the days before the Shiawase Decision, the government could send investigators onto corporate property with the necessary search warrants and drek to go through the files and dig out the real story. But because extraterritoriality put a corp's offices and its computer system outside national jurisdiction, the government can no longer send legal snoops to ferret out the truth.

>>>>>[No, it can't. But extraterritoriality cuts both ways. The UCAS government has no laws constraining the behavior of an IRS investigator when he's not in the UCAS. So if I infiltrate a corp facility physically or virtually and steal their real financial data, I haven't broken any UCAS laws because I'm not in UCAS jurisdiction. I'm breaking corporate laws. If I get caught I'm in deep, deep drek, so the trick is not to get caught. I did that for a living before I quit government service and came to Seattle. In effect, I worked as a shadowrunner for the UCAS government.

The shady legal issue comes down to whether my employers could order me to go break the law in another jurisdiction. The IRS argued that the end justified the means, but the corps tended not to agree. Anyway, the IRS kept the whole thing real quiet. Just like the old "*Mission Impossible*" schtick, if we got captured or killed, the government would deny all knowledge of our existence.

In the years since I left government service, I haven't kept in touch with my old colleagues. People like me may or may not still draw salary from the government payroll. Just before I left, I heard some talk about disbanding my department and hiring freelance shadowrunners for specific missions. I don't know whether that policy's in place, or whether the service had another change of heart.]<<<<<
—The Chromed Accountant (14:54:29/5-3-54)

>>>>>[Jeez, Chrome, why didn't you stay in the biz? Your Johnson was the fragging president of the UCAS. You knew where he lived; you knew he couldn't pull the fade on you. If the corps you burned came after you, you had the Secret Service to protect you, right? And because you spent all your time taking a quick shufty through corp files anyway, you could pretty well line your own credstick while you were at it, right? Frag, if somebody offered me that kind of job I'd think I'd died and gone to shadow-heaven.]<<<<<
—Phoenix (18:42:21/5-4-54)

>>>>>[No. You'd just think you died, and you'd be right. The Secret Service didn't protect us. Protection would have amounted to an admission that the government backed our activities. No, they left us on our own. Oh, and let me tell you why I came to Seattle. After I almost got scragged a few times by corp payback squads, I considered applying for a transfer out of the field. Then I heard about what happened to one of the old bright lights of the department. This guy, something of a legend when I joined, had applied for a transfer. A couple of weeks after moving, he died. According to the unofficial buzz I heard, he hadn't died of natural causes; he died because the government decided he knew too much about their black ops against the corps. The fragging government offed this guy who'd survived everything the corps could throw at him for a couple of decades.

I pulled the fade, ditched my SIN, covered my tracks and came to Seattle]<<<<<
—The Chromed Accountant (19:31: 42/5-4-54)

>>>>>[Payback time, Chrome?]<<<<<
—Kat (19:07: 57/5-5-54)

>>>>>[Revenge is a dish best served cold.]<<<<<
—The Chromed Account (13:09: 31/5-6-54)

>>>>>[Hey, where's that shadowsnoop trash who kept posting a while back ? This kind of scoop sounds like his meat, if he's got the *cojones* to go after it.]<<<<<
—Whacker Dan (03:45: 34/5-13-54)

The government also requires disclosure of corporate ownership. If any single entry owns more than a certain percentage of a public or private corporation, the corp must officially report this fact to the government. The percentage varies from jurisdiction to jurisdiction; in Seattle, it's 35 percent. Also, a corp that is a wholly owned subsidiary of another corp must report its status to the government. If the owning corp does business in the same jurisdiction ans a third corp owns a significant chunk of the second, the government must know the favt as well. Theoretically, such reporting allows the goverment to trackwho owns what in order to better evaluate whether the local corp has paid its fair share of taxws. The government can also use this information to prevent a corp fromfunneling revenue up the corporate structure to avoid taxation.

As usual, theory differs big-time from practice. Legally, only corps based within a government's jurisdiction need report their ownership to that government. Because off shore organizations own most subsidiaries, governments can trace ownership only one step up the corporate pyramid. Also, not every country in the world requires such reporting. Singapore doesn't, for one. So if one of a corp's divisions operates out of Singapore, the ownership trail ends there.

As an example of how disclosure of ownership really works, take Yamaguchi Technologies Inc. This Seattle-based corp reports officially and truthfully that it belongs to 12584AG Ltd., based in Singapore. Singapore has no reporting requirements, so the Singapore-based corp discloses nothing. Who owns 12584AG Ltd.? Null program, chummer. Nobody knows. Anyone can tell it's a holding company, but no one can find out whose.

>>>>>[You can get these ownership reports through the same freedom-of-information channels as financial reports.]<<<<<
— Keynesian Kid (10:38:35/3-24-54)

>>>>>[I truly believe that governmental agencies and public opinion have begun to bring the corporations to heel. I also believe the process is only just beginning. The corporations that gouge the consumer and flout the laws will weed themselves out in time through social Darwinism.]<<<<<
—Millennia (12:55:43/4-17-54)

>>>>>[What planet are *you* from?]<<<<<
—Zork (15:04:52/4-17-54)

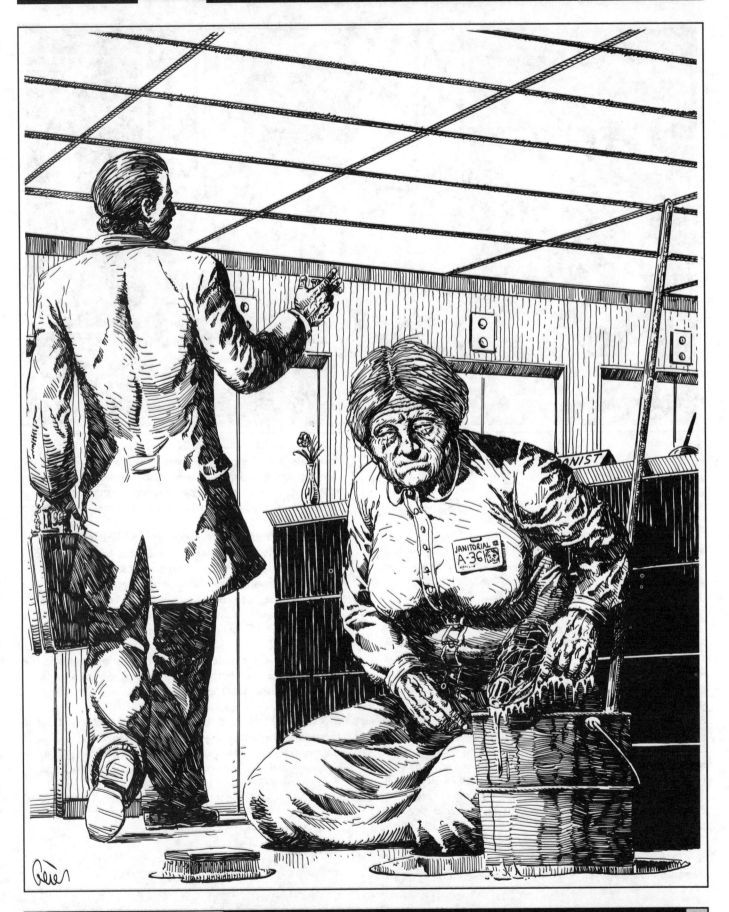

COMPETITION

A fter scanning gigapulses of info about corp structure and the many ways corps gouge money from Joe Citizen, all you Shadowland readers know all you need to know about the Almighty Megacorps. Right?

Wrong. More than one corp exists in the world, and they don't operate in isolation (big surprise). No, this sorry ol' world has hundreds of first- and second-tier corps, and Great Ghu knows how many thousands of smaller fry. Most of these smaller corps fall into empires run by maybe a dozen top-drawer megacorps, and members of one empire constantly pit their money and power against members of other empires. Now throw the independent small fry into the corporate mix. They may be tiny, but fragging *buckets* of them exist out there, all scrapping for much the same market as everyone else. Everyone competes with everyone, starting up an "every-corp-for-itself" feeding frenzy. Entertaining? You bet . . . unless you get caught in the middle. In the previous file, we talked about the ways corps pretend to compete while bilking the consumer. This file deals with how they really compete, against each other.

>>>>>[Corps even hit members of their own empire, chummer. Sometimes they do it because it suits the owning corp to have two divisions play off against each other. Even scarier, sometimes they and their direct owners don't necessarily *know* they're part of the same fragging empire.

Chip-truth, this happens. Right in the middle of one of the nastiest corporate battles you've ever seen, the two corps look up and go, "Hey, wait a minute . . ." And then they back off and suddenly start cooperating. This corp trip of not letting the left hand know what the right hand's doing sometimes leads to arm wrestling with yourself.]<<<<<
—Nuyen Nick (17:11:32/3-18-54)

Despite a global pie large enough to let everyone have a good, healthy piece without fighting, the corps spend untold amounts of time, money, and other resources one-upping each other. Their constant pushing and shoving stems from one ugly fact of human nature: greed. To a great extent, corps want more simply because more exists to get.

>>>>>[Why climb a mountain? Because it's there. Yeah, right.]<<<<<
—Bung (12:05:52/3-18-54)

>>>>>[There's more to it than that. No matter what the law says about corps being discrete business entities independent of their owners and employees, people run the fragging things. Those people get lots of personal benefit out of scrapping for that slightly larger slice of the pie.]<<<<<
——Nuyen Nick (07:08:21/3-23-54)

>>>>>[Yeah, but how much money can one person spend? How about Richard Villiers, of Fuchi Industrial Electronics? He owns one-third, give or take, of one of the world's top-rung megacorps. How much net worth does that give him? The way I read it, Richard Villiers is a multi-*multi*-billionaire. He personally owns and controls wealth greater than that of any emperor in past ages. Villiers could buy Alexander the Great out of petty cred, and snap up the whole Holy Roman Empire on a couple of hours' notice. Yet he still fights for that one additional iota of control, one more scrap of market share. Why?]<<<<<
——QuickStick (23:21:13/3-25-54)

>>>>>[Get one thing straight first. I'm no apologist for the megacorps or the plutocrats who run them. But sometimes top corporate suits aren't acting out of pure greed, megalomania, and malevolence. (Not that I'd rule those out in all cases.) I don't know Richard Villiers personally, and I don't know much about him. But just off the top of my head, I can think of several reasons aside from unbridled greed that might keep him on the treadmill.

Three different factions control Fuchi. Villiers is constantly fighting for position with the other two controlling families, the Nakatomis and the Yamanas. Sure, Villiers might step back from the struggle and spend the rest of his life living off some tiny

fraction of the money he's made. But you can bet the Nakatomis and the Yamanas won't follow suit. If Villiers backs off, the Japanese families get to eat his lunch. Compared to his partners in crime, Villiers brings a rationalizing influence to Fuchi policy. I don't know about you, but the thought of a corp as powerful as Fuchi run by the two Japanese "business butchers" makes my blood run cold.

Also, what would Villiers do if he retired? He's done the biz thing all his life. He's lived under pressure to make the right decisions, always taking the big risks. What the frag can he do with himself if he stops? Get into flower arranging, maybe? Tell me another one, chummer. He'd go through the same kind of "decompression" that runners suffer when they decide to quit the shadow biz. So he keeps going because he can't stand to think about the alternative.

Again, I don't know if either of these possibilities even gets close to the truth. But I think they illustrate that suit behavior might sometimes stem from something more than greed.]<<<<<
——Nuyen Nick (12:49:04/3-29-54)

Taking everything into account, corporate competition benefits Joe Citizen. A high level of real competition, instead of something mocked up to sleaze antitrust laws, guarantees a few market forces to keep the value-price ratio high and gives corps some incentive to offer their customers better products and services. If the megacorps someday decided to share the global pie evenly, without competition, they would represent an oligopoly in every market segment with total freedom to fix prices in whatever way they fragging feel like. Though the corps probably don't see it this way, only competition keeps coercion of consumers to an acceptably low level.

>>>>>[You call this acceptable?]<<<<<
——QuickStick (23:22:58/3-25-54)

Corps engage in two types of competition, one based on the market and one involving high-finance takeovers to eliminate rivals.

MARKET-BASED COMPETITION

Market-based competition gets taught in biz school, and so-called scholars write terapulses of papers on it. Ideally for the consumer, corps compete by meeting market demand better than their rivals. They offer better products and services at lower prices, with more efficient customer service, and all that drek. As noted in the previous file, corps can finesse this by persuading their consumers that they offer better products and service, regardless of the reality. Marketing and advertising take care of altering consumer perceptions. And when it comes to the value of goods and services, perception *is* reality.

This kind of competition benefits the consumer; only market-based competition keeps the market sane and controls coercion. However, the interested consumer can learn about the good kind of competition anywhere. Anyone who wants to learn about how to penetrate a market, analyze customer need, provide value to consumers and all that drek, go check out any on-line business school anywhere in the Matrix. The more interesting and danger-ous type of competition has nothing to do with meeting a need in the marketplace. This kind of competition gets down and dirty, presenting dangers to be avoided and opportunities to be ex-ploited.

TAKEOVERS

With all the biz college sophistry stripped away, corporate competition takes two forms. You can either do a better job than your rivals at meeting consumer needs, or you can take away your rival's ability to compete with you. In other words, if you can't beat them, buy them.

MERGERS

Although not strictly a takeover, merging with a competitor offers an efficient way of dealing with him. Why should a corp spend the time, money, and effort required to compete, when as a single entity that corp and its erstwhile rival can cooperate in the vital task of parting the consumer from his hard-earned credit? Mergers have a long, august tradition; they created today's megacorps.

The term "merger" has a friendly, cooperative sound. It hints at two noble rivals, each with great respect for the other, laying aside their weapons and becoming allies in "Fighting the good fight." Such amiable joinings happened in the past, and still happen occasionally. For example, Saeder-Krupp formed through an amicable merger of two industry giants, Saeder Strategic Industries and Krupp Manufacturing.

>>>>>[Chrysler-Nissan's another good example.]<<<<<
—Timothy (01:35:45/4-2-54)

>>>>>[Are you drekking me? Nothing amicable about that one, omae. Pure, out-and-out absorption of a lame duck by an industry behemoth. Nissan absorbed Chrysler after a long, drawn-out fight. The Nissan empire only kept the Chrysler name to gull Americans into thinking that they could still support home-grown industry by buying a Chrysler-Nissan car.]<<<<<
—Screech (13:05:56/4-5-54)

>>>>>[Oh, and let's look at that "long, drawn-out fight." The Chrysler board tried every trick under the sun to fight off Nissan's attempts, except for the tactics that might actually have worked. Their strategy consisted of pumping up the stock premium so Nissan had to pay a much bigger price to acquire a controlling number of shares. Surprise, surprise, all the people sitting on Chrysler's board just happened to have enormous stock holdings in Chrysler. No matter how you cut it, they did great. They looked like heroes for holding off the Japanese takeover, then got sicken-ingly rich when they finally accepted the takeover bid.]<<<<<
—Ron Bacardi (04:52:18/5-10-54)

In reality, however, the vast majority of so-called mergers are actually hostile takeovers.

HOSTILE TAKEOVERS

>>>>>[Now we're getting into the good stuff.]<<<<<
—Block (20:32:55/4-1-54)

For corporations that cannot drive a persistent rival out of business by performing better in the marketplace, trashing the rival's reputation and his shares on the stock market offers a popular alternative. Once the rival's stock plummets, the first corp can buy them up and take over the company. Say Corp A finds its market share dropping because Corp B has just fielded a competi-tive product that's the greatest thing since sliced bread. Marketwise, Corp B is making Corp A look sick and depriving Corp A of sales revenue. "Traditional" ethics demand that Corp A improve its own products to make them competitive with Corp B's again, perhaps better. But that involves expensive market research, product research, and R&D. So instead, Corp A creates the perception that its product beats Corp B's after all. It hawks a repackaged version of the same old drek and calls it "new and improved," or convinces the public that only an idiot would buy Corp B's drekky product. Firing up a hot ad campaign can accomplish this much-desired end, and shooting Corp B's reputation out from under it makes its stock prices drop. If it wants to, Corp A can now buy up Corp B's stock at its leisure.

>>>>>[Advertising is notoriously unreliable, particularly when you want to cast a competitive product in a negative light. It's much more cost-effective to make the competitive product look shoddy or even lethal by resorting to sabotage. If you sell commuter helicopters and a competitor starts eating into your market share, arrange for the competitor's choppers to have a few high-profile "tragic accidents." It's easy enough to set up this kind of thing, chummer. You can bet your hoop you'll start getting your market share back (as long as the competitor doesn't pull the same drek on you).]<<<<<
—Virth (03:21:58/3-21-54)

>>>>>[And if he does?]<<<<<
—Bugsy (12:54:05/3-22-54)

>>>>>[An unspoken rule exists among the corps against killing customers unless no other option exists. That kind of practice hurts everyone if it gets out of hand. Sometimes the Corp Court steps in to stop it; other times, the corps involved just come to their senses and call off the hostilities.]<<<<<
—Markops (09:23:53/3-27-54)

>>>>>[Virth's example isn't hypothetical. I worked for the other side when it went down. I won't name names, for obvious reasons, but the competitor whose choppers dropped out of the sky hired me and some chummers to track down and stop the other corp's sabotage team. Preferably, my Johnson wanted us to stop them dead. It took us awhile, but we got a line on them and stumbled on their plans for another little "demonstration," this time involv-ing Governor Schultz. The Metroplex government had bought a couple of commuter choppers from the corp that hired me, and the rival hit squad had those choppers next on its list. We staked out

Schultz' chopper and caught the bad guys red-handed. After the smoke cleared from the firefight, we found out that the "bad guys" were actually another shadow team. I knew a couple of them from previous runs. That kind of situation really makes me hate the corps. I don't like geeking old colleagues.]<<<<<
    —March (12:15:29/3-29-54)

>>>>>[You're getting old, March. You've lost your edge. Why don't you let someone take on those runs who can actually do their job without getting all misty-eyed?]<<<<<
    — Caine (14:09:22/3-29-54)

>>>>>[Some ways of fragging with a competitor don't kill off paying customers. Regardless of all the trid shows, most corp suits avoid taking life if they can.
    First off, they can slot with the competitor's manufacturing or distribution channels. If he can't meet his distributors' orders because part of his assembly plant "accidentally" blowed up real good, he suffers in the marketplace. Same thing if a shipment of product "goes missing" via plane crash, hijacking, or whatever. Even better, sabotage can make it hideously defective. (Note that "defective" need not mean "lethal," Virth you butcher.) If 50 percent of the cellular "bonephones" a corp sells don't work, the corp's rep still gets trashed without having a couple of the phones geek their users.]<<<<<
    —Winter (13:59:28/3-29-54)

>>>>>[Can we please get this back on topic? We're talking about takeovers.]<<<<<
    —Tintagel (16:43:13/3-29-54)

>>>>>[Okay, little miss conscience.]<<<<<
    —Clarence (19:11:00/4-2-54)

Acquiring enough of an interest in the competitor to influence its policies has become another popular option. If "their" product beats "your" product on the open market, just buy enough stock to control "them." In fact if not in name, "their" product becomes "your" product.
    Acquisition of assets is another good reason for one corp to take over another. One corp knows that its rival has a to-die-for research arm that would cost billions and take years to emulate. So the first corp buys them out, takes over the research arm, and peddles the rest or just lets it rot. Also, some organizations and individuals make a tidy profit out of buying up struggling companies, breaking them up, and selling their various assets to different buyers. They then use that profit to buy out and gut the next prospective target they find.

>>>>>[More dirt on these corporate raiders later in this file.]<<<<<
    —Nuyen Nick (16:09:23/4-23-54)

>>>>>[This kind of corporate raiding, acquisition/divestiture cycle is yet another example of churning activities, where corps make money without producing or providing any good or service.]<<<<<
    — Keynesian Kid (16:45:52/4-23-54)

>>>>>[As I argue elsewhere, we provide a valuable service. We force corporations to become more efficient and to serve the public good.]<<<<<
    —Pirate (11:18:57/4-24-54)

>>>>>[Corporate raiders are fragging leeches.]<<<<<
    —Dallas Deb (14:10:54/4-24-54)

>>>>>[For better or worse, lots of people engage in takeovers these days. The twenty-plus years since the recovery after the Crash of '29 has seen the highest level of acquisitions and mergers since the last peak in the 1900s.]<<<<<
    — Keynesian Kid (16:42:24/4-26-54)

>>>>>[Don't you mean the 1980s? Wasn't merger fever at its hottest back then?]<<<<<
    —Nuyen Nick (04:35:28/4-27-54)

>>>>>[Surprisingly, I mean the 1900s. If you factor in the GNP, the 1900s and the late 1920s and early 30s had a higher level of mergers and acquisitions than the 1980s did. Anyway, the level's even higher now than in all those earlier periods. Not by much, but higher just the same.]<<<<<
    — Keynesian Kid (15:55:01/4-27-54)

MANAGEMENT BUY-OUTS
    The management buy-out, or MBO, is another twist on corporate acquisition. Though it works like any other takeover, the group behind it is different. Instead of another corp or an individual raider buying up all outstanding shares, the corp's own manage-

ment team does it. An MBO takes a corp off the public market and consolidates all outstanding shares in the hands of a small, select group. A public corp becomes a private one, controlled by its management team.

>>>>>[Quite a few of the major megacorps, or at least the significant pieces of them, have gone private through MBOs. For example, shares in the central holding company of Fuchi Industrial Electronics don't get traded on the open market. The Villiers, Yamana, and Nakatomi families took the corp private through an MBO a couple of decades back.]<<<<<
—The Chromed Accountant (12:36:14/3-28-54)

In its major benefit, an MBO consolidates management control over the corporation. The management team need no longer keep other shareholders happy in order to hold onto their jobs, because the management team has become the collective sole shareholder. The management team also need not worry any more about the exigencies of the market affecting its profits.

>>>>>[So why doesn't every corp do it?]<<<<<
—Barnstable (15:28:00/3-27-54)

>>>>>[Cost. In a full-fledged MBO, the managers have to buy up every outstanding share in the corp, not just the majority they'd need for a takeover. That takes a lot of nuyen. When Villiers, Yamana, and Nakatomi took Fuchi private, it cost them 42 billion nuyen. They didn't pay for it all out of their personal fortunes, of course. They leveraged their expenditures by borrowing heavily from investment banks around the world. Obviously, the banks that backed them figured the three families could keep Fuchi profitable enough to pay back the loans. A lot of management teams don't have that kind of rep to trade on. They might want to take their corps private, but they can't convince investment bankers to take a risk on them.]<<<<<
—Keynesian Kid (11:44:35/3-28-54)

>>>>>[Investment banks aren't the only source of backing. Management teams from smaller corps sometimes go to the megacorps for funding.]<<<<<
—Casper (19:00:28/3-28-54)

>>>>>[Only the idiots or the desperate. MBOs often happen in response to a takeover attempt. If you get your backing from a corp, you've essentially sold out to them. You owe them big-time, and when they croak frog you jump.]<<<<<
—Keynesian Kid (11:53:52/3-30-54)

>>>>>[Here's a good example of what the Kid's talking about. A Los Angeles-based corp got wind of a major takeover plan in the works against it by some major Japanese conglomerate. For various reasons, an MBO looked like the only takeover defense the management team had available. They couldn't get a major bank to back them, so they turned to Saeder-Krupp to help them out. Saeder-Krupp loaned them the megabucks they needed, and the management team pushed their MBO through. Leveraged to the

fragging hilt and so far in debt they couldn't even see out of the hole, they thought they'd staved off the threat and kept control of the corp.

Two months later, Saeder-Krupp called its loan. The management team couldn't pay, so Saeder-Krupp took over the corporation. The kicker is, no takeover bid existed. The oh-so-scary Japanese conglomerate existed only in disinformation spread by Saeder-Krupp. Joyful, huh?]<<<<<
—Nuyen Nick (22:15:59/3-31-54)

The actual procedure for making an MBO differs little from a standard takeover. Management prepares for the buy-out by undervaluing the corp, leaking information and acting in a way that hints at financial trouble. This activity both lowers the stock price and deflects suspicion away from management. Of course, the stock price goes up as soon as management starts buying up shares. This price rise reflects the higher premium caused by any obvious demand for stock, and the public's realization that the corp's supposed financial troubles amounted to so much smoke and mirrors. A successful MBO depends on pushing transactions through as quickly as possible, before the market can drive prices up even further.

>>>>>[Sometimes other corps prefer an MBO to fail, particularly if management tries a buy-out to block a takeover. Corps can sometimes block an MBO simply by convincing the management team not to go through with it. Methods of persuasion may include blowing up their cars, shooting out their porch lights, and so on. Needless to say, managers involved in an MBO hire all the security they can get. Almost as effective and less messy is any tactic that slows things down so the managers can't snap up all the stock before the price rises prohibitively high. To accomplish this, some corps commonly resort to computer or data sabotage. Pay dirt for deckers, chummers.]<<<<<
—Argent (18:08:42/4-3-54)

EXECUTING A TAKEOVER

To take over a corporation, a buyer has to acquire enough stock in the target corp to get voting control. Most purchasers acquire stock by buying it through one of the virtual markets located in different corners of the Matrix. At any given time, most corps have stock available for sale, though the amount a buyer can pick up varies depending on the business situation and the overall economic climate. Share price also depends on a lot of factors, but in the end it all comes down to supply and demand. If more people want to sell shares than buy them, share price goes down, and vice versa. As stated in an earlier file, to some degree share prices also become a self-fulfilling prophecy. They go up or down according to the market's expectations. Therefore, anyone planning on snapping up a few hundred thousand shares in a takeover target has a definite interest in making sure the share price of that stock drops as low as it can possibly get. The possibility of a takeover adds to the many reasons already mentioned for one corp to jack with another corp's share prices, such as turning a healthy profit or indulging in sheer bloody-mindedness.

>>>>>[So when Aztechnology starts selling Microtronics Aztlan stock short, it can mean one of several things. First, the Azzy investment managers might know that Microtronics is in financial trouble, or that its much-trumpeted research program has fragged itself big-time. If so, they're selling so they can rake in some cash before the rest of the market learns of Microtronics' woes and sends stock prices into the gutter. Second, Aztechnology might just be yanking Microtronics' chain by decreasing investor confidence in them just when they need it the most. Or third, the Azzies might be trying to force Microtronics' share prices into the drekker so they can buy a controlling interest in the smaller corp.]<<<<<
        —The Chromed Accountant (12:00:36/4-2-54)

>>>>>[Aren't other investors intelligent enough to figure that out?]<<<<<
        —Skitch (05:08:24/4-3-54)

>>>>>[Yes, provided they saw it happening. If Aztechnology openly sells another corp short, institutional investors like banks figure that something's in the works. So as part of a takeover, Aztechnology keeps its stock-dumping secret. None of the "sell" orders have Aztechnology's name on them. Instead, every transaction goes down through other corps that Big A secretly owns. They spread it around to keep anybody from guessing that one guiding intelligence (Aztechnology management) engineered the move.]<<<<<
        —The Chromed Accountant (14:53:11/4-3-54)

>>>>>[I know most people don't think of business news as exciting. But frag, if you break the story that Aztechnology orchestrated the crash in Microtronics stock, you've hit a major scoop, chummer.]<<<<<
        —Reid (19:03:27/4-7-54)

>>>>>[And you've probably got a bunch of Aztechnology goons on your ass to make sure you don't do it again.]<<<<<
        —Pyramid Watcher (03:29:16/4-8-54)

>>>>>[If that's the price you pay for breaking the story, that's the price you pay. Someone's got to do the job.]<<<<<
        —Reid (18:49:01/4-8-54)

>>>>>[Oh, wiz, a crusading reporter. I thought you guys went out with Brenda fragging Starr and Clark fragging Kent.]<<<<<
        —Xavier (17:17:46/4-10-54)

>>>>>[Remember, corps have other ways to depress a target's share price. If you happen to be in the right place at the right time, those more direct methods represent great ways for shadowrunners with the right skill-sets to score some lucrative runs.]<<<<<
        —Rover (20:39:52/4-15-54)

Of course, when and if word of the takeover gets out, share prices skyrocket. When somebody wants something that someone else has, such as shares of a target company, they'll pay a premium to get them. Because companies staging takeovers want

to keep prices down, they keep their dirty dealing as quiet and as quick as possible. They have to buy control before the market can react or the target's management can stage a takeover defense.

Once the corp attempting the takeover has possession or voting control of a majority of outstanding shares in the target, it can vote its own puppets . . . er, *representatives* onto the target's board of directors. The board controls company policies and activities, so control of the board completes the takeover. Despite the widely believed fallacy to the contrary, a company staging a takeover need not buy out its target lock, stock and barrel. As long as the raiding corp owns 51 percent of the target's stock, it has control. The raider can put its own people on the board, who can then hire or fire the corporation's officers. The President/CEO must report directly to the board, whose members can oust or replace him or her with a majority vote. With this kind of power, the raiding corp can execute any changes it wants, regardless of other people's votes to the contrary.

>>>>>[Of course, owning 51 percent of the target's stock doesn't mean you have to put your own people on the board right away. You may have reasons for keeping the change of control a secret, or maybe the key people you want on the board are involved in other projects at the moment. But your ability to replace the board at any time gives you a big stick to wave at the current board members, doesn't it? "Play things our way or you're gone," makes a pretty effective negotiating tactic.]<<<<<
        —Malcolm (11:45:02/4-2-54)

>>>>>[Frag, you don't even have to own 51 percent of a target's stock to influence the way the corp does business. Say you have enough votes to put five of your people on a twelve-member board. As long as you can find two other people who agree with whatever you want to do, like replacing the CEO, you've got the majority you need. That's any two people for any initiative you try. With that setup, you can make a lot of decisions go your way. Political maneuvering gets you the same control as stacking the board with your patsies.]<<<<<
        —Zero (12:00:41/4-1-54)

>>>>>[Remember that "influence" covers a lot more than logical arguments. To take just a few examples, personal threats, blackmail, intimidation, and magical influence do wonders. Of course, the corp suits who arrange for this kind of thing to happen sure as drek don't soil their own hands. So who do they hire to do the dirty work? Three guesses, and the first two don't count.]<<<<<
        —Pietr (02:35:51/4-3-54)

>>>>>[During my corporate days, bosses used these "nontraditional" ways of doing business on at least a dozen occasions. (Not that I could prove it in court, though.) My job involved finding runners capable of doing the work and then arranging it so the people I hired didn't know exactly what they were doing or why.]<<<<<
        —Hangfire (23:56:40/4-5-54)

>>>>>[Even one board member can end up controlling company policy. Say the board splits into two factions, neither of which has a clear majority. The remaining board member gets to play power broker, casting his or her vote with the faction that offers him the most benefit.]<<<<<
—Lewis (12:28:09/4-6-54)

>>>>>[That's a dangerous tightrope to walk. Frag one faction off too many times, and one of Hangfire's "subcontractors" might keep you from doing it again. Permanently.]<<<<<
—Pietr (04:29:37/4-7-54)

If a raiding corp replaces the CEO after a takeover, the new president usually removes everyone closely associated with his predecessor and replaces them with officers he believes are personally loyal to him. For obvious reasons, no CEO wants people loyal to or bought by the exec who just got drekcanned hanging around. All too often, a change in CEOs leads to major bloodletting in the executive suites and a complete shakeup of upper management.

>>>>>[That happened a while back with Crashcart.]<<<<<
—Pinhead (16:28:03/4-1-54)

>>>>>[And with Yamatetsu Seattle's ISP division at about the same time. Any connection? Does anyone know?]<<<<<
—TS (15:39:42/4-6-54)

Predictably, executing a takeover is one helluva lot simpler to talk about than to do. In the next couple of megapulses, we'll examine some of the major steps and considerations involved in executing a successful hostile takeover.

>>>>>[*More* fragging business-school drek? Don't know about you, *omae*, but I'm never going to take over a corp. Gee whiz, I don't even have a power tie . . .]<<<<<
—Gronk (17:17:22/3-29-54)

>>>>>[If you don't want to scan the file, Gronk old slot, don't scan the file; just shut the frag up about it. This stuff can help you track down some runs you might not otherwise know existed, but if you're too drekheaded and unimaginative to figure out how that can help your miserable career and cred balance, then you're probably in the wrong business and on the wrong board. There's a wizzer Neil the Ork Barbarian retrospective in another corner of the Matrix. Sounds like that's more your speed, ya brain-dead trog.]<<<<<
—Matthew (20:53:19/3-29-54)

TAKEOVER ENVIRONMENT

Certain business environments foster takeovers, mergers, and acquisitions. Takeovers hit a peak when a wide divergence of opinion exists about the prospects of profits for certain corps, types of corps, or industries. Without this uncertainty, takeover activity drops off. To see why, let's make an example out of the fictional corp Drekware.

If everyone believes that Drekware's performance and chances live up to its name (drek), then limited incentive exists for anyone to acquire it. Who wants to buy the corporate equivalent of a thousand-kilo ball and chain? Corps and investors with anything on the ball ignore it and wait for it to go out of business. If everyone sees Drekware as a novahot corp with a booming profit margin, other corps might want to acquire it, but the current owners and management team have every incentive to keep control of it by any means necessary. They'll wheel up every defense available to them to keep their mitts on a moneymaker. Though an individual corp keen enough on the acquisition might break down the current managers' defenses through bribery, intimidation, blackmail, and so on, few outfits have sufficient resources to pull that off. Either way, an environment of certainty makes fewer corps interested in spending resources on takeovers.

A high level of uncertainty has the opposite effect. If a prospective raider sees its target as profitable enough to warrant acquisition but the target's managers don't think it worth enough to keep, a lot of takeovers occur. Significant new advances in knowledge and technology, unexpected changes in economic conditions, or drastic and unpredictable changes in society can all foster this kind of environment. So when technology advances at a ridiculous rate, when the economy's in turmoil, or when sociologists tear out their hair trying to understand just what the frag's going on with the world, takeovers reach their peak. Tell me, boys and girls, what era of history does that sound like?

>>>>>[Well, since you ask, the time immediately after the Awakening. I can't think of any time when society got a harder kick in the yarbles, what with dragons and goblinization. Add to that the addition of a totally new "technology," magic, and everything must have gone berserk.]<<<<<
—Willis (17:06:36/3-20-54)

>>>>>[Yes, of course. But it didn't stop there, did it? Just when it looked like things might settle down, we had the Treaty of Denver, the Crash of '29, the Euro-Wars, independence fever, the New Terrorism, the Texas-Aztlan fragup, and so on and so on. Just when one major kick in the nuts settled down, we got another one. The uncertainty, and hence the "takeover fever" climate, continued for decades.]<<<<<
—The Chromed Accountant (13:10:34/3-22-54)

>>>>>[Things have been quiet for awhile now, though. Right?]<<<<<
—Landier (11:05:04/3-25-54)

>>>>>[Only partially right. No major catastrophes recently, but the incredible advances in technology and magic plus the synergies between the two have kept the level of uncertainty high. I expect the takeover fever to continue until at least the 2060s.]<<<<<
—The Chromed Accountant (11:30:24/3-25-54)

PREPARING THE BID

So say you're a corp that wants to buy shares. The business environment's right, and you've picked your target. The first step in your takeover is to find out who currently owns significant blocks of shares in your target corp.

Tougher than it sounds, chummer. Depending on the jurisdiction in which the target incorporated, the law might require anyone owning more than a certain percentage of a corp's outstanding shares to report the fact to the government. Reporting requirements range from 5 percent in Aztlan to nearly 40 percent in CAS, and you can certainly dig that information out of the government via the freedom-of-information process or just by bashing your way into the target corp's computer systems. Most corps don't consider this kind of data sensitive enough to warrant serious security, so hacking your way to it poses no problem. Unfortunately, all this effort only discloses who officially owns each major block of shares. And nine times out of ten, the official owner is not the actual owner of the stock. For example, official records might show that 1234AG Singapore Ltd., No-Ware Computers Inc., and System 1 Corp. each own 15 percent of the outstanding shares in the company you have your eye on. That total block of 45 percent can get you close to the 51 percent needed for voting control, so you plan to approach these three apparently independent owners one at a time with a buyout proposal. Easy pickings, right?

Not necessarily. The records might not show you that Fuchi Industrial Electronics actually owns all three of the "independent" corps directly or indirectly. In fact if not on paper, Fuchi owns the 45 percent of the shares you want to buy. And Fuchi may have more interest in your prospective takeover activities than you find comfortable. Unless you do enough research to figure out that the three owners are actually one, Fuchi will almost certainly tip to your takeover plan before you realize the size and power of the owner you're actually dealing with.

>>>>>[More to the point, you need to find out who really owns the shares you want in case you have to apply a little pressure to get him or her (or perhaps, these days, *it*) to sell. Finding some kind of lever or edge is a practical business technique.]<<<<<
—PostHaste (14:59:17/3-25-54)

>>>>>[I throw this question out to the assembled multitude in the hopes that someone can shed some light on my predicament. A corp whose name I shall keep confidential has contracted me to persuade a certain individual to part with some shares she has held for several years. I have recently discovered that this individual is a free spirit. A "player," I believe, is the common term. When I reported this fact, my corporate contact reminded me that my agreement to do the job had no contingencies, least of all the nature of the subject I was hired to persuade. I should very much like to know how one persuades a free spirit to do something against its wishes. I await your answers.]<<<<<
—Damien (16:43:04/5-13-54)

>>>>>[You're better off than a chummer of mine, Damien. She got hired to go put the lean on a fragging *dragon* (may she rest in peace).]<<<<<
—Rusty (03:03:15/5-14-54)

Having found out who owns the stock you want to acquire, you next take the appropriate steps to force those shares down in price. However, you can't afford obvious tactics. The moment you telegraph intent to stage a takeover, your target's share price starts to go up. The current ownership/management might also stage countermoves, and you might attract the attention of a rival who wants to frag you over for the hell of it. A raiding corp needs to manipulate the price of its target's stock without appearing to do so. Through the several techniques of stock manipulation discussed in the previous file, **Doing Business**, a corp can keep its takeover bid quiet for quite some time.

CONSEQUENCES OF A BID

Unless the raider is incredibly slick and sly, sooner or later the market will spot the takeover in the works. Once the corp initiating the takeover has offered a bid and everyone realizes it, the market responds with a sharp increase in the price of the target's shares. An attempted takeover creates a sudden, increased demand for the shares on the part of the corp trying to take control, and increased demand always makes prices go up. For example, say you know that Ares wants to take over Drekware, and you hold a few Drekware shares. Unless your brain is running on empty, you won't let them go without trying to hold out for a better-than-market price.

No corp running a takeover can conceal its intentions forever, but every day they can keep it secret gives them a better chance of pulling it off on the cheap. If they can snap up the majority of the shares they need while the price stays low, the whole scam costs them a lot less.

>>>>>[As I said earlier, corp maneuvering can be a major scoop for a reporter on the biz beat. Be the first to break the story about a major takeover, and you'll attract a lot of attention.]<<<<<
—Reid (19:10:19/4-7-54)

>>>>>[Not all from editors, and not all positive, Reid old buzzard. To stick with the Neo-A's example above, you think Ares will appreciate you blowing their quiet takeover of Drekware wide open? You just cost them a few million nuyen in the process by inflating Drekware share prices. Golly gee, I always wondered why the biz beat has such a high turnover . . .]<<<<<
—Thomasina (15:39:41/4-9-54)

>>>>>[Hey, chummer, if a world-girdling megacorp wants me dead, that means a world-girdling megacorp knows I exist. Gotta like that.]<<<<<
—Reid (16:09:17/4-11-54)

>>>>>[Hey Reid, ya loser. Wanta hear something real drekky? Remember that big scoop of yours in 2051 about Graz-Burya trying to take over that MosTrans manufacturing division? You were prouder than snot because you broke the story and forced Graz-Burya to back off on their attempt, claiming all the while they'd never meant to run the hostile takeover in the first place. Remember? And then, while everybody had their eagle eye on MosTrans, Ares Macrotechnology snuck up and bought out Graz-

Burya. Remember that, Reid?]<<<<<
—Vlasti (17:42:42/4-11-54)

>>>>>[Yeah? So what, you slot?]<<<<<
—Reid (13:18:46/4-18-54)

>>>>>[(You know what's coming, don't you?) That whole "scoop" was a setup, Reid. Start to finish, a setup orchestrated by Ares Macrotech. All that "evidence" pointing toward Graz-Burya making some runs against MosTrans to push the share price down, and the "fact" that G-B was using holding companies to snap up MosTrans shares on the sly—bulldrek. I manufactured the whole fragging thing. And Ares paid me top cred for the job. One of the most successful runs I've ever pulled, and I didn't cap off a single round. How d'you like them horseapples, pud?]<<<<<
—Vlasti (19:14:08/4-18-54)

>>>>>[Vituperation and drek aside for a moment, a takeover bid usually increases share prices by about 50 percent. At least, that's been the average premium over the past few years. That benefits shareholders. After all, when they sell their shares they see a bigger return on their investment, right? So how can people argue that takeovers harm the market as a whole, hm?]<<<<<
—Argyle (16:02:18/4-20-54)

>>>>>[For a whole drekload of answers to that, keep reading, Argyle.]<<<<<
—The Chromed Accountant (12:03:48/4-21-54)

FIGHTING A TAKEOVER

All hostile takeovers don't necessarily succeed. A target corp's current ownership and management has several options, legal and illegal, that offer differing chances of blocking the takeover. Despite their allowability by law, legal tactics can be as sickeningly immoral as the down-and-dirty "black ops."

>>>>>[Even the so-called "legal" tactics often include illegal components, little twists where shadowrunners can find a little extra work on one side of the question or the other. Read on, and you'll see.]<<<<<
—Tangent (23:42:08/3-21-54)

>>>>>[Here's an interesting question. Takeover bids raise share prices, and mounting a defense can push them even higher. So why do managers really try to block a takeover? Are they really refusing a lower-priced offer because accepting it would set aside the best interests of the shareholders? Or is the takeover defense just a bargaining tactic, to raise the price higher so they'll make more money from their shares when the takeover bid actually goes through?]<<<<<
—Gerard (00:32:07/3-22-54)

>>>>>[Oh, come on . . . a management team or board of directors actually concerned about the interests of shareholders other than themselves? Don't make me yarf. Most managers try to block

takeovers because they don't want to lose their cushy jobs. It's that simple.]<<<<<
—Ross (21:47:44/3-25-54)

>>>>>[Consider this small factoid. Managers with large stock holdings in their firms are less likely to oppose takeovers than are managers with small stock holdings. Why?]<<<<<
—Gerard (01:42:38/3-26-54)

>>>>>[No-brainer, chummer. Either managers with large stock holdings back off because they risk losing the stock premium's big payoff if they oppose the acquisition, or managers with small holdings fight hard to keep their jobs (like I said yesterday). Even with the increase in price, their itty-bitty stock holding can't make up for their loss of salary. It's that simple.]<<<<<
—Ross (20:03:14/3-26-54)

BEFORE THE BID

Corps use the following legal techniques before the takeover bid: in other words, before the raiding corp actually gives the shareholders its offer to buy. Some of these legal maneuvers exist as "standing orders," provisions put permanently in place to frag up would-be acquirers. The management team initiates others when it hears rumors of a takeover in the works.

>>>>>[Shadowsnoops and wannabes, pay attention to this drek, okay? If you're on the business beat or just into general news, watching stocks can often give you a lead to a real story. Sometimes it's a story on its own.]<<<<<
—Reid (17:05:02/4-1-54)

Staggered Board

A small minority of corps split their boards of directors into three groups, with only one group elected at each annual general meeting. This division of power has to be written into the corp charter. If a raider picks up a majority of shares in such a corp, it cannot take over immediately, but can only replace one-third of the board with patsies at the first shareholders' meeting. The raider can still acquire a majority of shares and thus eventual control, so the staggered board can't stop a takeover. However, it slows down the raider's attempt to remake the target corp in the raider's image. Those raiders who don't want to deal with such delay tend to concentrate on target corps without this attached aggravation.

>>>>>[Why not just change the charter?]<<<<<
—Mad Monk (06:19:02/3-27-54)

>>>>>[Most modern corps require a 75 percent majority of the board to change the charter. You can't change the charter until you have control of the board, and you can't control the board. . .got it?]<<<<<
—Keynesian Kid (14:20:05/3-28-54)

>>>>>[Of course, if board members from the next year's group resign prematurely or just vanish, you've got to have an election right away, right?]<<<<<
—Corcoran (02:48:19/3-30-54)

>>>>>[Right. That's why only a few corps use this technique. Would-be raiders find board members excessively tempting targets, and no one likes feeling like a fish in a barrel.]<<<<<
    —Keynesian Kid (13:59:34/4-2-54)

Poison Pill

In this favorite technique, the board issues rights to a new issue of stock, giving them out to all current shareholders. Typically, each shareholder gets one right per share that he or she already owns. These rights remain useless, worthless, and usually non-transferable until some specific event triggers them. Such triggering events usually include the tendering of a bid for a large fraction of the corp (say, 30 percent) or a single shareholder accumulating 20 percent of the firm. Either event probably signals a potential takeover. When this happens, the rights become active, and shareholders can exchange them one-for-one for the new shares. This means the raider suddenly has to buy up twice as many shares to take control of the target. The poison pill also dilutes any equity that the raider already has in the target.

>>>>>[The poison pill harms the target corp in the long run, whether the takeover goes through or not. Even if the raider backs away, the target corp still has to deal with the equity hassles the poison pill caused.]<<<<<
    —Judy (18:49:15/3-29-54)

>>>>>[Sure, but a board member or senior exec who stands to get tossed out on his rosy red if he can't block the takeover, doesn't worry much about the long term. He does whatever it takes to keep his position, then deals with the consequences.]<<<<<
    —Keynesian Kid (14:02:12/4-2-54)

>>>>>[You can disable the poison pill by making sure the trigger condition never happens. That means finding out what the condition is, but any raider does that kind of homework as a matter of course. If the trigger is a single bid for more than 25 percent of the outstanding shares, make sure that the takeover doesn't appear as a single bid. Buy the shares through a bunch of shell companies and intermediaries. After all, anybody can own the shares as long as they vote the way you want them to.]<<<<<
    —Rox (10:40:03/4-5-54)

>>>>>[Easier said than done. Plenty of people spend lots of time worming around, trying to find out who owns who and who works on whose behalf. Not just the shadowsnoops, either. Every major corp has its "market intelligence" department (they call it something different, of course), and these days the kind of work they do makes military espionage look tame.]<<<<<
    —Hangfire (14:52:50/4-6-54)

Dual-Class Recapitalization

This nice little legal trick almost manages to stay ethical as well. The company issues new shares to shareholders, with better voting rights but lower dividends and/or less marketability. The new shares pay less and have stringent restrictions on when and how to sell them, making them a lot less attractive to your average investor than standard common shares.

With the new shares out, the corp offers shareholders a deal whereby they can convert these new shares into standard common shares that sell easily and pay a nice dividend. So Joe Shareholder converts his special shares to common stock, but the management team hangs onto the new stock like grim death. This gives management the vast majority of special shares, complete with the better voting rights. Standard common shares give the owner one vote per share, but the new stock gives the owner as much as 10 votes per share. Because most shareholders trade those extra voting rights for higher dividends, the managers who hang onto the new shares acquire the majority of votes without having to own the majority of stock. In other words, dual-class recapitalization shifts the voting power of the corp to the incumbent management. Slick, *neh*? The only shares on the market are the common shares, because management won't sell their special shares to a raider. So even if a raider buys up all outstanding common shares, he gets nowhere near the controlling votes he wants.

>>>>>[Corps can beat this simply by making it worth some manager's while to sell his special shares. Offer a few of them something valuable if they sell, such as their lives or the lives of their spouses and kids. Don't get me wrong, I'm not advocating this kind of drek. But you can bet your hoop any serious-minded raider considers the option.]<<<<<
—Hangfire (14:57:49/4-6-54)

>>>>>[You can bet the managers know it, too, and take serious precautions. For instance, they may hire some runners to round out their personal defense provisions.]<<<<<
—Argent (15:42:48/4-6-54)

AFTER THE BID
More reactive than proactive, the following tactics come into play once an attempted takeover becomes public knowledge.

>>>>>[Meaning a proactive way to disable these techniques is to keep current management from knowing about the takeover until it's already happened.]<<<<<
—Nuyen Nick (04:39:46/4-17-54)

White Knight
This defense requires the cooperation of another corp that management can trust, making it a seldom-used option. As soon as a raider issues a takeover bid, the white knight corp rides up and offers a higher bid. The raider can either shell out the funds to top the white knight's bid or slink off in defeat. Of course, topping the bid might prompt another counterbid from the white knight, and the raider has no way to know how expensive its takeover might get. If the raider caves in, the white knight withdraws its bid, and the target corp gets back to business.

Of course, sometimes the white knight refuses to withdraw its bid. It smells the possibility of pulling its own takeover, and can't resist the temptation. Unless management takes extreme care in selecting a white knight, this option gets risky for the target corp.

>>>>>[Note that the target often gives the white knight information not openly available to anyone else, to make it easier and cheaper for the other firm to chase off the raider. Of course, this gives the white knight a major advantage if it decides to go for control. Trust doesn't come easily in the corporate community, so the white knight tactic has gotten a lot less common.]<<<<<
—Nuyen Nick (04:42:16/4-17-54)

>>>>>[The problem with trying a takeover against a megacorp subsidiary, assuming the megacorp doesn't already have ownership locked up, is that the parent corp often comes to the target corp's rescue. This means that the only ones capable of making grabs against megacorp subsidiaries are other megacorps, financial corporations, and individuals with deep pockets.]<<<<<
—Michelangelo (05:10:28/4-19-54)

Greenmail
This elegant scheme plays on the natural greed of a partner in a takeover attempt. Greenmail specifically targets takeovers where a consortium of corps make the bid, a common practice these days. The target corp goes to one of the raiding firms or individuals and offers them a huge premium for the target corp shares they already have. The raider has the interesting choice to continue with the takeover attempt and risk losing out to a poison pill or a more destructive defense, or pocket a healthy profit with zero risk. If the raider goes for the safe money, management has reacquired a block of shares and votes possibly large enough to block or at least slow down the takeover. Of course, greenmail depends on a member of the raiding consortium putting its own profit above the interests of the consortium as a whole.

>>>>>[Not too rare.]<<<<<
—Nuyen Nick (04:44:04/4-17-54)

>>>>>[Maybe. But the rest of the consortium's going to be mighty ticked, and the raider offered the greenmail payment has to take that into account. Profit's great, but only if you can live to spend it. *Honto*?]<<<<<
—Toshikazu (17:30:02/4-19-54)

>>>>>[Combine the carrot with the stick and you'll get more response with greenmail. Approach a consortium member with a double-barreled offer: "Sell me your shares and you'll make a healthy profit. Don't sell me your shares and I'll frag you up." Works all the time.]<<<<<
—Virgo (11:34:42/4-20-54)

Litigation
Ah, the old standby. Why block a takeover in the boardroom when you can do it in the courtroom? Litigation lets the target corp try to sue the raiding company into a smoking crater. It can charge fraud, violation of antitrust laws, securities violations . . . frag, even littering if all else fails. Criminal or civil charges both fill the bill, and the charges need not stick. Though winning the court case carries its own advantages, the point of litigation is less to win than to tie the raider up in legal knots. If the target corp can slot the raider off badly enough, it skulks off to take over someone else. Even a reputation for suing anyone at the drop of a hat can sometimes scare off potential raiders.

>>>>>[This one can work real well, because not many corps particularly want to come under any form of legal scrutiny.]<<<<<
—Nuyen Nick (04:46:50/4-17-54)

>>>>>[What about jurisdiction?]<<<<<
　　—Ano (13:02:24/4-19-54)

>>>>>[That can be a problem. To get around it, you've got to charge the raider with something that's illegal in the local jurisdiction, and that the local government can actually enforce. In some places finding the right charge gets tricky, but the tactic can still work.]<<<<<
　　—Nuyen Nick (10:03:39/4-20-54)

If a target feels particularly daring, it can charge the raider before the Corporate Court. Finding a charge becomes more of a challenge because the Corp Court has declared few things categorically illegal, but some alternatives still exist. As with conventional courts, the target corp need not prove the charges. It need only cause the raider extreme irritation. If the target corp can make the court situation messy enough, the raider loses its incentive to go through with the takeover. Losing a case before the Corp Court saddles the target with its opponent's costs, but a losing corp faces takeover and so ends up paying debts to itself.

>>>>>[Going to the Corporate Court can be a real crap shoot, depending on who controls it at any given moment. Obviously, if the raider has a lock on the Court, the target has lost before it starts. A smart corp finds another option and hopes the raider doesn't decide to charge it with something as payback.]<<<<<
　　—Nuyen Nick (04:49:41/4-17-54)

>>>>>[In some jurisdictions, an embattled corp can go to the national government and claim that allowing the takeover to go through will significantly harm national interests. This approach has a chance only for a national corp, not part of some multinational megacorporate empire. But because so few national governments actually have enough clout to stop a takeover, the chances are always slim.]<<<<<
　　—Bedlam (12:12:33/4-21-54)

>>>>>[Tir Tairngire and Aztlan come immediately to mind.]<<<<<
　　—Turner (02:14:42/4-22-54)

>>>>>[Yeah, but you've got to have big brass ones to approach either government. Neither one has much sympathy for corporate interests. Except for the ones they own themselves, of course.]<<<<<
　　—Reid (10:09:15/4-26-54)

>>>>>[Another reason to stay away from the Corp Court: passing off fraudulent "evidence" gets a lot tougher. After all, the Corp Court justices can all probably fake up evidence like pros. Most likely did it for a living before they took the bench.]<<<<<
　　—Grist (15:26:02/4-27-54)

Acquisitions and Divestitures

One of the more destructive takeover defenses, this strategy involves making decisions that will affect the target corp for years to come. It may avoid a takeover, but at the price of making permanent decisions based on considerations other than good business sense. Obviously, any raider wants a corp for a specific reason. If the target corp figures out what the raider wants, it can slot him up but good. A target corp can divest, or sell, an asset that the raider wants; or it can buy assets the bidder doesn't want and saddle him with them.

For example, say Corp A tries to take over Corp B because it wants Corp B's management consulting division. So Corp B turns around and sells that division to someone else, leaving Corp A no motive for a takeover.

>>>>>[Sounds like sour grapes to me. "You can't have it, so *there*!"]<<<<<
　　—Craven A (12:38:53/3-29-54)

Or say Corp A wants Corp B because it's a lean and mean organization, with no dead wood and no debt load. So Corp B buys a badly managed, underfinanced company and turns it into a division, making itself bloated and debt-ridden. Once again, Corp A no longer has any incentive to take over Corp B.

In both examples, Corp A loses interest in the takeover. But in the first case, Corp B has to function without its best division, and in the second it must cope with a useless division. Acquisition and divestiture are the corp-level equivalent of theft-proofing your flashy new car by taking a ten-kilo hammer and pounding the drek out of it. You've warded off the thieves, but made your car worthless in the process.

>>>>>[Aztechnology raised the divestiture tactic to a whole new level last year. Big A had a subsidiary in Japan with a terrific gengineering lab that Mitsuhama coveted. So Mitsuhama made its move, and Aztechnology *blew up its own fragging lab!* ("If I can't have it, *nobody* can! *Ha-ha-ha-haaa!!!*") Twisted. But that's the Big A for you.]<<<<<
　　—Pyramid Watcher (04:57:25/4-16-54)

>>>>>[You sure about that? I'd heard a run by another corp went wrong.]<<<<<
　　—Nuyen Nick (04:56:21/4-17-54)

>>>>>[As sure as I can be on something like this, Nick.]<<<<<
　　—Pyramid Watcher (06:12:29/4-18-54)

>>>>>[If so, let's hope that kind of "scorched earth" takeover defense doesn't catch on.]<<<<<
　　—Nuyen Nick (10:06:13/4-20-54)

>>>>>[In another tactic getting more common in the UCAS, the target buys assets that create antitrust or other regulatory problems for the raider when and if it completes the takeover. In a pinch, the target might buy crap to get itself in legal trouble. In fighting off a takeover, sometimes anything goes.]<<<<<
　　—The Chromed Accountant (13:44:52/4-23-54)

Safekeeping

For corps too rational to just sell off key assets to someone, another tactic accomplishes the same thing without irreversible consequences (at least in theory). Instead of selling its "crown jewels," the target corp locks them up with a friendly third party.

>>>>>[Like, "lock up" how? Give me an example, somebody.]<<<<<
—Drago (13:18:29/4-13-54)

>>>>>[Like sell the asset in question to another corp you trust, with the understanding that the other corp will sell it back to you after the takeover threat passes; either at the same price or at a slight premium to reimburse them for their trouble.]<<<<<
—Nuyen Nick (04:59:13/4-17-54)

As with the white knight tactic, the target corp can never count on the "friendly" third party staying that way. Unless the target has some hold over them, nothing much can stop them from taking off with the assets entrusted to them.

>>>>>[I described a classic example of this in a previous file, **Megacorporate Primer** [p.11]. The soap opera about MCT, Renraku, and Eastern Tiger makes for a real cautionary tale.]<<<<<
—Vickers (14:06:42/4-24-54)

that seems to be changing as corp execs figure out the advantages of "plausible deniability." Management may feel happier trusting people they have control over, or for whom they have an accurate address should "follow-up" of any kind be required. On the other hand, pulling dirty tricks using corporate operatives points straight back at the guilty corp if its personnel have the lack of consideration to get themselves killed or captured. Using shadowrunners to do the nasty stuff helps keep your biz rival in the dark.

>>>>>[Cortex bombs come to mind as a way around awkward confessions by captured corp ops. Those few corp suits who care to limit the collateral damage go with a tiny charge implanted on each side of the throat, just large enough to open both carotid arteries. The Red Samurai special-ops teams have these "cutthroat charges."]<<<<<
—Collins (13:40:22/3-26-54)

>>>>>[The Red Samurai might go with it, but finding people willing to suicide is tougher than trideo and simsense shows would have you believe.]<<<<<
—Hangfire (15:05:08/3-28-54)

>>>>>[Oh, perish the thought, I never suggested suicide. That's far too voluntary. Hook the cortex bomb or cutthroat charge to a little receiver for which you have the transmitter. If your assets don't report back on time, even if they're 5 minutes late calling in, assume the op's blown and push the little button. *Splat!* End of problem. If you feel really paranoid, you can push the little button whether they report in or not.]<<<<<
—Collins (15:43:45/3-30-54)

>>>>>[You disgust me, Collins.]<<<<<
—Cyn (12:30:24/4-2-54)

>>>>>[You don't always have to earn trust. A corp a lot larger than its third-party "friend" can demand trust. The smaller corp knows that if it tries to pull anything on the larger, it might as well start digging its own grave. In this biz, size counts. Also, don't forget that corps own many subsidiary corps through deeply buried connections. The target corp can transfer power to one of its own arms long enough for the raider to lose interest. Of course if they get caught, all bets are off.]<<<<<
— Jeffers (20:09:56/4-24-54)

SHADOW OPS

As habitual readers of Shadowland, you really want to hear about this kind of drek. Unfortunately, I probably can't tell you much more than you already know. Come to think of it, some of you can probably tell me stories that'll curl my hair. I can tell you that shadow ops play a significant part in corporate takeovers. If the buzz I hear these days is true, more and more corps are using runners to do their dirty work. Though a lot of this crap still gets pulled by security or special forces belonging to the corp involved,

To pull their black ops, more and more corp execs are turning to the shadow community for unattributable and expendable assets. They routinely make the contract "double blind," meaning that the shadowrunners never know who hired them or exactly why their mission matters. Whenever possible, the corps prefer them not to know precisely what it is.

>>>>>[That's why all you slags have got to understand some of the info in these files. Pay attention and you might avoid getting

caught in some double blind trap where you can't tell who's trying to geek you, let alone why.]<<<<<
—Hangfire (11:29:48/3-24-54)

>>>>>[Sounds like a hot market for shadowrunners.]<<<<<
—Tober (13:43:32/3-26-54)

>>>>>[Yeah. Particularly for the dumb-ass ones who jump at any run offered without doing their research first.]<<<<<
—Hangfire (20:22:43/3-29-54)

>>>>>[Man, the corps have used us as unattributable assets for years. That's what running the shadows is all about.]<<<<<
—Raven Red (09:13:59/3-30-54)

>>>>>[True. But the use of shadowrunners is proliferating. Once upon a time, the corps hired us only for the blackest of black ops, or if they needed a blunt instrument. Now the Johnsons have figured out they can use runners for more subtle maneuverings, like manipulating a rival's stock prices. One thing hasn't changed though, *omae*. They still don't tell us why we're doing this drek.]<<<<<
—Argent (16:06:32/4-2-54)

Off the top of my head, I've drawn up a list of some of the shadow ops corps typically pull on each other in the throes of takeover attempts and defenses. (Note: I'm sure you can play "top that story" with me all fragging year. Please resist the temptation. This list isn't meant to be exhaustive by any means.)
· Destruction of assets in another corp (or your own). "Assets" can be tangible, such as equipment; intangible, such as data; or alive and kicking, such as staff.
· Hostile extraction or elimination of key personnel.
· Fragging up a corp's manufacturing or distribution channel so they miss important shipments, thus destroying public confidence in them.
· Extortion or other intimidating moves against board members, key owners, significant managers, or anyone else with clout.
· Sabotage.
· Industrial espionage.
· Infiltration (*agent provocateur* stuff).

>>>>>[Hey, Neo-A, don't go giving the Johnsons all those wizzer ideas . . .]<<<<<
—Luke (09:41:00/3-29-54)

>>>>>[Don't know about you, *omae*, but my palms get all sweaty just thinking about all that work out there.]<<<<<
—Barre Sinister (23:44:08/4-6-54)

>>>>>[For every corp that uses these tactics, another corp defends against them. Set a runner to catch a runner, right, chummers? We probably make better hunters than a lot of the security firms out there, because we know how the shadows work and how other runners tend to approach problems.]<<<<<
—Kris (02:32:32/4-7-54)

>>>>>[Hey, I thought runners were supposed to be the "rays of light shining out in the darkness." All this drek sounds horrific.]<<<<<
—Thane (14:34:27/4-7-54)

>>>>>[Well, yes. Some runners, myself included, have ethical qualms about taking certain kinds of runs. I draw the line at wetwork, and if I'm doing close cover I've got to believe that the body I'm guarding is worth keeping alive. But plenty of slags out there don't haul around what they'd call obsolete emotional baggage such as morals, ethics, and conscience.]<<<<<
—Dirk (04:15:43/4-10-54)

>>>>>[I'd class those people as criminals, not shadowrunners.]<<<<<
—Zork (22:45:44/4-11-54)

>>>>>[Take ethics, morality, and good clean country livin' on your runs with you and you're dead. At some point all that baggage just gets in your way and you get geeked. If you let all that moral drek hold you back, then you picked the wrong career.]<<<<<
—Caine (01:19:45/4-12-54)

>>>>>["Industrial espionage" often equals "data sabotage." Sometimes a corp cares less about how a rival makes their new wizzer doohickey than about how to stop them from making any more.]<<<<<
—Barre Sinister (11:23:09/4-13-54)

>>>>>[An interesting twist on *agent provocateur* stuff. You know how the Aztlan government acts so much like it wants to protect the fragging rain forest? Well, they only act that way when it suits them. Other times they play cut-trees-and-move-on as much as Tsimshian does, for frag's sake. Couple of years back, Aztechnology started slash-and-burning an area of the Yucatán for some project or other, with the Azzy government's blessings (big shock). Some "hard green" outfits tried to block them through legal and ethical means, no dirty tricks at all. The greens wanted to keep the moral high ground; they'd learned their lessons from watching some of the European ecotage groups who turned everyone against them with dirty tactics. Big A wanted the greenies out of the way, so they hired a team of runners to conduct some ecotage against Aztechnology assets. That's right, to frag with their own people and blow up their stuff. Oh yeah, and to make sure some innocent bystanders got geeked in the process.
So when that drek went down, Aztechnology threw up its collective hands in outrage at the heinous crimes of the supposed eco-terrorists. With public opinion switching overwhelmingly to its side and with full government backing, Big A staged a major black op against the real green groups, geeking a bunch of them and destroying the groups as a cohesive force. Problem solved, Big A went right on clearing the Yucatán.
Nasty, huh?]<<<<<
—Jackal (01:30:39/4-21-54)

>>>>>[That's the kind of thing I meant when I said that corps are using shadowrunners in more innovative and twisted ways.]<<<<<
—Argent (15:20:22/4-25-54)

TAKEOVER PROS AND CONS

People have scrapped over this question for more than a hundred years. I recently ran across some old data scanned into the Matrix from hardcopy books, and discovered that the pundits were debating the pros and cons of takeovers in the 1930s, 1980s, and 1990s. Some people defend all takeover activities, and some condemn it all. In the middle are the moderates and the "it-depends" crowd.

Personally, I make a distinction between "acquisition take-overs" and "destructive takeovers." Acquisition takeovers, in which big conglomerates like the megacorps get larger by taking over smaller, independent corps (or even other conglomerates), lead to bigger and bigger corps and fewer independents. Because this makes for less competition and more coercion in the market-place, I'm heartily against acquisition takeovers.

Not so destructive takeovers, where the megacorps frag each other over. In this kind of maneuver, the targets of the takeovers are actually subsidiaries or divisions of other megacorps. Because the takeover targets existed as part of a conglomerate to begin with, this activity doesn't decrease the overall level of indepen-dence and competition in the world. It also distracts the megacorps from absorbing independents. The time, effort, and assets they invest in acquisitory infighting decreases the attention they can pay to expanding their empires. If all the megacorps choose to devote themselves to this kind of cluster-frag, my blessings on their efforts.

I hereby throw the topic open for discussion. Have at it, my children.

>>>>>[Takeover fever is just more churning, where the corps get involved in activity for its own sake. If they do it right, they can make money. But they don't produce anything. All this slotting around doesn't put a single good or service on the market. It's monetary masturbation: rewarding enough in the short term, but not productive.]<<<<<
—Carol (12:55:42/3-24-54)

>>>>>[Drek, Carol, a corp board only cares about maximizing the return on investment for its shareholders. The board's supposed to do that. The charter of every corp and the business law of every jurisdiction says so. Ever hear of fiduciary responsibility? If the board and corp management can make money for the sharehold-ers by churning, then they're just doing their job.]<<<<<
—Lee (10:44:13/3-26-54)

>>>>>[Some board members recognize a responsibility beyond that of keeping stock prices up for their shareholders. They also have responsibilities to their employees, to the environment, to the community, and to (meta)humanity in general.]<<<<<
—Lynne (15:06:47/3-28-54)

>>>>>[Newbies, no doubt. Business virgins. No grief, they'll get that ground out of them right quick.]<<<<<
—Wolverine (13:04:29/3-29-54)

>>>>>[Don't forget the professional corporate raiders out there who spend all their time finding suitable targets for acquisition. After taking them over, gutting them, and breaking them up, they sell the assets, take the money, and do it again. At the moment they're doing the most damage in Europe, but they still have significant clout in North America and even in Japan.]<<<<<
—Carstairs (22:15:56/4-1-54)

>>>>>[Good point. One snotty Brit elf, *Sir* Geoffrey Barthwaite, has come across the pond to throw his weight around on this continent. Jesus, but he scared the living drek out of the mid-size corps in the UK and on the Continent. He has such a terrific track record as a corporate raider than just about any investment bank in Europe gladly lends him millions or even billions the minute he hints that a particular corp's ripe for takeover.]<<<<<
—Lang (19:24:48/4-2-54)

>>>>>[So Barthwaite the fragging pirate has landed here, huh? That's got to have a lot of corp suits quaking in their Guccis.]<<<<<
—Monitor (21:04:02/4-2-54)

>>>>>[Count on plenty of them working together to force him back over the Atlantic. Individual raiders like Barthwaite don't dominate the North American market of the 2050s. "Takeover cartels" do, and those cartels won't relish the competition.]<<<<<
—Junior (21:29:35/4-2-54)

>>>>>[Barthwaite might find North American banks a little less willing to lend him meganuyen just on his personal rep. But go back a bit, Junior. What do you mean by "takeover cartels?"]<<<<<
—Lee (23:24:01/4-2-54)

>>>>>[Takeover cartel: a small group of large investors who take turns financing each other in takeover raids. It's a good scam; as long as the takeovers go through quickly, the group has deep enough pockets to overcome just about any takeover defense. The guy who plays point man for a particular deal takes a little more financial risk, but the other members of the cartel stay protected from losses even if the takeover bid fails. It's an all-American way of doing business: share the responsibility and the cost, and turn it into a committee process. Quite different from the European approach, where individual raiders trade on charisma, rep, and pure balls to do the job.]<<<<<
—Junior (21:13:12/4-4-54)

>>>>>[Remember the drek in an earlier file about junk bonds? Some of Junior's takeover cartels use junk bonds to fund their acquisitions. That's how they raise the money they need so fast.]<<<<<
—Nuyen Nick (13:34:58/4-5-54)

>>>>>[A good reason to outlaw junk bonds.]<<<<<
—Thomas (03:04:11/4-6-54)

>>>>>[If the corps didn't have junk bonds, they'd find something else. Anyway, the connection between junk bonds and takeover fever is vastly overblown. Sure, corps use junk bond funding for takeovers sometimes, but not that often.]<<<<<
—Markops (03:35:57/4-6-54)

>>>>>[Markops, you're a fragging apologist for the megacorps. It happens all the time, you slot.]<<<<<
—Thomas (16:45:32/4-6-54)

>>>>>[I like the Neo-A guy's slant on the issue. Takeovers are only bad if they're directed at independents. If the megacorps want to bugger each other blind trying to take each other over, let them go to it.]<<<<<
—Ratzo (13:44:28/4-7-54)

>>>>>[Yeah, but doesn't takeover activity pump up stock prices? That makes it good for the economy and for investors, right?]<<<<<
—Talis (14:07:38/4-8-54)

>>>>>[Finally, a rational approach to the issue. In answer to your question, Talis, yes, takeover activity aids the economy for the reason you cite. It has other benefits as well.

In my extensive experience, takeovers and the threat of them provide the only stimuli that force certain firms into becoming competitive. Under the threat of a hostile takeover, firms close down unprofitable divisions and facilities, improve their management and accounting practices, and generally restructure to make themselves more profitable. In other words, takeovers force "fat, dumb, and happy" companies to become efficient and competitive.

I grant you, corporate boards of directors should restructure and refocus the organization they run on an ongoing basis, as part of their fiduciary responsibility to their shareholders. But often only the threat of an impending takeover and the concurrent ouster of the board can force negligent management to do what it should have done all along. In general, takeover targets either become efficient or cease to exist as independent entities. This culling of the weak can only be beneficial to the economy as a whole.]<<<<<
—Pirate (11:23:45/4-9-54)

>>>>>[Screen-name "Pirate" is actually Sir Geoffrey Barthwaite, the Brit elf that Lang mentioned in his post a week ago.]<<<<<
—Skeleton Hunter (18:59:41/4-10-54)

>>>>>[Sir Geoffrey is talking out of his knighted hoop. No evidence whatsoever exists that all these takeovers positively affect the economy. Takeover fever isn't helping the economy the way he says it is.]<<<<<
—Reid (23:18:36/4-10-54)

>>>>>[Mr. Reid, approach this topic with your intellect rather than with your libertarian, American emotions. Mergers and takeovers do have a positive effect on the marketplace, and the fact that your figures fail to support this has more to say about the inadequacy of your data than anything else. Please, I urge you to think it through.

Takeovers have the following positive results. They force the replacement of poor management teams. They force contraction of any industry in which no firm has voluntarily "rightsized." Because they lead to new conglomerates, they create new and sometimes unexpected synergies that bring new products to the consumer. How can these results fail to have a positive economic effect?]<<<<<
—Pirate (11:26:00/4-11-54)

>>>>>[He sounds convincing.]<<<<<
—Bung (16:49:46/4-11-54)

>>>>>[Bulldrek. He's a snake-oil salesman, that's his job.

Try these negative results, Sir Geoffrey. Takeovers decrease competition and create oligopolies. Because most jurisdictions offer tax breaks to companies engaged in your kind of corporate raiding, the nation's treasury and its citizens are unintentionally subsidizing takeover activity. What else might they use that money for, if you and your ilk quit siphoning it off? Also, takeover defenses do considerable economic damage. When corps sell assets below their value or purchase them above their value simply to thwart a takeover, price and value suddenly have nothing to do with each other. And you tell me this is economically OK? And I won't even mention the damage caused by black ops on both sides.

Give us a break, you slot, and go home. And SysOp, tighten Shadowland security a little so trash like that can't get in.]<<<<<
—Turner (18:26:49/4-11-54)

>>>>>[From time to time, I hear about another interesting form of corp competition. If a rival corporation gets in a corp's face, that corp retaliates by going after another corp that the rival depends on. It buys (or torches) the rival's largest domestic distributor, or their major supplier. The target corp might not expect any trouble at all, making it easier to nail the drek out of them with a well-planned shadow up. Also, taking out a much smaller but strategically crucial organization can cripple a major corp at a lot less risk. I call that efficiency in action.]<<<<<
—Murgatroyd (09:21:34/4-14-54)

CORPORATE WAR

No discussion of corporate competition can possibly be complete without mentioning out-and-out corporate war, the ultimate form of competition. Unfortunately, corporate war is neither a myth nor something made up by the writers of potboiler simsense software. And I'm sorry, children, but it can happen even in these oh-so-enlightened times. To my personal knowledge, we have teetered on the brink of global corp war twice within the last three decades. Spirits know how many other times we've stumbled close to the edge and the Corporate Court has covered it up.

>>>>>[This drek happens in Europe, right? Yeah, I can believe that. Not here, though.]<<<<<
—LeVoi (16:13:29/3-21-54)

>>>>>[That's right, keep your head comfortably buried in the sand.]<<<<<
—Isvestia (11:42:14/3-22-54)

CAUSES OF CORP WAR
Locked in continuous competition, the megacorps strike at each other in ways both marginally legal and black as the deepest shadows. Though black ops get the job done, they pose considerable risks for the corp running them. If the victim can prove who hammered it, a charge before the Corporate Court can force the perpetrating corp to pay damages for "assets expended" and even for its victim's lost profits.

>>>>>[The Corp Court rarely goes that far out on a limb. Unless the case is cut-and-dried, or a single corp or axis has a lock on the court and feels particularly militant, the court usually makes conservative decisions.]<<<<<
—Legal Beagle (16:33:27/3-29-54)

Lacking proof acceptable to the Corporate Court, the victim usually resorts to payback, running its own shadow ops against the original perpetrator. This course of action can start a vicious cycle of retaliation if the first corp decides to strike again.

>>>>>[Sometimes the corps get a real charge out of yanking each other's chains. Say Ares stages a nuisance run against Fuchi, but sets it up to frame Shiawase for it. Fuchi retaliates against Shiawase, the corp it thinks fragged it around. From Shiawase's perspective, Fuchi has initiated hostilities for no reason. Good and slotted off, Shiawase stages a nuisance run against Fuchi. Figuring it's evened the score, Shiawase goes about its business. But Fuchi thinks Shiawase has fragged with it twice, and so retaliates. For as long as this little game goes on, mastermind Ares just sits back, watches, and laughs itself sick.]<<<<<
—Manx (21:45:09/4-7-54)

Much of the time, the corps involved eventually see reason. They decide that escalating the conflict stands to lose them more than it gains; after all, the assets they expend in payback make them no money. Unless some special issue or extraordinary circumstance changes the corporate mind, inter-corp conflict rarely goes beyond the equivalent of border skirmishes. The corps involved know they've got a lot to lose if the infighting gets out of hand. Also, the Corporate Court can bring some influence to bear. If two corps spend time butting heads for no apparent reason, the court can censure the corps involved. As I'll discuss in a later file, this kind of censure has almost no teeth to it, but most corps follow the court's edicts for various good reasons.

However, sometimes the corps don't see reason. The level of escalation may have risen so high or gotten so personal that the corps feel they can no longer back down without losing face. Or individual divisions and subsidiaries within the corps may choose to act on their own.

>>>>>[Or it gets personal for another reason, like when exec veep Alice Ho of Shiawase Manufacturing went ballistic over the death of her husband during a run some Aztechnology ops made on her division. Alice took all of the secret funds she had available for shadow ops and used them to mad-dog against Aztechnology Seattle. Things got nasty for awhile until Shiawase International hired an expediter to deal with Alice.]<<<<<
—Dwight (19:04:38/3-20-54)

More often, things get out of hand because of some bone of contention so important that the corps involved prefer to risk out-and-out war than to back off. No matter how satisfying it feels in the short term, playing payback for its own sake isn't worth the consequences of ongoing retaliation and escalation. But with something really worthwhile at stake, the balance point between corp war's costs and benefits can shift drastically.

For example, society reached the brink of corp war back in 2041 when Yamatetsu broke into the first tier of megacorporations. It challenged the traditional lock that the "big three," Ares, Fuchi, and Mitsuhama, had on the Corporate Court and the Zurich-Orbital Gemeinschaft Bank. The other major megacorps had

reconciled themselves to the three-way control structure for several years, but refused to tolerate the "upstart" Yamatetsu challenging the Powers That Be for its own place in the pecking order. Yamatetsu's power bid forced the other first-tier corps and even a couple of the smaller fry to realize that a situation they had believed graven in stone could change after all. Not surprisingly, they failed to appreciate this rude awakening. They dug in their heels, determined to keep control of the Corporate Court and the Z-O Gemeinschaft Bank. Meanwhile, Yamatetsu remained equally determined to grab its share of influence and participation in court and bank decision-making. Both sides wanted a big prize, and neither wished to compromise. Skirmishes flared between megacorporate security assets throughout the world, as each side used special ops, industrial espionage, and sabotage against each other. Each new black up got nastier and nastier, and the conflict threatened to spiral completely out of control.

>>>>>[What about shadowrunner involvement?]<<<<<
    —Tenmace (11:01:10/3-29-54)

>>>>>[I worked in the corp world back in '41, but I didn't hire many runners. You've got to understand that the shadow community twelve years ago had nowhere near the level of development and sophistication that it has today. With a few exceptions, the "shadowrunners" of '41 were either habitual criminals or street punks, not the pool of skilled "freelance professionals" we usually

think of. Also, the corps hadn't figured out how to use the "shadow assets" efficiently. We lived in a different world back then, believe me.]<<<<<
    —Hangfire (15:57:16/4-2-54)

Only when a couple of corps began to mobilize their Desert Wars assets did the execs of the major megacorps realize they stood on the edge of a precipice with a long way to fall. Luckily, common sense abounded that year. Everyone backed away from the edge very carefully, all keeping a close eye on each other. By 2042, the corporate world had accepted Yamatetsu and gone back to business as usual.

>>>>>[Interesting that this screed ignores one of the most fascinating events in corp history, by my standards at least. Despite the statement above, not everyone backed off simultaneously. A large second-tier corp, an East Jerusalem-based outfit called QZE Corporation, chose not to call off its dogs. (God knows why. Jihad mentality, maybe?) Anyway, QZE saw an excellent opportunity to get a few more licks in, trash some of the big boys, and leapfrog its way into the corporate top tier.
    Well, the Corporate Court looked down from on high and realized that QZE threatened what little stability the corporate world had regained. So they put out an edict that some people call an Omega Order. I don't know if that's an official term or just something that sounds wiz. Anyway, this Omega Order declared open season on QZE Corporation. Anybody could strike at all of its

assets with impunity, everywhere in the world. Using the Omega Order as justification, all the major corps that had recently been at each other's throats teamed up to wipe QZE Corporation off the face of the earth.]<<<<<
—Link (23:05:00/4-13-54)

>>>>>[I've heard unconnected and unconfirmed rumors that the corps almost went to war for a bigger prize than control of the Corporate Court. The way I've managed to reconstruct it, somebody developed technology to eavesdrop on and even alter fiber optic communications. I know, conventional wisdom says you can't tap fiber without someone detecting your interference. But conventional wisdom doesn't know everything, right? Apparently, one corp either had the technology or data or whatever, or was real close to getting it. Of course, everyone else would risk just about anything to get it. Or suppress it, if they couldn't abscond with it.

Big prize, huh? Think about what a corp could do with the ability to tap into every competitor's communications anywhere in the world, and even diddle a few bits here and there. Within a couple of years everyone would develop and use a completely different technology to safeguard their secrets. But for that couple of years, exclusive control of the tapping technology could make a corp king of the drekheap. For some reason, though, the incipient corp war fizzled out. No one's made any obvious move away from fiber optics, so I don't know the full story.]<<<<<
—Walesa (18:44:00/4-18-54)

>>>>>[The full story, slot, is that no such tech ever existed. Your story's as full of drek as you are.]<<<<<
—Tec (05:30:14/4-19-54)

>>>>>[You sure of that?]<<<<<
—TS (09:32:10/4-19-54)

TYPES OF CORP WAR

Some people categorize full-fledged corp war as just more of the same shadowruns and black ops that corps always run against each other, increased in frequency and severity. People holding this view draw no distinction between corp war and heightened undercover activity. To them, such activity becomes war only when one of the participants, outside corps, or the Corporate Court finds the undercover ops unacceptable and takes steps against them. Many of the activities in a full-on corp war certainly resemble "business as usual," except that destruction of assets has escalated beyond so-called "acceptable" levels. Personally, I believe the following criteria differentiate corporate war from "acceptable" corporate skullduggery.

Action Against Uninvolved Assets

This activity serves as the corporate equivalent of strategic bombing against population centers. Most "action" such as terrorism, sabotage, assassination, and hostile extraction occurs against assets relevant to the dispute at hand. For example, say two corps get into a scrap over a new development in black IC technology. Direct action targeted against each other's programming or Matrix

security divisions qualifies as "business as usual." But as soon as one corp takes action against something unrelated to the dispute, such as its rival's simsense distribution network, that corp has crossed the line into corp war. Taken to extremes, corps use this kind of direct action to destroy the rival's ability to do business in any area or to sap its will to continue the competition. Obviously, strikes against family and friends of a rival corp's personnel fall into this category.

>>>>>[Corps have an unwritten rule against geeking the family and chummers of a rival unless they also work for the target corp. It's okay to terrorize, intimidate, threaten, brainwash, even injure friends and family: but the corps draw the line at killing. That's why Alice Ho went ballistic when her husband bought it. He was waiting in his car to pick up Alice when he got gutted by a stray burst.]<<<<<
—Dwight (19:12:43/3-20-54)

>>>>>[Of course, "uninvolved assets" comes down to a judgment call, doesn't it? Some people might consider any part of the same corp "involved," and therefore a legit target.]<<<<<
—Harmony (16:44:05/3-29-54)

Core Wars

Corps run deckers at each other's systems all the time, but this kind of game has certain unwritten rules. Hacking in to steal a rival's information qualifies as a fair tactic, but going in just to trash data becomes dirty pool. Actual destruction of program code and/ or hardware goes right out of the brawl zone. The rules allow corps to use or abuse components of a rival's computer system, but not to use them up. Otherwise, any decker who gets into a subsystem on the Matrix could "seed" that system with viruses a lot more damaging than the simple watchdog stuff that every decker plays with. Potentially, a decker could riddle a corp subsystem with tailored viruses that purge a whole system or even cause hardware damage.

>>>>>[How can viruses cause *hardware* damage? Come on . . .]<<<<<
—Victor (18:49:00/3-31-54)

>>>>>[I can think of a couple of dozen real examples, all too technical for a general-interest audience. So I'll toss out a couple of old-tech examples to get the point across. Remember what a hard disk is? (Going way back, I know.) If I want to, I can write a code fragment to take direct control of your hard disk and drive the heads back and forth across the disk surface as fast as possible. On a fast enough drive, they can go a couple of hundred times a second and keep it up for hours on end. Eventually, something wears out. Your disk crashes, and you lose data.

Or say you have a CRT monitor attached to your computer instead of a crystal matrix screen. I can write a virus to suppress the horizontal hold on your monitor. That virus can make your computer try to write all the screen data in an area one pixel wide. In maybe 20 seconds, some component or other in the back of your monitor burns out, and once again you crash.

That kind of fragging around gets a little tougher in the real world, but the idea remains the same. A hot decker could do it, but nobody actually does, if you get my drift.]<<<<<
—FastJack (00:53:06/4-1-54)

Every corporation in the world depends on its own computer systems and on the Matrix. All the megacorps use the shared resources of the Matrix, putting up with the minor risks of occasional decker incursion and trusting in the unwritten rules against full-fledged core wars to protect them against major destructive assaults. Though the Corporate Court has strict laws against direct destruction of computer and data assets, the main incentive for "playing by the rules" remains the knowledge that any corp starting a core war risks a devastating counterattack.

>>>>>[One of the concords promulgated by the Corporate Court allows the court to issue an Omega Order (I've heard the term too, Link) against any corp that initiates outright computer assaults. To the best of my knowledge, no one has ever used the provision because proof of guilt is so hard to come by.]<<<<<
—Legal Beagle (08:53:32/4-18-54)

>>>>>[Because of that, the Corp Court issues its Omega Orders based on reasonable suspicion. That gives the corps another reason to shy away from any connection with core wars.]<<<<<
—Hangfire (14:38:52/4-21-54)

Mutual risk and vulnerability maintain the minimal level of trust that keeps the megacorps connected to the greater Matrix. If any of the major corps should for some reason disengage from the Matrix, its fellow corps might well suspect it of preparing to wage core war against a rival by protecting itself from electronic retaliation. In reaction to such a move, all the other major corps would launch a fast, brutal, preemptive strike to blow the perpetrator off the face of the earth. Fear of such an extreme response keeps even the most security-paranoid corp from setting up independent, shielded systems invulnerable to decker penetration. Such an act would bring down the wrath of all the other corps, leaving the perpetrator a pile of corporate rubble.

>>>>>[I find it highly amusing that the corps operate on mutual trust in one area while slagging each other down in every other facet of their operations.]<<<<<
—Barkley (21:01:12/3-29-54)

>>>>>[That's life, Bark. You can find parallels in our existence as well, if you think about it.]<<<<<
—Big Z (04:05:16/3-31-54)

>>>>>[If anyone did decide to fight a core war, a tailored computer virus makes the perfect weapon. Slip it into a rival's system inside a smart frame, or have a decker carry it in. Assuming you know exactly what hardware the target's running, the right code can give you a lethal virus that can't spread outside the system you infect.]<<<<<
—TS (09:43:28/4-5-54)

>>>>>[Easier said than done. Considering the level of anti-viral protection built into most systems, only a self-modifying, evolving "smart" virus can do the job right. And no one can guarantee how it might evolve. Limited but compelling evidence exists that the historians got it wrong about the Crash of '29. Spontaneously generating viral code had nothing to do with it; the culprit was a rudimentary, self-modifying virus that got too smart. In other words, someone lost control of a core wars weapon and it took everyone out.]<<<<<
—FastJack (03:08:48/4-6-54)

>>>>>[Why doesn't the Corp Court outlaw research into "smart" viruses? Everybody might feel a little safer.]<<<<<
—Mulch (20:12:15/4-16-54)

>>>>>[Just try enforcing it, chummer. Having an unenforceable law on the books weakens the whole body of law.]<<<<<
—Legal Beagle (09:14:21/4-18-54)

Destruction of Strategic Assets
One step up from going after uninvolved divisions or personnel, strategic asset destruction matches core wars for militancy and viciousness. All major corps have so-called "strategic" assets vital to the corp's continued ability to do business. A private communication satellite network makes for the most common example; each of the major megacorps owns its own comsats and associated uplink/downlink sites. (No one wants to entrust their vital communications to someone else's hardware channels if they can avoid it.) Like computer systems, communication channels are vital and vulnerable. The level of technology available to any megacorp, particularly those with a major military presence in Desert Wars, makes knocking down satellites a relatively easy task. One battlefield-grade laser can burn the receptors off a low-Earth-orbit (LEO) comsat, and a battery of two or three can slag the sucker down.

>>>>>[Ground-based interception isn't as easy as this slot makes it sound. Plenty of corporate satellites have ASAT capabilities built into them because when push comes to frag, killer-sats have a better intercept ratio than any ground-based system.]<<<<<
—Blade (19:38:41/4-1-54)

Certain situations can strongly tempt a corp to knock down one or two rival comsats. For example, during a heavy-duty takeover or proxy fight, delaying crucial communications for a couple of minutes or even seconds can make the difference between success and failure. On the face of it, pranging up a rival's comsat network by simply laser-dazzling one or two of their birds for a minute or two looks like an easy option with a big potential payoff.

The danger lies in the response such action provokes. Eliminate even one of a rival's strategic communications assets and you're begging for instant retaliation. Tit-for-tat escalation becomes a frightening probability. Through the common practice of leasing sidebands on one another's satellites, other corps can also get involved. Sidebands purportedly allow corps to maximize

communication bandwidth, but also let them track the disposition of each other's satellites. If a corp takes out an Ares satellite that also carries Aztechnology datastreams, that corp has made two enemies with one shot and invited massive escalation. To keep this kind of chaos from happening, Corp Court laws prohibit corps from jacking around with each other's strategic assets.

>>>>>[See my earlier comments on core wars. The court can issue an Omega Order based solely on reasonable suspicion.]<<<<<
     —Hangfire (14:46:16/4-21-54)

>>>>>["Strategic assets" also include the headquarters buildings of rival corps. Blow up factories, research labs and branch plants, not HQ buildings. That's not kosher.]<<<<<
     —Talis (09:48:43/4-26-54)

Military Action

Some people mistakenly blur the distinction between "security assets" or street ops and military assets. The big difference between fielding a group of black ops professionals and mobilizing a Desert Wars division marks the distinction between business-as-usual and corp war. The personnel involved have a different level of training, and mil-spec gear can wreak infinitely greater destruction than the most lethal weapons available on the street. More to

the point, the two different types of forces allow the corps to pursue vastly different objectives. When a corp calls up the military, direct confrontation becomes inevitable. Corp war has begun.

>>>>>[Translation: when the army mobilizes, it's hoop-kicking time for real.]<<<<<
     —York (10:06:36/4-2-54)

>>>>>[OK, get your insults in now. But can somebody fill me in hardcore about Desert Wars? Everybody bats the term around and I've watched the trideo show (blast!), but what's the chip-truth?]<<<<<
     —Gabber (19:13:41/4-3-54)

>>>>>[Some time back a couple of megacorps came close to getting, shall we say, physical with each other. Instead of trashing each other's important physical and fiscal assets, they decided to set their security and military personnel against each other. Each side drew up contracts resolving the problem at hand to the benefit of whoever won the private war. Just before the blowout started, one of the international networks got wind of it and made a bid to cover the fight with a live entertainment feed. Never ones to turn down substantial money, the corps agreed to let their private war go public. When the war actually occurred, the winning corp made almost as much money on their cut of the advertising revenues as they did from the resolution of the original conflict.

Regularly scheduled corporate warfare became the next logical step, so we got Desert Wars. Twice a year in the North African desert, the corps pit their military assets against each other in a mix of lethal, quasi-lethal, and simulated combat. Big bucks. Big ratings. They occasionally settle actual disputes using those forces, but mostly Desert Wars serve the following four purposes:
     • Raising public corporate awareness. (Keep the corp name in the public's face.)
     • Bringing in advertising revenue. (Usually enough to at least defer operational costs.)
     • Merchandising. (Money for nothing.)
     • Training of security assets. (Security and paramilitary forces rotate through the Desert War camps as part of their training, in a manner similar to the old National Guard system of training with the mainline armed forces.)
     Fun stuff, *neh*?
     —Wittworth (03:13:44/4-6-54)

FALLOUT OF CORP WAR

If corp war remained entirely between corporations without involving anyone else, it might serve a beneficial purpose. If the big, bad megacorps oppressing the populace start offing each other whenever they feel like it, the rest of us might live and breathe a little more freely.

>>>>>[My sentiments exactly.]<<<<<
     —Lash (11:05:10/3-28-54)

Too bad it doesn't really work that way. Almost by definition, corp war causes worldwide consequences, up to and including possible nuclear war. First of all, the global economy has merged with and become dependent on megacorporate profits and business activity. If the corps go to war, they can't do business. Instead, they commit all assets to combat, or to prevent the destruction of key strategic assets. If enough assets get trashed despite precautions, the corps go belly-up. Without the corps to prop it up, the global economy crashes. Food shipments to the megaplexes stop, because the megacorps handle almost every aspect of the food industry. Food riots come next, like the ones that damned near brought down New York in 1999.

>>>>>[Oh, come on. I figure a full-fledged corp war might last a week at most before the weak sisters get cleaned out and the dominant corps grab total control. Food riots in a week? *Null!*]<<<<<
—Dude (15:20:15/3-23-54)

>>>>>[Oh? Ask yourself this, Dude. How much food do you have on hand right now, in your fridge and cupboards? If you don't own a fridge and cupboards, think it through for a chummer. (Assuming you have chummers.) On average, most people keep a couple days' food supplies on hand. When that runs out, they head for the stuffer shack or the food store. By that third day, the people who had less than two days' food or who knew what was coming have already cleared the shelves. Nothing left for you, *omae*. After 72 hours you start to go hungry, and you don't know when you might see food again.

Some people will hoard food, and others won't like that. Angry people tend to indulge in robbery, looting, and violence. Over the next 24 to 48 hours, the violence escalates. Nobody's really starving yet, but the hunger pangs feed the fear and anger, which in turn feed the hunger. From this point, full-fledged food riots are a pretty short step away. I figure all the cities of the world are 48 hours from revolution.]<<<<<
—Larry (20:10:28/3-25-54)

As the food riots escalate, civil law and government control break down. Hunger-driven civil insurrection takes over the streets, and governments watch their control evaporate. Rather than letting it go easily, they take draconian action to re-establish their power. But because the corp war has knocked out other parts of the social infrastructure dependent on corp involvement, any government strong-arm move has a minimal chance of success.

>>>>>[Utilities collapse. The phone companies are committed to the war as well, so that knocks out communications. The Matrix falls into chaos. Decker sabotage squads roam free, killer viruses float around everywhere. Not a pretty picture.]<<<<<
—FastJack (23:43:00/3-29-54)

At this point, the governments try to take action against the corporate instigators of the trouble. But the corps don't take kindly to government interference even at the best of times. The corp war has them all cranked up and out on the pointy end, ready to rock and roll with anyone who slots with them. Confrontations arise between corps and governments, with the governments facing a rout unless they mobilize their own armies. Military engagements flare up between national armies and corporate troops.

By this time, "digital bloodletting" in the Matrix and uncontrolled ASAT activity has crashed the global communication net. For the first time in more than a century, governments cannot communicate instantly with each other, *and they have armies on the move*. Suddenly, horrific levels of global chaos become frighteningly possible. Unless the world's governments collapse before the conflict escalates to nuclear exchanges, (meta)humanity can't hope to survive. And even if events sweep national governments away, isolated spasms of military or corporate activity can still lead to nuke strikes. Even without a global holocaust, civilization as we know it grinds to an end because the corp war has destroyed the Matrix, the communication nets, and the rest of the data-based infrastructure we've come to depend on.

Clearly, no one on this earth can afford the consequences of uncontrolled corporate war.

>>>>>[Frag . . .]<<<<<
—Luke (10:29:27/3-29-54)

>>>>>[Bulldrek. Pure, unadulterated bulldrek. Catastrophism. Paranoia. Idiocy. Alarmism. Forget it, it could never happen. It never has, it never will. Forget about it.]<<<<<
—Honker (03:33:01/3-30-54)

>>>>>[As I said earlier, I think we almost had a corp war start up pretty recently. I don't think we'd actually reached it, because I didn't notice any of the Neo-As' warning signs, but we came much too close. Remember those reports about pitched battles between corp security forces in Seattle, Cheyenne, and other cities? I call that a serious escalation from "business as usual."]<<<<<
—Walesa (18:49:09/4-18-54)

>>>>>[Those weren't sec-forces. Yak and Seoulpa Ring muscleboys scrapped it out for awhile. Just criminal turf wars, maybe with some hired shadowrunners. I'm not sure.]<<<<<
—Skip (03:42:45/4-19-54)

>>>>>[That's the corporate party line, hammered out by every fragging corp-owned news agency in the world. I say bulldrek. Corp forces fought those battles, chummer. I've heard some buzz that MCT and Ares damned near mobilized a few Desert Wars forces. I think Walesa's right, we walked right up to the edge of the precipice.]<<<<<
—TS (07:19:37/4-19-54)

>>>>>[But the corps backed away from it, didn't they? I guess Zurich-Orbital and the Corp Court have a few things going for them.]<<<<<
—Lola (09:50:11/4-19-54)

>>>>>[I don't think the Corp Court pulled the corps back from the brink. I don't know what did, but I doubt the court had anything to do with it.]<<<<<
—Hangfire (13:58:38/4-20-54)

ZURICH-ORBITAL HABITAT

Neither the only orbital habitat nor the largest, the Zurich-Orbital habitat occupies its position of importance solely because so much corporate power resides in it. Home to the Corporate Court and the Gemeinschaft Bank, Zurich-Orbital contains two of the most potent agents of megacorporate influence.

As well as the dirt on those two august organizations, this file includes a little history lesson to help all you dedicated readers understand how Zurich-Orbital became a corp power center. And because I know a lot of runners read this board, I include all the info I have on the habitat's layout, facilities, security, and residents. I sincerely hope to discourage any half-baked plans to strike the place.

HISTORY

After the breakup of the USSR in the early 1990s, the Commonwealth of Independent States (CIS) that replaced it inherited the *Mir* space station. The CIS had enough problems without figuring out what the frag to do with *Mir*, so when Harris-3M offered to buy it outright in the mid-1990s, the Commonwealth government jumped at the prospect.

>>>>>[What did a *Mir* go for back then?]<<<<<
—Virgo (12:55:35/3-25-54)

>>>>>[Don't know, Virgo; the data got lost in the Crash. I'd guess maybe five hundred million, no more than eight (converted into today's nuyen, of course). A fire-sale price, particularly when you consider that a Federated-Boeing Eagle costs about 50 million nuyen. A space station for the price of a squadron of Eagles; the idea boggles the mind.]<<<<<
—Bowers (21:57:31/3-31-54)

Harris-3M acquired launch capabilities from various sources, including China (whose *Long March* rockets had finally started to work worth a drek). Then they shipped research personnel up to *Mir*. (The Harris people unofficially renamed the station *Wheelchair*, apparently in honor of some science fiction writer.)

>>>>>[Doesn't anyone remember Robert A. Heinlein? Tragic.]<<<<<
—Friday (13:00:47/3-29-54)

At the time, nobody understood why Harris-3M wanted *Mir*, even though the company got the bargain of the century. The small, cramped station made a poor platform for the hot research topics of the day, such as growing microcrystals and synthesizing new proteins. The Hubble Space Telescope (recently "fixed") and other satellites made *Mir* redundant for astronomy or Earth analysis. Thinking ahead, Harris-3M figured to acquire more space assets in future. Their *Mir* "training station" taught them what they needed to know for future operations. Of course, they did some research on the side. Key topics of investigation included ways to prevent the progressive deterioration of muscle and bone caused by protracted time in orbit. As part of this research, a couple of so-called "volunteers" remained in zero gravity for more than five years.

>>>>>[The experiment didn't work, by the way. All the drugs, electrostimulation, and so on didn't keep the poor sods from being crippled when they returned to Earth.]<<<<<
—Laker Girl (10:13:40/4-2-54)

>>>>>[Crippled, hell. Of the four "volunteers," three died of heart failure within four months of their return to Earth. The fourth vanished. I suspect Harris took him apart to find out what went wrong with their program.]<<<<<
—Gregoire (18:52:31/4-5-54)

>>>>>[The research work proved that people could stay in orbit for about three years without irreversible damage, a lot longer than anyone had managed in the past. So it wasn't wasted effort.]<<<<<
—Kent (01:20:10/4-6-54)

>>>>>[Tell that to the poor slots who got expended in the program.]<<<<<
—Gregoire (19:05:43/4-6-54)

Just after the turn of the century, the CIS turned militant again. Reform came crashing down, and the hard-liners swept away all traces of democracy except for those they could pervert to their own ends. As a nuclear power, the Russia-dominated CIS had too much clout to take lightly. The Commonwealth "asked" for *Mir* back and Harris-3M politely refused. For the next few months, relations between Harris and the CIS remained tense.

>>>>>[Nice understatement. During this "tense" period of several months, the Russos prevented Harris from launching resupply or rescue missions to the station. Also, Harris never knew if Moscow might lob a missile at the station just for the frag of it. This all went down just after the Shiawase Decision, so the newly extraterritorial Harris was kind of feeling its oats. It had minimal military assets, but as a powerful conglomerate it still had the economic clout to make things really unpleasant for the Russians. If it had, of course, the Russos would have retaliated. Because the CIS hadn't gotten with the extraterritoriality picture, it would have struck not Harris, but the US. The Russos still considered Harris-3M a tool of the capitalist oppressors, or some such revolutionary jargon.

I'd call that a little more than "tense."]<<<<<
—Graves (13:27:39/3-21-54)

Eventually, the CIS decided it had no real use for *Mir* and dropped its demands. *Mir* remained Harris-3M's private station. The *Mir* station met its end in 2008, when a meteor impact holed the hull. The spaceborne rock killed two of the crew outright, and the rest died within a week because Harris failed to launch a rescue mission.

Experts at Harris decided that repairing the damage and returning the station to full operation cost too much for a limited return. The impact had perturbed the station's orbit, making it unstable and dooming the structure to atmospheric re-entry within four years. Instead of stabilizing the orbit, Harris management chose to perform a "public service" by destroying the doomed station before it could re-enter. A shuttle crew installed a powerful Fuel-Air Explosive (FAE) device in the *Mir* as a scuttling charge. On November 25, 2008, Harris detonated the FAE bomb and obliterated the station.

>>>>>[FAE, my butt. They used a nuke. They had the nuclear toys and wanted to play with them. Call it a "test" all you want; I call it boys playing with their toys.]<<<<<
—Yolanda (13:47:30/4-1-54)

>>>>>[I've heard that rumor again and again, even from people who should know better. A nuke couldn't have taken out the *Mir*. If it had, the electromagnetic pulse (EMP) would have fragged with communications and unshielded computer systems all over the world and in space. As it happened, not even the most sensitive RORSAT or astronomical CRsat recorded so much as the tiniest transient. So get off the story, Yolanda. I'm not saying Harris-3M didn't have nukes. They might have, as far as I know. But they didn't use one on *Mir*.]<<<<<
—Blade (04:52:38/4-4-54)

>>>>>[What about a clean, EMP-free nuke?]<<<<<
—Hipp (11:14:39/4-4-54)

>>>>>[Oh yeah, the kind designed by the same people who brought us crop circles, perpetual motion machines, and the 5,000-klick-per-liter carburetor. Ri-i-i-i-ght.]<<<<<
—Larch (00:56:08/4-9-54)

>>>>>[Why scuttle at all? Why not let the sucker burn up?]<<<<<
—Khan (21:43:46/4-10-54)

>>>>>[My great-grandfather lived in Australia when Skylab burned up in the 70s. It scattered crap over a huge footprint, but luckily nothing hit anyone. We're packed so tight these days that 3M figured the odds of someone getting beaned were too high.]<<<<<
—Boomer (20:56:52/4-13-54)

For several years after the *Mir* went down, the United States space station *Freedom* was the only real space station in orbit. Unfortunately, severe budget cutbacks pretty much prevented the

US government from using it. In 2015, as the "Indian Question" became a burning issue on Earth, *Freedom*'s orbit began to decay rapidly. To this day no one knows why. The leading theory points to a solar flare, but no one knows for sure.

>>>>>[Why would a solar flare dick with the orbit of just one orbital object? Why didn't it affect comsats and navsats?]<<<<<
　　—Lydia Free (15:24:41/3-20-54)

>>>>>[If you figure it out, let someone know.]<<<<<
　　—Ralston (03:18:18/3-21-54)

Though the cause remains a mystery, everyone predicted the effect; they expected *Freedom* to brush the upper fringes of the atmosphere by early October of 2017 and burn up within a couple of days. Having committed the bulk of its resources to dealing with Daniel Howling Coyote's Ghost Dancers, the US government couldn't divert the resources needed to save *Freedom*. Instead, they sent a shuttle up to evacuate it.

>>>>>[Even that almost didn't work. Some TerraFirst! eco-terrorist hosed off a man-pack SAM at the shuttle as it came in for a landing. Clean hit, but those ceramic tiles turned out to be tougher than anyone thought.]<<<<<
　　—Blade (05:06:10/4-4-54)

At this point, Ares Macrotechnology's predecessor Ares Industries entered the story. Foundering for years, the US space agency faced yet another funding cutback as a result of the severe United States budget crunch. By 2016, the shuttle program had degenerated into a series of intermittent launches, the agency had all but abandoned its troubled *Freedom* station, and the Hubble continued to experience severe technical problems. Ares stepped in and offered to purchase NASA's physical assets: the shuttle and cargo fleet, the Cape Kennedy launch facilities, installations in Florida and Texas, tracking stations, and so on. Though the US government initially resisted, economic realities and the threat of a falling *Freedom* forced the issue. In mid-2016 Ares Industries took possession of the National Air and Space Administration, and stabilized *Freedom*'s shaky orbit.

Immediately following the stabilization of *Freedom*, Ares and Lloyd's of London together began salvaging billions and billions of dollars worth of lost or abandoned satellites and other orbital material. Ares leveraged itself so deeply to buy up NASA that most observers predicted its failure within two years, but the steady influx of cash from the salvages kept the company afloat.

>>>>>[Just think about that salvage deal. Ares found millions and millions of dollars of lost or disabled communications drek up there, and also plenty of secret military stuff. Ares sold some of that, often back to the original owner, but I heard they kept most of the really really black stuff for their own R&D labs. Also, unlike NASA they actually got the cargo and shuttle operations working efficiently and profitably. Those two things together made Ares a going concern again in less than a decade.]<<<<<
　　—Deiter (20:58:49/4-3-54)

Ares actually used *Freedom* only for a brief time. From 2016 to 2018, Ares expanded the station and used it as its primary staging area for orbital salvage. During that time, Ares also began construction on their own platform, named the *Apollo* for the original United States lunar program. By early 2020 *Apollo* had become Ares' principal space platform, surpassing *Freedom*. *Apollo* later served as the starting point for Ares Macrotechnology's massive *Daedalus* platform. In late 2020, *Freedom* became Zurich-Orbital. Three years later the Corporate Court installed itself there, and the Zurich-Orbital Gemeinschaft Bank established its primary offices in the station in 2034.

IMPORTANT FEATURES

From its beginnings as a relatively small scientific facility, Zurich-Orbital has expanded considerably to become the behemoth we all know and love. The following sections of this file include facts, observations, and best guesses about Zurich-Orbital's location, size, facilities, and other important features.

LOCATION

Zurich-Orbital follows an equatorial orbit around the Earth, as close to perfectly circular as anything its size can achieve. It has an apogee and perigee identical to within less than 1 percent and orbits at an altitude of roughly 560 kilometers. That puts it in low Earth orbit (LEO). One complete orbit of the Earth takes about two and a half hours. I know the number's vague, but the corps keep the habitat's actual location close to their paranoid little chests. Of course, every national government that has space-track equipment has Z-O pegged within the millimeter, and the corps that run the lifts to and from the station have to know its location if they want their ships to get there. But because the corps don't talk about it, nobody without a good data source deep within a military establishment ever knows exactly where Z-O is.

>>>>>[Why, for frag's sake? It's not as if some slotted off shadowrunner can fire a missile at the place . . .]<<<<<
　　—VanZandt (16:25:59/3-21-54)

>>>>>[All chuckling aside, surface-to-orbit missiles (SOMs) can make the boost from the ground and knock out a LEO target. Milspec all the way, these babies are designed to take out an enemy nation's strategic surveillance and nav satellites. Not much of a warhead, really, but if somebody hosed off three at Zurich-Orbital they'd leave a piece just about big enough to make a nice paperweight. Of course, nobody outside a national military complex has the facilities to handle a SOM, even if they could lay hands on one or two.]<<<<<
　　—Blade (02:42:55/3-29-54)

>>>>>[Don't be too sure. Some of the bigger European policlubs might arrange access. Der Nachtmachen could, for one.]<<<<<
　　—Vitale (15:24:05/4-1-54)

>>>>>[Why wouldn't some national military decide to cap Z-O some bright day?]<<<<<
    —Nan (21:42:55/4-1-54)

>>>>>[Can you say "retaliation?" From all corps, everywhere in the world? No. No government would take that risk.]<<<<<
    —Hangfire (01:40:46/4-2-54)

>>>>>[Why is Z-O LEO? Why not geosynchronous?]<<<<<
    —Timmins (13:28:56/4-5-54)

>>>>>[Theoretically, Ares could easily have moved *Freedom* (a.k.a. Zurich-Orbital) out that far. But why should they? Costs more to boost cargo, takes longer to get there, and they get no substantive benefit from the move.]<<<<<
    —Carmen (00:27:05/4-7-54)

SIZE

Most people seeing Zurich-Orbital for the first time, whether for real, in a simsense, or on trid, are struck by its apparently huge size. Though some of the "orbital factories" are several times as large, Z-O's sprawling, almost haphazard design makes it look larger than it is.

Essentially, Zurich-Orbital is just a larger version of the old *Freedom* design. Its most common structural elements match those that made up *Freedom*. The station looks like a series of cylinders, about four meters in diameter and ten meters long, joined together like a kid's erector set. Because all the connection hardware specifically fits the cylinder design, the corps constructed most additions to the habitat in the cylindrical shape.

>>>>>[Note that all these structural elements are modular. If they want to, Z-O personnel can rebuild their habitat to meet changing needs.]<<<<<
    —Flash (05:05:01/4-2-54)

With new launch capabilities, the original station's restrictions on size and mass have changed drastically. The current design of Zurich-Orbital reflects that change. For example, the central element of Z-O's current design, known as "the Rotunda," is an asymmetrical dodecahedron about 30 meters in diameter.

>>>>>[Lift capability still hasn't gotten good enough to lift the Rotunda in one piece. But sure, it's still impressive.]<<<<<
    —Flash (05:06:02/4-2-54)

The accompanying illustration shows a "slice" through Zurich-Orbital to illustrate how the structure fits together. Remember that because Z-O is three-dimensional, you can't image it in two dimensions. If you want to see the thing in its full glory, duck on over to the three-dimensional rendering in another Shadowland node. Also remember that the layout changes according to need. The 3-D rendering is accurate as of 1-14-54, but station personnel may have reconfigured the modules.

Apart from the Rotunda, Z-O has five other significantly atypical structural elements that look more or less like "mini-Rotundas." The 2-D illo only shows two because the others are out of the plane of the illustration. As far as I can discover, a couple of these mini-Rotundas serve as meeting areas or private residences for the habitat's most important inhabitants. The rest look like equipment areas.

>>>>>[Kinda vague . . .]<<<<<
    —Rox (19:55:11/3-29-54)

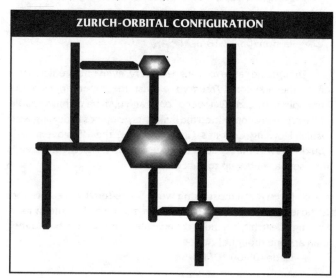

ZURICH-ORBITAL CONFIGURATION

>>>>>[Look, *omae*, why don't you sleaze up there, have a quick boo around, and come back and tell us all about it? And if you can't, quit bagging about "vague" data, scan me?]<<<<<
    —The Neon Antichrist (21:40:24/3-29-54)

FACILITIES

Predictably, Zurich-Orbital's living and working space has remained relatively cramped even for the "primary residents," discussed later in this file. Most of the staff lives in "residence tubes," barracks–like arrangements with four or five people to a single unit. The habitat doesn't spin, so all parts of it have zero gravity. The zero gravity makes normal bunks unnecessary, considerably decreasing space requirements. People hang themselves from hooks on the wall to keep from drifting away, which doesn't sound like a particularly comfortable or spacious environment. Certainly the grunts who actually run the place don't find it so.

>>>>>[Why not spin the sucker?]<<<<<
    —Max (09:31:27/3-21-54)

>>>>>[Couple of reasons. First, NASA never designed *Freedom* for spin, and the corps followed that old design paradigm with every addition they made. Spin it up, and bits fly off. Also, it's asymmetrical so it has no axis around which to spin. Finally, Ares didn't design structural elements such as the residence tubes with the concept of "down" in mind.]<<<<<
    —Flash (15:46:05/3-23-54)

>>>>>[Also, adding gravity would eliminate one of the great attractions of Z-O for the rich old farts who use it to carry out personal experiments in gerontology.]<<<<<
—Doc Dicer (21:02:22/4-5-54)

For others like the primary and secondary residents, accommodations get better. They still have short space, but I hear their quarters are positively luxurious. A secondary resident might have one or even two residence tubes to herself, or for her and a playmate if she wants it that way. A primary resident might have an entire subsection of half a dozen tubes, perhaps including an atypical larger structural element as well. For example, Eiji Yakamura, Z-O's most important primary resident, has personal quarters with a cubic volume equal to a large condo on Earth. Because Zurich-Orbital has zero g, he can use all of that volume, not just the part adjacent to the floor (if you know what I'm getting at).

Other facilities include a medical clinic with a focus on gerontology ("keeping old sods alive") and exercise facilities for staff who rotate back to Earth, to help keep their muscle mass from atrophying. Entertainment facilities are largely simsense-based, because just about everyone up there has a datajack. The staff has a commissary; primary and secondary residents have a gourmet kitchen. (I'd enjoy watching a gourmet chef try to cook in a weightless environment . . .) Air and water recycling facilities, docking facilities for various types of surface-to-orbit craft, similar arrangements for flitters and drek designed only to fly between the different habitats, communications equipment out the hoop, and wiz computer facilities round out the picture.

>>>>>[How about emergency equipment like space lifeboats? Are there enough to hold everyone?]<<<<<
—Barkis (04:02:42/3-23-54)

>>>>>[Thinking about an orbital version of the *Titanic* disaster? You dog, you. Yeah, it has emergency facilities. They're big, reinforced mylar balls, silvered on the outside to reflect sunlight and (some) radiation, that one person climbs inside and inflates. You float around in this ball until someone comes to pick you up. Better than nothing, but not what I'd call overly reassuring.]<<<<<
—Flash (08:58:18/3-25-54)

For Zurich-Orbital's official functions, the communications and computer facilities are the most important. The habitat's communications capabilities rival those of a military comm center, and it has more pure processing horsepower than any other single computer installation, on Earth or off. That computer installation is the Zurich-Orbital Gemeinschaft Bank, and that august organization demands only the best for its operations.

PRIMARY AND SECONDARY RESIDENTS

The primary residents of Zurich-Orbital are a group of high-ranking corporate executives, all retired, all stinking rich, and all older than Methuselah. Based on rumors and hints that living in microgravity can prolong the human life span, these "corporate gods" retired to the habitat, trading in freedom of movement on the Earth for a shot at a few more decades of life.

>>>>>[If I had the money, I'd probably make the same decision.]<<<<<
—Hangfire (11:51:32/4-1-54)

I know nothing about the cost or the process of selecting who gets to buy living space on Z-O. The habitat might have a waiting list fifty names long, or the six slots aboard might be the only people who've ever considered living there. Knowing the corp mentality, candidates most likely have to pay the Corporate Court an astronomical fee for the right to live in the habitat.

>>>>>[The way I hear it, you apply to the Corporate Court for a berth. If they accept you, you don't have to pay a single nuyen. But they make you alter your will so that on your death, every asset you own reverts to the Corp Court. (If you're lucky, they might let you leave your kids a paltry billion or two.) Imagine what that means for someone like Yakamura, who still owns a huge voting block of Mitsuhama stock. When he kicks off, the Corp Court gets that block of Mitsuhama. Depending on who controls the court at that time, that could be an incredible stroke of good luck or the worst conceivable catastrophe for MCT.]<<<<<
—Vargas (15:53:04/4-2-54)

Though retired, most of the primary residents continue to influence the corps that made them rich enough to live out their last days in orbit. Some own huge voting blocks of stock; others presumably know where the bodies are buried and which closets contain skeletons.

>>>>>[Could some people have gone "up the well" to avoid others who'd like to see that knowledge eliminated? Interesting thought.]<<<<<
—Gerard (02:00:58/4-7-54)

>>>>>[According to a rudimentary traffic analysis performed by some chummers in Denver, almost half of all communications between Z-O and Earth come from these old farts trying to control their empires from 500 klicks above their underlings' heads.]<<<<<
—Icebreaker (10:03:55/4-9-54)

I personally know about the six primary residents in the following list. Predictably, Zurich-Orbital issues no press releases discussing their VIPs, so this list could be out of date. Some other bigwig suits may have taken the boost, or some of these slags might have finally shuffled off this mortal coil. I only know for sure that none of these primary residents can ever return to Earth except in a box.

The *éminence grise* of Mitsuhama, **Eiji Yakamura**, 87, still owns a block of voting shares representing anywhere from 15 to 27 percent of the company, depending on whom you believe. Arguably the richest man alive, Yakamura is also the most powerful. Though he no longer attends meetings personally, he remains an honorary member of MCT's board of directors.

>>>>>[Yakamura has tight, tight connections with the yakuza. As I understand it, he's been the yak equivalent of a "made man" ever

since his teenage years back in the late 1970s. He spent the last seventy-odd years as a front man for yak money, and the yaks still own his soul.]<<<<<
—Yuri (23:42:39/3-20-54)

>>>>>[That rumor's floated around for decades, but nobody's ever dug up one iota of concrete proof. Personally, I keep an open mind. It could be true, or it could be an attempt at character assassination made by one of Yakamura's rivals or enemies.]<<<<<
—Reid (23:12:22/3-24-54)

The only woman among the primary residents, **Wilhelmina Graff-Beloit**, 89. may be the most Machiavellian of a Machiavellian crowd. One of the prime movers behind Saeder-Krupp's development into its present glory, she lost voting control when the dragon Lofwyr bought her out.

>>>>>[Back in 1990 or so, Mina Graff worked for an "executive escort service," which means exactly what you think it does. Through her "work" she met and married Michel Beloit, an up-and-comer (no pun intended) with BMW. That company, of course, became the seed around which the Saeder-Krupp empire crystallized. Mina turned out to be a real asset to her husband's career, partially due to the professional skills she learned as an "escort." She rode his coattails into the corporate stratosphere. When Michel died in 2016, Mina took over his position. Much to the disgust of the other execs, they could do sweet frag-all about it. Michel had bequeathed his considerable stock holdings to Mina, and by god she planned to vote them. A couple of people claimed to have evidence that Mina had offed Michel, but they conveniently vanished before producing it. So Mina connived and manipulated herself to the top of Saeder-Krupp, and chaired the board for five years. During her term, she executed corporate purges that made Joe Stalin and Roger Smith look like pikers until Lofwyr appeared on the scene and bought her out. Today she's a bitter old slitch who'd love to frag the dragon somehow. Of course, she's either too scared or too smart to take any action against him.]<<<<<
—Reid (20:18:37/4-5-54)

Sakehisa Tajika, 94, is unique aboard Zurich-Orbital for his background in science rather than business. As a young, rising-star Genentech researcher fresh out of university in the early 1980s, he rode the genetic engineering and biotech wave to its crest and then moved into management. He turned out to be an even more brilliant manager than researcher. Throughout the 1980s and '90s he moved from company to company, starting up new organizations and growing them, then moving on to new challenges. By 2005, he had a rep as a latter-day Midas. Anything he touched turned to gold. In 2010 Ares Industries absorbed his organization, EoTech, and he started his climb up the Ares corporate hierarchy. From 2023 through 2028 Tajika served as CEO of Ares, getting out just before the Crash. He served on the board from 2029 through 2040, and as chairman of the board from 2041 to 2043. Despite his wealth and power, his fellow board members eased him off the board in 2043 when he started getting senile.

>>>>>[The way I hear it, the board arranged for Tajika to take the lift to Z-O. Calling it a "retirement gift," they got him out of the way and freed themselves at least partly from his influence.]<<<<<
—Reid (20:20:28/4-5-54)

Another ex-MCT exec and board member, **Agatamori Kihara**, 94, had a plodding career, working his way up from corporate counsel to CEO and eventually to the board through sheer hard work and dedication. All this effort earned him incredible wealth and four stress-induced heart attacks. He chaired the MCT board until 2037, when he got caught in random gang violence and took three rounds to the chest. Citing health reasons, he resigned from the board.

>>>>>[. . . to be succeeded by Eiji Yakamura, who could easily have orchestrated the "random gang violence" to remove a rival. In any case, Kihara has the same yak connections as Yakamura, though his personal patrons seem to have less clout than Eiji's.]<<<<<
—Reid (20:22:26/4-5-54)

>>>>>[So Yakamura might have arranged for Kihara to get shot? Must lead to some interesting dinner table conversation.]<<<<<
—Bung (16:03:21/4-9-54)

One of the many princes of the Kingdom of Hawaii, **Prince Donald K. Ho III**, 83, was so far down the succession that only pandemic could have seated him on the Throne of Kamehameha. A lawyer and world-famous economist, Ho's a real cutthroat when it comes to corporate climbing. He leapfrogged from corp to corp, riding out the Crash with Renraku and then jumping to Yamatetsu. There, he climbed to the peak and became chairman of the board when the corp moved its headquarters from Tokyo to Kyoto.

>>>>>[He had no more competence than other Yamatetsu chairmen. His power and influence came not from his business smarts, but from his colossal wealth. During his leapfrogging days, he acquired stock in every corp he worked for. He remains an honorary member of the board at Yamatetsu (no surprise), Ares, and Renraku. Through intelligent trading, old Prince Ho makes money no matter which megacorp takes the lead in the ongoing intercorp rivalry.]<<<<<
—Reid (20:25:48/4-5-54)

The youngest primary resident of Zurich-Orbital, **Yuri Severenko**, 80, is also the most mysterious. Nobody seems to know how he got up there. He sat on Renraku's board of directors during the late 2030s, but apparently did nothing to distinguish himself from countless other seat-warmers. He never served as chairman, and apparently owns little Renraku stock. Despite this total lack of distinction, he lives in Z-O. There's a fascinating story here, and I wish I knew it.

>>>>>[It galls me to admit that I don't know it, either. I've checked out Severenko's history, and found nothing unusual. He's a moderately successful corporate climber and a plutocrat, of

course, but his known assets don't even put him on the list of the 100 richest people in the world. I can only guess that he has unknown assets or some greater influence than his track record shows. If I find out anything I'll post it, but I don't hold out much hope. I can't even find any leads to follow up on.]<<<<<
   —Reid (21:10:12/4-9-54)

Though they're nowhere near as rich, Zurich-Orbital has some pretty fragging influential secondary residents as well. Unlike the six old farts above, these guys don't live permanently in Z-O. None of them ever spends more than a year in the habitat before rotating back to Earth. They act as managers assigned by the Corporate Court to run Zurich-Orbital and all its facilities, and as members of the court itself.

Much sketchier information exists on these guys than on the primary residents. Not surprising, considering that secondary residents make up the Corp Court and the Z-O Bank. Because of the steady turnover of the court and the bank board, anyone able to dig up the orbital's next rotation of seat-warmers can gain significant control over the entire corporate world through blackmail, bribery, or intimidation. For this reason, the corps keep as quiet as possible about who's taken the boost recently and who's due in the near future. Even the total number of secondary residents changes with every rotation. I think about 20 live up there now, but don't anyone quote me. I only know there must be at least the thirteen justices sitting on the Corporate Court.

>>>>>[Wrong. Contrary to popular misconception, not all of the Corporate Court justices live aboard Zurich-Orbital during their

tenure on the bench. Some shuttle back and forth between the surface and the habitat; others never even set foot on Z-O. After all, they don't have to. The justices can meet virtually through a secure corner of the Matrix anytime they feel like it. Physical proximity isn't necessary.]<<<<<
   —Manx (11:24:54/3-21-54)

>>>>>[True, but sometimes it's useful. A little while back, something weird went down in the corporate world and all thirteen of the Court justices took the lift to Z-O for consultation. I can only figure that the subject of discussion had to be totally secure from surveillance, and Z-O's about the only place in the world with guaranteed security. Think about it. The habitat controls its own comm channels, and can isolate itself temporarily if necessary. It did that for three hours, soon after the last justice arrived in orbit. Also, mages and shamans can't function outside the Gaiasphere if they value their sanity, and magical surveillance doesn't work from ground to orbit. So Z-O is safe from that kind of spying as well.]<<<<<
   —PointBreak (00:42:53/3-24-54)

>>>>>[Anybody know what they were jawing about up there?]<<<<<
   —Den (21:02:29/3-25-54)

>>>>>[No, huh?]<<<<<
   —Den (20:43:37/4-10-54)

STAFF

These guys actually keep Zurich-Orbital functioning. They tweak the computers, maintain the environmental plant, swab the decks, cook the food, and patch the holes made by high-velocity dust specks. Grunts they may be, but they're highly specialized grunts, trained specifically for their jobs on the habitat. They have a level of training and professionalism equal to the enlisted crew aboard a nuclear sub.

In fact, duty aboard a nuke sub makes a good analogy for Z-O service. (Wow, glad I thought of it.) Both have the same confinement, isolation, and close quarters, plus similar tours of duty. Z-O staff typically work 90 to 120 days, then rotate groundside. Apparently, some of these guys prefer Z-O to planetside work, probably because they get paid constant overtime and special-duty pay. And because they have no place to spend their money while in orbit, they can stash it all away in savings.

Understandably, Z-O vets its staff under incredibly tight security. One terrorist on a suicide mission can ruin everyone's day, so security checks are as stringent as modern technology allows.

>>>>>[Z-O has flip-flopped on one of their selection criteria. In the early days, they chose staff without families on the assumption that terrorists might threaten those families and force the staff in orbit to do something heinous. That changed a few years ago, when the corp bigwigs who own Z-O realized that they could use families as leverage. Now only family men and women get tapped for Z-O duty. For as long as any given staff member stays in orbit, his or her family resides within a corporate enclave. The families act as hostages to ensure the staff's good behavior, even though the corps pitch it to candidates as a perk. "While you work in orbit, your family lives in luxury for free," and all that drek.]<<<<<
—Turner (12:19:42/4-1-54)

>>>>>[This tactic makes it exceptionally difficult to bribe or otherwise force habitat staff to do anything not perfectly kosher. If they do something bad, their family gets drekked upon. Exactly what the corps had in mind.]<<<<<
—Argent (21:02:15/4-6-54)

As far as I can tell, all candidates for Z-O service have worked for their current megacorp for at least five years and have spotless employment records. Almost no one can manage to sleaze into Z-O service from outside the megacorporate environment.

COMMUNICATIONS

Access channels to Zurich-Orbital have equally tight security, no surprise. Though in absolute terms a lot of information gets channeled back and forth between Z-O's systems and stations on the ground, in relative terms Zurich-Orbital has much lower comm requirements than your average corporate headquarters. Also, only a small percentage of the communication load is highly interactive, such as VR connections to the Matrix. Most communications are actually financial transactions to and from the Gemeinschaft Bank, and few bankers and brokers use full VR Matrix "presence" for this kind of work even when they can. This means

that Z-O can funnel its communications load through a handful of downlinks, each of which they've loaded with some of the nastiest IC in existence.

Zurich-Orbital works entirely on dedicated lines, with full handshaking between the two ends of the link. It has full confirmation with limited re-establishment . . . oh, frag the technical details. In English, all the technoese means that Zurich-Orbital only establishes a communication line with ground stations that it already "knows" about. That database of acceptable stations is in a datastore that gets isolated whenever Z-O is actually on-line with the ground. This setup prevents people from decking in and telling Z-O to expect a call from any old portable satlink.

>>>>>[Theoretically, you could send a smart frame in. In practical terms, the ice is so thick and so black that nothing like a frame can possibly make it through.]<<<<<
—FastJack (12:58:10/3-23-54)

In other words, even if you know the communication frequency and parameters, protocol, and encryption algorithms, you can't communicate with Zurich-Orbital from any unauthorized uplink and expect to crack into the habitat's computers. The habitat does have radio and laser comms with the ground, and you could send a voice message to the station if, say, you wanted to inform them that your chummers had launched a SOM at them. But you'd get no answer back, and no data linkup no matter how much you whine, cry and lie.

>>>>>[So you icepick your way into one of the authorized uplinks and piggyback on a signal that they expect.]<<<<<
—API (15:01:48/3-29-54)

>>>>>[Yah, sure. Easy . . . null. The uplink nodes, which are the SANs you've got to crash through, have a fragging ridiculous amount of security layered onto them. If any single corp ran them, the cost of installing enough processing juice to handle the traffic *plus* the level of ice would put them out of biz. But because the same megacorps that maintain the Corp Court and the corp bank run them cooperatively, cost ceases to be an issue.

The SANs usually have Matrix icons that look like little radio telescopes, and are considered "ultra-secure." That gives them ratings of Red-6 and up. Be warned.]<<<<<
—Icebreaker (11:44:28/3-30-54)

>>>>>[And that's just on the groundside end of the link. Expect even tougher security at the Z-O end of the datapipe.]<<<<<
—The Kernel (12:56:23/3-30-56)

>>>>>[Just try finding the uplink nodes in the first place. They're located in restricted regions of the Matrix, and you've got to go through at least one SAN to even get into the "neighborhood." That SAN alone has tough security, and you've also got to know which SANs take you where you want to go. You can bet that the corps haven't installed signposts reading, "This way to Zurich-Orbital."]<<<<<
—TS (03:14:42/4-1-54)

ACCESS

Supplies and replacement personnel reach the habitat mainly via suborbitals with strap-on tanks and boosters, and occasionally by shuttles based on the old American or Russian design. More frequently nowadays, they go up on task-designed lifters specifically constructed for the boost to LEO. By long-standing tradition supported by largely unenforceable contracts, all of the key megacorporations that support the Corp Court and the Gemeinschaft Bank take turns handling and paying for provisioning and personnel flights. Rare flights between Zurich-Orbital and the other habitats do occur, but only under exceptional circumstances and only when initiated by Z-O.

On the North American continent, lifts to orbit most frequently depart from Kennedy International in New York (formerly JFK), O'Hare in Chicago, and Dallas/Fort Worth in Texas. Less frequent flights boost from Sky Harbor in Phoenix. SeaTac handles occasional special-mission lifts, but has no scheduled service. Missions heavier than suborbital flights must depart from special launch facilities, most often the Ares-run Cape Kennedy site in Florida, CAS. Some lifts also go up from the CalFree SkyLift facility, built on the remains of the US Military orbital launch facility at the former Vandenburg Air Force Base. Lifts also depart from other sites such as French Guyana, North Africa, and so on.

>>>>>[How does someone catch a boost to Z-O?]<<<<<
—Panther (17:45:09/4-13-54)

>>>>>[He doesn't, unless that "someone" has really hot connections. You can't catch flights to Zurich-Orbital like you'd catch the old semiballistic missile from SeaTac to Narita. Flights don't lift every hour on the hour. They get scheduled weeks in advance. The realities of orbital mechanics such as launch windows and all that drek mean that everyone has to know precisely who and what goes aboard long before the actual lift takes place. That allows plenty of time for security provisions.]<<<<<
—Flash (03:46:58/4-14-54)

>>>>>[Flash is dead right. Say you want to catch the lift to Z-O. First, you've got to get on the passenger/crew list. That means the corp handling this particular lift has to know everything about you, from height and fingerprints to DNA and retinal patterns. They've also got to know your exact mass and the mass of everything you plan on taking with you, damned near down to the gram. Granted, I'm restricting my discussion to suborbital lifts. But all you oh-so-bright jokers can forget about getting aboard a shuttle or special-craft flight. You've got as much chance of pulling that off as of conning your way aboard a 1990s-era shuttle flight.

So you arrive at the terminal processing station twelve hours before the lift. Even if you're a high muckamuck, the processing station personnel put you through the most stringent security checks of your life. They run you over with every detector known to mankind: chemsniffers, metal detectors, X-rays, maybe even a quick NMR scan just for the frag of it. They have to make sure that you aren't willingly or unwillingly, consciously or unconsciously, carrying anything that might pose a problem during the flight or once you reach the habitat. And they know just what to look for.

They've seen people pass through with devices implanted in their flesh and bones, some without knowing it. Just as an example, Greenwar tried booby-trapping a computer technician with a belly bomb in the mid-40s. They'll also check your identity by every means available, including retina scan, fingerprint, voiceprint, and DNA typing. Then the mages give you the once-over to make sure no one's put you under a magical compulsion to simultaneously open both doors in an airlock or any other such drek. They take these precautions even though magic becomes totally undependable once you leave the Gaiasphere. See how seriously they take their jobs? Meanwhile, your luggage undergoes the same process with even more bulldrek, because it can't whine and bitch. So forget about smuggling something lethal, chummers. They'll find it, and they'll nail you for it.

With safeguards like that, only official passengers can take the lift from Earth to Zurich-Orbital. If anyone figures out a way to beat the system, please let me know.]<<<<<
—Hangfire (06:57:07/4-16-54)

>>>>>[They only want to make sure that the person who turns up in the flesh is the one authorized by their computer records to take the flight. So just alter the records to authorize yourself.]<<<<<
—Truman (09:40:52/4-16-54)

>>>>>[Do you really think the same corps that are so fragging paranoid about computer security on access lines to Z-O will get lax about protecting their passenger manifests? Give me a break! Processing before the lift means plenty more than an airline employee carrying a pocket secretary with a list of names. These guys use an Ultra system built around dedicated fiber optic lines, multi-cyclic encryption, and tell-me-four-times redundancy on each data packet sent. If I had to guess at a benchmark for the security, I'd put it at a minimum of Red-5. Possibly plenty higher.]<<<<<
—Icebreaker (18:09:00/4-16-54)

>>>>>[Going back to the original question, Panther, presumably you want to go to Z-O for a run. Not a particularly interesting vacation destination, is it? So some corp must have hired you. Can your Johnson certify you through the corp's channels? (Assuming your employer has a presence on Z-O, of course.) You just might make it that way.]<<<<<
—Hangfire (06:52:52/4-17-54)

>>>>>[How about stowing away? Try hiding in a crate marked "Toilet Paper" or something, with a registered mass equal to you plus your gear.]<<<<<
—Tiger (14:17:18/4-17-54)

>>>>>[There's one in every crowd. You want an answer to that one, brainwipe, go back and reread the previous posts. Everything that goes aboard the lifter gets run through every kind of security check known to man. One of those is *bound* to distinguish between 85 kilos of drekwipe and 85 kilos of drekhead, *neh*? Frag, the first mage who assenses the contents of your crate can blow your cover. And by the way, don't try setting up a hermetic circle

to keep you hidden. That mage will wonder mightily why toilet paper needs astral protection.]<<<<<

Thinking of going aboard with the maintenance team and not coming off? Hiding in the equivalent of the closet? No go there, either. They know the mass of everything and everyone going aboard. They won't overlook 85 kilos of additional, unaccounted-for mass.]<<<<<

—Flash (16:20:00/4-23-54)

>>>>>[Think about this, chummers. A few people have hinted at it earlier on this board, but never stated it strongly enough. Practicing mystics of any stripe, whether shamans, hermetics, druids, or anything else, don't exist aboard Zurich-Orbital. Some people up there might be magical adepts, but they can't do anything that connects them to astral space. No throwing spells, no assensing, no nothing. If they try, they'll go incurably mad. If they're lucky, the attempt will kill them outright. No one can have magical items like fetishes or foci up there, because leaving the Gaiasphere drains the objects of power. So for those of you who dream of going back to the "good old days" before magic returned to the world, the habitats are the place for you.]<<<<<

—Kombi (13:42:04/4-25-54)

>>>>>[Actually, rumor has it that magic does work outside of the Gaiasphere, but not in the way earthbound magicians expect. I don't know the specifics, but supposedly it's a different metamagical technique.]<<<<<

—Mr. Mystic (10:13:53/4-26=54)

>>>>>[Impossible. Magic requires mana, lots of it. Only life has mana, and it takes more than a couple of dozen people and a few plants in zero-g to create a biofield. Sorry chummers, modern myth.]<<<<<

—Theorist (21:59:51/4-27-54)

>>>>>[The lack of mana also affects how long staff and secondary residents can stay on Z-O. You can prevent zero-g atrophying of muscle mass and skeletal structure regardless of the length of exposure, but all the methods depend on magic!]<<<<<

—Mox (23:01:16/4-28-54)

CORPORATE COURT

Compared to the length of time that megacorporations have dominated world affairs, the Corporate Court is a relatively recent innovation. Its precursors include organizations such as OPEC, the 20th-century oil-producing cartel. Though limited when compared to the modern-day Corp Court, its influence still affected the actions of major corporations much as the court's actions do today.

HISTORY

In the heady years after the Shiawase Decision, the megacorporations explored the limits of their newfound freedoms. Conflicts and confrontations ensued, too limited to qualify as corporate war but still disruptive to the business community. By this time, corporations fell into two rough categories: the so-called

megacorporations and everyone else. Though the megacorps had attained nowhere near the size or influence in the years before 2010 that they have in the 2050s, they had vast power compared to run-of-the-mill multinational conglomerates.

>>>>>[Simplification. No cut-and-dried distinction between megacorporations and "everyone else" ever existed. Marginal cases abounded everywhere you looked.]<<<<<

—Nuyen Nick (11:32:45/3-21-54)

When confrontations between minor corps flared up and interfered with the profligate moneymaking of the big boys, said big boys usually cooperated in pressuring the fractious small fry to quit drekking in the corporate pot. This collective strategy worked quite efficiently to keep brushfire-level corporate conflict from interfering with business. But when the megacorps themselves became combatants, no coalition of "big boys" existed that could put the lean on them and remind them to play nicely with other children. On the rare occasions when groups of uninvolved corps tried to apply pressure, one or both of the combatants invariably perceived the outsiders' attitude as favoritism or a display of partisan interests. In fact, the very presence of outside corps threatened to widen the conflict by drawing them into it. The corps soon realized that any attempts by independent megacorps to break up conflicts risked escalation into full-fledged corp wars; but in the interests of a healthy business climate, they could not simply allow the squabbling parties to strike each other with impunity.

>>>>>[Particularly as megacorps started to build and equip military forces.]<<<<<

—Lynx (12:27:32/3-24-54)

After a particularly unpleasant tiff between the megacorp Keruba (prior to its absorption by Renraku) and the fast-growing "extended" BMW conglomerate that existed just before BMW spawned Saeder-Krupp, the megacorps realized that they had to impose collective controls on their own behavior. After Keruba reduced one of BMW's major research establishments to a smoking crater, BMW retaliated by trying to take out one of Keruba's key comm satellites. (Barely missed it.) By the time the two corps skulked back to their respective corners, they'd both lost billions of petrodollars in the exchange of hostilities. The other megacorps were out of pocket too, having spent all kinds of money on defensive schemes to prevent the unpleasantness from spreading to their operations. All in all, the dust-up had cost megacorporate society well over one trillion petrodollars. Regarding such a cost as unacceptable, the megacorps scrambled for a way to stop the infighting. The so-called "Big Seven" megacorps of Keruba, BMW, Ares, Shiawase, Mitsuhama, ORO (which became Aztechnology), and JRJ (later absorbed by Fuchi) agreed to form a central committee to represent the interests of all megacorporations. In 2012, as the world reeled from the consequences of the Awakening, representatives from the Big Seven formed the Inter-Corporate Council (ICC), a seven-member corporate board.

>>>>>[Actually, the Awakening itself forced the megacorps to do something to scale back damaging conflict. Remember the stuff posted earlier about how social and economic uncertainty leads to more takeovers? Well, the time directly after the Awakening had the highest level of uncertainty the world had seen for a good few centuries. Rampant takeover fever led to further megacorporate conflict, and endless possible repetitions of the Keruba-BMW antagonism on an even more destructive level.]<<<<<
—Keynesian Kid (16:24:00/4-2-54)

In its original form, the ICC had no real authority. It had no assets of its own, no security personnel, no police force, and no military. It could only draw on assets seconded to it by the megacorps that created and supported it. In effect, the vaunted ICC served solely as a secure, organized forum for reps of the megacorps to discuss issues that arose between them. Predictably, such a toothless organization didn't work worth a drek. If one corp had a beef with another, raising it in the ICC got them nothing but denials and arguments from the subject of that beef. In many cases, the offending corp's ICC rep knew nothing about the problem. At the time, standard corporate practice assigned minor execs to the post of ICC rep, and kept them in the dark about any shady activities. That way, the rep could honestly get up on his hind legs and claim ignorance of any activity with which another rep took issue.

In 2013, the ICC met and failed its first major test. Keruba and ORO went at each other with knives out, for reasons never adequately explained in the history books. When the cutting wound down and Keruba and ORO retired to lick their wounds, the other corps concluded that in order for the ICC to have a prayer of working, the CEO or his personal designate from each corp must sit on the council.

This solution didn't work, either. The ever-so-busy CEOs couldn't take time from their full schedules to get together for a regular blather with their opposite numbers. After the first meeting of the redesigned ICC, every single CEO sent a personal designate who didn't know squonk about his corp's business and interests. Despite these unpromising starts, after the ICC went through three or four more incarnations the megacorps realized that the dang thing finally seemed to be working. The mere existence of an independent body intended to help defuse tensions, even one that lacked clout, seemed to make a significant difference in the level of corporate bloodletting.

>>>>>[Not to say that inter-corp conflicts disappeared during this time. Some of them got pretty nasty. But they seemed less frequent than before, and they also seemed to peter out before they did as much damage.]<<<<<
— Keynesian Kid (16:27:01/4-2-54)

During the years when the Big Seven fiddled around with the ICC, the corporate situation changed drastically enough to affect a couple of the Big Seven themselves. Keruba got absorbed into a Johnny-come-lately called Renraku, which took over Keruba's position on the ICC. Meanwhile, BMW evolved into Saeder-Krupp. Some of the small fry such as Yamatetsu grew into

significant megacorporations. As for the minor corps, they had grown large enough to make spats between them almost as damaging as the megacorporate Keruba-BMW dust-up had been. Belatedly, the Big Seven realized that the ICC might help them keep other fractious organizations under control. Of course, a name as dull as the Inter-Corporate Council didn't sound particularly daunting. To give the council a more imposing air, they renamed it the International Corporate Court. (No reason to change the letterhead and business cards, after all.) Within a few months, the name was simplified to Corporate Court.

During its first few years, the court underwent several more changes until it settled into its modern, familiar form. The megacorporate environment also underwent changes; ORO Corporation became Aztechnology and Yamatetsu made its successful bid for prominence. In 2023, the Corporate Court relocated to Zurich-Orbital and has remained aboard the habitat ever since.

COURT STRUCTURE

The Corporate Court of 2054 consists of thirteen justices selected from the major megacorporations of the world (actually the old Big Seven plus a few newcomers such as Yamatetsu). An extensive clerical and research staff supports them, but the court still has no police or security forces of its own.

>>>>>[In fact, even the clerical/research personnel are officially on the payroll of the different megacorps. Theoretically, the corps can withdraw them at any time. The Corporate Court exists solely on the megacorps' good graces. Does that really surprise anyone?]<<<<<
        —Vark (14:21:51/3-29-54)

Justices serve a six-and-a-half-year term, though they can be recalled. Used only once, the recall process took so long that someone greased the slag in question before it ended. Judicial terms are staggered, with a new justice coming to the bench every six months. That means the entire court changes every six and a half years. A justice can serve any number of consecutive terms.

A special commission made up of representatives from each of the so-called "AAA" megacorporations selects Corporate Court justices. Each time a justice comes up for election, these representatives vote to confirm or reject him. Unlike the standard one-man-one-vote of a democracy, the vote of a more powerful corporation's rep counts more than the vote from a rep belonging to a less powerful corp. A ridiculously complicated formula weighs votes based on the characteristics of each corporation, including asset mix, revenue, net worth, and so on *ad nauseam*. With this kind of set-up, a corp significantly more powerful than its rivals can stack the court. The practice of confirming only two new justices per year makes such stacking a slow process, but a corp long-sighted enough to bide its time can make itself even more powerful by controlling the court.

>>>>>[Which adds a lot more incentive to keep every corp's membership on the Corp Court at about the same level. If someone like Ares starts pulling far enough ahead of the pack to give it a lock on the court, every other megacorp will do whatever it can to pull Ares down before it can capitalize on its advantage.]<<<<<
        —Turner (14:47:58/4-2-54)

>>>>>[What a stupid, drekheaded idea. As if the corps needed another reason to compete.]<<<<<
        —Tenmace (01:42:33/4-3-54)

>>>>>[I figure the megacorps did it on purpose to keep things evened out. It seems to have worked. The "Big Eight" seem pretty evenly matched in influence.]<<<<<
        —Turner (13:59:48/4-3-54)

>>>>>[Who decides who's a triple-A megacorp anyway?]<<<<<
        —Pip (14:50:36/4-3-54)

>>>>>[The Corporate Court. Incestuous, isn't it? A great way to make sure that the "old boys' club" controls things and keeps Johnny-come-latelies out. Actually, the Corp Court charter guarantees that the founding seven corps Ares, Aztechnology, Fuchi, Mitsuhama, Renraku, Saeder-Krupp and Shiawasecan never be disenfranchised by losing their AAA rating.]<<<<<
        —Nuyen Nick (02:49:08/4-4-54)

Personnel

The latest roster of the Corporate Court justices on the following pages include each one's megacorp affiliations and anything else the Neo-Anarchists could dig up about them. All of the sitting justices are experienced corporate lawyers, but in fact a place on the court requires no formal qualifications.

Dosan Aburakoji: About 55, he's close to the median age for this court. This hard-charger rose from MCT's arbitrage department after making a killing selling deutschemarks short in 2038.

Marlene Carstairs: The youngest justice at 43, she's also the newest. A Saeder-Krupp rep, Carstairs got elected to the bench in December of 2052.

>>>>>[She has known ties to various European policlubs, including one called Alte Welt.]<<<<<
        —Reid (15:35:40/4-2-54)

>>>>>[Alte Welt is a front for another poli, but I don't know which.]<<<<<
        —Magister (16:05:21/4-2-54)

Domingo Chavez: Like most Aztechnology suits, he might as well have been magically created when he took his seat on the board last year for all the history we could dig up on the slag. No age available, no background, no nothing except that he's apparently never actually visited Zurich-Orbital. That might mean he's a mage who doesn't want to curtail his activities. On the other hand, it could mean something completely different.

Korekado "Corey" Doi: Look up "charisma" in a hypertext dictionary and you'll find Corey's hologram. He's charming, easy to talk to, has a great sense of humor and a self-effacing style. He's also an absolute cutthroat. Affiliated with MCT, he has suspected yakuza ties (no surprise), and probably some close chummers in the Kyoto shadow community.

Paul Graves: At the age of 50, he looks about 30. In top shape, this Ares rep looks like an urban brawl player wearing a 5,000-nuyen suit. Graves comes across as the archetypal blunt instrument, acting on such inspiring mottoes as, "Why use one word when a lawsuit will do?" and "Politeness is for pukers."

>>>>>[Graves has something deep and dark buried securely in his past. I suspect he got his law degree late in life, perhaps after protracted military service.]<<<<<
        —Blade (15:43:50/4-1-54)

Yoshiko Hino: From Yamatetsu, she's drop-dead gorgeous even in her early 50s (ah, the wonders of cosmetic surgery). A slender lady with a classically beautiful face, her voice would turn a eunuch on. She knows it, and she uses it. Behind all that beauty, her heart's a pocket computer. Rumor has it she sold her blood for a healthy profit and replaced it with ice water.

Jonathan Msaki: Unique among the justices, he also serves as a director of an MCT subsidiary. That position puts him more "in the loop" than his colleagues on the bench. He may actually believe that corporations have some responsibility to the Earth and (meta)humanity at large, or he may simply be a champion liar.

>>>>>[Which do you think is more likely?]<<<<<
   —Gray Cloud (03:10:48/3-26-54)

Francesco "Paco" Napoli: He comes from the European side of the Renraku operation, and has a rep as one of the megacorp's better expediters. However, we haven't succeeded in digging up much to prove or disprove this rumor.

>>>>>[No wonder, if you're searching under the name of Napoli. Try "Tomba" and you'll find more. Ricardo Tomba has had a long career as an executive trouble-shooter of sorts. He spent years moving around within Renraku's latticework of divisions and subsidiaries, rearranging programs and structures, bringing executives into line, firing incompetents, and so on. A real hatchet man. He has no problem bringing in shadow assets when necessary, and he's not above "negating" them afterward. A real charmer.]<<<<<
   —Hangfire (14:52:26/4-5-54)

Beatrice N'guma: Apparently a real disappointment to her masters at Fuchi HQ, she's been a nonentity on the bench. Her term ends in June, and she has a slim to nonexistent chance of serving another.

>>>>>[Fuchi's already wired about having only one justice, and the one they've got seems mute. N'guma hails from the Yamana-Fuchi camp, so that gives the Nakatomi and Villiers pieces of the Fuchi mess some more leverage.]<<<<<
   —Victor Victor (12:51:54/4-6-54)

Akae Ono: Yet another Ares affiliate, Ono seems to like life aboard Zurich-Orbital. He may be trying it on for size in case he ever becomes a primary resident. As yet he's old enough, but nowhere near rich or powerful enough. The week after he got booted up to the bench in December 2051, he took the lift to Z-O and has never come back down. A competent old snake, Ono has an uncanny ability to read people.

>>>>>[Ono and Carstairs, the babe from Saeder-Krupp, hate each other big-time. I don't know why, and that picks me. It looks more complicated than just a personality clash. Instead, it reads like they know each other from earlier in their careers and never got over bad blood.]<<<<<
   —Louis White Owl
      (07:01:46/4-3-54)

>>>>>[I can't tell for sure, but I can guess at a reason. Carstairs has links with the European polis, and I've heard hints that Ono had some connection with Japan's Red Band terrorists. The Red Band got badly mauled when they tried to run some ops in Germany. That might be the Ono-Carstairs connection.]<<<<<
   —Turner (10:04:25/4-9-54)

Jean-Claude Priault: A Saeder-Krupp affiliate, Priault is considered the elder statesman of the current court even though he's a couple of years younger than Ono. His face looks like a classical master sculptor carved it out of marble. Apparently, he knows everything worth knowing about corporate and tax law and the eccentricities of different jurisdictions. Also, he's supposed to have an absolutely wicked sense of humor, dry as dust but scalpel-sharp. His idea of a good insult is the kind where the victim sits up in bed at 3 a.m. two days after Priault nailed him, going, "Oh, *yeah*?"

Samuel "Violent" Violet: Seattle-born and bred, Violet believes that some legal questions are best settled with a bullet to the brain, preferably fired by an "unattributable asset" hired out of the sprawl's alleyways. (And eliminated immediately thereafter, of course.) One of Renraku's bright boys, he's something of a womanizer. According to rumor, he and Marlene Carstairs have a thing going.

>>>>>[Old news, *omae*. Carstairs dropped him like a drek-soiled dishrag last week, and arranged things so that Mrs. Violet found out about the affair. Sammy's one unhappy justice at the moment.]<<<<<
   —Reid (04:21:29/3-23-54)

>>>>>[News flash: Samuel Violet decided yesterday that his responsibilities called him to Zurich-Orbital for the entire year and a half remaining in his term of office. His lovely wife, needless to say, remains groundside spending his credit.]<<<<<
   —Reid (21:34:03/4-11-54)

Lorraine Wakizaka: Shiawase's justice is a cold one. Margarine wouldn't melt in her mouth, but she excels at her job. Until her election to the bench, she sued people for a living. Anybody. As often as possible. Another corp cut into your market share? Sue the bastards. Somebody stole a march on you in research & development? Sue the bastards. Somebody mentioned in passing that their products are marginally compatible with Shiawase's? Sue the bastards. Nice lady, Ms. Wakizaka.

PAN-CORPORATE LAW

Because of their extraterritoriality, multinational megacorporations need only obey those laws promulgated by the Corporate Court. On paper at least, national divisions must obey national laws such as tax law and so on, but only the Corporate Court has jurisdiction over the corps as a whole.

Predictably, the court promulgates few laws that actually mean anything. A whole body of law exists concerning the committee that elects justices to the court, the structure and management of the Gemeinschaft Bank, and the payment of salaries for the Corporate Court's support staff. The court has all kinds of laws governing what they consider important, such as who handles next month's reprovisioning flight to Zurich-Orbital and who pays the tab if the habitat gets hit by a high-velocity Hasselblad left behind by a previous space mission. But all these laws essentially maintain the Corp Court's infrastructure, and have little effect on megacorporate activity. The following statements represent the few considerations that actually affect corporate behavior.

•Don't try to overthrow a national government unless you can get away with it.

Corps tend to frown on knocking over governments, because bringing down a government means that somebody gets stuck dealing with garbage collection and other background noise. Taking care of such minutiae in lieu of a legitimate government distracts the corps from their manifest destiny of making grotesque amounts of nuyen.

•If you break it (or geek it), pay for it.

If another corp can prove that you "wastefully" expended some of their assets by blowing up their lab or killing their people or whatever, you have to pay them a sum equal to the replacement cost of the assets.

>>>>>[Note that the wronged corp has to prove it, and proof lies entirely in the eyes of the court justices. If one corp has a lock on the court as MCT does at the moment, that corp's justices tend not to accept any evidence as proof of that corp's wrongdoing.]<<<<<
—Legal Beagle (22:41:05/3-24-54)

>>>>>[This is the closest thing pan-corporate law has to a murder charge. If Corp A kills Corp B's personnel, Corp B can't charge Corp A with murder. It can only try to recoup the cost of hiring replacements. And pan-corporate law has no rules against killing your own assets.]<<<<<
—Knocker (14:22:21/3-26-54)

•Don't go to war.

The actual legal text concerning this no-no comprises several terapulses of data, all of which boils down to forbidding any actions definable as corp war.

These three points comprise the only portion of corp law that actually applies to megacorp activity. Beyond that, the corps can do what they fragging well please. Really.

Authority and Enforcement

In this interesting area, we see a classic example of the difference between theory and practice. In theory, the Corporate Court has total authority over everything that the megacorporations do. In practice, it has little authority to enforce its own rules. The Corp Court can promulgate pan-corporate laws until it's blue in the collective face, but no matter how draconian the penalities of those laws or the implied enforcement, the court can do squonk about it if anyone breaks those laws. This schizoid state of affairs exists because the Corporate Court has no enforcement assets. None; zero; nada. It has no "Pan-Corporate Police" or "Pan-Corporate Army," not even a "Pan-Corporate Scolding Team." The Corp Court has as much real power as the old United Nations.

>>>>>[Worse than that, *omae*. The old UN had peacekeeping forces, seconded by national armies but under UN orders. The Corp Court doesn't even have that much.]<<<<<
—Blade (17:09:59/3-27-54)

What power the Corp Court has over megacorporate activity comes not so much from the strength of the court as from the insidious nature of the megacorporate environment.

Infringement against pan-corporate law falls into two basic categories: infringement by minor corps and infringement by megacorps. The first case is a no-brainer. If the Corporate Court decides that a minor corp (any corporation not classified as AAA) has broken a law and warrants punishment, it gives mandate to one or more of the major corps to a given degree. This mandate gives the megacorp official authorization from the Corporate Court to use its security assets against the guilty corporation, to the specified extent. A mandate can range from relatively minor destruction of selected black-ops assets to "open season," where the enforcing megacorp can destroy the target corp.

>>>>>[The dreaded "Omega Order" differs from this "total mandate" only in that an Omega Order lets every megacorp, and anyone else who wants to play, have open season on somebody.]<<<<<
—Hangfire (09:29:58/4-22-54)

Of course, prosecuting a mandate costs money. If the corp given mandate in a particular case had to pay for it out of general revenue, nobody would follow through with disciplinary action. To avoid this problem, when it grants a mandate, the Corporate Court authorizes the Zurich-Orbital Gemeinschaft Bank to pay the selected megacorp a certain sum to defray expenses. Specified at the time that mandate is granted, this sum is not negotiable.

>>>>>[The sum is usually more than fair as long as the selected megacorp prosecutes the mandate efficiently. If the megacorp plays dumb and loses assets because of command-and-control frag-ups, for example, the bank won't reimburse that extraordinary expense.]<<<<<
—Hangfire (09:32:36/4-22-54)

>>>>>[So "mandate" gives a megacorp the right to legally beat on a smaller corp that wronged it? Institutionalized vengeance?]<<<<<
—Pavel (18:02:27/4-24-54)

>>>>>[It used to work that way, until the court noticed that the "wronged" megacorp tended to overstep the terms of its mandate. In other words, the wronged megacorp went beyond the limits laid out by the mandate and reduced the target corp to a smoking crater. These days, the court grants mandate to a megacorp not involved in the original infraction. Say MiniCorp Inc. breaks pan-corporate law by trashing one of Ares' comm satellites. Instead of letting Ares hit back, the court grants mandate to someone else such as Yamatetsu, and orders Ares to stay out of the scrap. That system has cut down on attrition among minor corps.]<<<<<
—Legal Beagle (13:56:07/4-25-54)

>>>>>[Officially, overstepping mandate contravenes pan-corporate law. If you get a mandate to inflict one billion nuyen worth of damage on a target and you inflict three billion, you've officially broken the law, and the court can punish you. In reality, of course, the court has total discretion on enforcing that law. Depending on such circumstances as who currently controls the court, the authorities might turn a blind eye even if the megacorp with mandate obliterates the target.]<<<<<
—Hangfire (01:48:04/4-26-54)

Procedures work a little differently if a AAA megacorp violates corporate law. Because most of the these corps are more or less evenly matched in power, granting mandate to another megacorp could lead to untold unpleasantness. On the other hand, no reasonable set of court justices can expect Corp A to sit still without retaliating if Corp B trashes it's assets.

>>>>>[And it's reasonable if the target's not a triple-A corp?]<<<<<
—Kanada (18:55:21/4-24-54)

>>>>>[Betcherass. Take my example from a couple of posts ago. Say Yamatetsu has mandate against MiniCorp. MiniCorp might desperately want to strike back rather than just sit there and get drekked on, but it's fragging *Yamatetsu* doing the drekking. MiniCorp ends up like a hiker in the Cascades who finds herself facing a hungry piasma (you know, one of those metabears). Sure as hell she'd like to do something to the bugger rather than flinging herself on the ground and playing dead, but the piasma's a lot tougher than she is. Putting up with whatever it feels like doing is the smartest play if she wants to survive.]<<<<<
—Legal Beagle (13:57:50/4-25-54)

In this case, the Corporate Court has various options. Because all of the triple-A megacorps use Zurich-Orbital Gemeinschaft Bank facilities for short-term loans, brokerage services, access to money markets for arbitrage, and so on, the Corp Court can punish a AAA corp by increasing the fees for any of these services. For example, it might increase the interest rate at which the corp bank loans money to the guilty party for a given period of time.

>>>>>[A triple-A corp can always find other sources for all its financial needs. But to use them, it has to set aside the confidentiality and convenience of dealing with the Gemeinschaft Bank. That loss alone increases the cost of doing business, the worst punishment a corp can suffer.]<<<<<
—Nuyen Nick (15:42:08/3-27-54)

>>>>>[But doesn't that mean the Gemeinschaft Bank loans money to different corps with more or less identical credit ratings at different interest rates? Isn't that illegal?]<<<<<
—Luce (16:50:54/3-27-54)

>>>>>[Have we all been watching the same trideo here? "Illegal" in the corporate context only means "against the laws promulgated by the Corporate Court." Because the Corp Court is ordering the Gemeinschaft Bank to charge higher rates to different corps, that activity is legal by definition. Look, jokers, unless you give up the idea that national laws have any bearing on Zurich-Orbital and its dealings, you'll never understand this drek. Wake up and smell the soykaf!]<<<<<
—Carlo (07:14:18/3-30-54)

In extreme cases, the Corporate Court can issue mandate against any megacorp that breaks major rules. Depending on the severity of the infraction, the court issues mandate to two or more other corps in order to guarantee that the enforcing corps have enough security assets to do the job. If possible, the court avoids giving mandate to the corp or corps initially wronged by the guilty party's actions, but this becomes impossible under certain circumstances. If the guilty corp's actions have harmed the interests of every other triple-A megacorp, or if a single subset of megacorps cannot inflict the degree of damage allowed by the mandate, the court may issue mandate to all triple-A megacorps. Though seldom used, this provision invites such massive retaliation that few corps care to call its wrath down upon their heads.

In practice, the Corporate Court rarely has to issue even a minor mandate against a triple-A corp. The threat alone carries enough weight to keep most corps at least nominally in line. Each megacorp realizes that its rivals would love to have mandate against it, and that they might easily find the temptation to inflict damage beyond the terms of the mandate too enticing to pass up. Inviting mandate by breaking pan-corporate law represents too large a risk for any halfway sane corp to take.

>>>>>[So what happens if a group of megacorps decide to cooperate in breaking major pan-corporate laws? Bet the court couldn't touch them.]<<<<<
—Harker (03:15:10/3-27-54)

>>>>>[You got it, chummer. If the Corporate Court can no longer enforce pan-corporate law, its authority disappears. That's why the corps don't pull that kind of drek. The Corp Court serves an important, productive purpose; it holds the megacorporate environment back from the edge of chaos. Flaunting the rule of the Corp Court would tell every other corp that it can go ahead and break any pan-corporate laws it pleases because the court no longer matters. The result? Anarchy. Eventually, the full-out corp war that most corps want like hell to avoid. It's tough to do business and make money when the world's coming apart around your head.]<<<<<
—Hangfire (14:33:20/3-29-54)

>>>>>[A few events prove that we've almost reached that point a couple of times, once pretty recently. If trashing the court's rules offer a big enough payoff, the megacorps have no qualms about flirting with the utter disaster of corp war. Fortunately, they've always pulled back from the precipice before things spun totally out of control. So far.]<<<<<
—Turner (23:05:08/4-2-54)

Concords

The term concord refers to a super-secret agreement signed by every triple-A megacorp and binding on all corporations regardless of whether or not they know about it. If anyone knowingly or unknowingly breaks a concord, the Corporate Court automatically issues an unlimited mandate against the transgressor to every AAA megacorporation. In effect, it authorizes the megacorps to obliterate the guilty party to the last asset.

>>>>>[Because only the triple-A corps know about the concord, theoretically a smaller corp only figures out that it's broken one when all the major megacorps suddenly come gunning for it. Scary.]<<<<<
—Arnesen (11:35:22/4-11-54)

>>>>>["Unlimited mandate" is the Omega Order people talked about earlier.]<<<<<
—Link (23:57:08/4-13-54)

>>>>>[Could the Corp Court issue an Omega Order against Aztechnology, or somebody big like that?]<<<<<
—Pud (11:51:29/4-15-54)

>>>>>[Theoretically, yes.]<<<<<
—Magritte (18:31:42/4-15-54)

>>>>>[To the best of my admittedly incomplete knowledge, pan-corporate concords don't exist. I figure them as an urban myth retold so many times that it's picked up an aura of reality. Remember the old chestnut about the woman who washed her dog and then tried to dry it in the microwave? *Pop!* People believed that one, too. I can't see any benefit in having unwritten laws like these secret concords. And the Corporate Court doesn't do anything without some benefit.]<<<<<
—Hangfire (18:14:40/4-17-54)

>>>>>[Beg to differ, Hangfire. I can think of a *fragging* good reason for unwritten laws. Publicly declaring something illegal also publicly declares that it's possible. To use a simple example, no law exists against breaking the speed of light because no one can pull it off. Laws of nature see to that.

So think about this reason for unwritten laws. Everybody knows about the Crash of '29, right? Well, a lot of data got lost when the computer systems went down. The viral code had a weird propensity for encrypted data, which suggests it might well have been a core-wars weapon gone haywire. Because of the virus' preferred snacking pattern, the corps lost the data that they considered the most important and most sensitive. They lost stuff on secret corp drawing boards before '29 that never reared its head afterward. Ten to one, some of that lost data probably had enormous potential to destabilize the balance of corp power, and I'm sure most of the megacorps prefer that it remain lost. Secret concords could make certain of that. Say the triple-A megacorps all know that details on a particularly destabilizing technology disappeared in the Crash. The court establishes a concord making research into that technology illegal so the major megacorps don't pursue it, and an Omega Order wipes out any minor corps that do. Makes sense, doesn't it?]<<<<<
—Hersh (23:05:57/4-17-54)

>>>>>[Try this for size, Hersh. How about a technology that lets you tap into fiber optic communication channels undetectably?]<<<<<
—Ringer (08:42:53/4-18-54)

>>>>>[I keep hearing about this drek, but nobody's got any hard data. Another one of Hangfire's urban myths?]<<<<<
—Lord (16:39:41/4-18-54)

>>>>>[If this lost data really has the potential value of Ringer's fiber-optics tapping drek, no fragging concord will stop the

megacorps from digging into it. "Oh, yes," says Corp A, "it would be valuable. But the Corp Court says no, so I guess we shelve our research." *Null.*]<<<<<
—Archangel (19:02:00/4-18-54)

>>>>>[Of course it won't stop them, you slot. But it will slow them down. Sure, every corp that knows about it may go hunting for the holy grail of lost data. But knowing an Omega Order awaits them if they're caught makes them keep their research quiet, *neh*? Keeping mum makes research much less efficient because it eliminates the normal synergy between research establishments that comes from scientists talking shop over the Matrix. Maybe a concord can't stop this kind of behavior, but it can postpone the destabilization that might result.]<<<<<
—Larkspur (05:33:56/4-19-54)

>>>>>[It's all fragging drek.]<<<<<
—Lobo (11:14:49/4-19-54)

ZURICH-ORBITAL GEMEINSCHAFT BANK

As the megacorps' major bank, the Zurich-Orbital Gemeinschaft Bank has become the world's premier financial institution. Like most major banks, the Z-O Gemeinschaft is a data- or interface-bank, colloquially called a face-bank. As such, it deals almost exclusively with data. Its currency consists of bits and bytes in heavily secured and encrypted datastores, rather than concrete valuables or cash. Pay attention to that last statement, chummers. No matter how many trideo shows and simsense programs say otherwise, Zurich-Orbital has no huge, hidden vault bursting with a king's ransom in bullion, bearer bonds, or stock certificates. (Sorry.)

>>>>>[A little common sense tells you that. I can't tell you exactly how much it costs to lift one kilogram of mass to Z-O, but it costs a fragging lot, okay? Only a bimbleheaded drekbrain would expect to find bullion floating around somewhere in the habitat. *Bullion*, for spirit's sake! Get real.]<<<<<
—Marchand (13:02:19/3-21-54)

>>>>>[If the Gemeinschaft Bank deals with anything as crass as hard currency or concrete goods, it does so through one of its legions of groundside subsidiaries. A set of arm's-length transactions helps to keep things nice and secret.]<<<<<
—The Chromed Accountant (12:05:33/3-23-54)

HISTORY

The Zurich-Orbital Gemeinschaft Bank evolved from a Zurich-based financial corporation called Global Financial Services. Back in the 20th century, the World Bank provided a central source for the financial services needed by multinationals and by governments from time to time. In the 20-teens, Global Financial emerged to challenge the World Bank, which had taken staggering losses from bad loans to various so-called "Fourth World" nations. These once-developed nations had been part of the old Soviet Union, and the turbulence of independence had thrown them back into

poverty and instability. Global Financial Services offered them and other nations a level of service that the struggling World Bank could not equal.

>>>>>[Mainly because Global used the latest cutting-edge data transfer and processing technology that the World Bank didn't have. It had never faced real competition before, so it hadn't bothered staying current. It also had to keep some kind of backward compatibility between its old and new datafiles, even when it realized that Global's high tech allowed it to eat the World Bank's lunch.]<<<<<
—TS (13:19:36/3-28-54)

Although it clung to survival for almost a decade after Global's emergence, by 2020 the World Bank had given way to its competitor as the dominant force in international finance.

>>>>>[From what I've dug up, Global in the 2020s was hideously efficient, but also corrupt. It had a lucrative clientele of chip dealers and money launderers, and Global offered them whatever services they needed. By 2035 or so, Global had cleaned up its act considerably.]<<<<<
—Nuyen Nick (13:27:08/3-22-54)

>>>>>[Beg to differ, Nick. Before the corps took it over, Global continued to offer those "special services" that kept clients like chip dealers, money launderers, and a few nasty policlubs coming back for more. In the 2030s it cleaned up its image and glossed over its shadier operations and connections, but not much else.]<<<<<
—The Chromed Accountant (12:09:56/3-23-54)

The collapse of the world computer network in the crash of 2029 brought down the faltering World Bank and many other financial institutions. Hit as hard as everyone else by the catastrophe, Global almost followed its major competitor into oblivion. As it teetered on the brink of collapse, so did the world economy. Experts claim that if Global had gone butt-up in 2029, the world would have gone to hell in a handcart much faster than it actually did. Fortunately, Global managed to keep itself together, and the battered international corporate economy reformed around it the way crystals form around a seed.

>>>>>[Some economists argue that Global's demise would have taken down the whole megacorporate environment. If it had re-formed at all, it would have done so along totally different lines.]<<<<<
—The Neon Antichrist (10:04:43/3-24-54)

>>>>>[Bulldrek. At most, it might have taken longer than ten years to rebuild and the actual identities of the players might have changed. Instead of Ares, MCT, Renraku, and so on, some other bunch of corps would have taken center stage. But the structure would have stayed exactly the same. Don't anyone try to claim different.]<<<<<
—Samuel (21:09:51/3-24-54)

In an unbelievably fast recovery, Global had regained a fairly even keel by 2032. At the time, the Big Seven megacorps comprised its major creditors. As they poured money into building up the Zurich-Orbital habitat, which had become home to the Corporate Court nine years earlier, the megacorps realized that their future fortunes had become almost completely dependent on Global Financial Services. If anything ever happened to Global, they'd be up drek creek without an outboard. Not surprisingly, this realization scared them green. In late 2032, the largest megacorps that would later be classified as triple-A pooled their resources and staged a takeover of Global Financial Services.

>>>>>[They made the owners the stereotypical Offer They Couldn't Refuse?]<<<<<
—Bung (10:04:22/3-21-54)

>>>>>[All yuks aside, yes. They pulled a typical hostile takeover, with a disturbing level of black ops. Those of Global's major shareholders who survived, of course, became colossally rich.]<<<<<
—Keynesian Kid (19:54:23/3-24-54)

When the dust of the takeover settled, the triple-A corps owned the bank that held most of their loans and handled the vast majority of their financial transactions. By buying Global Financial, the megacorps had landed themselves in an interesting situation with dire possible consequences for the rest of the world. Each corp faced an overwhelming temptation to use that ownership and control to benefit itself, balanced by the knowledge that any attempt to use the bank that way would invite retribution from the other corps. Any corp stupid enough to grandstand with everyone else's money risked triggering a corp war that would annihilate it and rob the world of what little stability it had regained.

>>>>>[A couple of corps tried it in the first couple of months, and the world drifted close to corp war before everyone got smart.]<<<<<
—Bowers (18:27:52/3-27-54)

>>>>>[You know who I think came out on top? Ares Macrotechnology. The corps bought the bank right after Ares' CEO Damien Knight pulled his infamous nanosecond buy-out and acquired control of Ares Industries. Ares just happened to be financing the bulk of its long-term debt through Global, which had given it most of the funding it used to acquire NASA back in 2016. So in 2032, Ares suddenly became part owner of the financial institution that it owed gobs of money to. Can you say "refinance?" I knew you could.]<<<<<
—Hangfire (10:14:34/3-29-54)

To eliminate the temptation to misuse the bank and to minimize vulnerability to such misuse by others, the AAA megacorps agreed to let the Corporate Court handle the day-to-day running of Global Financial Services. In 2033, the court relocated the bank to its own home base aboard the Zurich-Orbital habitat, and renamed it the Zurich-Orbital Gemeinschaft Bank.

>>>>>[Why change the name, and why "Gemeinschaft?"]<<<<<
—Necro (00:01:22/3-28-54)

>>>>>[Why not? "Zurich-Orbital Gemeinschaft Bank" has an impressive, conservative, Old World sound to it. Just the thing to inspire confidence, or fear of crossing up the big boys.]<<<<<
—Laser's Edge (21:04:36/4-2-54)

OWNERSHIP

Ares Macrotechnology, Aztechnology, Fuchi, Mitsuhama, Renraku, Saeder-Krupp, Shiawase, and Yamatetsu each own 12.5 percent of the Zurich-Orbital Gemeinschaft Bank's shares. The corporation charter forbids these corps to trade in these shares. Selling or buying such shares violates pan-corporate law.

>>>>>[And breaking that law earns an Omega Order. Bet on it.]<<<<<
—Link (00:13:15/4-14-54)

In the only exception to this stringent restriction, the Corporate Court has the power to confer triple-A status on another corporation. Should this ever happen, the Big Eight corps must each sell the new AAA megacorp approximately 1.4 percent of the outstanding shares, so that each triple-A corp owns one-ninth of the Gemeinschaft Bank.

>>>>>[If you ask me, the Big Eight are holding onto their prerogatives much too hard for this ever to happen.]<<<<<
—Nuyen Nick (11:20:53/4-1-54)

>>>>>[If the Court ever names a ninth AAA corp, their reasons for such an extraordinary step ought to prove enlightening.]<<<<<
—Hangfire (13:52:00/4-3-54)

MANAGEMENT

The Corporate Court manages the Zurich-Orbital Gemeinschaft Bank through a board of directors. A special standing committee that comprises the CEOs of the Big Eight corps elects the directors from among each AAA megacorp's employees. During their term on the board, however, the directors are solely responsible to the justices of the Corporate Court. The corps still pay their salaries, supplemented by a healthy stipend commensurate with running the major bank on the planet, but the Corp Court constitutes the only authority they must submit to. However, the court's "hands-off" management style makes that restriction more theoretical than practical.

>>>>>[Okay, okay, how does it really work? Am I supposed to believe that Director Doe, a loyal Aztechnology employee, conducts her responsibilities as bank director without favoring the Big A?]<<<<<
—Lobo (14:19:22/4-14-54)

>>>>>[Believe it or not, it actually works that way. The directors know that the court can nail them with a mandate if they abuse their responsibilities. Should said abuse benefit the corp that a

director belongs to, both that director and the corp are disciplined by the court. For the corp, punishments range from temporarily downgraded bank credit to an Omega Order, depending on the severity of the offense. As for the director, what little I've managed to dig up implies a death penalty for abuse of authority. Facing that kind of sanction makes honesty a smarter policy. And it really seems to work, *omae*.]<<<<<
—Legal Beagle (19:08:45/4-17-54)

Bank directors hold their seats for a nine-year term. Though no director may serve two consecutive terms, he or she can serve multiple non-consecutive terms. Every year, one new director replaces a current board member. Legal provisions exist to remove a director before his or her term expires, but using them requires a unanimous vote by the Corporate Court justices.

>>>>>[Which means it ain't gonna happen, at least not that way. Like Madrid said in a previous file, it's easier to arrange an "unattributable accident" for the unwanted board member than to oust her legally.]<<<<<
—Hangfire (13:05:31/3-19-54)

Officially, board members can possess any variety of credentials or qualifications, but the vast majority have at least a master's degree in economics or a similar discipline. As with the justices on the Corporate Court, board members decide individually whether or not to spend any time aboard Zurich-Orbital during their term of office.

The following list of current board members includes each one's corporate affiliation and current residence as of 1-14-54.
    Derek Abernathie, Saeder-Krupp. London.
    Choy-Mu Laubenstein, Shiawase. Zurich-Orbital.
    William Marcus, Ares. New York.
    Sakehisa Noro, Yamatetsu. Kyoto.
    Kamako Otaku, Yamatetsu. Zurich-Orbital.
    Jeanne-Marie Roulleau, Saeder-Krupp. Zurich-Orbital.
    Xavier Talbot, Ares. Seattle.

>>>>>[Oho!]<<<<<
—Lockjaw (14:28:35/3-21-54)

    Samuel Wirth, Fuchi. Berlin.
    —Atsutada Yogo, MCT. Denver, Pueblo Sector.

>>>>>[??!??]<<<<<
—Troika (03:44:05/3-18-54)

>>>>>[Just like the justices, these guys have personal security like you've never seen before. Unlike the justices, the sheer volume of corp bureaucracy beneath the directors means that bribing or otherwise influencing one of these guys doesn't buy you much. Keep that in mind before you plan an intimidation or extortion campaign.]<<<<<
—Nuyen Nick (14:38:29/3-21-54)

>>>>>[You jerk around with the directors of the Zurich-Orbital Gemeinschaft Bank, and all the megacorporations will come gunning for your sorry ass. Also, remember that malfeasance and breach of fiduciary responsibility on the part of a director earns the poor sap a death sentence. The Neo-A guy writing this file didn't use those big words, but that's what he meant a little while back. With that kind of penalty, intimidating a director into malfeasance gets a little difficult. If you snatch one, most corps won't care if you keep the slag or kill him. The megacorps just have to replace the kidnapped director with another one; he's no loss to them. For all the money you'd get, you might as well render your prisoner down

to his component chemicals and pocket about 3 nuyen for them at the going rate.]<<<<<
—Bull (18:20:20/4-3-54)

The triple-A megacorps and others draw on the Zurich-Orbital Gemeinschaft Bank for loans, arbitrage, and brokerage services. The bank's official charter takes up almost a megapulse of impenetrable legalese, and its mission statement needs a fragging translation and glossary for anyone besides a corporate lawyer to understand it. So free of charge, as a public service, your friendly neighborhood Neo-Anarchists have paraphrased the Zurich-Orbital Gemeinschaft Bank's charter and stated purpose.

1. Maintain the status quo.
2. Keep everyone making money.

Beyond those two statements, all else is commentary.

"Everyone," of course, includes the Big Eight triple-A megacorps. If the bank can further the interests of other corps without harming the interests of its owners, it does so. If it can help out the occasional credit-strapped national government without impacting the Big Eight's rosy profit picture, it does. The corp bank might even think of looking out for the little guy, if it can actually help the little guy afford more products forced on him by the megacorps. Under those circumstances, it might consider the possibility. As for protecting the environment, the question only arises when some corp slag figures that the global extinction of (meta)humanity just might be bad for business. The Gemeinschaft Bank's priorities lie in exactly one direction, and everybody had by god better understand that.

Ugly, but true.

>>>>>[Ugly and overstated.]<<<<<
—Horvath (16:51:11/3-29-54)

>>>>>[Maybe, but not by much.]<<<<<
—The Chromed Accountant (13:30:01/3-31-54)

ASSETS

As mentioned earlier, as an interface-bank the Zurich-Orbital Gemeinschaft has no piles and sacks of filthy lucre lying around in vaults. Its assets amount to a bunch of zeros and ones recorded in one of the most secure distributed data storage/retrieval networks known to man. Because the Gemeinschaft Bank is extraterritorial, it need not report its asset mix, revenue, or profit to anyone. That fact plus the security of its computer systems make it virtually impossible to find out what kind of assets the bank possesses.

Despite the haziness of the details, one can safely assume that Z-O Gemeinschaft's assets are vast. Outstanding loans probably amount to a few terabucks. It probably also holds title to huge chunks of real estate such as buildings, factories, and so on as collateral, but no one can reliably guess how much.

Wealthy as it is, however, the Gemeinschaft Bank still has finite assets, and therefore cannot always meet the megacorporate community's demand for loans. Though most of the time the triple-A megacorps can get the loans they need, sometimes even they can't get the credit they want. Because they own the bank, they usually find a way to sleaze around this problem. Invariably, the bank forecloses on a couple of smaller corps' loans and

liquidates the assets backing them. It then slides the megacorps the money they need, and business goes merrily on.

>>>>>[If you ever wanted to crash the world economy to liven up a slow Sunday afternoon, just wait for the Gemeinschaft Bank to overextend itself a little and then trash its data files. I'm not talking about decker incursion, of course. Wouldn't do any good to send some poor sod traipsing in to erase the data file by file. The security would make dead meat of him but quick. No, I'd suggest slipping a killer virus into the Zurich-Orbital system, then cutting off the comm links between the habitat and the rest of the Matrix to keep the virus from spreading. Down comes the bank, down come the megacorps, and down will come baby, cradle and all. Pleasant thought.]<<<<<
—Phage (19:42:55/4-7-54)

>>>>>[Pleasant if you're a fragged-in-the-head, twisted sicko. Crash the Zurich-Orbital Gemeinschaft Bank and the megacorps couldn't get the credit they need to stay in business. Just to keep from collapsing, they'd have to acquire assets from the only remaining available source, each other. Crashing the bank would set off full-fledged corporate war, firing up within a couple of hours at the most. The Corporate Court might stave it off if the bank only crashed temporarily. But your plan, Phage, includes disconnecting the court from the rest of the world as well. If you need something interesting to do on a slow Sunday afternoon, why don't you blow your sick brains out?]<<<<<
—Mags (09:48:32/4-8-54)

>>>>>[Touchy . . .]<<<<<
—Phage (16:59:12/4-8-54)

SECURITY

To protect its vast assets, the Gemeinschaft Bank uses predictably extreme security. The security provisions placed around the bank's datafiles start with the nasty suckers protecting the Zurich-Orbital habitat and the Corporate Court, and build on them. In short, the Gemeinschaft Bank's portion of the Matrix is a black hole, the ultimate zero-zone. Don't say we didn't warn you, chummers.

>>>>>[Sound exaggerated? Not so. As I said elsewhere, the security on the bank's computers benchmarks out at Red-10 and up. Key nodes are loaded with cascading black ice, Pueblo-style "party ice," you name it. The load of the ice alone would slow to a glacial crawl any hardware less beefy than what the bank actually uses. I hear they've got a couple of ultracomputers with massively parallel architecture. Can your cyberdecks match that, chummers? If I were you, I wouldn't even think of approaching the bank's system. Chip-truth.]<<<<<
—Red Wraith (06:16:38/3-19-54)

>>>>>[For those who don't know the Wraith, he's the kinda guy who decks into the "black hole of Mitsuhama" just for the frag of it. Keep that in mind as you re-read his last post.]<<<<<
—Dead Deckers Society (10:14:30/3-24-54)

FORD	1150	120	120	
FORSYTH	3800	400	375	
FREEWEST	11670	320	276	+5
FUCHI	unavailable			-½
GTC	56594	$10	10½	
GANDALF	140450	400	360	
GEAC COMP	2334	$12	$11	+1
GMC	15221	$57	55	+2
GENOM	10950	$16	15½	+½
GLOBAL STN	85200	350	325	+2
GOLD CORP	83375	$8½	7⅞	+¼

RATING CORPS

This section provides gamemasters with tools for rating a corporation's performance against its competitors. Rather than simulating the complex financial wheelings and dealings of a megacorporation, the information in this section compresses a few key concepts into a straightforward set of rules. These rules allow the gamemaster to bring corporate interplay into focus during the game and provide him or her with a way to track a corporation's ongoing success or failure. This tracking may suggest several interesting directions for many shadowruns. In the context of an adventure involving a corporation, the following game rules also provide a useful means of gauging an individual shadowrun's effects on the corporation and its assets.

GAME TERMS

The gamemaster must take into account four elements of corporate activity, translated into the following game terms: the quarterly posting, the Posted Asset Rating (PAR), the Adjusted Asset Rating (AAR), and resources.

A corporation's standing is assessed quarterly, or every three months. At that time, the corporation tracks its numbers and determines whether or not it made money during that quarter. The determination and finalization of those numbers is called the quarterly posting.

At each quarterly posting, every corporation determines its final value in the following areas: its interests and holdings, and its internal operations and structure. Each of those areas has an Asset Rating that quantifies how well the corporation is doing in that area. The quarterly value for each major interest or operation is known as the Posted Asset Rating (PAR).

In any given quarter, the effects of shadowruns both for and against a corporation can change the PAR of a particular area. These increases or decreases in the PAR create the quarterly Adjusted Asset Rating (AAR) for each interest or operation.

Finally, every corporation has certain internal resources that it allocates to its operations. These resources derive from the PAR of various corporate operations. During the normal course of business, these resources enhance the corporation's performance in a specific area. A corporation can also allocate resources to counteract or lessen the effect of a damaging shadowrun on the corp's PAR for any given interest or operation.

ASSET RATINGS

Corporate Asset Ratings correspond to a corporation's various business interests and areas of operation. Each major interest and operation has an Asset Rating that represents the corporation's potential and actual worth, output, and productivity in that area.

MAJOR INTERESTS

Every corporation has an Asset Rating in the fourteen major interest categories described below. The Asset Ratings associated with each interest represent all of the corporation's holdings in that category, including subsidiaries, research, patents, and licenses. These assets may physically exist in any one of a number of cities or countries, or may only exist as datafiles in the Matrix.

Aerospace

This category covers all aviation-based interests, including production, research, and development. It encompasses conventional aircraft, space-capable craft, and aerospace technology.

Agriculture

This category encompasses all aspects of food production and distribution, including farming, animal husbandry and processing, and distribution.

Biotechnology

This area includes most medical technologies and research, from pharmaceuticals to advanced bioware.

Chemicals

This area includes chemicals and chemical-related products of all kinds, from cheap plastics to space-age carbon polymers. It also encompasses common chemicals for consumer and industrial use.

Computer Engineering

This category includes research, development, production, and distribution of computer and computer-related hardware.

Computer Science

This category encompasses research, development, production, and distribution of computers and computer-related software.

Consumer Goods

This area includes common goods of all kinds, from toasters to telecoms to hair dryers.

Cybernetics

Cybernetics includes all technology related to man-machine interfacing, from simple reactive circuits to advanced cyberware.

Entertainment

This field includes trideo, simsense, music, theater, book and magazine publishing, and related industries.

Finance

This field includes money-based concerns such as investing, banking, insurance, and brokering.

Heavy Industry

Heavy industry encompasses construction and production, including heavy manufacturing, waste processing, and related industries. It also covers power generation and distribution, including conventional, nuclear, hydroelectric, geothermal, and solar power.

Mystical Goods and Services

Still coming into its own, this area principally covers research and development, as well as a few marketable end results. Look for this business field to expand in coming years.

Military Technology

This area includes various industries and technologies geared specifically toward research, development, and production of weapons, defensive measures and countermeasures, and other military interests. Corporations rated in this area often have similar ratings in one or more of the Aerospace, Computer Engineering, and Computer Science assets.

Service

Service includes service and support industries such as fast food, transportation, security, data management, police and fire, and so on.

OPERATIONS

Corporate operations fall into five major categories: fiscal, intelligence, management, reputation, and security. Security is further subdivided into physical, magical, and matrix security operations.

As with major interests, each area of operations has an Asset Rating. This Asset Rating represents the corporation's performance in each category of operations.

Fiscal

Fiscal operations involve the corporation's financial worth and stability, determining its ability to conduct all of its operations. Reflecting the importance of money to business, the Fiscal Asset Rating determines the maximum Asset Rating for all other operations with the exception of reputation. No matter how extensive a corporation's assets are, under-funding means under-producing. For this reason, no Asset Rating for any operation except reputation can exceed the Fiscal Asset Rating.

Fiscal assets also serve as resources that a corporation can use to increase productivity in a major interest, counteract losses in a major interest, or affect fiscal, intelligence, management, or security assets. The allocation of fiscal resources can also affect corporate reputation. For more information on allocating resources, see **Managing the Corporation**, p. 116.

Intelligence

Corporations keep close watch on each other, and intelligence operations allow each corp to conduct espionage. The Intelligence Asset Rating represents the corporation's potential and actual intelligence performance. As with fiscal assets, intelligence assets can also function as resources to bolster interest areas, counteract losses, or enhance the corporation's fiscal, intelligence, management, and security operations. Unlike financial resources, intelligence resources cannot affect reputation. See **Managing the Corporation**, p. 115, for more information.

Management

Management operations refer to the management activities of a corporation's executives and middlemen. The Management Asset Rating reflects the quality of their performance. Management assets also serve as resources to bolster productivity in a major interest, or to enhance fiscal, intelligence, management, or security operations.

REPUTATION ASSET RATINGS	
Rating	**Reputation**
1–2	The corp is slime, the lowest of the low, disreputable and immoral.
3–4	The public regards the corporation with disfavor.
5–6	The public neither likes nor dislikes the corporation.
7–8	The public thinks well of the corporation, but few think it perfect.
9–10	The public regards the corporation with almost universal favor. It can do no wrong.
11+	The corporation is god.

Reputation

The public perceives every corporation in a certain way, and reputation refers to that public perception. Much like the Asset Ratings for the other operations, the Reputation Asset Rating indicates how positively or negatively the general public perceives a corporation. Unlike other Asset Ratings, the Reputation Asset Rating directly affects a corp's Fiscal Asset Rating. No corporation can afford to ignore its Reputation Asset Rating, because a corporation's Fiscal Asset Rating cannot exceed a number higher than twice the corporation's Reputation Asset Rating. This rule reflects the financial trouble that a corporation disliked by the public can expect to deal with. Customers refuse to purchase its products, it cannot recruit quality employees, existing employees hate working there and do a poor job, the corporation finds it harder to get certain kinds of funding or acquire certain resources, and so on. The Reputation Asset Ratings table explains the different ratings.

For more information on how to use and change the Reputation Asset Rating, see **Managing the Corporation**, p. 115.

Security

Corporate assets require protection, mostly from other corporations. Security operations cover four sub-areas of protection: magic, matrix, physical, and military security. The first three of those four areas help determine a corp's power and influence, and each therefore has its own Security Asset Rating. The ratings are designed to give players and gamemasters a general feel for the level of protection present in each area of security. A future **Shadowrun** product will focus on the area of corporate security in greater depth.

Each sub-area discussed below addresses the general level of protection present in each different category of security. When determining security Asset Ratings (see **Determining Asset Ratings**, p. 116), the gamemaster must tailor the level of corporate

SECURITY ASSET RATINGS	
Rating	**Security Level**
0	The corporation has no security worth the name.
1–2	Poor security; simple protection, rudimentary opposition.
3–4	Adequate security; the corporation is prepared for most occurrences. Challenging for amateurs, but routine for professionals who do not slip up.
5–6	Good security; the corporation protects its sites with well-trained and prepared forces. Those going against these security measures need to be careful and equally prepared.
7–8	Excellent security; effective and creative security measures that pose a challenge for top professionals.
9–10	Outstanding security; these extensive, effective, well-integrated systems require craftiness and thorough planning to beat.
11+	Dominating security; only the highest-caliber professionals or the most creative and crafty runners have any hope of penetrating these defenses.

security to the capabilities of his or her own group of **Shadowrun** players to find the right level of challenge for the individual game. Because the Security Asset Ratings are designed as overall evaluations of a corporation's capabilities, these ratings do not determine the level of security at a specific site or around a specific person, project, or datafile. However, gamemasters can use the general Security Asset Ratings to gauge the level of opposition that the corporation can field or support when it has to. The Security Asset Ratings table gives the gamemaster an idea of the various levels of protection possible in each area of security.

The gamemaster should view these general levels of protection and opposition as an average. Depending on the value of the assets needing protection, some locations may have lighter security, whereas those safeguarding important projects, key personnel, and so on tend to have greater security. Unlike many assets, security cannot be used as a resource.

The security Asset Rating also serves another function. The PARs for each security sub-area have little importance in and of themselves, though they may occasionally serve as the target of a shadowrun. However, an overall Security PAR is drawn from the average (round down) of the ratings in three of the sub-areas listed below. The gamemaster factors this overall Security PAR into the Net Rating of each corporation. For more information on Net Ratings, see **Determining Net Rating**, p. 117.

Magical Security: In this rapidly changing area of the corporate security picture, the frequent advances in technique and theory make accurate tracking difficult. Lower levels of magical security involve off-site magical resources such as hired mages, or limited on-site presence such as part-time wage mages and limited, site-specific magic protection. Mid-level protection involves on-staff mages, active spirit or other astral patrols, lower-level wards, and anchored spells. High-level protection involves powerful on-staff mages, strong wards, aggressive astral patrols, and so on.

Matrix Security: As with other areas of security, Matrix security varies depending on the assets being protected. Low-level protection involves high green Security Ratings and white IC that triggers alerts to outside security agencies. Mid-level protection involves orange Security Ratings, white and/or gray IC that triggers alerts to internal security assets, and on-staff corporate deckers. High-level protection involves red Security Ratings; white, gray, and black IC; and active internal Matrix security assets.

Physical Security: For game purposes, physical security refers to both living security assets such as guards or paranimals and technological assets such as alarm systems and countermeasures. Low-level protection involves simple entry restrictions and the occasional guard patrol. Mid-level protection involves more sophisticated entry protection, active security surveillance, frequent security patrols, and active internal post-entry alarm systems. High-level security involves advanced entry restrictions, constant surveillance, active security patrols (possibly including paranimals), and incredibly sophisticated internal post-entry alarm systems.

Military Security: The largest megacorporations field military units in addition to their regular security forces. Unlike magical, matrix, or physical security, military security forces have no Security Asset Rating because military assets do not help to determine a corporation's day-to-day influence. The various force sizes are listed below:

- Squad (9 men, usually Special Forces)
- Platoon (3+ squads, about 30 men)
- Company (3+ platoons, about 100 men)
- Battalion (5 companies, about 500 men)
- Light Regiment (2 battalions, about 1,000 men)
- Full Regiment (4 battalions, about 2,000 men)

Currently, no corporation fields more than a full regiment of military forces. In almost all instances, the battalion and larger units are combined-arms forces incorporating air, ground, sea, and possible space elements.

The six general levels of quality are poor, below average, average, above average, excellent, and exceptional. Note that these quality levels can represent a mix of training and outfitting. For example, a unit with average training but exceptional equipment might end up with an above average or an excellent quality level.

NET RATING TABLE

Standing	Net Rating
First-tier megacorporation	100+
Second-tier megacorporation	75–99
Third-tier megacorporation	50–74
Lesser corporation	less than 50

DETERMINING ASSET RATINGS

The simple procedure described in the following pages allows the gamemaster to determine initial Posted Asset Ratings when creating new corporations and subsidiaries. Asset Ratings for the Big Eight megacorps are listed in the **Big Eight Corporate Profiles**, p. 118 of this section.

CREATING CORPORATIONS

The gamemaster first chooses the new corporation's size and position, then consults the Net Rating Table below to find the appropriate Net Rating for the corp's standing. For example, if the gamemaster wishes to create a second-tier megacorp, its Net Rating according to the Net Rating Table falls between 75 and 99 Rating Points.

CORPORATE ASSET RATINGS

Rating Points	Assets
0–1	No assets worth mentioning
2–3	Poor assets
4	Adequate
5	Above-par
6	Good
7	Very Good
8	Extensive
9–10	Superior
11	Extraordinary
12+	Dominates interest/operation

To determine the corp's initial Posted Asset Ratings, the gamemaster allocates these points to the corporation's various major interests and operations, keeping in mind the following few guidelines.

1. No interest or operation can have a PAR that exceeds the Fiscal PAR.

2. The Fiscal PAR cannot be greater than twice the Reputation PAR.

3. For Security Asset Ratings, multiply the allocated points by three and distribute those points among the three rated security sub-areas.

Assets are rated on a scale similar to Attributes or Skills. When allocating Rating Points, the gamemaster should consult the Corporate Asset Ratings table below to find the number of Rating Points for each level of assets. For military assets (if any), the gamemaster simply chooses and notes them.

CREATING SUBSIDIARIES

Because corporate subsidiaries usually function as smaller, separate corporations, they have their own Net Ratings. A subsidiary's Net Rating is usually less than 25 Rating Points, and its business usually encompasses only one or two interests. However, the gamemaster should keep in mind that a subsidiary always has a full set of operations Asset Ratings. As with corporations, the gamemaster allocates the subsidiary's Net Rating Points to the appropriate interests and operations for its Posted Asset Ratings, following the same guidelines with regard to fiscal, reputation, and security interests and operations.

For those gamemasters inclined to figure out just how each subsidiary's Asset Ratings fit into the parent megacorp's overall profile, note that a controlling corporation's or megacorporation's ratings in its various interests and operations amount to more than a simple total of the respective ratings of all of its subsidiaries. However, any relative-value ranking system sophisticated enough to compile, track, and rank all of a megacorp's assets and resources would be too complicated and difficult to maintain without detracting from the game. The gamemaster should feel free to make the numbers up; no one will ever know the difference.

ADJUSTED ASSET RATINGS

Shifts in the Asset Ratings, also known as Adjusted Asset Ratings, are determined on a quarterly basis (see **Managing the Corporation**, p. 116) and represent the growth and/or decline of a corporation's interests in each area. A corporation's Asset Ratings can change for a variety of reasons. In addition to normal internal advancement or decline, these shifts can reflect external forces such as inter-corporate espionage or the effects of shadowruns. This section offers game mechanics for determining exactly how shadowruns affect a corporation's Asset and Net Ratings, and how the corporation can attempt to counteract losses and enhance gains.

SHADOWRUN EFFECT TABLE

Effect	Potential Loss
Negligible (corp barely notices)	0*
Minor (corp can easily compensate)	1*
Appreciable (corp can compensate with difficulty)	2
Major (corp has extreme difficulty compensating)	3

*These two ratings remain the most common for shadowruns. Anything greater on a regular basis leads to big inter-corporate trouble.

EFFECTS OF SHADOWRUNS

Using the following guidelines, a gamemaster can rate the potential effects of a shadowrun carried out for or against a particular corporation. The gamemaster should keep these ratings secret from the players; letting them figure things out for themselves adds interest to the adventure. Obviously, the guidelines given in this section do not cover all circumstances. Gamemasters must gauge the effects of a shadowrun in terms of how much impact they wish it to have. Does the gamemaster actually want to damage a corporation seriously enough to potentially alter the balance of power in the world? The gamemaster should make his or her choice after deliberate consideration, not just because players want to be in on something big.

Any run, from a seemingly simple data-grab to a full-blown "crash and burn" operation intended to destroy a corporation's valuable assets, can have potentially significant impact. As shown in the following table, the potential effect of a run determines how many points any given Asset Rating might drop because of it.

For example, the gamemaster may decide that a run targeted at a corporation's biotechnology interests will have an Appreciable effect. According to the Shadowrun Effect Table, such a run could potentially cost the corp 2 points from its Biotechnology Asset Rating unless it manages to compensate for the damage.

Because the gamemaster decides how damaging a run actually is, the loss remains potential rather than actual until the gamemaster determines otherwise. As part of its normal operations, the corporation has the chance to compensate for the potential loss or some portion thereof. Depending on the circumstances and the gamemaster's decision, the corporation may lose the full potential number of points from its Posted Asset Rating, a lesser number of Asset Rating Points, or no points at all. In some circumstances the corp may even come out ahead. However, the gamemaster should keep in mind that if the corp successfully compensates for some or all of the potential loss, it has almost certainly allocated or assigned resources to compensation that it could have used elsewhere.

Gains From Shadowruns

Depending on the nature of the run in question, another corporation usually stands to benefit from the potential losses of the targeted corporation. However, the gaining corporation does not necessarily acquire a number of points equal to those the target corp lost. In this case, value is relative.

ASSET GAIN TABLE

Target Corp Asset Rating	Net Asset Gain
·Less than half the gaining corp's PAR	Base Value x .5 (round down)
·50 to 100 percent of the gaining corp's PAR	Base Value
·150 percent of the gaining corp's PAR	Base Value x 1.5 (round down)
·More than 150 percent of the gaining corp's PAR	Base Value x 2

For example, a corporation with a low Military Technology Asset Rating stands to gain a lot more from a run against a corporation with a significantly higher Military Technology Asset Rating than from a run against a corporation whose Military Technology Asset Rating equals the gaining corp's. The multipliers given for Net Asset Gains in the table below vary according to the difference in Asset Ratings between the gaining corporation and its target. To find the appropriate multiplier, compare the target corporation's Asset Rating for the affected interest or operation against the Asset Rating for the same area of the corporation profiting from the shadowrun. The Net Asset Gain column of the Asset Gain Table gives the equation with the correct multiplier. Next, consult the Shadowrun Effect Table to find the effect of the shadowrun in question. This number equals the base value of the change in Asset Ratings. Multiply that base value as directed by the Net Asset Gain. The sum of that equation represents the profiting corp's Net Asset Gain.

This Net Asset Gain can boost the gaining corporation's Asset Rating significantly in a particular area, but such profits also carry potential risks. For example, if a shadowrun costs Ares Macrotechnology 2 points from its Military Technology Asset Rating and its competitor, Big Guns Inc., shows a 4-point jump in its own Military Technology Asset Rating in the next quarter, the suits from Detroit might get suspicious. Big Guns Inc. may lose more than it gained simply protecting itself from retaliation.

Though all Net Asset Gains determine a corporation's Adjusted Asset Rating (AAR) for the appropriate interests or operations, no actual increase occurs until the actual AAR is determined during quarterly posting (see **Managing the Corporation**, p. 116).

Viable Targets

Only the following areas make viable targets for shadowruns: the major interests Aerospace through Service, and Fiscal, Intelligence, and Management operations. Though shadowruns can occur against a corp's security and military assets, targeting those

areas means more significant opposition than the average group of runners would be hired to provide. A corporation only resorts to directly attacking another corporation's defenses if it means serious business. Though shadowruns cannot occur directly against such an intangible thing as reputation, every shadowrun potentially affects reputation, as described below.

REPUTATION LOSS TABLE

Public Perception	Potential Loss
No interest (revelation does not matter)	0
Momentary interest (riles special interest groups)	1
Public concern (activity mildly unacceptable; some media coverage)	2
Public outrage (conduct flagrantly violates accepted moral and legal codes; extensive media coverage)	3

Affecting Reputation

A shadowrun's effect on a corp's Reputation Asset Rating is gauged in the same way as other run-related damage to assets, but with potentially vast differences in values. A shadowrun that depletes few assets for a potential loss of 0 might have a value of 3 for its effect on a corp's reputation. For example, pulling a meaningless corp datafile documenting immoral genetic research on metahumans might deplete no tangible assets (potential loss of zero), but if made public could cost the corp 2 or 3 points from its Reputation Asset Rating.

In rating any particular run, the gamemaster should keep in mind its potential damage to the corp's reputation as well as its potential asset damage. As with losses from asset damage, the gamemaster decides just how much a run may damage a particular corporation's reputation. Generally speaking, the higher the corp's Posted Asset Rating for its reputation, the more damage a particular run might do. To determine potential loss of reputation, consult the table below.

Loss of reputation is always applied to the reputation Posted Asset Rating, to determine the Adjusted Asset Rating. The actual Adjusted Asset Rating is determined during quarterly posting (see **Managing the Corporation**, below).

MANAGING THE CORPORATION

All tracking of a corporation's assets occurs quarterly, or every three months, with the fiscal year beginning in January. Four postings are made per year, on the first of January, April, July, and October. Each posting reflects the corporation's performance in various interests and operations during the previous three months. In game terms, a quarterly posting serves as the public declaration of a corp's Adjusted Asset Ratings (AARs).

The steps listed below comprise the quarterly posting procedure. Each step is outlined in detail in the following sections.

1. Assess damage.
2. Allocate resources.
3. Determine Asset Adjustments.
4. Declare quarterly posting.
5. Determine Net Rating.

ASSESSING DAMAGE

The effects of shadowruns carried out against or on behalf of a particular corp apply to a given area's Posted Asset Rating (PAR) from the previous quarter. The change in that rating creates the Adjusted Asset Rating (AAR) for the current quarter.

As described in **Effects of Shadowruns**, p. 114 of this section, corporations targeted by shadowruns have an AAR for the target interest or operation that reflects the appropriate reduction in the PAR, and corporations that benefit from a shadowrun have an AAR that reflects the appropriate increase in the PAR. Remember to track the Adjusted Asset Rating for each interest and operation separately from the previous quarter's Posted Asset Rating, as the gamemaster will need both numbers for the quarterly posting procedure. For example, a corporation with a PAR of 10 for Agriculture loses 2 Rating Points when a competitor launches a run against that interest. The gamemaster subtracts 2

from 10 for an Agriculture AAR of 8. At this point in the quarterly posting process, the loss is potential rather than actual, so the PAR remains 10. The gamemaster marks both the PAR and the adjustments on the corporation's Corporate Profile Form.

These adjustments do not actually affect the corporation until the gamemaster has calculated the potential changes in all the Asset Ratings and determined the actual Adjusted Asset Ratings as part of the posting procedure. This system allows a corporation being battered by espionage or shadowruns to initiate runs of its own to counteract those effects and regain as much of their losses as possible before posting.

ALLOCATING RESOURCES

As noted in **Operations**, p. 110, the fiscal, intelligence, and management operations also function as resources. These resources can be applied to other areas of the company to compensate for losses or simply to increase their productivity. The Resource Rating for each operation is equal to the Posted Asset Rating (PAR) for that operation at the time of the previous quarterly posting. To apply resources, the gamemaster allocates a number of Resource dice from the corporation's fiscal, intelligence, and management operations equal to each operation's Resource Rating. The gamemaster distributes these dice according to the system outlined below; he may allocate any number of the total Resource dice to any interest or operation unless otherwise noted. The Resource dice come into play during the next step of the posting process, determining Adjusted Asset Ratings.

1. Allocating Fiscal Resources: The gamemaster may allocate fiscal Resource dice to any interest or operation.

2. Allocating Intelligence Resources: Intelligence Resource dice may be allocated to any interest or operation with the exception of reputation.

3. Allocating Management Resources: The gamemaster may allocate management Resource dice to any interest or operation with the exception of reputation.

Allocating Fiscal Resources

In many ways, fiscal resources are the corporation's lifeblood. By allocating fiscal Resource dice to the other interests and operations, the gamemaster is reflecting the corp's use of financing to counter problems or enhance profits in those areas. Such uses may include purchasing new technologies, picking up research grants, offering employees salary incentives, and so on. Note that fiscal resources can also be applied to fiscal operations.

Allocating Intelligence Resources

A corporation's intelligence assets and resources gather and analyze information on other corporations. Such activity ranges from espionage to more mundane efforts such as analyzing public statements or movements by key corporate figures. It can also include tracking personnel transfers or purchasing technology. Allocating Intelligence Resource dice to any interest or to fiscal, intelligence, or management operations reflects use of intelligence techniques to enhance performance in those areas. Note that intelligence resources can also be applied to intelligence operations.

Allocating Management Resources

The corporation's management resources represent the corporation's managerial capacity and ability to manage its assets. Allocating management Resource dice reflects the corporation's administrative priorities. For example, allocating more dice to agriculture than to heavy industry indicates that corporate management pays closer attention to the former area. The gamemaster may allocate management Resource dice to any interest or to fiscal, intelligence, and management operations.

DETERMINING ASSET ADJUSTMENTS

At this point, the gamemaster determines the actual effect of the damage assessments to each interest and operation's Asset Rating. Also at this time, he determines any gains and losses resulting from the natural business cycle. Without damage, a corporation's assets can still fluctuate on their own. Damage simply makes the changes more severe.

To determine these actual Adjusted Asset Ratings (AARs), the gamemaster makes a Success Test for each interest or operation in question. The gamemaster rolls a number of dice equal to a given area's Adjusted Asset Rating, plus any Resource dice allocated to that area, against a target number equal to the area's Posted Asset Rating (PAR) from the previous quarter.

ADJUSTED ASSETS TABLE	
Successes	**Result**
0	Reduce the previous quarter's Posted Asset Rating by 1D6 ÷ 2 (round up).
1–2	PAR value remains the same.
3–4	Increase the PAR by 1.
5+	Increase the PAR by 2.

Fuchi Corp. has a PAR of 8 for its intelligence operations. The effects of shadowruns made against Fuchi's intelligence assets in this quarter have cost it 2 Rating Points, for an Adjusted Asset Rating of 6. The gamemaster has allocated no Resource dice to intelligence, so he would roll 6 dice (equal to the current AAR) against a Target Number of 8 (previous quarter's PAR). The number of successes rolled determines the actual AAR for the quarter.

For the effects of this dice roll, consult the Adjusted Assets Table, p. 116. The number of successes rolled determines the actual change in the PAR.

The gamemaster applies the resulting gain or loss to the affected area's previous quarterly PAR to determine the actual AAR for this quarter. Any net gains or losses in any interest also apply to the Adjusted Asset Rating for fiscal operations, raising or lowering the previous quarter's PAR appropriately. See **Operations**, p. 110, for more information. When adjusting Asset Ratings for operations, the gamemaster should always resolve fiscal operations last. Net losses or gains in operation Asset Ratings are not applied to the fiscal Adjusted Asset Rating. Also note that this Success Test does not apply to military operations.

DECLARING QUARTERLY POSTING

At this point in the posting procedure, the gamemaster officially declares the final Adjusted Asset Ratings (AAR) for each interest and operation as that area's new Posted Asset Rating (PAR) for the current quarter, subject to the following limitations:

• The fiscal PAR cannot be higher than twice the reputation PAR.

• No interest or operation can have a PAR higher than the fiscal PAR.

DETERMINING NET RATING

Having noted the new PARs, the gamemaster must determine the corporation's Net Rating for the quarter. The net rating represents an evaluation of the corporation's overall quarterly performance and standing. To determine the Net Rating, the gamemaster adds up all the PARs except those for security. To find the overall PAR for security, average the PARs in each security sub-area and round down. Add this value to the total of all the other PARs. The final sum is the corporation's Net Rating for the current quarter.

This Net Rating determines a corporation's standing in the business world. To determine a corp's standing as a first-tier megacorp, second-tier, third-tier, or lesser corp, consult the Net Rating Table on p. 113. Note that a corp must have a Net Rating at least 10 points higher than a competitor to have a true advantage over it.

Closing The Books

After calculating the Net Rating and completing the quarterly posting, the gamemaster closes the corporation's accounting books for the quarter. As the next quarter begins, corp accountants and analysis programs across the world renew their silent watch

on the shifting numbers that dictate megacorporate profit or loss. To begin accounting for the next quarter, go back to step 1 on p. 115 and repeat the process.

ADDITIONAL GUIDELINES

The following notes provide the gamemaster with a few additional guidelines for using corporate rating rules in a **Shadowrun** adventure.

•Allow the players to see the Posted Asset Ratings made public at the start of each quarter, but keep the Adjusted Asset Ratings secret during the posting process.

•Ignore the effects of shadowruns that the player characters do not participate in. Assume that gains and losses from other runs even out for each corporation.

•If he wishes, the gamemaster can omit quarterly posting Success Tests (see p. 116) for those interests or operations not affected by player-character activity. This significantly reduces the number of dice rolls needed and also allows the players to track the immediate effect of their characters' actions on corporate fortunes.

•Keep down the number and severity of shadowruns valued at 1 or greater (see Shadowrun Effect Table, p. 114) against any one corporation during a single quarter. Share the pain as well as the wealth. The player characters can actually make a dent in the corps' standings using this system, so be careful not to overdo it. The more damage the player characters do to a corp, the swifter and nastier its revenge.

•As always, the gamemaster may adjust or modify these rules as he sees fit. Additionally, if the dice rolls ever get in the way of good storytelling in the game, feel free to change the result. As with all aspects of **Shadowrun**, rules should enhance the fun, not squelch it.

BIG EIGHT CORPORATE PROFILES

	Ares	AZ	Fuchi	MCT	Renraku	S-K	Shiawase	Yama
Major Interests								
Aerospace	11	6	7	3	3	6	6	6
Agriculture	2	5	2	6	6	7	6	7
Biotechnology	2	6	3	6	6	7	8	8
Chemicals	5	7	2	8	5	9	7	6
Computer Engineering	6	5	11	9	10	7	5	8
Computer Science	5	5	10	8	10	5	5	6
Consumer Goods	7	6	7	6	5	6	5	4
Cybernetics	3	6	8	4	4	4	3	7
Entertainment	5	3	5	7	4	3	2	2
Finance	4	5	5	6	5	8	5	6
Heavy Industry	7	8	7	9	5	10	9	3
Mystical Goods/Services	3	8	5	7	4	3	4	3
Military Technology	10	8	8	3	6	7	6	6
Service	7	6	5	2	7	6	8	7
Operations								
Fiscal	10	8	10	9	10	10	9	8
Intelligence	6	6	8	9	6	6	8	6
Management	8	4	6	6	8	6	6	6
Reputation	10	4	6	5	9	7	8	8
Security	7	8	8	8	7	7	6	8
Magic	7	9	6	8	6	9	6	6
Matrix	7	8	11	9	9	5	6	8
Physical	9	7	8	9	7	9	7	8
Total Net Rating	118	114	123	121	120	124	116	114

Quarterly Posting Period: April 1–June 30, 2054
Note: The megacorps listed in this table represent the major players in the world of **Shadowrun**. Because of their notoriety, these corps have the predetermined Asset Ratings listed on this table for the time period noted above. The gamemaster need not create Posted Asset Ratings for these well-known corps. AZ refers to Aztechnology, S-K to Saeder-Krupp, and Yama to Yamatetsu.

CORPORATE PROFILE FORM

Corporation:

Status:
Quarter Beginning: Ending:

Interests Profile

Area	PAR		AAR	
Aerospace	[	]	[	]
Agriculture	[	]	[	]
Biotechnology	[	]	[	]
Chemicals	[	]	[	]
Computer Engineering	[	]	[	]
Computer Science	[	]	[	]
Consumer Goods	[	]	[	]
Cybernetics	[	]	[	]
Entertainment	[	]	[	]
Financial	[	]	[	]
Heavy Industry	[	]	[	]
Military Technology	[	]	[	]
Mystical	[	]	[	]
Service	[	]	[	]

Operational Profile

Area	PAR		AAR	
Fiscal	[	]	[	]
Intelligence	[	]	[	]
Management	[	]	[	]
Reputation	[	]	[	]
Security				
Magic	[	]	[	]
Matrix	[	]	[	]
Physical	[	]	[	]

PAR: Posted Asset Rating
AAR: Adjusted Asset Rating

UNAUTHORIZED POSSESSION OF THIS DOCUMENT IS A VIOLATION OF APPLICABLE
CORPORATE LAW AND PUNISHABLE ACCORDING TO THE LAWS AND REGULATIONS
OF THE CORPORATION.

ACCESS RESTRICTED
Authorized Eyes Only

AZTECHNOLOGY

·FIN·

>>>>>[Jam it and **scan** it, chummers. The file's my **gab** and **grab** total true. So's this, 'cause boredom kills. Like it or not, I care little. **Download or die.**]<<<<<

—Black Isis (10:22:59/4-13-54)

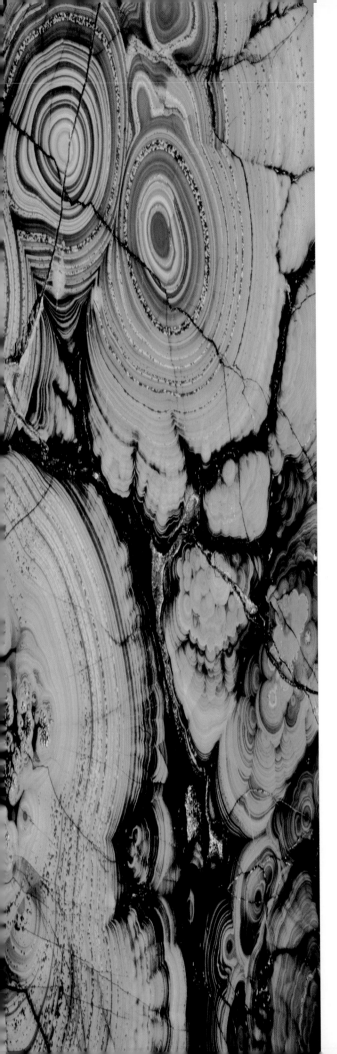

PROFILE:

HOME OFFICE LOCATION: DETROIT, MICHIGAN, UCAS

PRESIDENT/CEO: DAMIEN KNIGHT

CHAIRMAN OF THE BOARD: LEONARD AURELIUS

CORPORATE STATUS: PUBLIC CORPORATION

MAJOR SHAREHOLDERS:

> DAMIEN KNIGHT (22 PERCENT APPROX.)
>
> LEONARD AURELIUS (22 PERCENT APPROX.)
>
> GAVILAN VENTURES (12 PERCENT APPROX.)

Net Rating: 118

MAJOR INTERESTS:

AEROSPACE: 11

AGRICULTURE: 2

BIOTECHNOLOGY: 2

CHEMICALS: 5

COMPUTER ENGINEERING: 6

COMPUTER SCIENCE: 5

CONSUMER GOODS: 7

CYBERNETICS: 3

ENTERTAINMENT: 5

FINANCE: 4

HEAVY INDUSTRY: 7

MYSTICAL GOODS/SERVICES: 3

MILITARY TECHNOLOGY: 10

SERVICE: 7

OPERATIONS:

FISCAL: 10

INTELLIGENCE: 6

MANAGEMENT: 8

REPUTATION: 10

SECURITY: 7

MAGIC: 7

MATRIX: 7

PHYSICAL: 9

MILITARY: LIGHT REGIMENT/EXCEPTIONAL

ARES MACROTECHNOLOGY

>>>>>[Note that in all the profiles, "Major Shareholder" refers to any individual or corporation owning more than 10 percent of outstanding voting stock. An individual might control 50 percent of a corp's shares, but unless he personally owns more than 10 percent, he's not a major shareholder. Keep that in mind, chummers.]<<<<<
—The Answer Man (03: 51:14/3-21-54)

>>>>>[What the frag is Gavilan Ventures?]<<<<<
—Lew (10:55:51/3-21-54)

>>>>>[Holding company incorporated in Singapore. So far, no one's found out who it belongs to. Who owns Gavilan? Anybody know?]<<<<<
—Ladner (12:03:07/3-31-54)

PRIMARY BUSINESS

Ares Macrotechnology Inc. has interests in a wide range of industries. Major divisions and subsidiaries such as Knight Errant Security, Inc., Ares Arms, AresSpace, and Ares Global Entertainment make the parent corp a healthy profit in security, weapons, munitions and other military/security equipment, aerospace, entertainment, and many other areas. A wide-ranging business empire, Ares extends its interests through minor subsidiaries to such diverse markets as simsense, utilities, fashion, biotech, automotive engineering, and scientific research.

>>>>>[A scattergun approach, but it works. Most people think that all divisions of Ares' empire have "Ares" or "Knight" in the name. Not so; Ares doesn't care much about uniformity of image. As long as the money gets funneled into the Ares hoppers, individual subsidiaries can have any name that spins their jacks.]<<<<<
—Ladner (12:04:53/3-31-54)

>>>>>[Ares also has more internal competition than some other megacorps. To take a minor example, Ares owns Hard Corps Inc., a UCAS-based private security provider. At the high end of its services, Hard Corps competes with the low end of Knight Errant's business. Knight Errant is Ares CEO Damien Knight's pet project, so the two security outfits go at each other hammer and tongs even though they're both under the Ares umbrella. I've heard unsubstantiated rumors that they sometimes stage shadowruns against each other.]<<<<<
—Lykes (23:34:38/4-2-54)

>>>>>[Consider it substantiated. Hard Corps hired the old Wrecking Crew for a run against KE back in 2050.]<<<<<
—Argent (02:35:27/4-4-54)

CORPORATE STRUCTURE

The parent corporation, Ares Macrotechnology Inc., is a public corporation based in Detroit, UCAS, with 11 series of shares and 9 of debentures trading on virtual stock exchanges around the globe. At present, company president and CEO Damien Knight is the prime shareholder in the corporation, with the current chairman of the board, Leonard Aurelius, holding marginally fewer voting shares. Several million registered shareholders divide the remaining shares between them.

>>>>>[Hell, I own Ares stock. Part of my bulging portfolio (yeah, right).]<<<<<
—Stuff (11:49:08/3-18-54)

Knight and Aurelius seem to be carrying on a bitter personal feud. Up until 2049, Knight served as both chairman of the board and CEO of Ares. Through a cunning proxy campaign, Aurelius gained control of the board and ousted Knight, taking over the chairman's position. Knight apparently took this maneuver as a personal slight, and has done everything in his power to make Aurelius' life as miserable as possible.

>>>>>[Well, no wonder. Aurelius' father founded Ares Industries, the company that grew into Ares Macrotechnology. Nicholas Aurelius engineered the NASA buyout in 2016 and made Ares a megacorporation prior to Knight's involvement. Knight himself only appeared on the scene in 2033, when he acquired 22 percent of Ares' stock through his infamous Nanosecond Buyout. Knight's cluster of expertly programmed computers in Stockholm executed a series of transactions so complicated that even today only another computer can figure out what he did. By the end of the minute or so that the transactions took, three corporations ceased to exist. Two multi-millionaires lost their fortunes, three others made theirs, and Damien Knight acquired 22 percent of Ares Industries. From that point until Leonard Aurelius' inspired proxy campaign of '49, Knight has dominated the company.]<<<<<
—Double Janet (12:02:14/3-20-54)

>>>>>[Why didn't Aurelius go all the way? As chairman with an apparent lock on the Ares board, why didn't he kick Knight out as president and CEO? That's standard procedure, right?]<<<<<
—Vlasti (14:52:00/3-21-54)

>>>>>[Right, but Knight and Aurelius control almost exactly the same number of voting shares. According to my calculations, Knight owns about 22.3 percent of the corp and Aurelius owns 22.1 percent, and they also control about the same number of proxies. With that balance of power, Aurelius can't get board support for drekcanning Knight, and Knight can't get rid of Aurelius. As for why Aurelius didn't chuck Knight when he had the upper hand, that's another question. . .]<<<<<
—Nuyen Nick (18:17:52/3-24-54)

>>>>>[Knight probably has a hold over Aurelius. Not enough to break him or control him, but enough to keep his position as CEO. What that hold might be, I couldn't begin to guess.]<<<<<
—Targa (19:01:06/3-27-54)

Major Divisions

Because of its wide range of business interests, Ares is structured differently from most other megacorps. Instead of basing its divisions solely on region or function, it does both. Ares UCAS is one of its regional divisions, whereas Ares Arms is a functional division.

Under this system of organization, different functional areas such as Ares Arms, AresSpace, Knight Errant, and Ares Global Entertainment operate as independent megacorps. For example, AresSpace has its own international HQ located in Houston. That division also has regional and functional subdivisions, such as AresSpace CommSat and AresSpace Lifters UCAS.

The parent company's Detroit HQ has an additional set of subdivisions based entirely on region. For example, Ares-CAS spawns subdivisions such as Ares-Atlanta. These regional divisions serve as management corps and holding companies for the many subsidiaries Ares owns or controls in hundreds of industry segments.

>>>>>[So getting back to KE vs. Hard Corps, here's how the reporting structure works for the Seattle area. KE Seattle reports to KE UCAS, which in turn reports up the line to Knight Errant Security and its boss, Roger Soaring Owl. A puppet of Damien Knight, ol' Rog can't even visit the drekker without a go-ahead from his boss. Hard Corps Seattle is a subdivision of Hard Corps Inc., based in N'Yawk, which reports to Ares-UCAS. Ares-UCAS reports directly to Ares Macrotechnology's Detroit

HQ, and the datajack of Damien Knight. See?]<<<<<
— Lykes (23:38:32/4-2-54)

>>>>>[By the by, a lady named Karen King is the veep of Ares-Seattle. If anyone cares.]<<<<<
— Tommyknocker (18:09:37/4-9-54)

>>>>>[In an interesting aside, Ares based its vast aerospace holdings around the old NASA facilities that Ares Industries acquired from the U.S. government back in 2016. According to the provisions of that deal, Ares agreed to return elements of the facilities to the U.S. government in 2055. Course, the U.S. government doesn't exist any more. (Grin)]<<<<<
— Double Janet (04:15:52/4-10-54)

Execs

Officially, Roger Soaring Owl serves as executive VP in charge of Knight Errant Security. In practice, the ubiquitous Mr. Knight controls nearly all facets of the division's day-to-day business.

>>>>>[Sometimes to the detriment of his responsibilities to the core corp. KE is Knight's personal baby, and it shows. If Aurelius eased him out of the CEO chair and put him in Soaring Owl's spot, Knight would probably be a happy camper once his bruised ego healed.]<<<<<
— Suzy Q (16:07:14/4-3-54)

>>>>>[What's Knight's background, anyway? He's something of a mystery man.]<<<<<
— Andante (14:32:21/4-6-54)

>>>>>[Hard to trace. I doubt Knight is his birth name, but that ident's so deeply entrenched that it's become his real name. He hit it big during the Crash of '29, and parlayed his way to the CEO's chair. I'd peg him as a former corporate raider, but I don't really know.]<<<<<
— Maurice (11:03:42/4-9-54)

>>>>>[For a corporate raider, he's got a real knack for security operations. My guess is a merc background. He might have been a warboss with one of the more militant Euro-polis.]<<<<<
— Raver (21:20:54/4-9-54)

>>>>>[Oh? And on what (non-existent) evidence do you base this wondrous conclusion?]<<<<<
— Cliff (13:25:05/4-11-54)

>>>>>[I've spent years digging into Knight's background, and I think I've found his birth name. At least, I've found the name he used before he took Knight. The name's David Gavilan. That's right, Gavilan. Ten to one he has some interest in Gavilan Ventures, the third major shareholder in Ares Macrotech.]<<<<<
— Turner (00:40:43/4-13-54)

>>>>>[If so, Knight/Gavilan could outvote Aurelius, so he'd still be chairman of the board. I think there's some drek going on here that we don't know about.]<<<<<
— Alix (18:03:01/4-13-54)

>>>>>[Wait a minute! David Gavilan? Doesn't anybody remember David Gavilan??? I can't believe this didn't occur to me before! Major David Gavilan of the United States Air Force, liaison to the National Security Agency, headed up the Echo-Mirage project back after the Crash of '29! He disappeared in late 2031 after the Echo Mirage team purged the computer virus and the project closed. This has some really nasty implications, folks! Turner, can you dig some more??]<<<<<
— Eddie Monster (23:15:49/4-14-54)

>>>>>[If you're right, Eddie. . .Yes, I believe I will dig some more.]<<<<<
— Turner (03:42:15/4-15-54)

General Guido Cantarelli, retired from the UCAS Marine Corps, serves as exec VP of Ares Arms. We suspect that Cantarelli is a figurehead, trading on his reputation to gain points with military clients while a body of advisors makes the actual business decisions for the division.

>>>>>[Or maybe Knight does—the fragging eminence grise behind Ares.]<<<<<
— PKzip (19:35:22/3-30-54)

>>>>>[Cantarelli has a terrific rep in military circles. He's the single most-decorated, still-living officer in UCAS history. His personal legend mentions that he took a sniper round to a major nerve trunk during one engagement, but refused treatment until his men had won the battle. Immediate treatment would have left him the full use of his legs; the delay gave him a major limp. He apparently refuses cyber replacement.]<<<<<
— Blade (23:56:00/3-30-54)

>>>>>[Doesn't sound like the kind of guy who'd play figurehead. Hmm. . .]<<<<<
— QB (13:27:30/4-1-54)

Dacia Lucas is the exec VP of AresSpace, and Amir Lakha serves as exec VP of Ares Global Entertainment.

SECURITY

Each major division within the Ares hierarchy takes care of its own security. Not surprisingly, the effectiveness of security varies from one division to another, although overall security remains admirably high.

>>>>>[No wonder. Ares Macrotech may not have a central internal security agency, but any division can hire the services of either Knight Errant or Ares Arms to help it out. KE and Ares Arms personnel constantly get seconded between divisions, paid for by internal fund transfers. So if AresSpace needs top-notch corporate security against an expected shadowrun, it hires KE forces to do the job. Meanwhile, if Ares Global Entertainment's Germany division happens to expect a wave of major sabotage from some policlub, Ares Arms' military "advisors" show up to guard its facilities, armed with "prototypes" of mil-spec hardware. Not easy to crack, chummers.]<<<<<
— Vagabond (12:35:04/3-29-54)

Physical and Magical Security

Though generalizations get dangerous when it comes to discussing Ares security provisions, physical site security generally depends more on personnel than on hardware. The people on-site may have the best gear available in their hot little hands, supported by comm nets and other infrastructure. But most of the time, if either trained personnel or a remote sensor can handle a particular security task, Ares puts its "wetware" on the cutting edge with the hardware and software backing them up, rather than vice versa.

>>>>>[Military thinking, I guess. More countermeasures work against high-tech sensors than against a good pair of eyes and a trained brain.]<<<<<
—Blade (23:58:13/3-30-54)

In terms of magical site security, Ares has a well-deserved reputation for efficiently integrating its magical assets with its physical security provisions. Rather than concentrating its mages in a single band of magical shock troops, Ares spreads them among mundane units to back up the non-magical security forces.

>>>>>[Again, good military practice. Classic combined-arms ops.]<<<<<
—Blade (23:59:50/3-30-54)

>>>>>[Ares tends to have fewer magical assets than other corps.]<<<<<
—Crunch (20:46:26/4-2-54)

>>>>>[If that was ever true, it's definitely changing now.]<<<<<
—Wyse (13:13:28/4-6-54)

Matrix Security

In this one area, Ares has fallen behind the other megacorps. Ares simply has less sophisticated Matrix security than that established by corps such as Fuchi. Ares tends to use IC at least one generation behind the cutting edge, and its hardware generally works a bit more slowly. To make up for these drawbacks, a typical Ares system has considerable layering, often uneven, with data choke-points that look like glaciers.

>>>>>[Who is this guy? Chummer, you go breezing into an Ares high-security or ultra-security stem looking for a cakewalk, and your neurons will never know what hit them. May whatever gods there be protect your soul. Sure, you might not find individual programs and chunks of hardware as wizzer as the nasty things in a Fuchi system, but that doesn't make the system vulnerable. Other corps design their systems around insecure paradigms and make up for it with heavy ice. Ares uses intelligent, secure system architectures so they don't need bleeding-edge ice to keep yobs like me out.]<<<<<
—Icebreaker (16:50:01/3-25-54)

>>>>>[So you've got to plan your penetration a little smarter. Pick the right SAN to enter the system through, and find the datapaths that avoid as many of those nasty choke-points as possible.]<<<<<
—Nora (20:15:29/3-27-54)

>>>>>[If Knight headed up Echo Mirage, then Icebreaker's point makes sense. David Gavilan/Damien Knight saw the fraggin' Matrix born. He knows exactly how it works. Smart design wins out over smartframe, I guess.]<<<<<
—Eddie Monster (23:27:09/4-14-54)

Military Security

Ares Arms' Military Systems Division provides the megacorporation's military assets. These include a competitive Desert Wars force; an extensive set of trained "test and evaluation" personnel capable of putting any new weapon or support system through its paces; and a team of "end-user consultants" assigned to train the purchasers of Ares' military products to use them most efficiently. With the possible exception of Aztechnology, Ares has the most extensive military capability among all the megacorps.

>>>>>[Yeah, well, Big A's a special case. Hard to tell where Aztechnology's military ends and Aztlan's begins.]<<<<<
—Pyramid Watcher (05:23:49/4-13-54)

>>>>>[Okay, Ares has a Desert Wars force. Also a group of slags who test weapons. Think they might have some fragging lethal prototypes kicking around? Gotta test something, right? Ares also has consultants who train armies how to slaughter each other using Ares weapons. Think they just might have some of those weapons lying around? After all, the best way to teach someone is to demo the skill. So that gives Ares three fragging armies, equipped with the best that Ares Arms can crank out. Scary…]<<<<<
—Durandel (14:03:06/4-16-54)

Extended Security

Officially, Ares has limited "extended security" assets on staff. It appears to use few street ops, and even fewer special forces. Of course, its widespread range of subsidiaries means that nobody can watch them all. Instead of keeping a black-ops team on Ares' payroll where someone might notice, Damien Knight buries them in the payroll of a distant subsidiary not publicly acknowledged as part of the Ares corporate empire. That way, Knight can honestly claim that Ares Macrotechnology Inc. employs no black-ops teams.

>>>>>[For the same reason, Ares frequently employs shadowrunners.]<<<<<
—Hangfire (23:18:43/3-29-54)

>>>>>[In my personal experience, you're least likely to get fragged by your own Johnson on an Ares run. The corp pays top cred, and it usually does right by its temporary employees.]<<<<<
—NewWest (00:29:58/4-1-54)

>>>>>[Your naiveté is fragging touching. From your post, I'd call your personal experience limited and unlikely to get much more extensive. Chummer, every corp frags its shadowrunners over if and when it suits them to do so. No matter who pays the tab or claims to pay the tab, you do your fragging homework and find out what's behind the goddamn run. If you want to keep sucking air past your teeth, find out what you're really in for and whose toes you'll be stepping on. Never mind what your Johnson tells you, whether it's an Ares run or not. Got me?]<<<<<
—Argent (02:38:19/4-4-54)

> "KNIGHT... WAS THERE WHEN THE FRAGGIN MATRIX WAS *BORN*. HE KNOWS HOW IT WORKS, AND DOESN'T."

AZTECHNOLOGY

PROFILE:

HOME OFFICE LOCATION: Mexico City, Aztlan

PRESIDENT/CEO: Juan Atzcapotzalco

CHAIRMAN OF THE BOARD: Unknown

CORPORATE STATUS: Private Corporation

MAJOR SHAREHOLDERS: Unknown

NET RATING: 114

MAJOR INTERESTS:
Aerospace: 6
Agriculture: 5
Biotechnology: 6
Chemicals: 7
Computer Engineering: 5
Computer Science: 5
Consumer Goods: 6
Cybernetics: 6
Entertainment: 3
Finance: 5
Heavy Industry: 8
Mystical Goods/Services: 8
Military Technology: 8
Service: 6

OPERATIONS:
Fiscal: 8
Intelligence: 6
Management: 4
Reputation: 4
Security: 8
  Magic: 9
  Matrix: 8
  Physical: 7

MILITARY: Regiment or larger/ Above average

>>>>>(Unknown chairman, unknown shareholders. Neo-A's don't know much, do they?)<<<<<
   —Harvey (10:39:38/3-23-54)

>>>>>(That always happens with Aztechnology, chummer. Get used to it.)<<<<<
   —Pyramid Watcher (15:23:34/3-25-54)

PRIMARY BUSINESS

The most diversified of the triple-A megacorps, the Big A is into everything from diapers, to nerve gas, to consumer electronics, to heavy munitions.

>>>>>(So just about all its operations step on the toes of some other megacorp. Aztechnology seems to like it that way. Confrontational bunch.)<<<<<
   —Hiberia (13:43:58/4-2-54)

>>>>>(Hardly surprising, considering their background. Aztechnology started out as a coalition of the most aggressive, corrupt, and unethical corps that ever did biz, and the megacorp still has a lot of those characteristics.)<<<<<
   —The Chromed Accountant (12:05:58/4-5-54)

>>>>>(How the hell did a motley crew of technopirates turn into the world's most militant megacorp?)<<<<<
   —Moxie (12:15:47/4-5-54)

>>>>>(Mainly by forming alliances. First and foremost, they hooked their tentacles into the Aztlan government. Considering the personalities of the people involved, I'd bet that "alliance" depends on the sheer amount of dirt Aztechnology suits dug up from government members' pasts. The Big A loves blackmail. Whatever the case, the line between "Aztechnology" and "the Aztlan government" tends to shift with the winds.

Though this is wild speculation, ongoing rumors claim that the original founders of Aztechnology got some heavy-duty magical help. Depending on what version of the rumor you hear, their allies range from feathered serpents to some mucho mysterioso "Aztec spirits." The featherheads are less impressive than great dragons like Lofwyr, but still smart and powerful enough to help out a struggling corporation. As for the Aztec spirits, no one says nothin'.)<<<<<
   —Carpe Diem (00:14:00/4-7-54)

>>>>>("Aztec spirits," my hoop. Big A got where it is today through the most unscrupulous business practices anyone ever went a long way to avoid. If you want a textbook of dirty corp tricks, get your mitts on an Aztechnology policies and procedures manual.)<<<<<
   —Lucas (21:33:55/4-7-54)

CORPORATE STRUCTURE

Publicly, no one knows much about Aztechnology's ownership. The government of Aztlan may have a major equity position in the company, or that relationship may be reversed. No one outside Aztechnology's topmost levels knows for sure.

>>>>>(More than a few colleagues of mine have tried to find out. They've either gotten stonewalled until they gave up, or they died in convenient "accidents.")<<<<<
   —Turner (15:04:03/4-2-54)

>>>>>(I heard a rumor that a consortium of feathered serpents owns Big A, and that Atzcapotzalco is just a figurehead.)<<<<<
   —Lucas (21:33:55/4-7-54)

>>>>>(Well, I heard that Atzca-whatever has been dead for six or seven years. The real bosses of Aztechnology use magic to puppet him around. They want the (meta)humans to keep believing that they call the shots, instead of realizing that they're just pawns in some weird game.)<<<<<
   —Rat Dancer (22:57:05/4-9-54)

>>>>>(Where'd you hear that? A fragging insane asylum? No no, don't tell me. The datatabs, right? And the real bosses of Big A are Elvis, Jimi Hendrix, Jetblack, and Jim Morrison. Su-u-u-re.)<<<<<
   —Loree (03:28:33/4-12-54)

Major Divisions

Aztechnology has six continental divisions: North America, South America, Europe, Asia, Africa and Australasia. Within these divisions are regional subdivisions such as Aztechnology Northwest, Northeast, Central, and so on. Aztechnology divisions range widely in size, from monolithic corps as large as some multinational conglomerates to small holding companies that control wholly owned subsidiaries.

Execs

No information.

>>>>>(Hey, what's happening here? Are the Neo-As getting lazy, or what?)<<<<<
   —Harkness (11:03:03/4-1-54)

SECURITY

World-renowned for efficient security, Aztechnology forces are well-trained and carry state-of-the-art equipment. At every level, the corp integrates its mages with physical security, frequently also using parabiologicals. Aztechnology uses high-technology sensors, though the corp avoids lethal threat-suppression systems.

>>>>>(Bulldrek it does. Big A uses a ton of autonomous gun systems, the kind with miniguns slaved to fire-tracking radars and tactical computers. They also like land mines and lasers. I thought these Neo-As knew what they were talking about.)<<<<<
—Harkness (11:03:59/4-1-54)

Physical and Magical Security
No information.

>>>>>(What the frag is this?)<<<<<
—Harkness (11:04:35/4-1-54)

Matrix Security
>> FILE ACCESS ERROR
>> DATA MAY BE CORRUPTED
>> ATTEMPT ACCESS ANYWAY? (Y/n)—y
>> UNRECOVERABLE FILE ACCESS ERROR

Military Security
Aztechnology has no military assets.

>>>>>(Wrong wrong wrong! Big A's a major player in Desert Wars, chummers. You can't play in that league without military assets.)<<<<<
—Branigan (11:13:07/4-2-54)

>>>>>(Maybe they're talking "officially," Branigan. As in, "They're not our army units, they belong to the Aztlan government. We just get to play with them." That kind of drek.)<<<<<
—Roger Dodger (21:03:46/4-5-54)

Extended Security
>>>>(I heard a rumor that a consortium of feathered serpents owns Big A, and that Atzcapotzalco is just a figurehead.)<<<<<
—Lucas (21:33:55/4-7-54)

>>>>>(Lucas, you already said that.)<<<<<
—Raiko (05:32:25/4-8-54)

>>>>>(I never said that.)<<<<<
—Lucas (21:33:55/4-7-54)

>>>>>(I just scanned the file. Lucas you slot, you're up to something. Every posting you've made in this section has the same fragging time-date stamp. Every fragging posting, even the last one, which appears to be out of sequence. Either you're fragging around, or somebody else is.)<<<<<
—Whistler's Mother (14:20:49/4-8-54)

>>>>>(Okay, jokers, be warned. Someone's penetrated Shadowland. Considering the state of the Aztechnology file, this shouldn't come as a total shock to most of you. The board's not completely compromised, but I advise you all to take care and practice safe computing. (Always wear a write-protect chip.) Here at Shadowland,

we're very careful. Deckers and IC cover most access channels. The Neo-Anarchists managed to huck this drek onto our board without our say-so, but we cleared that up. It was an inside job, and the person involved is no longer associated with Shadowland. 'Nuff said. Because a good "stealth" virus could crash our system but good as well as the system of anyone who logged on to the BBS, we take pretty stringent precautions against infection.

For one thing, we keep comments uploaded by you fraggers in a different file on a different computer, completely separate from the real Shadowland data. (The wonder of distributed file structures lets you see them merged when you scan our files.) Anyway, anything anybody uploads that might contain a virus, like executable code or certain types of text file, gets run first in a "virtual machine." (For null-heads, that means a "machine within a machine" that has real restrictions on memory allocation, hardware access, and so on.) Any code running in the virtual machine is completely isolated. If a virus wants to do something unpleasant within the VM, we let it; we detect its activity and purge the file, no love lost and no risk.

Over the last couple of weeks, a really nasty virus got onto Shadowland from an unknown source. The person who coded the virus knew about our practice of running uploaded data in a virtual machine, and wrote his code specifically to "escape" from inside a VM. We think it's an inside job because the virus seemed tailored specifically to the paradigm of VM that we use. We tracked down the virus and eliminated every copy of it, as far as we can tell. But don't take that for granted. We might have missed one.

Having warned you, our responsibility ends at this point. Thank you.)<<<<<
—SYSephan OPus (04:06:38/5-2-54)

>>>>>(Frag, this is nothing new. Aztechnology penetrated Shadowland once before. They blew up the fragging server hub, crashed the whole network but good.)<<<<<
—Ginny (18:18:08/5-4-54)

>>>>>(You mean back in May '51, the Grodin's Tavern explosion? Chummer, Aztechnology didn't pull that drek.)<<<<<
—Lady Blues (11:35:57/5-5-54)

>>>>>(Who the frag did, then?)<<<<<
—Ginny (19:42:41/5-5-54)

>>>>>(Don't know, but not the Azzies. I know that much.)<<<<<
—Lady Blues (23:23:13/5-5-54)

>>>>>(Best you should not ask further.)<<<<<
—Man of Many Names (16:32:00/5-6-54)

>>>>>(Who the frag's this geezer?)<<<<<
—Ginny (20:21:13/5-6-54)

FUCHI

INDUSTRIAL ELECTRONICS

FUCHI INDUSTRIAL ELECTRONICS

HOME OFFICE LOCATION: Tokyo, Japan
PRESIDENT/CEO: Richard Villiers
CHAIRMAN OF THE BOARD: NA
CORPORATE STATUS: Private corporation
MAJOR SHAREHOLDERS:
    Richard Villiers (approx. 35 percent)
    Shikei Nakatomi (approx. 32 percent)
    Korin Yamana (approx. 30 percent)

NET RATING: 123

MAJOR INTERESTS
    Aerospace: 7
    Agriculture: 2
    Biotechnology: 3
    Chemicals: 2
    Computer Engineering: 11
    Computer Science: 10
    Consumer Goods: 7
    Cybernetics: 8
    Entertainment: 5
    Finance: 5
    Heavy Industry: 7
    Mystical Goods/Services: 5
    Military Technology: 8
    Service: 5

OPERATIONS
    Fiscal: 10
    Intelligence: 8
    Management: 6
    Reputation: 6
    Security: 8
        Magic: 6
        Matrix: 11
        Physical: 8
    Military: Company/Excellent

PRIMARY BUSINESS

The consummate high-tech company, Fuchi develops state-of-the-art hardware and software for the corporate, industrial, and military markets. Through its various divisions, the corp handles all facets of the process, from pure research and development to mass production and marketing. Numerous smaller divisions also sell certain products directly to end-users. Sidelines include management consulting, contract programming and development, and technical troubleshooting services.

>>>>>[Fuchi developed the first ASIST technology, the tech that opened up cyberspace and paved the way for the Matrix as we know it. Any decker can tell you that Fuchi makes some of the better cyberdecks on the market, and even non-Fuchi products such as Fairlight decks use tech patented by Fuchi Electronics. In a way, you could call Fuchi the patron saint of deckers and the spiritual parent of Shadowland.]<<<<<
    —Electron Warrior (18:11:41/3-19-54)

>>>>>[Sure, you could call them that…if you're a fuzzy-minded slot. Let me point out that Fuchi also develops wiz ice, right out there on the bleeding edge. A full assortment of colors, too: white, gray and black. Fuchi personnel developed the initial IC concept, and they're still pushing the edge of the envelope.]<<<<<
    —BugHunter (23:01:57/3-19-54)

>>>>>[It takes smarts to avoid the "NIH" (Not Invented Here) problem. Fuchi's IC labs know just how to get around it. Instead of developing stuff from scratch, they sometimes license wizzer new algorithms from other developers. For example, they got their mitts on some particularly nasty "smart" ice developed at the University of Cheyenne, in the Sioux Nation.]<<<<<
    —Nora (08:47:06/3-21-54)

>>>>>[Flash! Fuchi has just pulled off a hostile takeover of FTL Technologies Inc., a Sioux-based software developer. FTL developed the popular "Warpdrive" language, and holds patents on a lot of breakthroughs in cyberdeck technology. (To give just one example, Fuchi, Fairlight, and others have used FTL's code for years in Persona chips.) FTL managed to hold off takeover attempts by MCT and other big boys for quite a time, until Fuchi caught them in a credit crunch. The megacorp drove FTL's share prices into the drekker, then bought up voting control. No dirty tricks that I've heard of, just plain business smarts. Expect some hot products to come out of Cyberspace Development Corp., the Fuchi subsidiary that engineered the FTL snatch.]<<<<<
    —Larkspur (05:43:42/4-24-54)

>>>>>[Cyberspace Development Corp.? That puts FTL cleanly in the Villiers camp. CDC is one of Villiers' babies.]<<<<<
    —Turner (13:42:28/4-24-54)

>>>>>[Hey, I thought Sioux had laws against foreign corps taking over its so-called "strategic" companies.]<<<<<
    —Xist (21:09:04/4-24-54)

>>>>>[Well, yes. I simplified the story. FTL actually got taken over by Laramie Resource Development Inc., a Sioux-based outfit incorporated in Cheyenne. Through three intermediaries, Cyberspace Development Corp. indirectly owns Laramie. That makes it a Fuchi takeover, but done at arm's-length to avoid local restrictions.]<<<<<
    —Larkspur (04:54:48/4-25-54)

CORPORATE STRUCTURE

A consortium of the Villiers, Nakatomi, and Yamana families owns Fuchi Industrial Electronics Corporation, the heart of the Fuchi industrial empire. Though various members of the three families own stock, only the heads of the respective clans vote all of the shares owned. The percentage ownership figures for Richard Villiers, Shikei Nakatomi, and Korin Yamana in the Profile above reflect voting control, not personal ownership.

>>>>>[The figures don't add up. Who owns the rest of the stock?]<<<<<
    —Ballyhoo (10:15:03/3-27-54)

>>>>>[Different individuals, possibly the Gemeinschaft Bank (collateral, you know). Most of the remaining stock is non-voting, or else one of the three principals has the owner's proxies.]<<<<<
—Maurice (09:10:12/3-29-54)

>>>>>[Samantha Villiers, Richard's ex and VP of the Fuchi Northwest division, owns about 2 percent of voting stock. She always backs her ex-husband, but by choice rather than through coercion.]<<<<<
—Ladner (12:38:30/3-31-54)

Richard Villiers officially resides in New York, though he spends most of his time at Fuchi HQ in Tokyo. Though he currently wields the greatest power over corp policy among the three factions, this balance between Villiers and his partners has changed in the past and may change again. The three families who own Fuchi have an efficient, but far from cordial, relationship requiring a constant tightrope act by each family head. Each group has its own "empire," a group of divisions and subsidiaries that it either owns outright or controls. Like any group of good little corporate moguls, each family tries to expand its empire at the expense of the others without triggering infighting that might damage the profits of the corporation as a whole. No sense fighting for a bigger slice of a shrinking pie, after all. So far, this uneasy balance between division profit and corp-wide profit has kept Fuchi's three families from crossing the line into no-holds-barred conflict.

>>>>>[Fuchi works kind of like the Politburo in the old Soviet Union. (Any historians out there?) The Soviet troika was the Party, the Red Army, and the KGB; Fuchi's is Villiers, Yamana, and Nakatomi. To keep their outside rivals off their back, the three factions need to show the world a unified front. Show any weakness to MCT, for example, and MCT might rip you up. Meanwhile, a major power struggle goes on behind closed doors. The balance of power can shift at almost a moment's notice.]<<<<<
—Jackson (19:03:29/3-24-54)

>>>>>[Sometimes the power struggle gets a little out of hand. Fuchi has actually made runs against itself, as divisions in one empire target parts of other empires.]<<<<<
—Hangfire (21:11:10/3-27-54)

>>>>>[Just now, it looks like Villiers is in the catbird seat. Nakatomi owes him big-time for his help in resisting a move by Yamana. Villiers seems to have a lock on things, at least until Nakatomi gets his empire back on an even keel.]<<<<<
—Rat (01:13:21/4-10-54)

Major Divisions

Fuchi Industrial Electronics Corporation follows a straightforward hierarchical structure. The central corp has three continental divisions: Fuchi Americas, Fuchi Pan-Europa, and Fuchi Asia. Fuchi Orbital, the fourth major division, handles the corp's considerable assets located in low earth orbit. These include various manufacturing facilities run by computer and telepresence operators and two small orbital habitats. Under the current division of power, the Yamana faction runs Fuchi Pan-Europa (renamed from the old Fuchi Europe division), Nakatomi runs Fuchi Asia, and Villiers controls Fuchi Americas. Control of the new Fuchi Orbital division fluctuates between all three families.

>>>>>[Predictably, things aren't really that clear-cut. Yamana runs Europe but also has his fingers into Asia, and both Yamana and Nakatomi have some influence on the east coast of North America. Right now, Villiers has an edge in the orbital operations, but it might not last. Watch the box scores, boys and girls. Fuchi's internal power games can provide endless entertainment.]<<<<<
—Maurice (09:15:23/3-29-54)

At last count, Fuchi's major continental divisions comprised thirty-one regional subdivisions such as Fuchi Northwest, Fuchi Caribe, Fuchi Nihon, and so on. These subdivisions encompass smaller functional divisions, such as Fuchi Internal Security and Fuchi Orbital Transport. As their names imply, the former acts as the megacorp's primary intelligence-gathering arm, and the latter handles communication and transportation between Earth and the corp's orbital assets.

>>>>>[Interesting point: Richard Villiers more or less controls both of those functional divisions. His control of Fuchi Orbital Transport gives Villiers his lock on the entire Fuchi Orbital division; through the transport company, he controls access. At least, he does for the moment. After all, any suborbital with strap-on tanks and boosters can get to low earth orbit. Other Fuchi divisions own suborbitals, and both the Yamana and Nakatomi factions are busy acquiring the strap-on hardware to give them orbital capability. Once they've got it, Villiers may have a fight on his hands. Then again, Villiers controls internal security for the whole corp. That must make Yamana and Nakatomi more than a little twitchy, and may stop them from making any major moves.]<<<<<
—Link (09:45:48/4-1-54)

>>>>>[You can bet the other two families have their own intelligence-gathering and security assets, whether or not those assets exist as divisions. You can also bet that they shut out Fuchi Internal Security from any sensitive operations they've got going on.]<<<<<
—Hangfire (20:22:53/4-3-54)

Execs

San-yo Ohara, a tough operator who once worked as Yamana's personal expediter, serves as executive VP of Fuchi Pan-Europa. Shikei Nakatomi's daughter-in-law Noriko Sakai holds the exec VP position at Fuchi Asia. Jacques LeMer serves as executive veep of Fuchi Orbital.

>>>>>[Poor, embattled SOB. LeMer backs Villiers to the hilt. He used to work in the Pan-Europa division, but skipped to Fuchi Americas some years back and asked Villiers for political asylum. Supposedly, the two of them have a close, personal friendship. LeMer's a top manager, and received a master's degree in astronautical engineering from MIT&M before getting a doctorate in business administration. Those sterling qualifications made him a natural for the exec veep spot at Fuchi Orbital. Of course, both the Japanese factions are racking their little brains for a way to bring him down.]<<<<<
—Ladner (12:40:31/3-31-54)

Surprisingly, Fuchi Americas has no executive VP. CEO Richard Villiers runs this key division himself.

>>>>>[In our neck of the woods, people pay attention to Ricky's ex-wife, Samantha Villiers. Stinking rich and frighteningly competent, she's also on friendly terms with Richard. She started as VP of Seattle-based Fuchi Systems Design, one of

Fuchi Americas' most profitable subdivisions. Recently, the corp bumped her upstairs to the VP slot at Fuchi Northwest. A slag by the name of Dr. Ben Bleiler took her place at Systems Design, and under his management that division has outperformed even its staggering success with Samantha at the helm.]<<<<<
—Ladner (12:41:58/3-31-54)

>>>>>[Systems Design and Fuchi Corporate Services, a management consulting outfit that belongs to the Nakatomi empire, have an ongoing feud. CorpServ staged a couple of runs against SD when Sam Villiers bossed the place, and hostilities likely won't cease with a change of personnel. Unless the Nakatomis had a personal motivation…now there's an interesting thought.]<<<<<
—Hangfire (20:03:35/3-31-54)

>>>>>[A guy named Miles Lanier runs Fuchi Internal Security. (He pronounces his name "Luh-neer," not "Lan-yeh" like the French do.) Everybody who knows him says he's an aristocratic son of a slitch with an attitude problem. He's arrogant as all hell, and apparently a pain in the hoop to work for. He's also hideously competent. This guy wrote the book on Matrix and physical site security.]<<<<<
—Rover (09:22:10/4-2-54)

SECURITY

Within the Fuchi organization, Fuchi Internal Security acts as a resource on which other divisions and subsidiaries can draw. Because IntSec belongs to the Villiers faction, however, divisions and subsidiaries controlled by Yamana or Nakatomi interests rarely use its services for anything beyond basic site security.

>>>>>[That means security provisions at Fuchi divisions vary quite a bit. That much variety can be a pain for runners planning an op, because experience with one Fuchi facility doesn't necessarily apply to another.]<<<<<
—Argent (15:10:34/4-5-54)

Physical and Magical Security

IntSec tends to provide physical site security almost military in its precision. Unlike other corps such as in-your-face MCT, Fuchi prefers to make more subtle security provisions. Not many personnel wander around sporting big guns, and massive firepower plays an equally small role. A typical IntSec site has layered defenses, with passive and active sensors that detect intruders and then direct countermeasures to the appropriate location.

>>>>>[IntSec tends to work by the book, as written by Miles Lanier. Lanier served time in the military as a sniper, which explains his focus on precision. Corps like Mitsuhama use a "minigun" approach to defense: put enough rounds in the air and they're bound to hit something. Lanier's approach goes the opposite way, recognizing that a single needle round to the temple drops a target more efficiently than saturation shooting.]<<<<<
—Blade (15:02:11/4-2-54)

>>>>>[IntSec is bloody good. A lot of their personnel have military training, and it shows. Not surprising, considering their chief's background. Fuchi security's one weakness exists in the realm of magic. Both Lanier and Villiers are mundane, and so are most of Villiers'

closest friends and advisors within Fuchi. They tend toward short-sightedness when it comes to magical possibilities and dangers.]<<<<<
—WizKid (21:43:08/4-3-54)

>>>>>[That situation is changing rapidly. IntSec got burned a few times recently by magically adept raiders, and Lanier and his lackeys learn from their mistakes pretty fragging fast. Expect more mages to get involved in IntSec projects, and also look for more parabiological beasties.]<<<<<
—Skywalker (22:32:33/4-8-54)

Matrix Security

Fuchi has a level of Matrix security unmatched by anyone else in the world, notwithstanding Mitsuhama's claims to the contrary. To protect its sensitive computer systems, Fuchi uses ultra-security that rivals mil-spec systems.

>>>>>[No surprise, chummers. Fuchi developed all that tech in the first place. The UCAS military uses Fuchi software and hardware for its own Matrix defense. Those divisions and subsidiaries working with IntSec resources supplement their high- and ultra-security installations with talented roving deckers.]<<<<<
—BugHunter (23:09:07/3-19-54)

Military Security

Though its military remains relatively small compared to other corps, Fuchi fields its exceptionally well-trained and well-equipped force in occasional Desert Wars campaigns. The Fuchi forces have a widespread reputation for innovative combined-arms operations that depend on split-second planning. Most units larger than platoons also use tactical expert systems, including the state-of-the-art TEX system that Fuchi recently sold to the UCAS, CalFree, and German militaries.

>>>>>[Fuchi has an army, but I doubt Villiers can trust it. As CEO, he's the official C-in-C of the corp's military arm. In practice, divided loyalty runs through the whole military. Some commanders are in Nakatomi's pocket, others back Yamana. Villiers could cope with the problem by organizing a purge of the officer corps, and he probably will at some point. Of course, that would tear the heart out of the military arm, which would take Fuchi years to rebuild. So don't expect to see Fuchi fielding military forces anywhere but in the Desert Wars theater.]<<<<<
—Blade (15:07:06/4-2-54)

Extended Security

Fuchi has the reputation for staging the most successful covert ops, using the best-trained company men. Among other things, Fuchi began deploying mages in all its combat teams before many of the other corps followed suit.

>>>>>[Interesting and somewhat contradictory, in light of Lanier's short-sightedness about magic.]<<<<<
—Nick (10:45:03/3-19-54)

>>>>>[Lanier's IntSec doesn't run covert ops, Nick. A different group takes care of those. Apparently, Lanier likes it that way. I don't know exactly what division handles covert ops, or who's in charge. Villiers supposedly has lots of contacts among shadowrunners worldwide, so he may well contract a lot of black ops out.]<<<<<
—Hangfire (23:47:43/3-23-54)

MITSUHAMA COMPUTER TECHNOLOGIES

Home Office Location: Kyoto, Japan
President/CEO: Toshiro Mitsuhama
Chairman of the Board: Samba Oi
Corporate Status: Public corporation
Major Shareholders:
   Samba Oi (approx. 13 percent)
   Yuriyasu Shin (approx. 11 percent)
   Oguramaro Saigusa (approx. 10 percent)
   Akae Uehara (approx. 10 percent)

Net Rating: 121
Major Interests
   Aerospace: 3
   Agriculture: 6
   Biotechnology: 6
   Chemicals: 8
   Computer Engineering: 9
   Computer Science: 8
   Consumer Goods: 6
   Cybernetics: 4
   Entertainment: 7
   Finance: 6
   Heavy Industry: 9
   Mystical Goods/Services: 7
   Military Technology: 3
   Service: 2
Operations
   Fiscal: 9
   Intelligence: 9
   Management: 6
   Reputation: 5
   Security: 8
      Magic: 8
      Matrix: 9
      Physical: 9
   Military: Company/Above average

>>>>>[Note that Toshiro Mitsuhama, son of the famed Taiga ("Tiger") Mitsuhama who created MCT in its present form, does not hold a major block of voting shares in the company he runs.]<<<<<
—Ladner (12:52:33/3-31-54)

>>>>>[Where's Tiger himself? Why isn't he on the list?]<<<<<
—Cibola (22:21:10/3-31-54)

>>>>>[Between them, Tiger and Toshiro Mitsuhama own maybe 2 percent of MCT. Even though Tiger's hard driving beat MCT into its present shape, he never had a strong equity position in the company bearing his name.]<<<<<
—Maurice (10:23:58/4-3-54)

PRIMARY BUSINESS

As its name implies, Mitsuhama Computer Technologies makes its money through various facets of computerization. Though it tends to follow Fuchi's lead in the area of direct neural interfaces, MCT is the pre-eminent designer and marketer of physical interfaces by which computers directly affect the physical world.

>>>>>[Meaning robotics, CAD/CAM, autonomously guided vehicles, and so on. If the computer's jacked into anything but a brain, MCT's in the forefront.]<<<<<
—Nora (12:06:11/3-24-54)

Numerous and varied subsidiaries also operate in many other industries, including such areas as entertainment.

CORPORATE STRUCTURE

Following a structure typical of average corporations, Mitsuhama has a management team distinct from the corp's owners. The major shareholders of MCT do not run the company; instead, they make their fortunes by investing in several large, growing, profitable corporations. For example, the chairman of MCT's board of directors, Samba Oi, sits on the board of six other megacorporations. However, MCT is the only triple-A megacorp on whose board he serves.

>>>>>[Oi, Shin, Saigusa, and Uehara make their meganuyen other ways, too. These four are the oyabun, the head honchos, of four of the major yakuza families in Japan. Believe it. The yaks funded Tiger Mitsuhama when he built his business empire, because they needed a superficially respectable outfit through which they could launder money. When Tiger turned his business into a staggeringly profitable megacorp, the yaks saw that as icing on the soycake. The yaks not only got to launder money through it, but they could also draw a significant legitimate, aboveboard income from the corp. Sort of the ultimate double dip.]<<<<<
—Ripper (10:50:21/3-29-54)

>>>>>[Oh, tox, not again! Anytime the conversation turns to Mitsuhama, people yammer on about yak connections. But talk's cheap, chummers. Sure, I'd love to believe that the yaks run big, bad Mitsuhama. I'd love to believe just about anything bad about the megacorps. But I need to figure out the truth. The TRUTH, scan me? And that involves finding evidence to support claims like this. Conjecture, suspicion, and wild-eyed beliefs don't cut it. I've looked pretty hard, and I can't find any concrete evidence linking MCT to the yaks. None.]<<<<<
—Turner (21:45:58/4-2-54)

>>>>>[Two possibilities, Turner. Either you're looking in the wrong place, or Mitsuhama pays you to play spin-doctor. The evidence exists; you just need the eyes to see it.]<<<<<
—Margeson (03:56:37/4-3-54)

>>>>>[Fine, then. Document it for me and post it here.

Then we can all review it at our leisure. Deal?]<<<<<
— Turner (20:04:38/4-3-54)

>>>>>[*I'm still waiting.*]<<<<<
— Turner (22:31:52/5-2-54)

MAJOR DIVISIONS

Mitsuhama divides its operations by region rather than by function. The corp's major divisions include MCT North America, MCT Western Europe, MCT Australasia, and so on. Each of these divisions has subdivisions specialized by function.

>>>>>[*Doesn't that lead to redundancy, like five labs working on robotics instead of a single one?*]<<<<<
— Marcia (11:29:20/3-26-54)

>>>>>[*Redundant or not, that practice doesn't seem to hurt MCT any. They just prefer distributed labs to having One Big Lab.*]<<<<<
— Panda (23:00:36/3-28-54)

>>>>>[*In the long run, lots of labs might prove more effective than the standard One Big Lab concept. Central research establishments develop larger, more stolid bureaucracies than smaller outfits. Any researcher who disagrees with the big boss doesn't get the resources he needs to continue with unpopular research. Even though lots of smaller labs may duplicate each other's work, they can often get more done just by avoiding bureaucracy. And as long as the labcoats talk on a regular basis, they won't duplicate that much. A central group might come in handy just to cross-correlate results from different labs, but constant communication could make that unnecessary.*]<<<<<
— David-John (00:21:04/4-1-54)

>>>>>[*Speaking of separate labs, every major MCT division has at least one department dedicated to pure research into magical principles. I'd estimate that this megacorp spends more on undirected magical research than any two of the other megacorps combined.*]<<<<<
— Spume (11:31:23/4-2-54)

>>>>>[*With the obvious exception of Aztechnology.*]<<<<<
— Pyramid Watcher (20:46:33/4-2-54)

>>>>>[*Well, yeah.*]<<<<<
— Spume (11:34:03/4-3-54)

Because the executive in charge of a particular division must direct all of that division's various activities, MCT execs can handle transfers between divisions more easily than execs at other corps. Where an executive VP moving from Ares Arms to AresSpace might be completely lost in his new position, an exec VP shifting from MCT Australasia to MCT North America would make the transition much more easily because his responsibilities remain largely the same.

EXECS

Senior Executive Vice-President Tamatsu Sakura heads MCT North America.

>>>>>[*He has yak ties.*]<<<<<
— Lola (23:57:52/4-1-54)

>>>>>[*Will you guys give it a fragging break? You have no evidence.*]<<<<<
— Turner (21:49:19/4-2-54)

>>>>>[*Beg to differ, Turner ole chummer. I shared a hot tub with Sakura, and saw the yakuza tattoos covering half his chest and two-thirds of his back. That makes him one important yak.*]<<<<<
— Lola (01:17:18/4-3-54)

>>>>>[*Tub time with Tamatsu, huh? Adds a whole new shade of meaning to the phrase "cozying up with the corps."*]<<<<<
— Markie (03:40:34/4-3-54)

>>>>>[*You're just jealous, Markie.*]<<<<<
— Lola (23:28:24/4-3-54)

>>>>>[*Hey, Lola. . .how big was it? The hot tub, I mean. . .*]<<<<<
— Carr (04:53:47/4-4-54)

>>>>>[*I always knew making a run against MCT could get you in hot water (ga-harf ga-harf)!*]<<<<<
— Diamond Dog (09:32:51/4-4-54)

Marli Bobinek serves as executive VP of MCT UCAS, and vice president John Chang currently heads MCT Seattle.

>>>>>[*I'd dive into a hot tub with Marli Bobinek anytime.*]<<<<<
— Rod (06:35:11/4-4-54)

>>>>>[*Enough about the fragging hot tub!*]<<<<<
— Lola (01:17:46/4-5-54)

SECURITY

Each MCT division has a sub-department that handles local security. Well-trained and well-equipped, Mitsuhama security forces can handle just about anything from a single intruder to a massive armed incursion.

PHYSICAL & MAGICAL SECURITY

Mitsuhama responds to any threat against its facilities swiftly and brutally. Unlike more subtle corps, MCT flaunts its security provisions. Sizable patrols of heavily armed guards travel the grounds at all MCT sites, many of them supported by biologicals. MCT also uses plenty of high technology, including active and passive sensors and threat-suppression systems.

>>>>>[*Runners, beware: MCT takes few prisoners. Because most Johnsons leave their hired shadowrun-*

ners in the dark about who really hired them to do what and why, MCT sees little profit in interrogating them. At least, that's the MCT party line. The corp also loves layered defenses, with each layer more lethal than the last. Particularly sensitive facilities have gun ports, lasers, and monowire, sometimes even war gasses like Seven-7. Anybody wants to know more about this stuff, look in the Shadowland file that some wit tagged **The Neo-Anarchists' Guide to Real Life**.]<<<<<
—Tonga (19:12:04/4-2-54)

>>>>>[MCT originated the often-copied concept of the "zero-zone." That means zero incursion and zero survival. Anyone outside doesn't get in. If someone does get in somehow, MCT goons bury him there.]<<<<<
—Harley (03:29:34/4-6-54)

>>>>>[MCT Seattle is pouring research funds into "smart" gun ports, miniguns linked to sensors and fire-control computers. If they get it right, they can dispense with flesh-and-blood sec-guards. Smart gun ports can detect unauthorized personnel and hose them down without (meta)human intervention.]<<<<<
—Daedalus (09:18:16/4-9-54)

In terms of magical security, Mitsuhama uses parabiological watch-critters whenever possible. They appear to prefer piasmae which are essentially Awakened metabears.

>>>>>[They use hellhounds too, from time to time.]<<<<<
—Mink (12:03:32/3-28-54)

MCT security forces also always include mages or shamans. Among the first corps to regularly use watcher spirits for site surveillance, MCT employs watchers and bound elementals to safeguard particularly sensitive areas.

>>>>>[MCT is good at this magic drek. Unlike a lot of corps, they integrate it into their planning from the get-go rather than handling it as an afterthought.]<<<<<
—Spume (11:39:03/4-2-54)

MATRIX SECURITY

As with its site security, MCT's Matrix security makes up in brutality what it lacks in subtlety. It loads all SANs leading into any MCT system with heavy ice, as much as they can possibly support without significantly degrading system performance. In all systems, black ice is the rule rather than the exception. Deckers also frequently patrol the most sensitive subsystems, ready to take out what few intruders the ice might have missed. As a further precaution, even the most seemingly innocuous data is encrypted.

>>>>>[Just what you'd expect from an outfit that fronts for a crime syndicate, hm?]<<<<<
—Hardcase (12:12:01/4-1-54)

>>>>>[Can you say, "No evidence?" Sure, I knew you could. . .]<<<<<
—Turner (21:52:02/4-2-54)

MILITARY SECURITY

Mitsuhama has a small but well-equipped and trained Desert Wars force. Unlike other corps with an effective military arm, MCT has never used its corporate army to supplement site security.

>>>>>[Not officially, anyway. Instead, they transfer military officers to internal security postings, sometimes at a moment's notice. Of course, the transferred personnel have to bring their lethal, mil-spec gear with them. After the crisis blows over, the military personnel go straight back to the Desert Wars force. So anyone making a major run against MCT facilities might find themselves facing Desert Wars veterans filling out those internal security uniforms, packing mil-spec weaponry instead of standard-issue guns. That's enough to ruin anyone's night.]<<<<<
—Blade (13:05:52/4-1-54)

>>>>>[Sometimes Mitsuhama doesn't even bother with transfers. They just hire a few weapons consultants from Ares to give them what they call a "live-fire evaluation." Yes, that means exactly what you think it does.]<<<<<
—Hangfire (13:48:21/4-1-54)

EXTENDED SECURITY

Officially speaking, Mitsuhama has no extended security assets. (Surprise, surprise.) Of course, anyone who has ever dealt with the megacorp realizes how far that official reality lies from the truth. Judging by results, MCT has one of the best extended security networks in existence. With the possible exception of Aztechnology, it can stage more black ops with greater success than any other corp. And even Aztechnology cannot rival MCT's ability to practice or resist standard business dirty tricks.

The assets required for this kind of activity do not appear in the corp's organizational chart. Either the corp contracts out all black ops to shadowrunners, or it has managed to hide an extensive special operations department where no analyst can find it. Of the two possibilities, the second is a lot more likely.

>>>>>[You can find it if you look in the right place. Try looking behind Oi, Shin, Saigusa, and Uehara. When necessary, MCT just turns to the yakuza clans that its big boys run. Hell, the yakuza have taken care of extended security and special operations for all kinds of paying customers during the past 500 years or so. By now, they've got it pretty well chipped.]<<<<<
—Yuri (12:42:27/4-1-54)

>>>>>[I fragging give up.]<<<<<
—Turner (21:53:59/4-2-54)

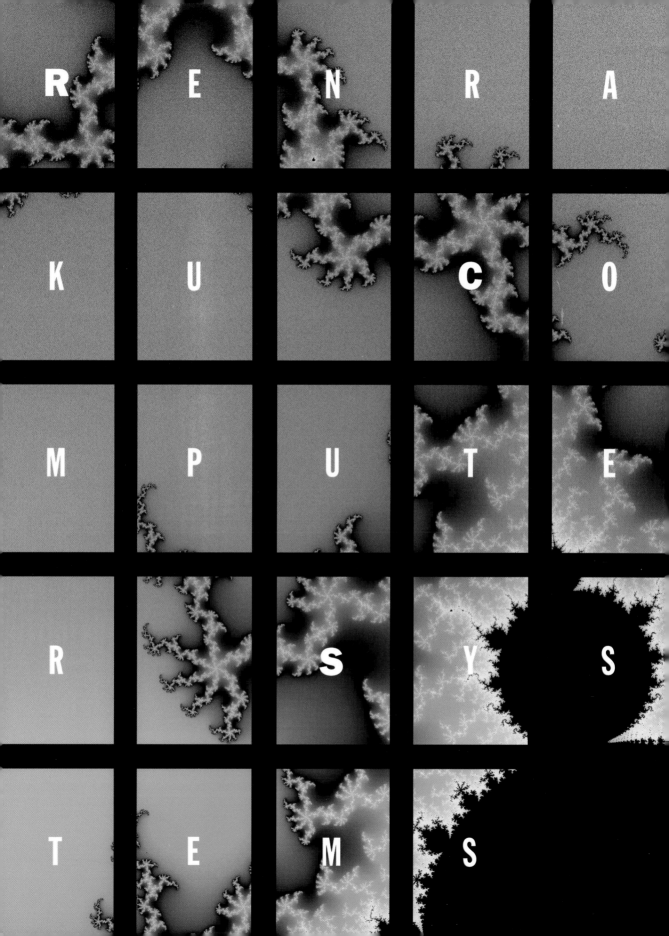

RENRAKU COMPUTER SYSTEMS

Home Office Location: Chiba, Japan
President/CEO: Inazo Aneki
Chairman of the Board: Yukiako Watanabe
Corporate Status: Public corporation
Major Shareholders: None (No recorded shareholder owns more than 10 percent)

Net Rating: 120

Major Interests
- Aerospace: 3
- Agriculture: 6
- Biotechnology: 6
- Chemicals: 5
- Computer Engineering: 10
- Computer Science: 10
- Consumer Goods: 5
- Cybernetics: 4
- Entertainment: 4
- Finance: 5
- Heavy Industry: 5
- Mystical Goods/Services: 4
- Military Technology: 6
- Service: 7

Operations
- Fiscal: 10
- Intelligence: 6
- Management: 8
- Reputation: 9
- Security: 8
- Magic: 8
- Matrix: 9
- Physical: 7
- Military: None reported

>>>>>[Just because ownership's spread around doesn't mean control is also, chummers. Some group or individual could well control a whole frag of a lot more than 10 percent of voting shares, ownership or no ownership.]<<<<<
—Markops (03:49:03/3-27-54)

>>>>>[Well, of course. That's standard corporate practice. The people in charge control shares through intermediaries, holding companies, shells, and all that drek to keep everybody from finding out who really calls the tune.]<<<<<
—The Chromed Accountant (12:28:22/3-29-54)

>>>>>[I finger Yuki Watanabe as a likely suspect. She's a tin-plated, cast-iron slitch with a hell of a business brain. If she's not the puppet-master, someone in Central Casting missed the obvious choice.]<<<<<
—Lucas (06:00:13/4-5-54)

>>>>>[Hold the phone a tick. Inazo Aneki founded the fragging corp, and he's not a major shareholder? Come on.]<<<<<
—Fox (13:03:53/4-6-54)

>>>>>[Aneki owns about 5 percent, which equates to a couple of billion nuyen. But he doesn't own a controlling block. Renraku got into real trouble back in the late '30s—corruption, scandals, mismanagement, the whole nine meters. A couple of Aneki's major investors tried to take control of the board so they could oust him before he brought the whole corp crashing down around their ears. Things had gotten so bad that they figured to lose their investments unless they took drastic action. Aneki managed to hold them off, and in a kind of reverse coup, he ousted them from the board. Slick as snake-oil. But because he needed a vast infusion of capital to keep things going, he issued a whole whack of authorized shares. Apparently he wanted to raise funds by issuing junk bonds, but realized that the corp had too poor a rep to make it work. Anyway, issuing so many shares diluted his equity in his own company something fierce. So now he sits on his 5 percent, and has no control.]<<<<<
—The Chromed Accountant (13:09:23/4-8-54)

PRIMARY BUSINESS

Leaving Fuchi to dominate the brain-computer interface market and MCT to concentrate on computer interaction with the physical world, Renraku focuses its resources on the guts of the machine. They make their nuyen in computer data storage and processing.

>>>>>[I guess "brain-computer interface" includes ice, huh?]<<<<<
—Xist (16:06:28/3-25-54)

Renraku holds patents on many fundamental algorithms for data compression, plus storage/retrieval schemes and systems to handle non-linear equations. The megacorp continues its considerable research in these areas, frequently licensing its discoveries out to others.

>>>>>[Renraku tends to produce modular code, but the modules interact correctly only with other Renraku modules. So if you use some Renraku algorithms, for maximum efficiency you need to use all of them. That includes paying licensing fees for all of them. So despite Renraku's constant claims that it favors open systems, its systems actually close the software architecture to a certain degree.]<<<<<
—Nora (13:04:20/3-28-54)

>>>>>[I hope that wasn't important. I didn't understand a word of it. (And don't try explaining it again.)]<<<<<
—Morrisette (10:47:08/3-30-54)

Renraku also operates as a service bureau, leasing computer processing resources, storage space, data transfer/conversion, encryption/decryption, and system analysis/design consultants to paying customers. If a small corp suddenly starts a project requiring more computer processing horsepower than it has in-house, it can rent the extra processing resources from Renraku. In keeping with its role as a service provider, Renraku Seattle maintains SeaSource, the Seattle public data base.

>>>>>[Hey, SysOp, Shadowland's been running slow recently. Too many users, too little capacity. Have you thought of subcontracting out some of your databases to Renraku?]<<<<<
—Bung (19:15:29/3-23-54)

>>>>>[Oh, har har.]<<<<<
—SYSephan OPus (23:56:04/3-23-54)

Inazo Aneki's lifelong fascination with experimental sociology has provided the corp with a sideline that might someday become a major money-maker. The CEO's interest in investigating (meta)human societies and cultures in the information age prompted him to set up the Renraku Arcology in Seattle.

>>>>>[Maybe someday the arcology can make some money. At the moment it's a big, unfinished money pit.]<<<<<
—Drogue (22:00:49/4-2-54)

>>>>>[So it's a money-loser, but not much of one. And if you take into account the spin-offs it's produced, like new building techniques applicable to other projects or improvements in fire

prevention/control technology, the Arcology has actually made Renraku a packet.]<<<<<
—Nuyen Nick (23:04:44/4-2-54)

>>>>>[Don't underestimate the value of a good tax write-off, either. If you look on the arcology as a big laboratory, as Nick suggests in his post, then tax write-offs subsidize its funding as Renraku enjoys the results that lab produces.]<<<<<
—The Chromed Accountant (13:23:05/4-4-54)

CORPORATE STRUCTURE

Renraku Computer Systems appears to have highly diversified ownership. As we mentioned above, the corp has no major shareholders (no one owns a 10 percent block of outstanding shares). Board chairman Yukiako Watanabe dominates the board, more because of her forceful personality than because of the amount of stock she owns. On most issues she and Aneki see eye-to-eye, so she lets him run Renraku pretty much as he likes. They disagree most often about Aneki's emphasis on the Seattle Arcology. Though Watanabe sees enough value in it that she's never tried to shut it down, she balks occasionally when Aneki diverts money from Renraku's more profitable divisions to shore up the arcology's sagging finances. In all such cases so far, however, Aneki has convinced her to see his side.

>>>>>[Makes me wonder whether Aneki knows where the bodies are buried. S'pose that's why Watanabe knuckles under to him?]<<<<<
—Holita (06:26:06/4-2-54)

>>>>>[Judging by what I know of Yuki Watanabe's personality, if Aneki or anyone tried something like that, she'd have him assassinated right fragging now.]<<<<<
—Lucas (06:04:54/4-5-54)

>>>>>[Maybe Aneki controls a lot more of the shares than he owns, and Watanabe has to toe the line to keep her seat on the board.]<<<<<
—Holita (04:01:35/4-6-54)

>>>>>[I still say she'd off him. Maybe they really do see eye-to-eye on everything, including the arcology, but she feels she has to put on a show of bringing him to heel. Maybe she has to satisfy other shareholders that she's not letting Aneki run off in weird directions. How's that theory sound?]<<<<<
—Lucas (06:09:19/4-6-54)

Major Divisions

Renraku organizes its major divisions along regional lines. Individual departments within those divisions specialize by function and/or by region, depending on specific circumstances. The major divisions include Renraku America, which covers both North and South America; Renraku Asia; Renraku Europa; and Renraku Australasia. In turn, Renraku America has regional subdivisions such as Renraku Seattle and functional subdivisions such as Renraku Pan-System Consulting.

Execs

Rather than the standard executive VP title, Renraku calls its top execs divisional managers. The formidable Sherman Huang serves as Divisional Manager of Renraku America, reporting directly to Aneki.

>>>>>[Ah, Dr. Sherman Huang. Brilliant, eccentric, and incredibly well-educated, he has at least three doctorates in subjects like computer science, math, and (believe it or not) Elizabethan literature. He may have a fourth degree by now in yet another subject. Apparently he and Aneki regard each other as close friends, almost as soul mates. They meet in the Matrix almost every day just to yak it up.]<<<<<
—Sydney (15:04:48/3-21-54)

>>>>>[All true, but the Renraku Arcology has become a snake in their personal little Eden. Officially speaking, the arcology represents a subdivision in its own right and comes under the direct authority of friend Sherman. But it's also Aneki's hot-button, so the CEO constantly goes around Sherman to talk to Donald Acres, the arcology project manager. At first that didn't bother Sherman. He doesn't care two squonks for typical management structure. But recently, Acres has started acting too big for his fragging boots, and sneaks around Huang to go directly to Aneki. That ticks Huang off something fierce, but Aneki refuses to pull the plug on Acres because the upheaval might damage the arcology.]<<<<<
—Turner (02:27:52/3-25-54)

>>>>>[Any other divisional manager would hire somebody to put a round in Acres' ear. Lucky for Acres, Sherman doesn't work that way. I hear he's managed to get some slag from Chiba HQ, Hiroshi Ushida, to ease Acres out. Officially, Ushida is there to stabilize the arcology's management. Guess that's ol' Sherman's way of making sure that Aneki can't accuse him of interfering with the progress of the precious arcology.]<<<<<
—Zapmeister (08:56:19/3-29-54)

The divisional managers of Renraku Asia, Australasia, and Europe are Tev Greenwaldt, Lucy Don, & Karl Stadt, respectively.

SECURITY

Once upon a time, Inazo Aneki had a schizophrenic attitude toward security. In recent years, it seems to have evened out and grown a little more rational, possibly under the influence of Yuki Watanabe. Aneki created the renowned Red Samurai, basing them at Renraku's Chiba complex. At the same time, however, he stinted on funds to pay for security at Renraku's other divisions and subsidiaries.

>>>>>[Not so schizophrenic when you understand a little bit about Aneki and the Red Samurai. The Samurai started out almost exclusively as a ceremonial guard. They looked tough and packed wizzer weapons and armor, but lacked the training to do much more than march around looking intimidating. Aneki created them as his personal Praetorian guards, but they couldn't do

much despite their "elite" reputation. Hell, any truly elite unit could have diced them up for catfood. They just got a lot of press and stroked Aneki's overblown ego. In spending money on them, Aneki stayed perfectly consistent. He hardly ever spent money on real security back in those days, and he didn't do it with the Red Samurai. The initial Red Samurai were flashy status symbols, not a real security force.

That's changed over the years, in spades. It started happening before Watanabe appeared on the board, but she certainly accelerated the process. The Red Samurai actually grew into their reputation, becoming the elite security force we in the shadows all know and loathe.]<<<<<
—Paragon (17:02:03/4-2-54)

Today's Red Samurai still operate from their base in Chiba, but units from the enlarged force sometimes travel to other Renraku installations to solve specific security problems. More often, however, they travel abroad as Aneki's personal bodyguard. Several of them patrol the arcology whenever Aneki drops in to check up on things.

At the divisional level, funding for security has improved drastically. In Renraku's case, the improvement means going from hopeless to marginally inadequate. In-house assets can provide basic security for normal situations. In high-risk situations, however, such as the incident when various "hard green" ecotage groups targeted the arcology, the corp hires outside forces.

Physical and Magical Security

The level of security at any Renraku site depends on how crucial corporate management considers that site. Other determining factors include the expectation of trouble and the site's current level of funding. Though those factors apply to any corporate site, they have a much greater effect on security at Renraku than at any other corp.

Renraku's in-house security assets are well-trained and reasonably well-equipped, but the corp has relatively few of them. (These particular security assets do not include the Red Samurai; in addition to their role as bodyguards already mentioned, I discuss them under military security, because they function more like soldiers than garden-variety guards.) Security forces are frequently understaffed, and attempts to compensate for insufficient personnel using wizbang tech don't always work well. At a critically important site, however, or if a site expects real trouble, Renraku augments its own assets with freelance security resources ranging from a small band of local shadowrunners to a full Knight Errant team. On occasion, they have even hired an Ares Arms military-grade force.

>>>>>[Moral of the story? Do your fragging homework before the run, chummers.]<<<<<
—Hangfire (08:32:58/4-1-54)

>>>>>[The degree to which Renraku integrates magic with physical defenses also varies, depending on who calls the shots. Renraku handles the integration nicely, but they tend to lack enough combat mages. Of course, combat mages also vary from site to site.]<<<<<
—Spume (11:46:35/4-2-54)

>>>>>[If you interpret all this drek to mean that Renraku has shabby and useless security, think twice. Even without outside help, the corp can take care of its assets and facilities in the vast majority of cases. Only under special circumstances do they fail to handle trouble themselves.]<<<<<
—Big Blue (03:20:59/4-4-54)

Matrix Security

Renraku has excellent Matrix security. Not only does the corporation license high-quality IC from Fuchi, but it has also developed its own smart IC to protect its most sensitive nodes.

>>>>>[Smart ice? Are we talking adaptive trace, or something worse?]<<<<<
—Onco (17:40:07/4-1-54)

>>>>>[Worse. Adaptive doesn't begin to describe it. I'd guess it's driven by powerful Expert Systems with an incredibly sophisticated rule-set. Anyway, if you meet black ice of any particular configuration in the Renraku system, expect the thing to benchmark at one rating point higher than its outward characteristics might indicate. As an example, Fuchi's "Black Samurai" line of ice benchmarks at around 7. In a Renraku system, that Black Samurai might be accessing the Expert System for on-the-fly instructions, which would kick its rating up to 8. On a Red system, that one point makes a big difference.]<<<<<
—Red Wraith (20:58:27/4-2-54)

>>>>>[Expert Systems, hell. There's a fragging AI in the arcology system, and it handles the wizzer black ice. It "lives" in the Matrix, and it knows more tricks than you ever will. No matter how good you are, it'll tear you apart.]<<<<<
—King (20:59:04/4-2-54)

>>>>>[I knew someone would bring that up. Bulldrek, King old pal. No such thing as an AI. Not today, probably not for another ten years. And if anyone ever creates one, it'll be so alien that it won't even recognize us as intelligent beings. So bet your hoop it won't sit around running ice for some corp.]<<<<<
—Red Wraith (21:01:26/4-2-54)

Military Security

According to Renraku's annual report, the corporation has no military forces. Needless to say, the corp's definition of military splits a few hairs. Renraku classes every Red Samurai unit as "security forces," even though many of them have military training and use mil-spec weaponry that includes tanks and fighters. Some of these "non-military" units even fight in Desert Wars.

Extended Security

From the early days when Renraku had a rep as the least predictable and most corrupt of the burgeoning megacorps, Inazo Aneki maintains an unbelievable range of contacts around the globe. He has friends and informants in many rival megacorps and national governments, and also remains in touch with fixers and individual shadowrunners. These contacts provide him with an extensive network of unofficial assets for extended operations.

>>>>>[Renraku even has certain shadowrunners on retainer. They can take other runs as long as they remain "on call" for Aneki's special missions. They can even take runs against Renraku, if they think they can get away with them. These guys frequently get tapped to serve as payback teams, an idea that the jealous and vindictive Aneki has used plenty of times during the past few years.]<<<<<
—Hangfire (23:41:32/3-22-54)

>>>>>[Believe it. Most of his "stringers" live in Japan, but he's got a couple in Seattle. Sorry, I don't name names.]<<<<<
—Argent (12:55:49/3-24-54)

Major Shareholders:

Sadato Shiawase (approx. 13%)
Tadashi Shiawase (approx. 11%)
Soko Shiawase (approx. 10%)
Ryoi Shiawase (approx. 10%)

Net Rating: 116

Major Interests

Aerospace: 6
Agriculture: 6
Biotechnology: 8
Chemicals: 7
Computer Engineering: 5
Computer Science: 5
Consumer Goods: 5
Cybernetics: 3
Entertainment: 2
Finance: 5
Heavy Industry: 9
Mystical Goods/Services: 4
Military Technology: 6
Service: 8

Operations

Fiscal: 9
Intelligence: 6
Management: 8
Reputation: 8
Security: 6
    Magic: 6
    Matrix: 6
    Physical: 7
Military: None reported

>>>>>[Nice little family affair, isn't it? I guess it's a public corp in name only.]<<<<<
—Zed (21:05:11/3-24-54)

>>>>>[Hold on. Let me explain this little soap opera (oh, joy). Yep, it looks like a tight little package ripe with nepotism. Chairman-of-the-Board Sadato is CEO Tadashi's father, Soko is his aunt, and Ryoi is his uncle on the other side of the family. Such a warm, family picture. . .until you look a little deeper and find out that brother Sadato and sister Soko hate each other's fragging guts. They celebrate each other's birthdays by dispatching

where h
(Didn't
Ar
that be
decision
and car
alist, a
Jerri H
to talk
—

>>>>>
cent of
Smarte.
that.]<<
—

>>>>>
Sadato
way.]<<
—

>>>>>
est in p
them ha
Howard
—

PRI

Ar
triple-A
in Shiaw
Shiawas
tion at S
Biotech
Shiawas

>>>>>
Atomics
rogation
Shiawas
(Shiawa
not.)]<<

>>>>>

mers. I'm just passing this drek on, okay?]<<<<<
—VU (06:06:27/4-1-54)

CORPORATE STRUCTURE

Members of the Shiawase family own most of Shiawase Corporation, with other significant blocks held by various investment banks. None of these other blocks represents more than 5 percent of the company's outstanding shares, and many owe loyalty to the Shiawase family.

>>>>>[With a group that fractured, family loyalty might mean anything.]<<<<<
—Requiter (17:22:09/4-1-54)

Between the votes they own and the votes they control, the Shiawases can stave off any takeover attempt that comes their way.

>>>>>[This situation makes those "loyal" voting blocks prime targets for corps planning a move on Shiawase. Think about it. Another corp gets some hold on a couple of these blocks. The happy, happy Shiawase clan still expects the blocks to vote with them when push comes to frag. Surprise, surprise, the vote tosses the Shiawases out on their keisters and the corp undergoes a major restructuring. If they have any sense, the Shiawases must make considerable efforts to guarantee that all those "loyal" voting blocks actually remain loyal.]<<<<<
—The Chromed Accountant (13:23:56/3-29-54)

>>>>>[Shiawase Corp differs from the other megas in its degree of employee ownership. Shiawase wants to gain and keep employee loyalty in a big way. They manage some of it through training and "personal education" (read brainwashing), but they get a lot of loyalty by offering a stock purchase plan. If a wageslave puts aside a slice of her salary to buy stock in the company, the corp matches her contribution, so she gets a kind of two-for-one deal. Nice setup for the employees, and it must make them feel at least a little warm-and-fuzzy toward good old Shiawase.]<<<<<
—Smoke & Mirrors (02:27:20/4-2-54)

>>>>>[It might sound like a good deal, but it's a crock, S&M (oooh. . .). First, Shiawase employees have to contribute something like 7.5 percent of their salary to the plan. They can fork over more if they want, but not less. Second, buying these shares doesn't put them in the wageslave's grubby little hands. Oh, no. Instead, the nice corp holds them in trust. This "trust account" doesn't vest with our hypothetical little wageslave, meaning she doesn't get the shares, until she's worked for the corp for 15 years. Anybody who quits before the end of this vesting period gets nada. Of course, as the trustee, the corporation gets to

vote the shares. The supposed employee-owner gets no say. Even after the shares have vested, a whole crop of tricky little restrictions makes it immensely easier for the wageslave to give the corp proxy votes than to vote the shares herself. All in all, this lovely policy gives Shiawase yet another way to control blocks of shares to help it fight off takeovers.]<<<<<
—The Keynesian Kid (09:29:21/4-4-54)

>>>>>[Under UCAS law, even before your shares vest with you, the half of them bought by the corp are subject to taxes. That asset gets added to your tax bill, not the corp's. In other words, you pay tax on a benefit you won't see for 15 years. Nice, huh?]<<<<<
—The Chromed Accountant (12:08:43/4-4-54)

>>>>>[So if this deal's so excrementally lousy, why do employees put up with this drek? A recent international survey put Shiawase wageslaves at the top of the employee satisfaction scale. Or is that another corp lie?]<<<<<
—Fargo (15:29:50/4-6-54)

>>>>>[Surprisingly enough, it's true. Most Shiawase wageslaves are perfectly happy with their lot. So either they're too phenomenally stupid to figure out that the stock purchase plan acts like a ball and chain, or the corp's "personal education" works better than most people think.]<<<<<
—Featherstone (17:34:45/4-9-54)

Major Divisions

Shiawase breaks down into primary divisions by function rather than by region. The key divisions that have the strongest presence in Seattle are Shiawase Atomics, Shiawase Biotech, and Shiawase Envirotech. (These Seattle corps presumably matter most to you slags out there reading this board.) Though all have a presence in Seattle, Shiawase Envirotech has the most impact on the Seattle region because that corp handles a big chunk of waste processing for metroplex industry.

>>>>>[Shiawase Envirotech has pretty much kept Elliot Bay from being more of a cesspool than it already is.]<<<<<
—Totness (08:40:27/3-27-54)

>>>>>[More to the point, Seattle generates untold tons and cubic meters of solid waste every single fragging day. Considering the state of nearby landfills and the understandable refusal of our Salish-Shidhe neighbors to let us dump our trash in their backyard, Seattle would be up a dataline without a program if not for Shiawase Envirotech. The corp takes solid waste from all the various minor contractors and processes it to reduce its volume by two orders of magnitude, simultaneous-

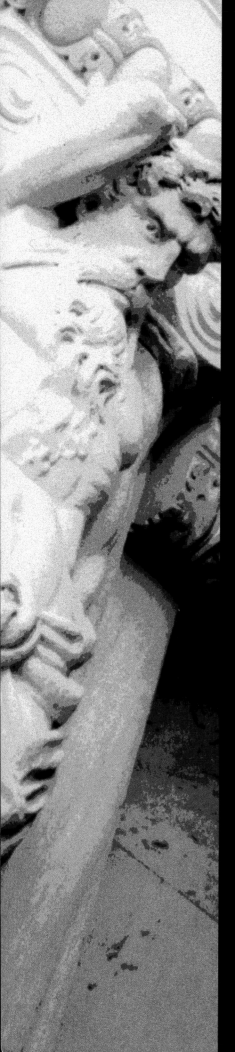

ly removing most hazardous materials. They do a hell of a good job.]<<<<<
 —Rimmer (16:44:09/3-29-54)

>>>>>[Like frag they do. Ever seen the toxic smoke belching out of the stacks at Shiawase's HAZMAT processing incinerator? Now you know where "hard rain" comes from.]<<<<<
 —Kermit (01:20:26/3-31-54)

>>>>>[A couple of corrections are in order, folks. Kermit, old slag, the concentration of known toxins in that belching smoke falls well within nationally accepted guidelines. To the Neo-A who wrote this part of the text, don't discount Shiawase Atomics' influence in the Seattle area. Gaiatronics may generate Seattle's power from their fusion plant on the Olympic Peninsula, but Shiawase Atomics delivers that power to the Seattle grid. They handle the high-tension lines that take the power from the fusion plants to its destination in the sprawl. So we depend on them for power as well as waste disposal.]<<<<<
 —Dana (23:53:01/4-1-54)

>>>>>[The rest of the UCAS considers Shiawase Atomics big news. Without them, much of the east coast would sit around in the dark.]<<<<<
 —Bowers (09:42:43/4-4-54)

>>>>>[No nukes is good nukes! Shiawase out!]<<<<<
 —Rex Mundi (13:58:58/4-4-54)

>>>>>[Save us from the neo-Luddites among us! Look, Rex, whaddaya want? The east coast needs power, right? It doesn't have enough mountains or water to get power from hydroelectric projects. It doesn't have enough sunlight to use solar power. Maybe little towns within a stone's throw of the Bay of Fundy can get energy from tidal power, but places like Manhattan and Boston sure as drek can't. So they can either use nuke plants or keep generating power by burning what little stuff they have left to burn. Of course, burning stuff pours tons of drek into the atmosphere, creating more acid rain and more air pollution. No thanks, Rex, I'll pass.]<<<<<
 —Manx (09:10:32/4-5-54)

In addition to its major divisions, Shiawase also owns subsidiaries that operate in a wide range of industries.

>>>>>[For example, Ressha Corporation, the outfit that runs the maglev-bullet to SanFran, is a Shiawase subsidiary.]<<<<<
 —Ladner (13:15:36/3-31-54)

>>>>>[True, but not widely known. Shiawase tends not to publicize which smaller corps it owns or controls.]<<<<<
 —Maurice (13:21:16/3-31-54)

Execs

Within Shiawase, managing directors (MDs) rather than the standard executive vice presidents head up each division. Within each division, vice presidents occupy the executive level directly below the MD.

>>>>>[Supposedly, Ryoi Shiawase came up with this structure six months after his death. I tell ya, this outfit is fragged in the head. . .]<<<<<
 —Ladner (13:17:52/3-31-54)

Christopher Keratsu serves as the MD of Shiawase Atomics. This high-powered manager made his mark in Shiawase Biotech before moving to his current, more prestigious position. Despite the fact that his previous experience had no connection to power utilities, he seems to handle the requirements of his job exceedingly well. His replacement as MD of Shiawase Biotech is Etsu Powicke, and Mariko Kiyonobu heads Shiawase Envirotech.

>>>>>[Mariko can claim active membership in half a bazillion environmental organizations, ranging from the insipid to the downright militant. She may be truly committed to the environmental movement, or just making a wise business decision. I leave that question up to others to decide.]<<<<<
 —Cerebi (09:27:30/3-28-54)

>>>>>[Mariko Kiyonobu actively sabotages the environmental movement she pretends to espouse. Her membership disgraces every group that accepts her. In the guise of environmentalism, her corporation has done more damage to the Earth than many others that don't pretend to be green.]<<<<<
 —Kermit (01:25:49/3-31-54)

SECURITY

In the absence of a central security department from which divisions can draw resources, individual divisions and subsidiaries each handle their own security provisions. Divisional managing directors have the power to hire outside security forces whenever necessary, without approval from corporate headquarters.

>>>>>[Shiawase may have no central pool of physical resources, but they do have a central information-gathering resource that gives them a lot more power than people think. The innocuously-named Market Intelligence and Forecasting Department, located in the Osaka HQ, looks into a lot more than market fluctuations and consumer demographics. MIFD is Shiawase's home-grown nest of industrial spies. They not only predict market fluctuations with amazing accuracy, but they also scope out their competitors' secrets with a frightening rate of success. If any of you chummers get hired to make a run against

a major Shiawase asset, I'd give odds close to 25 percent that the boys and girls at MIFD know about it. Runners take note: MIFD also excels at disseminating information like who's hitting whom to the places where it'll do the most good.]<<<<<
—Gene (22:19:49/4-5-54)

>>>>>[MIFD hires lots of shadowrunners, and not just street ops working in Japan.]<<<<<
—Hangfire (14:00:22/4-7-54)

Physical and Magical Security

Compared to outfits like Ares or Fuchi, Shiawase has relatively light physical security. Though well-trained, its forces generally carry only light arms and armor. During a confrontation, they prefer to drive off intruders rather than kill indiscriminately as many other megacorps do. However, Shiawase sec-forces *can* kill without compunction if the situation so warrants.

In keeping with the megacorp's high-tech focus, it supports its security guards with passive and active sensors as well as various threat-suppression technologies. Among all the megacorps, Shiawase tends to set up the most sophisticated layered defenses.

>>>>>[Shiawase seems to like the idea of non-lethal threat suppression. Instead of MCT-style killer gasses, gun ports, monowire, and lasers, Shiawase takes down intruders with knock-out gas, netguns, and anesthetic darts. They capture them and put them through the fragging wringer to find out who hired them and why.]<<<<<
—Zoom (05:06:24/4-1-54)

>>>>>[Pay attention to this point, folks. Shiawase puts any intruders it happens to capture through rigorous interrogation. They shy away from physical torture, but only because they don't see it as a reliable method of information extraction. Instead, they use drugs and magic. A Shiawase "mind probe" tends to leave a subject crashed out, physically and mentally weak as a baby for days afterward.]<<<<<
—Pink (17:40:21/4-2-54)

>>>>>[Better that than what happens if Aztechnology interrogates you, chummer...]<<<<<
—Pyramid Watcher (22:14:00/4-2-54)

In terms of magical security, most Shiawase security teams include hermetic mages. However, these security personnel often serve in separate squads or platoons from the security force rank and file.

>>>>>[A smart runner can exploit that weakness.]<<<<<
—Argent (13:55:24/4-3-54)

Matrix Security

Shiawase rarely uses killer ice, preferring to load its nodes with high levels of gray trace-and-dump or trace-and-burn ice. As far as anyone knows, the corporation has no ultra-security systems, so it relies on distributed processing and databases to make up for this relatively low degree of security. In other words, a decker making a datasteal on a particular key topic might have to visit four or five datastores located in different parts of the Matrix. Having to penetrate moderate security four to five times often proves just as difficult as beating extreme security once, and usually takes longer. Few Shiawase systems have deckers patroling on a regular basis; the corp sends in deckers to deal with threats only if the system goes on alert.

>>>>>[Distributed processing makes Shiawase's system more vulnerable than most to viral attack. If corp conflict ever turns into all-out core war, Shiawase'll be the first megacorp to crash in a smoking heap.]<<<<<
—Xist (19:45:58/4-3-54)

Military Security

Shiawase has no military assets, officially or otherwise. If it needs heavy-duty security forces for any reason, the corp contracts the job out to another organization such as Ares Arms.

>>>>>[They had to do that last year in Germany. Ares forces love this kind of job. Because they're rocking and rolling on someone else's turf, they don't have to worry about collateral damage. They blew stuff up real good over there.]<<<<<
—Sarge (10:00:44/4-1-54)

Extended Security

Shiawase has no significant extended security assets, though according to street buzz it occasionally hires shadowrunners for special missions.

>>>>>[Wrongo! Remember the MIFD I talked about earlier? A classic example of extended assets, they're about the best in the biz. Anyone interested in conducting industrial espionage could take lessons from the MIFD.]<<<<<
—Gene (22:23:45/4-5-54)

>>>>>[The MIFD is also Shiawase's primary weapon in hostile takeovers. They're past masters at driving a target's share price down.]<<<<<
—Nuyen Nick (10:08:44/4-6-54)

SAEDER-KRUPP CORPORATION

HOME OFFICE LOCATION: ESSEN, GERMANY

PRESIDENT/CEO: LOFWYR (GREAT DRAGON)

CHAIRMAN OF THE BOARD: LOFWYR

CORPORATE STATUS: PRIVATE CORPORATION

MAJOR SHAREHOLDERS: UNKNOWN

NET RATING: 124

MAJOR INTERESTS:
Aerospace: 6
Agriculture: 7
Biotechnology: 7
Chemicals: 9
Computer Engineering: 7
Computer Science: 5
Consumer Goods: 6
Cybernetics: 4
Entertainment: 3
Finance: 8
Heavy Industry: 10
Mystical Goods/Services: 3
Military Technology: 7
Service: 6

OPERATIONS:
Fiscal: 10
Intelligence: 6
Management: 6
Reputation: 7
Security: 7
Magic: 9
Matrix: 5
Physical: 9
Military: Battalion/Exceptional

>>>>>[Saeder-Krupp has the distinction of being the only corporation with a wizworm as its president. At least, the only one we know about...]<<<<<
—Wally (01:32:34/3-20-54)

>>>>>[You can bet your hoop that Lofwyr personally owns a nice, healthy chunk of the corp. Whatever he doesn't own, he controls. (Would you vote against a dragon, or try to oust him from the board? Null.)]<<<<<
—Tad (17:58:41/3-21-54)

PRIMARY BUSINESS

Saeder-Krupp is the largest corporation in the world involved primarily in industry and heavy assembly, as well as resource-based operations. In the last century, many "green" philosophers predicted that the growth of the information age meant the end of resource exploitation. Antecedents of these philosophers predicted the same thing in the mid-2020s, and again in the late 2040s. Saeder-Krupp's continuing success has proved them wrong on all counts.

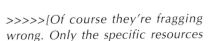

>>>>>[Of course they're fragging wrong. Only the specific resources exploited have changed. For example, nickel used to be a hot ticket, until changes in technology made thallium and molybdenum vital. But actually stopping resource exploitation? Give me a break here, folks.

And for all you neo-Luddites out there getting ready to bend my ear about recycling, shut the frag up. Sure, following the three fragging Rs can decrease your requirements and slow down resource exploitation. But eliminate it? Spirits, the Hungarians tried that in 2015 when the Greens controlled the government. Have you looked at Hungary lately? The economy's gone to drek. The standard of living's gone to drek. Health care crises run rampant, lots of people starve, the cities have no power. (But the shrubs look awfully healthy...)]<<<<<
—Locke (16:29:44/3-29-54)

CORPORATE STRUCTURE

Though Lofwyr controls just about every facet of Saeder-Krupp's corporate operations nowadays, the real mover-and-shaker behind the emergence of Saeder-Krupp was Michel Beloit, a young senior exec with BMW. Predicting some of the chaos that later occurred in Europe, Beloit ousted BMW's conservative management team in a palace coup of epic proportions. Once in control, he struggled to position BMW for growth in the challenging times ahead.

Beloit had either the devil's own luck or unbelievable competence. By 2010 or thereabouts, he had expanded BMW and made it Europe's premier industrial power. With a few well-selected mergers, Beloit developed BMW into a mighty corporate empire. Finding BMW's association with automobiles too restrictive a market, he restructured the megacorp around Saeder Munitions and Krupp Manufacturing to form Saeder-Krupp. He then spun off a leaner, meaner BMW as a wholly-owned subsidiary that could keep covering the market for automobiles and associated technology. In 2032, Beloit kicked the bucket. His wife, the glamorous and rapacious Wilhelmina Graff-Beloit, took over and ran the megacorp for five years.

Around 2037 or so, the great dragon Lofwyr appeared on the scene. Though Mina Graff-Beloit controlled the board and owned billions worth of Saeder-Krupp stock, she didn't hold anywhere near a majority of votes. She believed that no one else did, either. Behind the scenes, however, Lofwyr had spent years buying up Saeder-Krupp shares. When he emerged into the limelight, he announced that he owned a staggering 63 percent of Saeder-Krupp's outstanding shares. He immediately used them to vote himself into the chairmanship of the board, ousting Graff-Beloit and banishing her to Zurich-Orbital. In his next step, he named himself the megacorp's president/CEO.

>>>>>[Now hold on just a tick here. A fragging dragon buys up 63 percent of the corp and no one notices? Hard to believe.]<<<<<
—Monk McQueen (08:38:37/3-24-54)

>>>>>[The deal was more complicated than it sounds. Up until the day before he announced control, Lofwyr personally owned no shares in Saeder-Krupp as far as anyone could tell. He'd done all the purchasing quietly, via holding companies and shells that he controlled, but no share certificate had his name on it. When he figured he had what he needed, all those holding companies privately sold him their shares. At that point all the stock tracking systems lit up like Christmas trees, screaming takeover alert. But no one could stop him by then. Lofwyr owned more than half the company, so he became Saeder-Krupp by default.]<<<<<
—Nuyen Nick (11:40:16/3-27-54)

Following his assumption of all major offices, Lofwyr pulled off a management buy-out, through which he snapped up all remaining outstanding shares of the company. In 2040, hints emerged that Lofwyr had given or sold some shares to other individuals. Nobody knows for sure who he passed them off to, or why. To this day no one knows exactly who (or what) owns what percentage of Saeder-Krupp.

Major Divisions

Saeder-Krupp has multiple divisions made along arbitrary lines. Some divisions are based on region, some on function, and some using obscure criteria. For example, the Saeder-Krupp Prime division is based in the same Berlin complex as the megacorp HQ, under Lofwyr's direct control. It has regional and functional subdivisions, and seems to conduct exactly the same range of activities as the parent megacorporation. Apparently, no reason exists for S-K Prime to exist separately from the central corp.

>>>>>[Hey, chummer, don't expect a fragging wizworm to see the world the same way you do.]<<<<<
—Darryl (02:48:35/4-2-54)

To illustrate how confusing this corporate structure can get, consider the two major Saeder-Krupp operations based in

Seattle: S-K Northwest and S-K Aerospace. Despite their location in the same region, both subdivisions belong to separate branches of the megacorp's organizational chart and have completely distinct chains of command that link them with other divisions up the line.

>>>>>[Darryl hit it on the head. The organization must make perfect sense to Lofwyr, but "perfect sense" seems to be species-specific.]<<<<<
          —The Keynesian Kid (14:52:28/4-7-54)

In most corps, executives know how much autonomy they enjoy. They either run their divisions as independent entities or plan their operations around gaining HQ approval for every course of action. Lofwyr's Saeder-Krupp works differently. From one week to another, the same divisional manager might find himself calling all the shots, or find Lofwyr looking over his shoulder and micromanaging every facet of the business. Because of Lofwyr's degree of control, differing executives at different divisions have little input into corporate policy or actions. For this reason, this profile does not include Saeder-Krupp exec VPs.

>>>>>[This schizoid power structure leads to high stress and fast turnover among Saeder-Krupp execs.]<<<<<
          —Nuyen Nick (11:25:29/4-1-54)

>>>>>[The fact that Lofwyr can track the intricate business activities of a fragging megacorp all by himself hints that dragons have more intelligence than (meta)humans do, just like the datafaxes say.]<<<<<
          —Trollkin (00:03:05/4-7-54)

>>>>>[More intelligence than humans, perhaps.]<<<<<
          —Tal Gilgalad (17:13:56/4-10-54)

SECURITY

Though Saeder-Krupp's security force has relatively few personnel, its small size takes away none of its effectiveness. Unlike its fellow megacorps, Saeder-Krupp makes no meaningful distinction between military and civilian security assets. The megacorp maintains a considerable military force that participates in Desert Wars, and it cross-trains constantly between these units and its civilian security arms. Individuals and entire squads often get transferred between the two forces with little warning. The military and civilian forces do use different weapons, if only because anti-personnel cluster bombs do too much collateral damage for efficient site security. The personnel, however, have virtually the same capabilities.

>>>>>[Stress this point again, chummers. Saeder-Krupp security grunts have a lot more on the ball than the typical wannabes with guns, or even KE's pro civilians. These guys have top-notch military training, including communications and tactical skills. Collateral damage limits weapons choice a bit, but not enough to make a big difference. Nobody's going to call in rocket artillery against a group of shadowrunners caught coming over the fence, but the troops watching key installations might well pack MP pulse lasers and other serious death.]<<<<<
          —Midnight (20:44:23/3-29-54)

>>>>>[S-K does real well in Desert Wars. When you try to penetrate an S-K site, you're facing a military varsity squad.]<<<<<
          —Blade (03:35:55/4-1-54)

Physical and Magical Security
Saeder-Krupp's basic physical site defenses come from the corp's so-called civilian defense arm, equipped with the necessary materiel for the task at hand. Lofwyr seems to understand that popular opinion still carries weight in the business world, so site security teams rarely use weapons of mass carnage. (All that collateral damage makes a corp look bad.)

>>>>>[Dead innocents and bombed-out buildings aren't the only collateral damage. A corp's rep, or a dragon's, can suffer from collateral damage as well.]<<<<<
          —Turner (08:29:12/3-30-54)

Like some other megacorps, Saeder-Krupp integrates mages and shamans with its standard security teams. The corp uses more mages than shamans, and often sets bound elementals to guard important sites. The corp supports its security teams with the technology appropriate to the situation, and frequently supplements its (meta)human resources with parabiologicals.

>>>>>[Not surprising; their CEO is one.]<<<<<
          —Stim (19:36:58/4-2-54)

>>>>>[S-K uses a lot of paranimal watch-beasts. And not just hellhounds, either. I've heard of griffins and birdmen, even sirens staking out sensitive places. And enough watcher spirits to play a game of urban brawl.]<<<<<
          —Maro (23:57:09/4-4-54)

On occasion, Saeder-Krupp also hires special outside assets for specific missions. If shadowrunners or even petty criminals look like the best forces to use, the megacorp hires them without a qualm.

>>>>>[Saeder-Krupp, specifically Lofwyr, likes to play payback as much as Aneki does at Renraku. You mess with the dragon and he'll hire people to mess you up, even if there's no other percentage in it for him. And chummer, dragons have long memories.]<<<<<
          —Eastman (01:02:42/4-3-54)

>>>>>[Lofwyr calls retaliatory strikes "education." As an example, a European policlub hit a Saeder-Krupp subsidiary pretty hard some time back. So Lofwyr ordered the subsidiary president to hire a bunch of local criminals to track down and kill as many of the polis as they could find. Seems like it worked; S-K hasn't suffered from any significant poli attacks on its facilities ever since.]<<<<<
          —Carstairs (11:08:27/4-9-54)

>>>>>[You're talking about Alte Welt and Hamburg-Stein, aren't you?]<<<<<
          —JohnnyX (19:56:51/4-11-54)

Matrix Security
For a major megacorp, Saeder-Krupp has surprisingly limited Matrix security. Of course, it also makes surprisingly limited

use of the Matrix. Because Lofwyr has personal control over so much of the corp's day-to-day business, Saeder-Krupp needs to communicate and store much less sensitive data than any other megacorp. Though Saeder-Krupp has a lot of powerful computer systems in the Matrix, it uses them mostly for such mundane activities as running factories and maintaining inventories.

>>>>>[If I wanted to frag with Saeder-Krupp, that's where I'd go first. Hit 'em where it hurts, right? For a heavy manufacturer, it hurts to hit inventory and shipment schedules.]<<<<<
—Icebreaker (22:04:29/3-22-54)

>>>>>[True enough.]<<<<<
—Nuyen Nick (12:32:46/3-27-54)

Saeder-Krupp computer systems tend to be utilitarian, with little innovation. The system architecture has no adaptive killer or party ice or other cunning tricks. It does, however, have beefy trace-and-report programs starting at Rating 6 and going way up. Those programs exist everywhere in the system.

>>>>>[Saeder-Krupp does things this way so it can use its vaunted semi-military security people. T & R gives them a location; as you tap away on your cyberdeck, a squad of stormtroopers kicks in your door.]<<<<<
—Nora (15:13:21/4-3-54)

>>>>>[Don't get this guy wrong: Saeder-Krupp systems are still glaciers. Just smaller glaciers than the ones that'll geek you at Fuchi.]<<<<<
—Ricardo (23:00:39/4-9-54)

Military Security
As discussed under **Physical and Magical Security**, Saeder-Krupp makes no distinction between its civilian and military security assets.

Extended Security
Like its fellow megacorps, Saeder-Krupp has no official extended security assets. Despite this apparent lack, it still manages to pull a lot of black operations. As mentioned earlier, on occasion the corporation hires shadowrunners and other street ops for special tasks. Other times, the special missions just seem to happen without the corp taking any obvious action.

>>>>>[S-K's main contact with shadowrunners comes through a slag called Brackhaus. I don't know his first name. He hired me a couple of times. He always knows where to track me down, that's the scariest thing. A couple of chummers who've worked for Saeder-Krupp tagged Brackhaus as their Johnson. I've heard that sometimes Lofwyr himself goes out and hires runners, but I don't know if I believe that. You know what they say: never deal with a dragon.]<<<<<

—Jimmy Dean (08:21:47/3-29-54)

>>>>>[Hate to tell you, Jimmy, but Brackhaus is Lofwyr. He's one smart old wyrm, and he knows that (meta)humans prefer cutting deals with members of their own species or metatype. Brackhaus is his public persona. You want evidence, ask anyone else out there who's done some deals with Brackhaus of Saeder-Krupp. What metatype is he?]<<<<<
—Trevor (20:23:05/4-2-54)

>>>>>[He's human, of course.]<<<<<
—Jimmy Dean (08:02:24/4-3-54)

>>>>>[Hans Brackhaus? Dwarf.]<<<<<
—Talbot (13:31:19/4-4-54)

>>>>>[Hans Brackhaus is an elf of fine lineage.]<<<<<
—Finn (17:09:49/4-4-54)

>>>>>[An ork like me. Didn't think many of us made it that high in the megacorps...Oh, drek...]<<<<<
—Mung (23:56:00/4-6-54)

>>>>>[Oh drek is right. Get my point?]<<<<<
—Trevor (19:58:44/4-7-54)

>>>>>[Bulldrek! "Brackhaus" is just a floating identity that lots of company men use. Lofwyr may well walk the streets or the shadows in human guise, but not as Hans Brackhaus.]<<<<<
—Maus (02:34:47/4-10-54)

>>>>>[I heard that Saeder-Krupp once sent a great-form hearth spirit to deliver proxies to the shareholders' meeting of a rival corp. Sometimes the medium is the message, neh? I guess this kind of drek comes up when you deal with a dragon.]<<<<<
—Highwayman (00:47:59/4-2-54)

>>>>>[As a dragon and the CEO of a major megacorp, Lofwyr probably has two different sets of contacts and confidants to draw from.]<<<<<
—Tenmace (09:33:25/4-3-54)

>>>>>[Hey, Lola, why don't you go for a tub with Lofwyr? You might end up sharing the thing with a couple of water serpents or mermaids.]<<<<<
—Carr (05:01:36/4-4-54)

>>>>>[I fragging mean it; enough of the fragging hot-tub jokes.]<<<<<
—Lola (01:24:05/4-5-54)

>>>>>[No reason to get so steamed...(Nyuck nyuck)]<<<<<
—Hoss (17:36:40/4-7-54)

"THE FACT THAT LOFWYR CAN TRACK THE INTRICATE BUSINESS ACTIVITIES OF A FRAGGING MEGACORP ALL BY HIMSELF HINTS THAT DRAGONS HAVE MORE INTELLIGENCE THAN (META)HUMANS DO, JUST LIKE THE DATAFAXES SAY."

YAMATETSU CORPORATION

Home Office Location: Kyoto, Japan
President/CEO: Saru Iwano
Chairman of the Board: Tadamako
  Shibanokuji
Corporate Status: Public corporation
Major Shareholders:
  Tadamako Shibanokuji
    (approx. 14 %)
  Buttercup (approx. 11 %)
  Newton Chin (approx. %)

Net Rating: 114
Major Interests
  Aerospace: 6
  Agriculture: 7
  Biotechnology: 8
  Chemicals: 6
  Computer Engineering: 8
  Computer Science: 6
  Consumer Goods: 4
  Cybernetics: 7
  Entertainment: 2
  Finance: 6
  Heavy Industry: 3
  Mystical Goods/Services: 3
  Military Technology: 6
  Service: 7
Operations
  Fiscal: 8
  Intelligence: 6
  Management: 6
  Reputation: 8
  Security: 8
    Magic: 6
    Matrix: 8
    Physical: 8
  Military: None reported

>>>>>(Buttercup?)<<<<<
  —Sid (20:06:32/3-26-54)

>>>>>(Buttercup. She (he? it?) is a free spirit, an anima. Nobody knows exactly how long she's existed, but she has a tendency to drop names of people who died during the Renaissance. Of course, she could just be playing a game. Who knows anything about an anima's sense of humor? Anyway, Buttercup knows how to play the stock market smart. She owns big chunks of half-a-dozen major corps, though so far Yamatetsu is the only megacorp she has her mitts into. She sits on the board, but from what I hear she observes rather than actively participates.)<<<<<
  —Turner (08:47:30/3-29-54)

PRIMARY BUSINESS

A high-technology corporation, Yamatetsu focuses on what it calls "(meta)human factors engineering." One way or another, most of its research involves boosting (meta)human performance in a wide range of fields. In fact, its official mission statement goes on at tedious length about "pushing back the limits constraining the (meta)human spirit" and such drek. Yamatetsu has its fingers in such diverse pies as improved smartgun interface technology, various "performance boosters" such as modified wired reflexes and similar technologies, cutting-edge bioware, and ergonomically-designed teleoperation workstations.

>>>>>(Last year's annual shareholders' report described it best. The title read, "Yamatetsu—Pushing the Envelope.")<<<<<
  —Dodd (22:15:09/3-26-54)

CORPORATE STRUCTURE

A diverse range of shareholders owns Yamatetsu Corporation. Thirteen or so major owners hold roughly 72 percent of the corp's stock, with the remainder trading on the open market. Tadamako Shibanokuji, Yamatetsu's chairman of the board, directly owns only 14 percent of the shares but controls a considerably larger chunk. CEO Saru Iwano owns only 1 percent of the outstanding shares, giving him a relatively small equity position in the company.

>>>>>(That still nets him a personal fortune of a billion or so nuyen. "Small" my hoop.)<<<<<
  —Moxie (09:43:59/3-27-54)

Major Divisions

Yamatetsu organizes its divisions along regional lines. It has major divisions in North America, South America, Asia, Europe, and Australasia, with a limited presence in the Middle East and India. Each major division has regional subdivisions, such as Yamatetsu Seattle. Within those subdivisions, departments are structured by function.

>>>>>(Yamatetsu goes against all the conventional wisdom regarding corporate practice by basing all the heads of its first-tier divisions in Kyoto, Japan. Every management consultant the world over would scream at such stupidity, believing that any decent divisional manager must have personal experience with the region in which his business lies. Stupid or not, though, this weird little business practice doesn't seem to hurt Yamatetsu any.)<<<<<
  —McDermid (19:00:23/3-29-54)

>>>>>(True, partly because the divisional managers give an incredible level of autonomy to subdivisional heads. For example, the head of Yamatetsu North America checks the profit-and-loss reports from the slags who run operations in Seattle, New York, Chicago, and so on, and then leaves them alone. As long as the figures look good, the subdivisional managers can run their own little empires any way they see fit.)<<<<<
  —Nuyen Nick (12:49:14/4-1-54)

>>>>>(Yamatetsu uses matrix management big time, but sometimes they take it too far. For example, Yamatetsu Seattle used to have a sub-department called the ISP group, whose director had his own direct line of communication to the head of Yamatetsu North America. He still had to report to Jacques Barnard, who headed Yamatetsu Seattle at the time, but the ISP head could also play Barnard off against Barnard's boss at YNA. Barnard got wise last year and reorganized ISP to end that situation.)<<<<<
  —Marcus (22:52:05/4-2-54)

As a megacorp, Yamatetsu directly and indirectly owns many subsidiaries. Some of these subsidiaries report directly to corporate HQ in Kyoto, and others report to subdivisions much farther down the chain of command.

>>>>>(That happened when Yamatetsu took over Crashcart, DocWagon's upstart competitor. They made Crashcart a subsidiary of Yamatetsu Seattle, and it reports to that division head rather than to Yamatetsu North America.)<<<<<
  —Paragon (11:54:43/4-1-54)

>>>>>(I still don't understand what went down with that whole deal. One

day Crashcart was eating DocWagon's lunch. Next thing you know Yamatetsu took it over, iced the entire upper echelon of management, and then forgot about its new toy. Crashcart does frag-all in profits these days. Can anyone explain why Yamatetsu even bothered absorbing it?)<<<<<
—Barrett (20:08:46/4-3-54)

>>>>>(From what little I've heard, I don't want to know any more.)<<<<<
—Quincy (22:26:24/4-3-54)

Execs

Jacques Barnard currently serves as the executive vice president of Yamatetsu North America. Up until the end of last year, he headed Yamatetsu Seattle, but now he makes his home in Kyoto.

>>>>>(If you get a chance, check out a holo of Barnard from a year or so ago and then scan one from today. He looks older by a couple of decades. If promotion does that to you, I'm glad I'm not a corporate warrior...)<<<<<
—Crosshair (10:02:47/4-7-54)

>>>>>(He looks like he's learned some drek he prefers not to know.)<<<<<
—Blackguard (13:02:40/4-10-54)

>>>>>(Barnard's old comptroller, Mary Luce, took his place at Yamatetsu Seattle. He keeps in close touch with her, apparently still personally interested in his old territory.)<<<<<
—Nuyen Nick (20:08:37/4-11-54)

The other major executives include Mochikune Mibu at Yamatetsu Asia, Nadine Cross-Walters at the Australasia division, Pierre Debruille heading Yamatetsu Europe, John Eckert serving as exec veep in India, and Nahid Mostafavi at the corp's Middle East division.

SECURITY

The megacorporation has no central security office from which managers can draw resources; instead each regional subdivision takes care of its own security and that of its departments and subsidiaries. For example, Yamatetsu Seattle covers security for Crashcart and other subsidiaries in addition to its own security needs. Because subdivisional

managers have significant autonomy, security provisions vary considerably between locales.

Physical and Magical Security

In general, Yamatetsu facilities have effective but low-key physical security. Heavily armed guards keep a low profile, but respond rapidly to any threat. Few Yamatetsu facilities go in for such automatic threat-suppression measures as autonomous gun ports and the like, preferring not to risk collateral damage to innocent civilians.

>>>>>(Oh yeah, sure. A megacorp that cares about innocent victims. Pull the other one.)<<<<<
—Troika (12:00:42/3-24-54)

>>>>>(Strange to say, Yamatetsu does seem to care. They get good PR out of it, and that kind of consumer goodwill often translates into profit.)<<<<<
—The Chromed Accountant (13:13:48/3-26-54)

Though an average Yamatetsu security team uses few (meta)human mages and shamans to supplement its mundane personnel, the corp frequently uses trained parabiologicals such as hellhounds.

>>>>>(Yamatetsu Seattle, at least, has pulled up its socks with regard to mages. Mary Luce has organized a hiring blitz, picking up any good, bondable mage who's currently at liberty.)<<<<<
—Carnet (00:29:58/3-25-54)

>>>>>(Oh, great. Just when I thought I had an edge.)<<<<<
—WizKid (04:16:32/3-29-54)

Matrix Security

Every division of Yamatetsu has excellent Matrix security. Though the corp routinely uses black ice on particularly sensitive nodes, it uses far fewer killer programs than, say, MCT or Fuchi. Much like Shiawase, Yamatetsu seems to prefer protecting itself with high levels of trace-and-dump and trace-and-burn.

The corp has well-designed, clean system architecture without any of the weird anachronisms that appear in certain other corporate systems. It uses layered defenses and data choke-points to great effect against electronic intrusion.

>>>>>(Yamatetsu uses the textbook systems. They do it all right.)<<<<<
—Nora (10:52:31/4-2-54)

>>>>>(Plus they use top-flight deckers to patrol the more sensitive systems. These guys can't wait to trash an intruder in a dogfight.)<<<<<
—Icebreaker (20:28:30/4-5-54)

Military Security

Yamatetsu has no known military forces, and unlike other AAA megacorps it does not participate in Desert Wars. If Yamatetsu needs military force, the corp subcontracts outside organizations such as Ares Arms to handle the job.

Extended Security

Yamatetsu has an excellent and extensive network of extended assets, ranging from industrial spies to highly skilled assassins.

>>>>>(That's why they don't need a military. Greasing the right general gets you the same results as killing ten thousand troops.)<<<<<
—Blade (21:48:51/4-6-54)

Because many of these assets serve "on retainer," Yamatetsu rarely hires shadowrunners for one-shot missions.

>>>>>(When it does, watch your back because something twisted is going down. Make sure you find out the real lowdown and what consequences to expect before signing onto a Yamatetsu run.)<<<<<
—Argent (09:10:35/4-2-54)